Award-winning author Jo Goodman enchants readers with her unforgettable historical romances. Now she returns to the Hamilton family with the enthralling tale of two wary hearts coming together. . . .

IF THIS WAS LOVE . . .

Reclaiming her family's Carolina rice plantation from her ruthless stepfather was Bria Hamilton's only wish—and she was taking a chance by hiring Northerner Lucas Kincaid to help her. With her own painful scars still fresh ten years after the War Between the States, Bria couldn't trust any man—especially one as dangerously attractive as Luke—to understand that the legacy of Concord meant everything to her. More than a warm smile or a tempting promise, and more than the sudden, yearning hope that Luke might offer the kind of happiness she had never dared wish for . . .

IT WAS MORE THAN SHE WISHED FOR

Bound to his own past as surely as Bria was bound to hers, Luke had only one reason for working at Concord—a reason bound in secrecy. He couldn't afford to let his response to Bria distract him from his only chance to right his family's fortune—but when Bria proposed a marriage of convenience, he couldn't deny her. Just as he couldn't deny the laughter that sweetened their moments together, the passion he longed to teach her, and the love he never meant to feel. . . .

"Jo Goodman writes with a unique and impressive style."
—Virginia Henley

Books by Jo Goodman

THE CAPTAIN'S LADY

CRYSTAL PASSION

SEASWEPT ABANDON

VELVET NIGHT

VIOLET FIRE

SCARLET LIES

TEMPTING TORMENT

MIDNIGHT PRINCESS

PASSION'S SWEET REVENGE

SWEET FIRE

WILD SWEET ECSTASY

ROGUE'S MISTRESS

FOREVER IN MY HEART

ALWAYS IN MY DREAMS

ONLY IN MY ARMS

MY STEADFAST HEART

MY RECKLESS HEART

WITH ALL MY HEART

MORE THAN YOU KNOW

MORE THAN YOU WISHED

Published by Zebra Books

MORE THAN YOU WISHED

Jo Goodman

ZEBRA BOOKS
KENSINGTON PUBLISHING CORP.
http://www.zebrabooks.com

For Aunt Ev and Uncle Bill
and in fond memory of all those years at the kids' table
—Snowball

Chapter One

July 1875

She was not going to hire him. He had always known there was a risk involved in approaching her in this manner, but he had convinced himself the chance of success was worth it. Now there was no chance.

Lucas Dearborn Kincaid looked directly across the reflective surface of the desk separating him from his future employer. Ex-future employer, he thought. Had he been standing he could have made out the blurred edges of her image in the dark walnut. The distortion would not have softened her, only given an impression of softness and vulnerability where there was none.

Luke wondered at what point he had lost her interest, or if he had ever had it. He had watched her attention drift from the topic of their discussion and never once had her eyes left his face. They were beautiful eyes. For all the importance of this interview with her, he had not failed to notice that. Her eyes were the same dark shade of blue as sapphires. The deep color was a perfect match, but the stones themselves had more life.

He had been informed—no, *warned*—that she was different.

Some people had told him this while tapping a finger to their temple and nodding, head cocked a little to one side, trying to convey through a gesture something they seemed afraid to put into words. Others simply shook their heads, an eyebrow raised pensively, while they looked Luke over and announced he would never do. She would never have him. They made it seem as if the difficulty lay more with her than him, but they never explained.

He never asked for more detail. Expressing too much curiosity, he reasoned, would have roused suspicion. Luke did not want to be remembered. He'd observed that Charleston, for all its size and breadth of commerce, had the guardedness of a small town. He had the sense he was welcomed, but only because the community wanted to know the enemy in their midst.

He was, after all, a Yankee.

Bria Hamilton wondered why he thought she would hire an outsider. A *Yankee* outsider. Someone in the city was amusing himself by pointing Lucas Kincaid in the direction of Concord. No doubt there were wagers being made. *How long before he returns with his tail between his legs?* She could imagine that even now there was a goodly sum at stake. It occurred to Bria that hiring Mr. Kincaid was the surest way to confound Charleston's genteel wags.

There was a slight curve to Bria's lips as she considered this tempting course, but she had not brought Concord around by acting in ways that defied her own reasoning. Her smile vanished as if it had never existed.

Lucas blinked, startled by the change in her features. For the briefest of moments he had allowed himself to be encouraged by her smile. He had already realized she had not meant it for him. It had never once touched her cool and distant eyes, yet he thought it might portend some hope. On the contrary, Bria Hamilton's gaze never wavered as she continued to look right through him.

"You'll find I am a hard worker, Miss Hamilton," Luke

told her. He wondered if he'd already said that. He hadn't expected to lose his way through the interview because of a pair of sapphire eyes, but that was exactly what was happening. Luke could hear himself groping for words as he wondered if this was the end of it all. He could only hope that Bria Hamilton's remote study of him meant her attention had wandered again.

"So you've mentioned," Bria said. "Several times." She watched as he shifted uncomfortably in his chair and realized she had embarrassed him. He probably would have been more comfortable on his feet, standing on the other side of her desk with his hat in hand. It would have given him something to do with his fingers instead of nervously drumming them on the arms of the chair.

Bria did not apologize for her observation and she was not moved to alleviate his discomfort by adding to her own. Although he looked to be just under six feet and only a few inches taller than she was, Bria would not allow him to use the advantage of height, even across the expanse of the desk. "Where are you from, Mr. Kincaid?" Bria asked.

"New York."

"The city?"

"Is there any other place in New York?" He smiled then, a quiet, slightly crooked smile that came and went like sunlight chasing shadow across his face.

A small vertical crease appeared between Bria's eyebrows as they puckered. She had not expected him to have a smile quite like that. Moments before he had seemed ill at ease, even desperate for some sign of consideration. The smile, though, made her wonder if something else wasn't going on. She watched him rake his fingers through his dark, coffee-colored hair, a gesture that appeared more natural than the drumming fingers.

This line of thinking only served to raise her guard. "New York City," she said softly. New *Yawk* City. The sweet cadence of her voice made it sound exotic. "And what did you do in

New York City that makes you suited to work on a Carolina rice farm?''

Luke knew she was being a bit disingenuous calling Concord a farm. It was one of the largest plantations left standing after the war. It hadn't been sold piecemeal to pay for taxes as some estates had. The Hamiltons had found a way to keep their land. They just hadn't been able to keep it in their name. Bria Hamilton might manage Concord, but she didn't own it. "I don't believe anything I did in New York would be helpful to you," he said. "But it's been a while since I lived there. I've worked on farms in Maryland and plantations in Virginia and around Raleigh. I've done construction in Atlanta and Richmond."

"Construction?" she asked. "Or reconstruction?"

Luke did not miss the hint of sarcasm in her tone. He also did not miss the look of regret that touched her features, as if this brief emotional response had been too revealing. "You may call it what you like," he said. "But I'm no carpetbagger, Miss Hamilton. I don't have the money to invest in the misfortune of others, even if I had the stomach for it."

Bria's eyes narrowed slightly. Could she believe him? His manner of dress didn't suggest someone of means. Although he had made some effort to turn himself out, his clothes had a carefully tended look. One of the buttons on his jacket did not quite match the other three and the thread looked as if it might have been fishing line. The right sleeve was frayed at the wrist and the collar was shiny from being fingered in too many nervous attempts to keep it straight. His shirt was clean and white but the material was thin from more washings than it could properly bear. Small, even stitches closed a tear in one knee of his trousers. His shoes bore evidence of his long trek from town. The road dust would have been less noticeable if he had not tried to brush it away. Now it lay in bands and creases across the worn leather, left there when his fingertips had strayed from their task.

Bria remembered the hat Addie had taken from him before

he was ushered into the study. The housekeeper had held it away from her, the sweat-darkened brim caught between her thumb and forefinger as if the thing had given her offense. If Addie Thomas burned it before the afternoon was out, Bria wouldn't have been surprised.

"I'm passing good with my hands," Luke went on. He glanced at them and missed the stricken look that came to Bria's features as she did the same. "I can repair most anything and I can build what I can't repair."

Bria dragged her eyes away from his hands. She was no longer only aware of the steady tattoo of his fingers. He had made her notice him in a manner she had been trying to avoid since the outset of the interview. He had made her see him as a man, with a man's square-tipped nails and flat, powerful palms, with lean fingers that held a certain tensile strength, and knuckles that stood out in hard relief when the hand itself became a hammering weapon.

Bria's own hands slid from the desktop and came to rest in her lap. Out of Luke's line of sight she folded them into a single fist. Her palms were damp and the ridges that were her knuckles were white. "Is that what you've done on the farms where you've worked?"

Luke nodded, then added, "Yes, ma'am. I've learned some things about planting and harvesting along the way. There was no such thing as doing a single job at any of the places I worked, but mostly I know about building."

"You're a handyman." Bria had an opportunity to wonder again about the quiet, slightly crooked grin that made Lucas Kincaid's ordinary good looks suddenly seem extraordinary. That smile moved across his features like quicksilver and sharpened eyes that were very nearly that same reflective color. "Have I amused you, Mr. Kincaid?"

Luke felt himself pinned back in his chair, held there in equal parts by the sapphire eyes and the frosty accents. "No, ma'am," he said carefully. Bria Hamilton was easily the *least* amusing woman he had ever met. Until now he had always imagined his own grandmother forever being the person to occupy that place in his mind. Uncertain if she would take offense or embrace it as a compliment, Luke kept the observation to himself.

"Why south?" asked Bria. "Surely there is work north of Mason-Dixon and west on the railroads."

"I've been west. I built bridges for the Union Pacific and I've worked in Philadelphia and Pittsburgh."

"You don't appear to stay long in one place."

"That's a fact."

"Then I couldn't really depend on you here at Concord."

"I've never left a job undone, Miss Hamilton, if that's what you're afraid of. I finish what I start."

Bria heard conviction in the last. He was more than serious about it; it was a matter of pride with him. She gave an almost imperceptible shake of her head, reminding herself that she would not be swayed by this. What did his pride matter in the face of her own? She was not going to hire a Yankee. No one could expect that she would.

Bria's chin came up suddenly as if literally struck by the thought. There *was* one person that might expect it of her. Bria Hamilton came to her feet and braced her palms on the edge of the desk. Stiff-armed, her entire body rigid with the certainty that she was being played for a fool, she still spoke quietly, as if she were unable to give her frustration full rein. "Mr. Kincaid, I must tell you that you have wasted your time coming out here. I'm certain my stepfather had his own reasons for putting you up to this. No doubt Orrin would like to have someone he imagines as a compatriot living at Concord. I'm afraid that in short order you would find yourself as much a fish out of water as he does."

Lucas came to his feet more slowly than Bria had. "I don't understand," he said. But he did. She was dismissing him. "I don't know your stepfather or why Mr. Orrin needs a compatriot, as you say."

"Foster," Bria corrected him absently. "Orrin Foster is my

stepfather and the landowner here.'' Her eyes narrowed. "You did know that, didn't you?''

Lucas wondered how much he could safely say. Truth was best. Lying was dangerous. He offered something in between, a compromise that did not set well with him. "I've never met your stepfather,'' he said again. "But I heard a Yankee owned Concord. You're right that I thought it might help me find work. I never considered it would make me Mr. Foster's boon companion.''

She almost smiled at that. It surprised her that she would be tempted. The moment Lucas Kincaid had followed her example and come to his feet, Bria had anticipated the familiar tightening in her chest and was prepared for it, only to discover it had not arrived with the intensity she was used to. As though from a distance she heard herself say to him, "Orrin's boon companion is bourbon. Scotch if there's no bourbon. Madeira if there's no scotch.''

"Any port in a storm.''

Bria blinked and looked at Luke oddly, wondering if his wordplay had been intentional. If it was, he was doing his best not to let her see it. His eyes remained the implacable grey of a frozen lake and the vaguely off-kilter smile had been swallowed this time. "Yes,'' she said, nodding slowly, still watching him carefully. "Any port.'' When he still gave nothing away, Bria asked, "Do you drink, Mr. Kincaid?''

"Not often and not to excess.''

"You're a temperate man, then.''

"In some things.''

For the first time Bria felt his gaze penetrate the barrier she had erected. The look in his eyes was both deliberate and disarming and Bria's discomfort was immediate and intense. She felt the color drain from her face. Cold prickles raised the soft downy hair at the back of her neck.

Lucas took a step forward. His thighs touched the edge of the desk. Thinking to help her, he extended one hand.

Bria recoiled. His hand seemed to snake out of nowhere,

swift and threatening as it came toward her. She groped for the center drawer of the walnut desk, her fingers fumbling for the key.

Luke withdrew his hand and let it fall casually to his side. He straightened, inching back from the desk, and stood there loosely, calmly, his open palms turned slightly toward her. "There's no need to go for your gun," he said, dry humor edging his tone. "I meant no disrespect. For a moment it looked as if you were going to faint."

"I don't keep my gun in that drawer," she told him. Now that there was some distance between them again, Bria felt her breathing return to its normal rhythm. "That's where I keep the letter opener." Using fingers that no longer trembled, Bria found the key easy to manage. She drew the drawer open and removed the letter opener. The silver handle was beautifully etched with flowers and flourishes while the blade bore much in common with a stiletto.

Her eyes never leaving the man across from her, Bria's fingers closed over the handle slowly. "Won't you have a seat, Mr. Kincaid?"

Luke dropped like a stone in the chair behind him. "Yes, ma'am."

Bria shook her head as she replaced the opener and closed the drawer. She did not sit. "I don't believe for a moment that you're afraid of me," she told him. "Your retreat was a tad too quick. I only mention it so that you might improve your act—with the next woman you try to gull."

She was far too composed, Luke thought. How old could she be? Twenty-four? Twenty-five? That would make her six or seven years younger than he was. So why was he thinking of his grandmother? Perhaps because Julia Dearborn was the last woman he had tried to gull. On that occasion it had been the matter of convincing her he had washed behind his ears, when in truth he had enough dirt back there to plant parsnips. Nana Dearborn hadn't threatened him with a letter opener though. She'd taken him by the scruff of the neck and renewed his acquaintance with the washbasin. He'd almost drowned.

Even now the memory of it raised Luke's hand to the back of his neck. He absently rubbed Nana Dearborn's imaginary fingerprints from his nape.

"Is something wrong with your neck?" Bria asked.

A sheepish grin touched Luke's mouth. His hand dropped away and curved lightly over the arm of the chair. "No, ma'am." *Nothing that driving that stake through my Adam's apple wouldn't cure.* He swallowed. "I was just thinking." Luke could not fail to notice her silence. She was probably trying to decide if she could believe him. He had not given her much reason to suspect that he thought at all. "Might you know of another place that's hiring?" he asked, his earnestness not entirely feigned. If he could stay close to Concord, perhaps it would be enough. There might be opportunity to visit, to learn the things he needed to know. "One that's not fighting the war all over again?"

One of Bria's dark brows arched at this remark. "I hope you intend to explain yourself."

"You don't want to hear it."

"I assure you, I do."

Luke's posture had relaxed a little. He was of the opinion now there was simply nothing left to lose. He felt the self-imposed burden he carried ease from his shoulders. He stretched his legs, crossing them at the ankles, and leaned into the damask-covered chair in which he sat. For the first time since being shown into the great study at Concord, Lucas Kincaid permitted himself to take some small pleasure in his surroundings, imagining what it would be like to have the right to sit here at his leisure, even throwing one leg over the arm of the chair and resting his head in the curve of the back and wing. And on the heels of that thought came another, one he hadn't suspected was lurking but one he didn't try to turn away when it came to the forefront. He gave it free rein as his chin lifted and he studied Bria Hamilton with lashes at half mast, considering what it would be like to rise from his chair, circle the desk, and extend a hand to her that would not be met by a six-inch blade.

"I am not your enemy," he told her. "The war is ten long years in the past. I'm a Yankee, true, but it doesn't have to be an epithet. No matter what you think, it's not synonymous with viper."

"It is in my dictionary."

He noticed that she spoke unflinchingly, with a certain conviction in her tone that made him realize she would not be easily swayed. She accepted his study of her now without retreating. What appeared outwardly as composure was most surely resistance. If she had known he found her remote glance faintly mysterious, she would have drawn yet another icy curtain over it. If she had suspected he was intrigued by the dark honey coil of hair intricately knotted at the back of her head, he felt certain she would have hacked it off.

"And so you continue to fight the war," he went on. "Your slaves are gone. Your land is no longer properly yours. Sometimes I believe that Lee was only speaking for himself when he surrendered."

"He was."

Lucas nodded slowly, still thoughtful. "I see. Then you're saying no one else will hire me."

"Not in these parts. Carolinians are a trifle more discerning than the Georgians or Virginians or Marylanders."

"I generally find that people are discerning as it relates to their needs and their choices. I understand your need is great. Perhaps I misunderstood the number of choices you've had. I'm one of a long line of people wanting to work for you. Is that it?"

"I think you have been misinformed all the way around," Bria said. "I have no plans to hire anyone this summer. If you were told differently then I'll have to amend my thinking and trust that the trick was played on you, not me. Someone must have considered it vastly entertaining to set you walking out here. I'm sorry for your trouble and I'll see that Addie serves you a decent meal and gives you something for your trek back to town, but that's all you can expect from me, Mr. Kincaid.''

Lucas was not quite ready to give up. Like Bria, he didn't easily surrender. ''Then it wasn't true that you're looking to build a new stable?'' He saw the flash of annoyance in her eyes. For a moment he thought she was going to lie to him.

''There are always things that need to be done at Concord.''- Prevarication did not come easily to her. ''Oh, very well,'' she sighed. ''Yes, I want to build a new stable. And there are outbuildings to shore and timbers to be replaced and floors in need of repair. There's plastering and painting and bricklaying and paving and . . . '' Her voice had grown softer until it trailed away. For the first time since Lucas Kincaid had introduced himself, Bria avoided his eyes. ''There's plenty of work, Mr. Kincaid,''she said finally.

''And none of it for me.''

''Yes, that's right.'' She faced him again because she believed she owed him that. ''Do you have a family?'' she asked. ''Are there others depending on you?''

''Yes,'' he said. ''And yes. But not the way you mean. If I don't work, Miss Hamilton, then I'm the only one going hungry.''

''You have no children then.''

''No children. No wife. I have a mother and six aunts back in New York.'' He clicked them off on his fingers quickly. ''Mary—my mother. Aunt Nancy, Aunt Lyssa, Aunt Maggie, Aunt Laura, Aunt Livia, and Aunt Madelyn.''

So many women, Bria thought. But then the war had taken so many men. She knew that first hand. ''When was the last time you saw them?''she asked gently.

''Six months ago.''

That surprised her. For some reason, perhaps in light of the number of places he had worked, she had the impression he'd been away much longer than that. Without quite meaning to,

Bria heard herself ask, "Have you considered it's time to return home?"

"I'm on my way there now." He saw her confusion. "My current state of funds requires that I work to pay my way back."

"Oh. Then you haven't any savings."

"Not any longer." He pushed himself upright. "I'm a gambler, Miss Hamilton. Currently on a streak of astonishing bad luck. I hoped a job here would turn things around, be my ace in the hole, so to speak. I can see that's not to be the way of it."

Luke started to rise slowly, careful not to send her flying by jumping to his feet. An imperious wave of her hand pushed him backward as easily as if she had shoved him. Still wondering how she was able to exert that kind of influence with a mere graceful twist of her wrist, Luke was late realizing that she was talking to him. She had to repeat her question.

"I was inquiring as to whether you are a good gambler."

"You mean do I win more often than I lose?"

"Yes, I suppose I do."

Luke plucked at the front of his shirt. "Well, I haven't lost this yet." He saw her frown and followed her gaze down. He'd forgotten this particular shirt wasn't his own, or at least it hadn't been until very recently. It had cost him almost two dollars, but then the washer woman who bargained with him had the heart of a robber baron. If he'd been forced to purchase his entire wardrobe from her wash line, she'd have broken him.

Luke released the shirt. His grin was a trifle self-mocking. "I believe I mentioned my current streak of bad luck."

"*Astonishing* bad luck, I think you said."

"Yes, but it will turn around. It always does. In any event, I wouldn't be much of a gambler if I relied solely on luck."

"You cheat, you mean."

Luke was certain there was no judgment in her tone. If she thought less of him for stacking the cards in his favor, she gave no hint of it. "Let's say I play a skillful game."

Bria had no difficulty accepting that. She also did not think he was speaking solely of games of chance. At least she hoped he wasn't. Bria walked past the desk, away from where Lucas Kincaid was sitting. She imagined his eyes following her progress to the window, but she didn't turn to see if she was right. He must be wondering why her interest was piqued. She cautioned herself to go slowly, then again not to go at all.

Drawing back the heavy velvet drapes, Bria fixed them to each side of the window, letting sunlight flow into the study for the first time. It was Orrin who kept the drapes closed. He claimed sunlight ruined the fabrics on the sofas and high-backed wing chairs. It faded the deep maroon damask and lightened the leather bindings on the books. It was true, of course, and since he had paid for new furniture after Union Army stragglers had reduced the old to tinder, and since he had restocked the shelves with books when the same renegades had destroyed her own family's collection, Bria did not normally choose to fight this battle. She never thought for a moment that her stepfather cared particularly about fading fabrics and bindings. It was much more to the point that the sunlight hurt his eyes when he was deep into his cups or recovering from the same.

Quite deliberately now, Bria opened another pair at the second window and then moved on to the third. She lifted her face to the sunshine, turning her head so the warmth was absorbed by the slender line of her neck. She touched the hollow just behind her ear and felt the heat taken up by her fingertips. For a moment she allowed herself the luxury of closing her eyes.

"Would you say you're a better gambler or a better handyman?" she asked at last.

Luke had to lean around the wing chair to see her. She was visible only in profile, her features pensive. "Do you have need of one over the other?"

"That's entirely possible."

Which was no answer at all, Luke realized. "You'd be hardpressed to find a better laborer in all of Charleston," he said at last. "As for gambling, there I have a few equals."

Bria turned to face him. Her tone was soft but astringent. "They're all wearing better shirts, I take it."

"Yes, ma'am. If I won all the time it wouldn't be gambling."

She nodded, satisfied that he wasn't lying to her about his skills. "I would prefer if you would address me as Miss Hamilton." The servants called her Miss Bria or Miss Bree, but she wasn't going to allow Lucas Kincaid that familiarity. Even if she hired him—which she didn't think she would—Bria didn't believe she would change her mind about that. "No one at Concord calls me ma'am."

"As you wish." Luke wondered if his astonishing bad luck was on the cusp of turning. "It's just that you remind me a little of—" He stopped, realizing what he had been about to say.

"Yes?" she prompted.

So much for his luck turning. "My grandmother."

At first Bria could not believe she had heard him correctly. His *grandmother*. Could that possibly have been what he said? But it was. She saw him slip back around the curve of the wing chair, no longer straining himself to stay in her line of vision. He was probably relieved to have a hiding place.

Bria's laughter had the volume and rhythm of Gatling gunfire. Luke's eyes widened and he peeked around the chair again just to make certain he wasn't under attack from the high ground. No, she was laughing. Hard. It didn't seem possible that such a rich and hearty sound could be issuing from that slender body, yet that body was almost shaking with it. The sweeping curve of her smile had lifted Bria's cheeks so that her eyes were mere slits. Tears dampened her lashes and her face was flushed. He watched her draw in a breath only to have the startling sound escape again. *Tremble* was too delicate a word to describe what happened to her mouth when she attempted to hold back.

Luke slipped back around the chair as Bria reached for her handkerchief and put it to her eyes.

"Oh, forgive me," she managed on a tiny sob. "I cannot say

why that struck me so." Bria returned to the desk and sat down, shaking her head. "I suppose because it was such a startling comparison." She held up one hand when he looked as if he might explain. "Please don't tell me. I don't think I want to know."

Luke settled back in the chair, quite relieved to be able to keep his thoughts to himself. She was not reminding him at all of Nana Dearborn at the moment. Bria Hamilton's eyes were luminous now, bright with the effect of the tears that still dampened her dark lashes. The flush that had pinkened her complexion had not faded. Her smile was not so wide as it had been, but some evidence of it lingered in the high curve of her cheeks and the parenthetical creases at the corners of her full lips. Those lips parted slightly as she drew a steadying breath. She tucked her handkerchief under the tightly fitted sleeve at her wrist. Only an edge of lace was left to brush against her pulse.

Luke's eyes lifted when Bria's hands dropped under the desk. He saw her narrow shoulders brace as she sat up straight. Out of his sight he knew her hands were folded primly, even tightly, in her lap. Only an errant tendril of hair the color of dark honey was left to remind him of the other woman who sometimes shared the same air with Bria Hamilton.

"I believe we were discussing your success at gambling," she said. Bria eyed his clothes again but her expression was not disdainful, only thoughtful. "I wonder if you might be interested in a small wager."

Luke's features gave nothing away. He said, "I came looking for real work, Miss Hamilton."

Bria wondered if that were strictly true. She didn't entirely trust Lucas Kincaid. "Tell me," she said. "How did you know that I've been thinking about building a new stable?"

Although Luke was surprised by the change in subject, he was sure she had her reasons. He answered easily, "There's talk in the city that you're interested in developing the stud here at Concord. Folks were speculating that you'd want better accommodations for your horses. More fencing. Better runs. Were they wrong?''

"No, not wrong. I simply haven't discussed it with many people.'' Her voice fell off so the last words were just above a whisper. "Not even Rand.''

Luke realized she had not meant to be heard. She had spoken more to herself than to him. He said nothing, waiting to take his cue from her.

Bria drew herself back to the present. "If you're being truthful with me and have never met my stepfather, then that leaves a very short list of people who know about my plans.''

"Austin Tipping.''

She sighed. "I suppose I neglected to tell him I didn't want it bandied about. I'm sure he thinks he was helping me. Did he send you out here, Mr. Kincaid?''

"He didn't discourage me.''

"I'm certain he didn't.'' Bria could too easily imagine that Austin believed he would ultimately reap the benefits of any improvements she made to Concord. He and Orrin were as thick as thieves these days, plotting her future as though she had no say in any of it. Bria let them go on because it seemed harmless enough. It wasn't as if she could be forced to be a willing participant in their plans. *Forced to be willing.* Bria simply shook her head. Could even Austin and her stepfather fail to see the contradiction in that?

Bria went on, "Did Mr. Tipping suggest you speak to me or my stepfather?''

"He said I should speak to Mr. Foster,'' Luke said. "But when I asked around a bit more I got the impression I should speak directly to you. People seem to think you're the one who makes the decisions here.''

Bria was silent a moment, taking this in while she continued to study Lucas Kincaid. Was this last observation meant to flatter her? What made him suspect she *could* be flattered? "Mr. Foster will be leaving for the city later today. He's joining my mother there.'' At this time of year virtually all the landowners left their homes along the Ashley and Cooper Rivers for the relative safety of Charleston. It was, after all, the height of the malaria season, and nowhere was the danger greater than on the lowland rice plantations like Concord.

Bria's mother had begged her to leave more than a month ago, shortly after Rand and *Cerberus* had sailed for the South Seas, but Bria had declined. Her decision had everything to do with the fact that she thought her stepfather was accompanying Elizabeth to town. When she found out differently it was too late to change her plans, or at least change them without having it look as if she were running away from Orrin. She wouldn't have put it past him to follow in their wake just to spite her. Sharing the close quarters of their summer home in the Battery with Orrin Foster was not something Bria wanted to do. At least at Concord she could avoid him, and in truth there was a benefit to this current arrangement: while Orrin remained at Concord he couldn't lift a hand against Elizabeth. Every day away from Orrin Foster gave her mother an opportunity to heal.

Now that Orrin had made his decision to leave Concord, Bria knew little in the way of relief. She found herself wishing that when Orrin arrived at their summer home, Elizabeth would not be there.

"If Mr. Foster is leaving today,"Lucas said, "then you—"

Bria interrupted him. "I will be remaining here. Not that it concerns you particularly. The wager I mentioned earlier would mean you'd have to return to Charleston."

Lucas thought of the long walk back. He didn't believe she'd offer him a horse, what with having no guarantee that he'd return. After all, he'd told her he was looking for funds to make his way home. She probably hadn't forgotten he'd said that. Musing on the problem, Luke absently rubbed his chin with the back of his hand. The coarse growth was like the brush of nettles and a reminder that he hadn't shaved. He sighed, wondering if Orrin Foster would offer him a seat in his buggy.

"I haven't heard this wager yet," he said. "I might not accept it."

One corner of Bria's mouth curled in a patently derisive smile. "I very much doubt that, Mr. Kincaid."

She was too confident by half, he thought, and much too sure of him. Luke wasn't certain he liked it. Nana Dearborn. His mother. All six aunts. The family portrait they brought to mind raised his smile. He was ever at the mercy of women. Looking across the desk at Bria Hamilton, Lucas decided it was not entirely without its rewards. "Very well, Miss Hamilton," he said. "What is the wager?"

She held up one hand as though to stay his eagerness. "A moment."

Luke's eyes fell on her hand. The fingers were long and slender, the turn of her wrist, graceful. Yet it was very much a working hand. The nails were trimmed short. The palm was faintly reddened and coarse. Compared to her complexion the back of her hand was lightly tanned. He thought she wore gloves more often than not, but didn't stop to look for them when they weren't readily available. He imagined she had always flouted convention in small ways, not as a conscious act of rebellion perhaps, but simply because she did not acknowledge all manner of convention as serving any purpose. All six of his aunts would like her. His mother would come around quickly. Nana Dearborn would spin in her grave.

Bria's head tilted to one side as she regarded Lucas questioningly. There was that enigmatic smile again. On the surface it seemed genuine enough, a little self-effacing, as if he were a shade embarrassed by his own amusement, but Bria wondered about it nonetheless. A smile like that could hide things. A gambler would have a practiced smile, she reminded herself, and Lucas Kincaid's seemed very well practiced. The loose tendril of hair that had lain against her temple now fell across her cheek. She pushed it behind her ear, the gesture vaguely impatient.

"Is it your grandmother again, Mr. Kincaid?" she asked.

"No," he lied. He offered no explanation for his amusement

because he couldn't think of one. His mind was blank. Realizing he had no bluff at the ready, Lucas was instantly sobered.

Bria said, "What do you know of the Hamilton-Waterstone treasure?"

The way she posed her question, Luke realized, gave him little opportunity to make a denial. Clearly she expected something more from him. "I know the story,"he said. "It *is* a story, isn't it? A myth?"

"Tell me what you know."

He shrugged. "Two English pirates named—"

"Privateers."

"What?"

"They were privateers. It's an important distinction. They had letters of mark from Queen Elizabeth to prey on Spanish ships."

Obviously, Lucas thought, Bria Hamilton took the story seriously. But then she was a Hamilton. He had been warned about that when he was making his inquiries. In the minds of those he questioned the Hamilton heritage apparently went a long way toward explaining the family's peculiarities. *She's a Hamilton, you know. One of* those *Hamiltons.*

"Privateers," he repeated. "James Hamilton and Henry Waterstone." When she didn't interrupt him, Luke knew he had remembered their names correctly and went on. "They captured treasure from the Spanish government that was intended for the pope. I don't think they returned to England immediately."

"They didn't."

"They captured other ships?"

"Yes. Other treasures."

"And took it halfway around the world."

"That's what we think."

"Isn't there a map?" He frowned, trying to recall what he'd been told. "No, a riddle. Two riddles. Hamilton and Waterstone."

Bria smiled slowly but with no humor. "So you *were* paying attention to what people told you."

"It never hurts to listen. I didn't say I believed any of it."

"Didn't they tell you anything else?"

"Something about a brother of yours going off to find the treasure. Randall, is it?"

"Rand," she corrected. "Just Rand. He's been gone off and on since the end of the war. He was here for two weeks at the end of May."

Ten years, he thought. She was telling him her brother had been adventuring for a decade, chasing down a treasure that common sense and the passage of time said was no better than a sea tale to begin with. Was that why the responsibility of managing Concord had come to rest on her shoulders? Because her brother wanted no part of it? He had assumed it was because Orrin Foster was a drunk, but perhaps that wasn't the only reason Bria Hamilton had stepped into the breach.

Although Lucas offered no criticism of Rand Hamilton, he did not make an effort to keep his expression neutral. Something of what he was thinking was revealed in the tightening of his jaw and the icy shutter that was drawn over his grey eyes.

Bria was having none of it. "You don't know my brother well enough to pass judgment, Mr. Kincaid. I won't have it. He left this time with my blessing. My encouragement, in fact. Just as he's left on every other occasion."

She would hardly have been more than a child the first time Rand left her. Fifteen? Sixteen at the outside? "Then he believes the treasure exists," Luke said.

"Of course," she said simply. Bria regarded Lucas consideringly as she judged how much she could tell him. "You may as well know, Mr. Kincaid, you are not the first fortune hunter who has imagined the path to the Hamilton-Waterstone treasure is through me."

Both of Luke's brows rose. "I'm just looking for a job, Miss Hamilton, not a fortune. Certainly not marriage." He saw her give a start at his plain speaking. ''I'm assuming the route you're talking about is down the bridal path.''

There was no mistaking his word play this time. The distinct light of humor was in his eyes. Her lips twitched slightly. *Bridal* path, indeed. Bria acknowledged his cleverness with a small, almost regal nod. ''I believe the treasure exists, too,'' she said. ''And I believe if anyone can find it, it will be my brother Rand.''

''Others have tried?''

''Over the course of three hundred years there have been a number of attempts. Some from my forebears, some from the Waterstones. The two families have never worked together. They each have a riddle that was written by the man who buried the treasure. Henry Waterstone killed him to keep the secret.''

''You seem certain it was Waterstone.''

''That's because I'm a Hamilton. Naturally the Waterstones blame us, or they did until the last of them was murdered some years back.''

''At the hands of the Hamiltons?''

Bria was not offended. Given the enmity between the two families, the question was a reasonable one. ''Not that I'm aware. Someone simply trying to get the Waterstone riddle.''

''You know it exists?''

''I've never seen it, if that's what you mean. But I don't know why it wouldn't exist. Ours does.'' Bria did not miss his surprise. Clearly he had not expected her to tell him that. ''The man who drew up the riddles was a cartographer on the Waterstone ship. When he realized that his assignment to bury the treasure was as good as a death sentence, he wrote the riddles. James and Henry were more friendly rivals than friends and the mapmaker counted on that. He reasoned that since both commanders had already proven their greed—indeed, their decision to bury the treasure was in order to keep the lion's share out of the hands of the queen—he further reasoned they would be likely to haggle over recovering the treasure. Henry and James, not trusting each other, agreed to his plan that neither would know the precise whereabouts of the buried treasure. They accepted directions to it which contained but half the necessary information.

"The mapmaker thought he was negotiating a reprieve. He could not imagine the two pirates would—"

"Privateers," Lucas corrected.

One corner of Bria's mouth lifted in a smile rife with self-mockery. "He could not imagine the two *privateers* would agree to work together behind his back. I suppose their pact lasted until he handed over the riddles and was murdered for his efforts."

"He should have given them the directions they asked for. Substituting puzzles was reason enough to kill him."

"Apparently Henry thought so," she said dryly. "The plan was for the crews to return to England and set sail again some years later to recover the treasure. Henry's cartographer had the last laugh. He correctly surmised the two captains would never share their half of the riddle. To compound their problems, Waterstone couldn't keep silent about the treasure. Rumors reached the queen. There were attempts on Captain Hamilton's life and later on his son's. It was Henley, James's son, who secured land in the colonies and brought his children from England. That move separated the fortunes of both families. The Hamiltons did well enough without recovering the pope's treasure. The Waterstones fared none the worse under the watchful eye of the queen and all of her successors."

"Until the last of them was murdered."

Bria expressed no sympathy. "They never learned to remain silent about what they had."

"Unlike you Hamiltons," he pointed out wryly. "Who tell complete strangers the story of the riddles and treasure."

She shrugged. "I thought one of us should stop pretending we don't know why you're really here."

Luke pushed himself upright. *She thought he had come because of the treasure?* That had never occurred to him. Even while he listened to variations on the tale from the people he'd talked to, he hadn't considered how it might affect his coming here. The Hamilton-Waterstone treasure was just a myth. It seemed he had always known some version of the story the same way he knew that Icarus had flown into the sun or that Pandora's curiosity had loosed ills on the world. He had never thought of there being a *real* Hamilton family, one descended directly from Captain James Hamilton himself. Hell, he'd never been entirely convinced that James Hamilton had existed.

"I'm just looking for work," he said again.

Bria supposed it was too much to expect that he would admit anything different. "As you wish, Mr. Kincaid, but please do not delude yourself that my silence hence means I have accepted your explanation. I assure you, I have not." She paused, drawing in a short breath and then letting it out slowly. "One last thing about the riddle," she said quietly. "It's not here. Rand keeps it in a safe place, but not at Concord. From time to time my stepfather takes it into his head that it must be here and begins a search. If he has included you in his most recent scheme, it would be in your best interest to abandon it. You won't find anything."

"I'm not looking."

"Good."

He didn't think she believed him but he didn't bring more attention to his denial by denying it again. Instead he asked, "What about the Waterstone riddle?"

She shook her head. "Not here either, I'm afraid. Whoever killed the last Waterstone has that."

"Then your brother has but one piece of the puzzle."

"I didn't say my brother has the riddle with him." If Orrin thought she could be tripped up so easily, he was mistaken. He should have found someone less obvious in his delivery than Lucas Kincaid. In many ways Austin Tipping was a more worthy adversary. "Only that it was in a safe place. But, yes, he has but one piece of the puzzle *here*." She tapped one side of her head with a forefinger.

That explained Rand's decade-long absence. With only half

the riddle in his possession his search was best characterized as quixotic. That was if Lucas was being kind. *Foolish* was another adjective that came to mind. Lucas shared neither with Bria. She had already proved herself quick to come to her brother's defense. "When do you expect him to return?" he asked.

Her voice was wistful, a trifle young. "One never knows with Rand, but I suspect this voyage will keep him away longer than most." She smiled, thinking of Claire and the way Rand's eyes followed her, even though she couldn't appreciate the look in them. "He has a special passenger this time around," she told Luke. "Miss Bancroft is the niece of Rand's financial sponsor for this voyage, the Duke of Strickland. Rand is assisting in the search for her father and brother. It seems that eight months might be a reasonable time in which to see him again. A year would not be out of the question."

"And if he doesn't return with the treasure this time?"

"Then he'll leave again," she said matter-of-factly. "I told you, it's important to him."

Something about the way she said this caught Luke's attention. "Isn't it important to you?"

Bria placed both palms flat on the desk. For a moment she looked down at the spread of her fingers, appearing to study them while she considered her answer. Finally she looked up and said frankly, "The treasure is important to me because it's important to my brother. I do not want it for myself. He thinks he has to find it for all of us but he is the only one who needs it." She hesitated, then came to her feet slowly. Her palms remained flat on the desk, this time supporting her. "Rand envisions the treasure will allow him to buy Concord back from our stepfather."

"Won't it?"

"Orrin hates Rand. I don't know if he'll sell, even for the kind of jewels the treasure is supposed to contain. Rand thinks Orrin will accept an offer. I've never been so sure of it."

"So the treasure may not buy your brother what he wants."

"It's always been a possibility. This is Hamilton land, Mr. Kincaid. Or at least it was until the end of the war and a tax burden too enormous to bear. My mother married Orrin Foster and purchased a precious commodity with her vows. She bought time, Mr. Kincaid. Time for Rand to look for the treasure. Time for me to make the plantation sustain itself. It's my mother who can never be repaid. That's why I propose to take Concord back. For two hundred and fifty years this land was known as Henley. I want it to be Henley again."

Lucas understood most everything except what it had to do with him. He merely regarded her, the question in his eyes.

Bria's voice was serene. "I mean to hire you to get it back for me."

Chapter Two

Luke did not say anything for several moments. He sat there, unmoving, unblinking, absorbing what she had said. A number of thoughts eddied through his mind, all of them variations on a single theme, all of them questioning his sanity or hers.

I mean to hire you to get it back for me.

He supposed it couldn't hurt to ask. "And how do you propose one would accomplish that?"

Bria's glance slid toward the pocket doors. Could she trust that Orrin was not skulking in the hallway? More than any other room at Concord, Orrin had claimed this study as his own. Visitors, even his wife and stepdaughter, were trespassers and treated accordingly. She knew from experience that one could not eavesdrop on conversations in the study. Unless Orrin was banging around, searching for the last bottle of liquor he'd hidden, Bria had never been able to hear clearly what was going on. Even when Orrin was hosting a card game there was little Bria could surmise about the outcome from her position on the other side of the doors. There was the occasional curse, but she would have been hard-pressed to say if it had come from Orrin or one of his guests.

Knowing that she could not be overheard did not lessen

Bria's growing sense of unease. "I wonder if we might step outside, Mr. Kincaid."

At first Lucas thought she only meant to take him into the hallway and show him the door. It seemed a certainty that she was now thinking better of her rash proposal and wanted him as far from Concord as she could send him.

He accompanied Bria into the hall and anticipated her direction by taking a step toward the left and the front door. She confounded him by gracefully indicating the opposite end of the long hall.

"This way, please. For the river view." Bria preceded him out of the house and onto the wide verandah, stopping only briefly to appreciate the breathtaking canvas of gardens, water, and sky. She never tired of this view from the house, but in deference to what she believed were Lucas Kincaid's more plebeian tastes, she didn't linger to admire it.

Lucas stood on the lip of the flagstone verandah several moments longer than Bria. She was used to this, he thought, all of it. The carefully tended flower gardens were in full bloom. The effect was as if sunlight were being filtered through a prism. The full spectrum of color was scattered across the lawn. Iridescent petals of begonias maintained the borders in pastel shades of apricot, peach, and yellow. Pink ones filled in places where the tall oaks spread their shade. Roses, camellias and daylilies added more fireworks to the display. Dahlias in full blush and the deeper lavender hues of delphinium filled in circles made by carefully manicured boxwoods.

Bria glanced over her shoulder when she realized Lucas was trailing behind her. He was still poised on the edge of the verandah, one hand resting lightly on a thick white column, his left knee slightly bent as though he had been brought up in midstride. His features were cast boldly in a slant of sunlight and shadow. His rich, coffee-colored hair, overlong at the ears and a bit shaggy at the collar, appeared darker now than it had in the confines of the study. In contrast, the light grey eyes were more reflective.

He was looking out over the gardens and then beyond them to the river, and the expression on his face told Bria that he was more capable than she of enjoying this moment. Shamed, Bria turned away and held her ground, waiting for him to join her. She moved again, at a more leisurely pace this time, when she heard his feet crunch on the gravel path as he approached.

Lucas waved one hand to indicate the expanse of the grounds. "I understand why you want Concord returned to your family, but not what I can do to assist you."

"I'm not prepared to explain it to you just yet," Bria said. "You must allow that I have only just made your acquaintance. I'm not entirely convinced I can trust you."

Luke's smile was wry. He raked back his hair and looked at her askance. "I wondered about that."

"After all, you may be in my stepfather's employ."

"Yes, there is that. Perhaps you would tell me again what it is I would be doing for him."

"Finding the riddle, of course."

Luke nodded but was otherwise slow to respond. He pretended to give his response full consideration while he was actually occupied with the fragrance of lavender coming from her hair. Her peculiarities did not trouble him overmuch. Having spent most of his early and later years with his mother and six aunts, he was used to peculiarities in women. For the most part he found he was charmed more often than exasperated. His middle years, however, were a different story.

Luke grimaced. Nana Dearborn's peculiarities simply terrified him.

"Is something wrong?" asked Bria.

It took Luke a moment to realize she was speaking to him. He shook his head, not in answer to her question, but to clear the image of Nana Dearborn's stern countenance. "Wrong?"

"Mr. Kincaid, you looked as if you'd bitten into a persimmon."

Which was the single, sour expression his sainted grandmother used. For her a perpetual grimace covered the full range of emotion from joyful to despairing. Lucas concentrated on the scent of lavender again and felt the muscles of his face relax. He worked his jaw loose. "Nothing's wrong."

Bria accepted this without pressing. She pointed out the gazebo off to their right. It stood in a clearing of pines, a carpet of needles outlining its six-sided perimeter. "There used to be a cabin there. It was the first building erected at Henley. It was burned by Tories during the Revolution and never rebuilt. My grandfather had the gazebo erected."

They were close to the water now. The Cooper River lapped against the bank, providing accompaniment to their steps with its steady beat. Bria turned toward the gazebo. They were both silent until they reached it. Bria climbed the stairs to it first. She heard the boards creak under her weight and snap to louder attention under Luke's.

"These steps are starting to rot," he said. "They should be replaced before someone falls through." He began to look around. There were signs of mildew on the floor of the gazebo. The problem, he thought, was not so much due to the proximity to the river, but to a leaking roof. He glanced up and immediately saw two disjointed seams that could be the cause. His eyes followed the likely path of the water—and came squarely in contact with Bria Hamilton's interested gaze.

"Aaah," he said slowly. "It was a test of sorts."

"Of sorts," she agreed. "Although I would not say that it takes any great skill to surmise there are some repairs to be made."

"Repairs? I would tear down this structure and start again."

Bria shook her head. "Then Concord can't afford you. Orrin will not approve that sort of money."

Luke's gaze left Bria's face and focused on a point past her shoulder. The cascading branches of pines gave him a somewhat restricted view of the house but his keen eye picked out the salient features. He could see patches in the roof where the repairs did not quite blend in with the original. Panes of glass that had been used to replace what had been shattered were not of the same thickness and quality as the earlier ones. Sunlight lay flat against those windows while at others it winked and shimmered. The impressive columns supporting the balcony above the verandah were freshly painted, but Luke remembered the feel of one under his palm. A certain roughness underscored the paint. Strip it away, he thought, and he would find evidence of fire and insect damage.

In his mind's eye he stepped back into the house and passed through the hallway where the plaster had been reworked in patches instead of refinishing the entire wall. He recalled that the pocket doors to the study had been hard to open, first for Addie and later for Bria, a sure sign they were warping with heat and humidity and thickening with too many coats of varnish. The study was relatively recently furnished. The carpet and fabrics were undamaged by sunlight. The desk gleamed with polish and the surface itself was unblemished. But the shelves that held the burnished leather-bound books were starting to sag. When Bria had pulled back the drapes he recalled seeing evidence of water damage beneath the middle window.

There was no question in his mind that much had been done to give Concord the appearance of her former grandeur. No doubt a great deal of money had been spent toward that end. Orrin Foster's money, if he could believe everything he'd heard. Concord had been dressed up and turned out like Cinderella at the prince's ball. Somewhere, close by, there was a clock ticking inexorably toward the midnight hour.

Lucas swiveled his glance back to Bria. "Mr. Foster is willing to gild the lily, I take it, but not to nurture the plant."

Bria wondered where he had gone when his eyes had taken on that distant look. Now she knew. He had taken a closer look at Concord and found her wanting. "My stepfather had a vision of Southern life when he came here that ceased to exist during the war."

"Then he's not from these parts?"

"No. Philadelphia."

Luke's mouth twitched. "A carpetbagger."

Bria did not share his amusement. "He thought he could recreate a lifestyle of leisure and graciousness. The first is a myth—at least here it was. My father and brothers worked as hard or harder than any three bucks. And graciousness is bred in the bone."

"Obviously it can leapfrog a generation," Luke said dryly.

Bria gave a small start. Her mouth parted a fraction as her chin came up. Had he just said she had been something less than gracious? That she had given him any time at all was making herself hospitable to a fault. She could have directed Addie to show him the trader's entrance by way of showing him out and been done with him. Instead she let herself be swayed by his determination to reach Concord and find employment. She would have hired him at the outset if he had been anyone but a Yankee. It was a sad truth that there was a chronic shortage of workers, but the crisply accented edge of his speech grated across Bria's memory, turning up bits of flotsam like the tides after a storm.

"If I have given offense," she said carefully, "then I apologize."

Luke doubted she even knew what she'd said that raised his hackles. He debated whether to tell her or let it pass. "When you referred to the men who worked at Concord as bucks . . . well, yes, I found it offensive."

"My," she said quietly, more to herself than to him. "And you accused *me* of still fighting the war. What would you have me call them?"

"Slaves. That's what they were, weren't they?"

Bria didn't flinch from his tone but the words *self-righteous, abolitionist, Yankee prig* were tumbling through her mind. "There were all kinds of slaves on this plantation, Mr. Kincaid. House nigras like Addie and Jebediah, caretakers like Eb and George. Some, like Cutch and Mammy Komati, were free blacks, more like members of my family than you can possibly imagine, respected and revered, even loved. There were field hands and skilled workers but the strongest, best, and, yes, handsomest men were the bucks. My brothers would have been flattered to be called such. You know nothing about life here as it was before the war. You may even know less than my stepfather did. Perhaps you should learn more before you rush to judgment.''

Luke wasn't sure he could move after having been so firmly put in his place. She hadn't once raised her voice or given herself over to passion. There was no apology here. Clearly she thought he was the one who misspoke. It was on the tip of his tongue to fumble through some act of contrition when a disturbance off to the right caught his attention.

''What the—'' He broke off as a horse and rider cleared a stand of trees and galloped precariously close to the perimeter of the riverbank. Clods of earth churned up by the horse's hooves were thrown into the water. Sunlight gave the animal's lathered coat a blue-black sheen and sharpened the edge of the rider's weighted riding crop.

Luke spun on his heels to better follow the passing of the pair. The floor of the gazebo actually echoed the vibration of the ground. The wooden shingles overhead shivered in place as horse and rider thundered by. The canopy of pine boughs would have thwarted the progress of a less tenacious rider. The man seated astride the thoroughly frightened animal used his crop to slash at the boughs and alternately to slash at his mount. The rider's face was florid with his exertions. A bit of spittle flew from his mouth as he whipped the animal under him to greater efforts.

''Like the wind, you damn sack of oats! Fly!'' The horse raced between the trunks of two trees that Luke thought wouldn't permit the passing of his own shoulders. Horse and rider went through as easily as water through a sieve. Pine branches swayed in the aftermath and the sweet scent of sap lingered in the air.

Luke discovered he had been holding his breath. He let it out slowly as the labored sound of the horse and the curses of the rider diminished with distance. ''I've never seen—'' He stopped when he realized that Bria was no longer sharing the gazebo with him. He had a glimpse of delicately turned ankles and slim calves as she lifted her gown to clear the last step. Then she was running across the lawn at an angle, hurdling the hedge roses and boxwoods as if they were no more a nuisance than a puddle. The hem of her cream-and-red-striped gown was rucked up to her knees now and the lace trim of three petticoats fluttered just below it.

The intricate coil that held her hair in place with pins and a cherry red ribbon was starting to falter. One thick lock escaped and lay over her temple like the floppy ear of a basset hound. It was an improvement, Luke supposed, that she was no longer reminding him of Nana Dearborn.

Knowing himself to be much less chivalrous than curious, Lucas Kincaid threw himself into the chase. Vaulting over the side rail of the gazebo, he cleared the carpet of pine needles and darted past the pines for the open lawn. Until he started running he'd forgotten the shoes he was wearing weren't his, or at least that they had only recently become so. The worn leather had too much give in it and his feet slid forward with each step, jamming his toes, then rubbing his heels. Catching up with Bria was going to be more difficult than he thought, especially when he realized how very fleet of foot she was.

Luke did not know Bria's destination until he saw the crumbling wall of an old stone foundation. There was nothing to indicate what sort of structure the stones had once supported. It could have been a curing shed, an outbuilding for tools, or the old kitchen. The stones rose abruptly from the ground, mostly intact on one side to a height of four feet, and more raggedly on the two adjoining sides. One section of the wall had been removed altogether. Grass and wildflowers grew high around the shattered foundation and throughout its center.

Luke caught up with Bria seconds before she met the wall. He leaned against it to rest and catch his breath. Bria, he noticed, allowed herself no such luxury. She stepped up on one of the blocks and peered in the direction of the woods. Shading her eyes from the sun, she raised herself on another stone. Luke glanced down at her feet. They weren't winged after all.

When he looked up Bria was no longer staring off into the woods. She was watching him. She pushed at the skirt of her gown, smoothing it over her midriff as if that would lower the hem. That she was self-conscious now seemed out of character for a woman who had just raced across a lawn with her knees showing.

Bria accepted the hand he held out and dismounted from her perch.

"Why are we here?" Luke asked.

"I'm here because my stepfather is going to kill Apollo if I don't stop him. I can't speak for you."

Luke ignored Bria's faint jibe. Apparently she hadn't forgiven him for staring at her feet. If she had known what he thought about her stockinged calves she'd have boxed his ears. "That was Mr. Foster?" he asked.

She understood he wasn't really questioning her. It was simple disbelief that prompted him to speak. Orrin Foster's behavior did that to people. Just when Bria thought it was not possible for him to act in a more brutish manner he exceeded her expectations. "Yes," she said. "The master of Concord."

"Does he ride like that often?"

"Drunk, you mean?"

Luke hadn't realized Foster was drunk but he believed Bria. "Bruising, I was thinking."

"Bruising," she said softly. "Yes, that describes him exactly. The horse is mine this time. That's different for him. He's never dared it before."

"How do you know he'll come here?"

"Because he won't be able to help himself. This wall challenges him. Perhaps because I can clear it on Apollo's back. I'd let him break his neck if I didn't think he'd break Apollo first."

Luke's ears picked up the sound of a disturbance in the woods at the same time Bria did. She stepped around him to get a better look while Luke turned on his heel. Just as she predicted, her stepfather and Apollo emerged from a break in the trees and headed toward the foundation. Foster was bent low toward the horse's mane. Occasionally his right arm swung back with the crop. A practiced flick of his wrist snapped the whip over Apollo's hindquarters. Snorting, his ears laid back, the horse raced forward.

Waving her arms and crying Apollo's name, Bria ran ahead to meet them. Foster wasn't distracted by her antics but he felt Apollo veer off course.

"Goddamn you, Bria!" he yelled, giving Apollo his head. "I'll run you over, you devil's whore!"

Bria's arms fell to her sides. Beads of perspiration touched her forehead and upper lip in spite of the fact that she was shaking with cold fury. She stood as if newly planted, her hands trembling like leaves turning in a gentle breeze. Apollo bore down on her.

She heard Luke shout but only as she was diving into the grass. Apollo's hooves thundered close and then the animal and his rider were airborne effortlessly over her head. Bria felt the ground shake as both landed again. She twisted onto her side, fought off the tangle of her own petticoats, and pushed herself upright. Her stepfather was still driving Apollo toward the wall. She knew just by the angle of entry that they couldn't possibly make it.

Bria's heart could not sustain another loss. She had been so certain she was numb to all feeling, yet watching Apollo race toward his own destruction warned Bria she had not quite come to that pass. Seeing this valiant animal die in the service of pleasing Orrin Foster would leave her with no shred of emotion. Already she could feel herself stepping outside the pain and hurt and embracing the void.

She watched what was happening as though from a great distance, where she was an observer, even of herself. The farther back she reached into the emptiness, the wider the tableau became and the clearer her vision.

Bria saw herself sitting on the ground midway between the woods and the walls. One arm was outstretched, a gesture that was at once supplicating and horror-filled. Beyond her ability to reach them with either hand or voice, Apollo and Orrin plunged on. The great shining muscles of the horse bunched and shifted as he was driven forward. Above him Orrin held his seat with the foolish courage and dumb luck of a drunk.

Ahead of them still was Lucas Kincaid. He was crouched on the stone foundation some five feet about the ground. He had thrown off his jacket and his sun-bleached white shirt flashed brightly as he shifted his position. Then there was no movement at all from him as he took on the watchful stillness of a predator.

He leaped suddenly. His effort had the extraordinary agility of a mountain cat and the unerring accuracy of a falcon. Apollo reared, then changed direction, going along the wall instead of over it. Luke slammed into the horse and rider, making Foster bear the brunt of most of the attack. They went over Apollo's flank while the horse raced on, free of its onerous burden.

Bria's lungs filled with air as her body and mind connected with powerful force. She was propelled to her feet, stumbling at first as though being pushed from behind by tangible fingers of energy. She dashed to the site where her stepfather was rolling on the ground with Lucas Kincaid. It was hard to believe they both weren't unconscious.

"Let him up, Orrin," she said sharply. "He saved your life."

Foster grunted. "He tried to kill me."

Bria reached down, nimbly dodging the rolling bodies while she tried to grab her stepfather by the collar. For her efforts she had her arm slapped away. She tried again and this time provided enough distraction for Lucas to pin Orrin back. Luke swung one leg over Orrin's thick middle and pulled himself to a sitting position across the older man's stomach. When Orrin struggled, Luke lifted himself then sat down harder.

"Aaaooooh!" The air that rushed from Orrin's stomach was

a mixture of alcohol and fermenting foodstuffs. Had Lucas struck a match the result would have thrown a flame three feet in the air. "I can't breathe," Orrin groaned.

Lucas turned his face to one side. "That makes two of us."

"Yer squeezing my lungs."

"Take shallow breaths," Luke said. "You'll manage."

"I'm going to puke!"

That was the threat that dislodged Lucas, though he was sorely tempted to keep Foster on his back and let him drown in his own vomit. He pushed off him in disgust and rose to his knees, brushing himself off. His shirt, fragile as it was, had survived the altercation with nothing more than some grass stains. Luke doubted it would survive the washing necessary to remove them. It was a two-dollar loss, he figured, and mentally applied the debit to his streak of bad luck.

He was brushing the back of his trousers when he realized he had yet to hear the sounds of Orrin Foster being sick. The attack came a mere second after Bria shouted a warning and he realized his position left him vulnerable to a blow at the middle.

Foster drove the breath from Luke's lungs with a meaty fist to his midriff. This was followed in short order by a roundhouse punch to the head. Luke toppled sideways, heaving for air and seeing pinpricks of light on the edge of his vision. While he was trying to recover he felt Bria throw herself into the fray. He shook his head, intent on clearing the orbiting meteor shower, and saw *two* Brias clobber Foster with a piece of the crumbling wall. *Easy for her*, he thought as Foster was felled. *She has a friend.*

Lucas came around a few minutes later. Bria was sitting beside him at the level of his shoulders, tapping his face lightly. He imagined that she was peering at him with what passed as her anxious expression. The sapphire-blue eyes remained detached but her lower lip had been pulled in just a fraction. She would not want to affect too much concern, he thought, in the event he placed some meaning to it that she did not intend.

He raised his lashes to better than half-mast and felt Bria withdraw her fingers from his cheek.

"Good," she said, satisfied. "Is anything broken?"

Luke glanced at Orrin, remembering how Bria had taken him out with a piece of stone. There hadn't been two of her at all. "My pride," he said faintly.

"Nonsense. You gave a good account of yourself. How is your jaw?"

He moved it from side to side, gingerly at first and then with some vigor. "Not broken." Which was not to say that it was fine. He didn't clearly remember being hit there. When had it happened? Luke turned his head slightly in order to see Foster and felt the ground spin under him.

"It would be better if you simply kept looking at me," she said.

In so many ways. Luke grinned a little crookedly at her. "If I must." He noticed that Bria did not flush prettily as other women might have done. She did not acknowledge in any fashion that he had just flirted with her. Unless, he thought, the color draining from her face *was* her response. His grin faded. He kept his head steady and allowed only his eyes to shift in Foster's direction. From this angle he could make out the turned up feet and belly of the man.

Before he looked away he saw Orrin's chest rise and fall abruptly and a harsh sound, like the final bark of a frenzied, exhausted hound, caused his entire body to convulse. Both of Luke's brows arched as Orrin's feet fell sideways. The man remained still after that.

Luke glanced back at Bria. "Death rattle?"

"Snore."

"He's *snoring?*" Luke asked. He carefully raised himself on one elbow to get a better look at the man. In the time it took to do that, Orrin's chest heaved again as he dragged air into his lungs. The effort made his body twitch. Entire armies marched across cobblestone roads with less noise than Orrin Foster made sleeping. "Then you didn't kill him."

She shook her head. "Not this time."

"Pity."

Bria looked at him sharply. How seriously was she expected to take that comment? Uncertain, she decided it was best to ignore it. "Can you sit up now?"

Luke pushed himself into a full sitting position. His head didn't swim this time. He rolled his shoulders to work out the stiffness, then did the same to his neck. He looked up at the wall. From his current perspective the height seemed enormous.

Bria followed Luke's glance. "You earned every one of your bruises," she said. "You covered quite a distance."

Out of the corner of his eye Luke saw that Apollo had wandered into the clearing. He kept his distance, skittish still. He watched them warily, advancing a few feet only to be driven back by Orrin's rumbling snores. "Is your horse all right?" he asked.

"As near as I can tell. I haven't tried to get close to him."

"Your stepfather rode him hard. He needs to be rubbed down."

"I'll attend to that as soon as you're on your feet again."

Luke realized then that he was keeping her from making arrangements for her horse. He drew his legs under him and confirmed that nothing had been broken or even sprained, then he rose to his feet in a single fluid movement. He extended one hand to Bria.

"I forget that you're self-sufficient," he said when she ignored his outstretched hand and stood without assistance. Shrugging, he withdrew his arm. At least she hadn't reached for a weapon to fend off his attack. She may not have had the letter opener handy, but he only had to see Orrin Foster's prostrate form to remember that she was a resourceful woman.

"I've learned to be," Bria said.

Luke could detect no bitterness in her tone but he wondered at the lessons she had endured to reach this pass. He watched her brush herself off. Dust rose from her palms as she slapped them together. She left a trail of smudges when she smoothed the material across her midriff. There was a grass stain on her sleeve and another at the level of her knee. Her hair was repaired in short order although the effect was softer looking than if she had had a mirror. Luke thought that had she seen her reflection, Bria probably would not have permitted the stray blade of grass to remain. The end of it tickled the upper curve of her ear so that from time to time she pushed it back impatiently.

The fact that Luke valued his life was only part of the reason he didn't pluck it from her hair. The truth was, she looked delightful. It was astonishing, he thought, what a single, misplaced blade of grass could do for cold eyes, a severe mouth, and a sharp tongue. Truly astonishing.

Belatedly he noticed that Bria was looking at him oddly. He glanced down at himself, then back at her, a question in his own eyes.

"You were whistling," she said.

Had he been? He tried to remember. He could feel the residual pucker of his lips so it must have been true. *Mine eyes have seen the glory . . .* The tune went through his mind again and he understood the problem. *The Battle Hymn of the Republic* was not likely to endear him to Bria Hamilton. "My apologies," he said.

"At least choose another tune." With no more admonishment than that, she started off toward Apollo.

Lucas hastily grabbed his jacket from the wall and shrugged into it. He caught up to her when she had covered half the distance to her horse. "What about Mr. Foster?" he asked.

"He'll sleep it off," she said without a backward glance. "He'll be fine."

There was no mistaking the confidence in her tone. Luke supposed she spoke from experience. "Won't he be angry?"

"At me you mean? I doubt it. No more than usual, at any rate. Like as not Orrin won't remember it."

"Won't remember it? He was *that* drunk?"

"He's nearly always *that* drunk, Mr. Kincaid." She held out one arm sideways to halt his progress. "Now you really must be quiet else I won't be able to reach Apollo. And stay here. He's wary of you, you know. You did fly at him."

Luke thought he detected the faintest hint of amusement in her voice. He stayed where he was and took pleasure in the easy sway of her skirts as she walked on. She spoke to her horse gently, crooning a sweet song of nonsense words and encouragement. The big black gelding shied away at first, snorting and stamping his feet restlessly, but Bria gave him no quarter. The voice that was as thick and sweet as honey merely disguised an approach as relentless and powerful as the moon's tug on the tides.

There was something to be learned here, Luke decided. Something about her, and something to be gained for himself as well.

Bria caught Apollo's bridle and held it firmly. When the horse would have pulled away, she brought him back. She was careful not to jerk or yank and engage in a battle of brute strength she could not possibly win. Bria knew that his mouth was sore from Orrin's rough handling and she softened her hold, not in fact, but with gentle words. She stroked his nose and forelock and held one palm flat under his mouth. Apollo snuffled, searching out a treat.

"In a little while," she said. "I promise. When we get back to the stable I'll have something for you."

The gelding snorted, unmoved by vague promises.

"Sweet oats," she said. "Perhaps an apple?"

Apollo shook himself out and pranced a little.

Still holding the bridle in one hand, Bria stroked his mane with the other. Her palm slid along his damp neck. Apollo tossed his head and cords of muscle rolled under her fingertips. "Shhh," she whispered. "You're safe with me. I won't let him have you again." She released the bridle and continued to stroke him, moving closer to the saddle to prepare to mount. Apollo had to take her as a rider again and soon, else he might never accept her. She did not want Orrin's hard handling to be what Apollo remembered.

"Would you like a leg up?"

Bria spun on Luke, glaring at him as Apollo bolted ten yards closer to the woods. She pointed toward the house.

In spite of the fact that Luke regretted his ill-timed offer, he was not going to skulk off like a shamed puppy. It was not as if he had just dirtied her carpet. Luke stood his ground. A small measure of the same gentle encouragement she used with Apollo would have had an even more profound effect on him. Luke thought it was just as well this approach did not seem to occur to Bria. He really had no wish to turn cartwheels for her.

One corner of Bria's mouth curved upward, her smile unamused and derisive as Luke folded his arms across his chest and told her without words that he would not be moved. "Then . . . be . . . *quiet,*" she told him.

Luke did not signal his intention to obey one way or the other.

Bria shook her head and stalked off after Apollo. It took only a little less time to gentle him again. When she believed he would stand for it, Bria hiked up her gown and petticoats and put one foot in Apollo's stirrup. The gelding balked and shuffled sideways. Bria held on and pulled herself up and over the saddle.

Although she was used to riding astride, she'd never done so in a dress. Yards of material settled around her. Without glancing in his direction she knew Lucas Kincaid was watching her. It was bad enough that she looked like a cake ornament without making a cake of herself. She gathered the cream-and-red fabric of her skirt along with her petticoats and tucked it around her legs as best she could. Apollo danced under Bria, testing her resolve to stay in the saddle. She realized that he was not so gentled that he wouldn't try to make her lose her seat.

Bria abandoned doing something with her gown and took up the reins in both hands. She patted Apollo on the neck and crooned softly to him again, then she nudged him firmly with her heels. He obediently began walking. The stables were on the far side of the house. Bria turned him in that direction and gradually let him pick up speed until his pace was a brisk trot.

Luke watched them go. A small smile softened the curve of his mouth as he lowered his arms to his sides. He glanced at Orrin Foster and saw he had fallen into a more restful slumber. The sun was lower in the sky and the wall's shadow extended to where Orrin had dropped. The shade must have provided him a modicum of comfort—his breathing was regular and much less labored. Luke went closer and stood over the man, studying him for several long minutes. In sleep he looked extraordinarily peaceful. "Not that you deserve it," Luke said quietly. "Bastard."

He stepped over Orrin Foster and started to walk.

Bria was in the stables when he arrived there. He thought she might still be lecturing the stable hands but she was occupied rubbing down Apollo. Her strokes were vigorous and beneath the tight sleeve of her gown, Luke could make out the definition of taut muscle. Though she was flushed pink, the work did not appear to tire her.

"Have you no one to help you?" asked Luke.

Bria pulled the brush harder across Apollo's flanks. "I sent them out to look after Orrin."

"Aaah," Luke said, remembering the two hapless fellows who'd passed him without speaking. "Punishment enough for their carelessness."

Bria paused and glanced over her shoulder. "I don't blame Tad and Geordie for what happened. I am the only one at Concord who might have stopped Orrin and I was occupied with you."

"So it was my fault."

She grimaced at this facetious line of reasoning. "If you're so eager to accept fault, then you may have it." Bria twisted around and picked up a brush that was lying on the divider between the stalls. She tossed it to Luke.

He caught it easily but didn't move from his place in the gated doorway. "Am I being punished?" he asked. "Or are you asking for help?"

"Either," she said. "Both, if that's more to your liking."

"I'd rather you said it."

"Oh, very well. I would much appreciate your assistance."

Her delivery was left of the target but the words themselves were on the mark. He entered the stall and pulled the gate closed behind him. He saw the steady rhythm of Bria's brush falter, then resume the stroking with less vigor. She had no liking for sharing this small space with him, that was clear enough to Luke. Was it him? he wondered. Or any man?

He casually opened the gate again.

Bria shot him a glance.

"In the event this beast of yours needs a quick way out," he offered in explanation. "I'd rather it wasn't through me."

Bria nodded. "Give him a piece of that apple over there and make friends."

Luke took a slice of apple from the stool in the corner and fed it to Apollo. The horse shook his head and poked at Luke's hand. "How would you have stopped him?" he asked idly.

"What?"

"You said you were the only one at Concord who could have stopped your stepfather. How would you have done it?"

"Can I assume from that that you weren't impressed with my flailing-arms diversion?"

Luke grinned. She had a sense of humor after all. "I had better hopes for success when you threw yourself prostrate on the ground." In fact, he'd been terrified she'd be trampled.

"You'll understand if I don't employ that particular strategy often."

Thank God, he thought. He patted Apollo on the nose again, then moved to the opposite side and began brushing out the blue-black coat. "So what strategy would you have employed?"

"I find that simply keeping an eye on him works best," she

said. "If his antics can't be nipped in the bud then there is always the point of a gun."

Luke bent down and stared at her from under Apollo's neck.

Bria intercepted his glance, made no effort to smile, and continued with her work.

Luke resumed as well. "You're serious."

"I have to be. You can see for yourself that he's dangerous. I can't always play the nursemaid, Mr. Kincaid."

"Your mother? I believe you mentioned he was going to join her today."

"It will be tomorrow by the looks of it now. My mother does better staying out of his sight than in it. I prefer it that way as well."

"And yet you're not going with him to Charleston."

Bria did not answer immediately. She was troubled by the same line of thinking, but she owed no explanations to Lucas Kincaid. "Will you join us for dinner, Mr. Kincaid?" she asked. "We're informal here. It's late now for you to be starting back to town. Jeb can find a place for you in one of the old slave cabins. You'll be comfortable enough there. In the morning, who knows?" She shrugged lightly. "Orrin might offer you a ride with him."

Luke very much doubted that. "I thought you meant to hire me," he said.

"I haven't changed my mind," she told him. "But I never said *when*."

Jebediah Brown showed Luke where he could wash up. "This here used to be the overseer's place," Jeb told him. He was tall enough that he had to duck in the doorway as he entered the house. He brushed a cobweb out of his salt-and-pepper hair. "I'll have Martha and the girls take their brooms to it directly. Lay down some fresh linens, too, since you'll be staying the night." He scratched his head, his wide brow furrowed as he studied Lucas.

"What is it?" Luke asked.

Jeb seemed to remember his duties suddenly. He hefted the bucket he was holding and carried it over to a washstand. He made a cursory swipe of the bowl with his free hand, then poured half the bucket into it. The other half went into a pitcher that had been turned upside down. He remarked under his breath that it was probably clean enough. "Don' make no kind of sense," he said to himself.

"What's that?"

"Oh, I gets to talkin' to myself sometimes," Jeb explained. "On no account should you pay attention."

Luke looked around him. The quarters consisted of two rooms. The one he was in had a hearth, a table and three chairs, the washstand, and a wood stove. Some pots and pans hung from a rack above the stove. A few utensils lay along the back of it. Luke craned his head a bit to get a peek at the other room. He saw a bed in there that had been stripped to the mattress. It did not look particularly inviting but his choices would have been a pallet of straw in the stables or a spot of hard ground somewhere between Concord and Charleston.

Luke's eyes wandered back to Jebediah. The man had just muttered something under his breath again and was now engaged in shaking his head slowly from side to side. For someone who claimed he wanted no attention, Jeb certainly had a way of bringing it upon himself. "You were saying?" Luke prompted dryly.

"Was I?" Jeb asked. "Don' rightly know. Don' listen much. Don' nobody else, either. 'Cept you. I reckon you have a powerful curiosity." He glanced down and saw a cobweb had attached itself to his arm. It lay spread like a tangle of veins across his dark skin. With another long-suffering sigh, he brushed it off. "No kinda sense," he said. He looked directly at Lucas now. "Why would Miss Bree invite you to dinner in the big house and offer you these quarters for the night?"

"Because I'm a Yankee?"

Jebediah snorted. "You bein' a Yankee shoulda got you

pullin' jackstraw outta your behind on account of the broom she took to you. It would have been passing simple if she'd put you up at the house for the night.'' Both of his brows arched and the look in his black eyes was frank and somehow conspiratorial. ''You want to know what I think?''

''I've *been* asking.''

''Something is rotten in the state of Denmark.''

Luke blinked. Jebediah had just quoted Shakespeare. And correctly. Before he could ask how that had come to pass, the man had ducked under the doorframe again and was hurrying across the lawn. Luke resisted the temptation to call after him. Jeb would probably have denied knowing the passage's origins. *There* was a man who was dumb as a fox.

Luke shrugged out of his jacket. He folded it carefully over one of the chairs, then stripped off his shirt. He found a sliver of soap in the bottom of the washstand and used it to gingerly scrub the grass stains from the sleeve. He was sluicing water over his face and chest, waiting for the shirt to dry, when he was interrupted by a parade of young negresses. They marched into the cabin single file, a half dozen strong, all-business except for the sly glances they stole in his direction. The youngest among them actually giggled when he hastily retrieved his shirt and put it on.

One was tall, another pleasingly round. Two had the look of Jebediah Brown about them. They made quick work of making his living quarters habitable. It was Martha, he assumed, who was swinging the broom with real vigor. The cloud of dust they created was absorbed by the wet mops and sponges. If the rooms were still relatively barren when they left, then at least they were clean. Fresh water had been poured into the basin and the floor had been scoured. The bed was made up with clean, white linens and on the table top was a package that had been left by one of Jeb's daughters.

''Miss Bree says you should wear these,'' was all she said before she ran out to join the others.

Now Luke unfolded the thin blanket that had served as wrapping for the contents. He stood back, whistling softly and raking his hair with his fingers. No matter what the girl said to him, Luke had been more prepared to find a snake under the blanket than these fine garments.

He picked up the jacket that lay on top and unfolded it. He held it up and judged the fit to be a good one. His nose picked up the faint scent of cedar. The clothes, whoever they belonged to, had been in storage. The jacket was tan cotton broadcloth, a good choice for the Carolina heat. The trousers were of the same material. The silkaline undergarments were more comfortable than what he was currently wearing. Bria, if indeed she had chosen the clothing, had included brown high-topped shoes and a black satin striped silk waistcoat. The pristine white shirt was as fine as anything he had ever owned.

Luke closed and barred the door against further interruptions, then carried his bounty into the bedroom. In short order he was dressed, this time in clothes that fit him remarkably better than the ones he came to Concord wearing. His quarters had no mirror but Luke caught his reflection briefly in the window and pronounced himself turned out well enough for dinner in the big house.

He approached the house this time from the river side. Bria was on the verandah sipping lemonade. She gave a small start as he came up the wide steps.

"Oh, Mr. Kincaid," she said, recovering quickly. Her smile was faintly apologetic. "I didn't hear you."

But that wasn't cause for her start, he thought. It was something about his appearance that had done that. She might have wanted him to wear these things, but she wasn't prepared for the way he looked in them. Lucas Kincaid was not unaware of his good looks. He had a mother and a half dozen aunts who never failed to tell him how handsome he was. He had always accepted their pronouncements with a few grains of salt, understanding that their doting led to effusive praise. Thaddeus Prichett's mother said the same thing about her son and Thaddeus had a face that made horses bolt. But then Nana Dearborn told Lucas the same thing and she hadn't meant it as praise. He was too handsome by half, she'd said, and peacock proud. His eyes were full of deviltry and he had a smile that would make Saint Joan herself recant.

When Luke had merely grinned back at her, too surprised to know what to say, she'd slapped that smile away. After that, Luke just figured he was handsome but took no special pleasure in it.

"Did I misunderstand?" he asked. "You meant me to wear these things, didn't you?"

How like him to lay the subject before her when she would rather have walked around it. "Yes, I meant you to wear them. You may consider them yours."

"Then thank you," he said. "They're a good fit."

She nodded. Through some considerable exercise of her own will she managed not to let her gaze roam all over him. "At first I thought David's clothes would be best, then I remembered the trunk Mother kept of Shelby's things. Father's clothes were out of the question. Would you care for something to drink?" She turned her hand in one of those graceful gestures that came so naturally to her. "I was having lemonade."

Luke saw that she had anticipated his acceptance by having another glass at the ready. He nodded and bent slightly to take it from her.

"Please, won't you sit down? You'll find the air from the river cools things off a bit."

Luke sat in the empty wicker chair. A small round table that held the pitcher of lemonade separated them. He sipped his drink, wondering if he should acknowledge that he knew who David and Shelby were. He supposed his silence spoke for itself. He did not know the details of their deaths, or that of her father, except to know that none of them had lived to see the end of the war. Of the Hamilton men, only Rand had survived the fighting. Bria and Elizabeth Hamilton were left to survive the surrender.

Bria set down her glass and picked up the paddle fan lying

in her lap. She waved it lightly in front of her, raising her chin to let the moving air touch her arched throat. "Would you like one?" she asked Lucas. "I imagine this heat is difficult for you."

"I've been working in the South for some time now, Miss Hamilton. I find it tolerable."

She lowered her head and gave him a frank look. "My step-father hates it."

"That's because he drinks so much."

"I know. My mother has tried to tell him that he'd be more comfortable leaving his bourbon in the decanter."

"How is he doing? Will he be joining us for dinner?"

"Oh, yes. It takes a bit more than a knot on the head to keep Orrin on his back for long."

"Does he know how he got the knot?"

"When you tried to kill him, of course."

Chapter Three

"*When I tried to kill him?*" asked Luke. "I thought you said he wouldn't remember that."

"Really, Mr. Kincaid. You must be more cautious in your phrasing. You make it sound as if you *were* intent on murder."

Luke raised his glass in a small salute. She had reeled him in again. He used to think he was a smarter fish. Evidently it was an opinion in need of revision. What was odder, he didn't think he particularly minded. Who was to say he couldn't pull on the line hard enough to yank her in the drink with him? It was a notion worth entertaining.

Smiling to himself, Luke sat back, comfortable with the silence that settled between them. The breeze from the river carried the scent of roses mingled with the fragrance of lavender in Bria's hair.

She'd changed, as he had. The blade of grass had been plucked from her hair and the ribbon wound in her coil was blue now, not red. Even under the wafting air of the paddle fan, not a strand dared move out of place. The dress was muslin printed in a pattern of delicate blue and white flowers. Three tiers of flounces repeated the pattern in the jacket. The particular shade of Delft blue was no match for her eyes but made them somehow seem a deeper and richer blue for the contrast.

She sat in the middle of a wide wicker chair, her back regally straight, her long legs postured primly together beneath the spread of her skirt. Her arms rested flatly on the arms of the chair. Bria's only movement was the hand that bent back and forth at the wrist waving the paddle fan.

She seemed oblivious to his presence as she stared out toward the river. Beneath lids and lashes that shielded most of his eyes, Luke studied her three-quarter profile, knowing all the while that divining her thoughts was impossible. Bria's carefully composed features did not lend themselves to interpretation.

There was a trace of color in her cheeks but Luke believed it was a product of the evening's warmth, and not to be confused with either embarrassment or excitement. She had full lips, parted fractionally now and faintly damp with a hint of lemonade. He imagined the taste of them would be more tart and less sweet than the drink she served, although he would have been willing to be proved wrong.

"Is it your grandmother again?" she asked. Bria turned her head fully toward him. "You have the oddest expression on your face."

"No, I wasn't thinking of her just then, though now that you mention it, you rather sit like her." When Bria arched a single brow, Luke chuckled. "Your disdain is noted," he said. "Again, very much like Nana Dearborn."

"I think I approve of your dear Nana."

"She was never my dear Nana. You may as well know she only endured me."

Bria bit back the rejoinder that came immediately to mind and instead offered softly, "I'm sorry. Grandmothers should be a place to go when no one else understands you."

"Were your grandmothers like that?"

She shook her head. "My mother's mother died when I was very young. I have no memory of her. Grandmama Hamilton passed on before I was born, just around the time my parents were married. I never knew her. But I had Mammy Komati and she was very much like I would expect a grandmother to be. My father had to accept her when he married my mother. Mother wouldn't come to Henley without her." Bria's smile was wistful. "Father always said he was forced to start a family right away in order to give Mammy something to do. She snorted at that and told him on no account was she taking blame for his lustful ways. *'Givin' my baby babies.'*" Bria affected the deep, throaty timbre of Mammy Komati's rich baritone. " *'Why, t'ain't fitting that she should have so many in a row like some bitch throwing a litter. You'll break her, Master Andrew. Mark my words.'* "

"Mammy was a plain speaker, I take it."

"Very. Whether by accident or design my father appeared to heed her. David, Rand, and Shelby were the ones in a row. I came along some years after. Mammy, of course, took a contrary view. ' *'Bout time Henley had itself a girl child. Don' know what you were thinking sirin' all these young ruffians first.'* " She paused as Lucas laughed. "I think Father came to realize there was no satisfying her, at least not so that she would admit to it. He did better than endure her. He respected her. Naturally, my brothers and I adored her. She was strict and loving and told the most remarkable stories about Africa. She was a Christian woman when it served her and a practitioner of healing rituals and sacrifices when she thought prayer was taking too long. We could come to her with broken birds and injured possums and she'd make them well again. For most of their lives, she kept the young ruffians on the straight and narrow. She was marginally less successful with me."

Luke took a sip of his lemonade. The edge of the glass hid his deepening smile. How wild would she have become in less formidable and capable hands than Mammy Komati's? "And how did you try her patience?"

"I trailed after my brothers," she said simply. When this

explanation was met by Luke's blank expression, she added, "Do you have sisters, Mr. Kincaid?"

"No."

"Aaah." Bria nodded once, wisely. "Then you don't know how very trying and determined we can be."

He was beginning to have an idea. Luke set his glass aside and stretched his legs. In contrast to Bria's rigid position he felt as if he were sprawling in his chair. He crossed his legs at the ankles to contain himself. "I'm willing to be enlightened," he said.

Bria wondered what she really wanted to tell him. It was not that she was particularly secretive about her family; it was just that she did not often have the opportunity to talk about them. Rand's recent visit had stirred some memories that she thought had been lost to her. It wasn't Rand who drew her out, but Claire Bancroft, his passenger on the voyage. Claire had a way of asking questions without prying and a way of listening to the answers that made Bria hear herself, on occasion for the first time.

Lucas Kincaid was a little like that, Bria thought. He was watchful in a quiet manner. He observed things around him, not with the wariness she recognized in herself or Rand, but with a rather restrained curiosity that she found interesting. He was not guarded, but he was alert and probably saw much more than he commented on. That meant he could be circumspect when he chose to be. His eyes were not always entirely implacable; she had seen glimpses of his humor in their depths.

Though he looked completely at ease half-reclining in his chair, Bria wondered if that could possibly be the case. He seemed to be always thinking, his minding churning away in deep waters while his body remained motionless in the current.

He turned that slightly crooked smile on her then and she almost gasped at the arrogance inherent in it. The sound, though, remained locked in her throat as an unfamiliar heat unfolded in her chest. The flush was an uncomfortable and unwelcome response to that smile. She had not anticipated finding it attractive or being moved by it. His eyes were locked on hers, warmer now, the color of smoke. She would not look away but neither would she acknowledge that something had passed between them. In a few moments she had convinced herself it was true.

"I followed my brothers wherever they went," she told him as if her thoughts had never drifted anywhere but back in time. "Mammy's young ruffians didn't want me around but they had little choice. I knew too much, you see, and I was not above tattling to get my way. When they included me in their mischief no amount of cajoling or threatening could make me give up their secrets.

"My mother despaired of their influence and Mammy only a little less so. She lectured the boys about their duty by me—which they suffered as much as my presence. When she would turn her back I'd trail off after them again. Rand suggested a leash for me once and Mammy scolded him roundly for that. *'On no account are you boys going to be tying her up. I never heard of such a thing.'* Later that evening she found me trussed to a tree, indigo and yellow ocher on my face. Captured Indian Princess I believe was the name of the game my brothers invented. In the meantime they had taken a skiff upriver to High Point, to spy on Emily Tipping's governess. Mammy threatened to leave me there for being so gullible. I can tell you, it was the last time I was such an easy target for David, Rand, and Shelby."

Lucas chuckled deeply. "You make me wish I'd had a sister."

Bria's look conveyed her disbelief. "Then I must not be telling it right."

Luke's heartfelt reply to the contrary was interrupted by the doors to the verandah swinging up. Addie Thomas stepped out. She smoothed the front of her clean white apron as she spoke to Bria.

"Dinner's on," she said. Her dark eyes rolled sideways to indicate the hallway to her right. "*He's* just come poundin'" down the stairs and looks fit to eat it all if you don't come directly."

Bria nodded. "Thank you, Addie. Mr. Kincaid and I will be right there. Don't try to keep Mr. Foster waiting." She stood as Addie disappeared into the house. Lucas was already on his feet beside her, waiting for the least indication from her that she desired an escort. Bria kept her arms at her sides. "This way, Mr. Kincaid."

Luke fell in a half-step behind her. Bria's steely spine and haughty chin only had the effect of deepening his grin. It was no wonder her brothers had tied her to a tree. The proof that they loved her lay in the fact that Mammy Komati had been able to find their hitching post at all. He would have made a better job of it.

Orrin Foster was already seated at the head of the long walnut table when Bria and Luke entered. He rose halfway out of his chair, more in deference to their guest than his stepdaughter, before the effort became too much for him. He sank back down heavily, causing the chair to shudder.

"I'm on Orrin's right," she whispered to Lucas. "You will take the opposite chair." Bria raised her voice slightly to capture her stepfather's attention. He was pulling his linen napkin toward his lap. "Mr. Foster," she said. "I believe you will be pleased to meet, Mr. Kincaid. He is the man responsible for saving your life this afternoon."

Foster's eyes opened a fraction wider. They conveyed no hint of the amount of liquor he had consumed. The whites were not bloodshot and the lower lids were not rheumy. There was a faint heaviness to the upper lids but it was more a result of Orrin Foster's recent rise from the dregs of sleep than an indication of inattention. Indeed, his green eyes were sharply fixed on his guest. "Kincaid, you say? Not one of those damnable Kincaids from up Summerville way. The ones that are always trying to sell me their worthless horseflesh."

Bria flashed Lucas a questioning glance.

"We're not related, sir," Lucas said easily. Out of the corner of his eye he saw a bit of tension seep out of Bria's shoulders. "Not that I know of. There are no horse traders anywhere in the family that I can recall."

Orrin Foster nodded once. "Glad to hear it." He tossed his napkin back on the table and rose again, this time ending up on his feet. He held out his hand and pumped the one Luke put into it. "I don't much like the Kincaids," he said. "Always wanting something for nothing. They think I have money to burn or that I don't know the value of their stock. It's damn insulting either way." He dropped Luke's hand. "Have a seat, my boy. We don't stand on ceremony too long here. Mrs. Foster makes me mind my manners but she's not about just now. And my stepdaughter doesn't care too much for them, do you, Bria?"

Bria smiled wanly and accepted the chair that Lucas pulled out for her. She eased it under the table and waited until he was seated before she unfolded her napkin. She signaled to Addie that she could begin serving.

Lucas was surprised by Orrin Foster's open, affable countenance. He had a round face, a wide smile, and the steady pink of drink in his cheeks. The light flush made him appear healthy. This man seated beside him was a far cry from the florid, sonorous drunk who had passed out in the field.

"So you're the man who saved my life," Orrin said, dropping back into his chair. He rubbed the back of his head. "You might have been more gentle about it. You put a knot on my head."

Lucas managed not to falter in ladling soup into his bowl. Orrin Foster remembered rather more than Bria had led him to expect. Beside him Addie patiently held the tureen. She moved on silently when he finished. "I believe the knot was courtesy of the ground."

"Just so," Orrin said. "What the deuce were you doing out there?"

It was Bria who answered. "I told you, Mr. Kincaid has come to Concord inquiring about work."

Orrin's attention did not stray from Lucas. "That's what she told me. I didn't say I believed her."

Luke noted that Bria gave no indication that she was bothered by the slight. His mind went back to the epithets Orrin hurled at his stepdaughter as he tried to run her down. She hadn't flinched on that occasion, either. "It's true," Luke said. "I came looking for work. In town there was some talk of new stables being built here at Concord. I thought you might be in need of laborers."

"You needn't worry," Bria interjected hastily to Orrin. "I haven't hired him."

"Is that right?" asked Orrin. "She hasn't hired you?"

"That's right."

Orrin chuckled. "You shouldn't have saved my life this afternoon, Mr. Kincaid. Not when my stepdaughter was trying so hard to end it. That set you back in her good graces." His head swiveled and his gaze fell sharply on Bria. "I'm considering having that gelding put down," he said. "He's dangerous and unpredictable."

Bria swallowed her mouthful of soup. "I will put *you* down, Orrin, before I will let you take Apollo out again."

Laughter made Orrin's broad chest heave and tears gather at the corners of his eyes. He slapped the edge of the table hard. "See what I mean, Kincaid?" he said, enjoying himself. "She thinks nothing of threatening me. Plotting my demise is one of her pleasures."

"Everyone must have diversions," Bria said without inflection.

Orrin used his napkin to wipe his eyes, then smoothed it across his lap again. His smile remained stamped on his face as he lifted his spoon. "Did you think I wouldn't clear the wall, Mr. Kincaid?"

"I didn't think anyone could clear that wall. Not at the point you seemed to be attempting to take it."

"Bah!" A bit of liquid dropped from his spoon as he waved

his arm expansively. "It was that fool horse and Bria's antics that nearly cost me my neck."

Lucas did not gainsay him. Addie stepped forward to offer more soup but Luke shook his head.

"Still," Orrin continued, "I remember being pulled from that damn beast before it took the jump. Good thinking, that. I wouldn't have made the jump then. Was that you, Kincaid?"

"Yes."

"Then I suppose I do owe you my neck."

"You're welcome, sir."

"I wasn't thanking you," Orrin said. He waved churlishly at Addie to take his bowl. "The main course," he said. "And some wine for me. Whatever is in the sideboard. Would you care for wine, Kincaid?"

"Yes, I believe I would."

At the sideboard Addie opened a bottle of red. She carried it to the table and poured it for Orrin first. He tasted it, pronounced it satisfactory, and waited for his glass to be filled. Addie poured Luke's next. She would have returned the bottle to the sideboard but Orrin tapped the edge of the table with his forefinger, indicating she should set it down there. Over the top of Foster's head, Addie Thomas looked for guidance from Bria.

Orrin caught the housekeeper's glance. His large hand shot out and circled Addie's wrist. He held it firmly, not hurting her but applying just enough pressure to remind her that he could. "Who owns Concord, Addie?" he asked pleasantly.

"You do, Mr. Foster." Addie's complexion was suffused with high color, deepening it from coffee to ebony.

"And who is master here?" he continued.

"You are."

Bria sighed. "Stop it, Orrin. You've made your point."

"Have I?" He released Addie's wrist. She left the half-empty bottle on the table and scurried away to retrieve the meat platter. "Mr. Kincaid, you're hired." Orrin looked back at Bria, his graying brows arched, his slight smile fully satisfied.

"There. Now I've made my point *and* thanked Kincaid properly."

Bria started to rise.

"Sit down, girl," Orrin snapped. "And rein in your temper. I know where that beast of yours gets it."

Luke's observation was that Bria was hardly having a fit of temper. If anything, she looked a shade more in control than normal, her sapphire eyes brilliant because of their iciness. It was as if her anger imploded, leaving her frigid at the center rather than a hot, fiery mass that would have to be vented from time to time.

"Sit *down*," Orrin said again.

This time Bria's knees folded under her and she returned to her chair. She held her hands rigidly in her lap.

"I can make decisions here as well as you," Orrin told her. He helped himself to the thinly sliced roast beef that Addie held out on a bone china platter. "Do you think I don't know why you didn't want to hire Kincaid? It's because he's from my neck of the woods. Did you know that, Kincaid? She wouldn't hire you because you're a Yankee. Did she tell you that or just lead you to believe there's no work for you here?"

"Actually it was a bit of both," Luke said. He helped himself to a generous portion of meat, realizing for the first time how ravenous he was. "Are you serious, sir? About the job. You haven't just done it to—"

"To spite her?" asked Orrin. "Of course I have. She's not supposed to like it. Just live with it. That's the nature of spite, isn't it?"

"I believe so."

"Good. Then I've done it right." He toasted himself with his entire first glass of wine and poured another. "Now, what part of my woods are you from?"

"New York," Lucas said. He noticed that Orrin Foster reacted in no way to this information. "Manhattan."

Orrin tucked into his roast beef, then still chewing, added

the potatoes and sweet green beans that Addie proffered. "Big place, Manhattan," he said around a mouthful of food.

"Five Points," Luke said for clarification.

"Never heard of it," Orrin replied. "But then I've never been to New York. Are you familiar with Philadelphia?"

"I worked there briefly after the war."

"We don't mention"—Orrin's rich baritone dropped to a whisper—"*the war.*" He cocked his head toward Bria and rolled his eyes in that direction. "The natives don't like it."

"I understand." He almost sent an apologetic glance in Bria's direction but she was calmly looking at her plate, seemingly unaware and unmoved by the conversation going on around her. It was just as well, he thought, because he had no idea what he was apologizing for. It was her stepfather who was behaving in a boorish manner. That was hardly Luke's fault.

"I'm from Philadelphia," Orrin said. "Germantown, really."

"I know the area."

"Don't establish your connection to me too strongly. I'm leaving for Charleston tomorrow. Bria would have no qualms about letting you go."

"She could do that?"

Orrin nodded. He glanced at Bria. There was a vaguely smug smile about her mouth as she cut into her meat. "She appears to be contemplating it now." He picked up his own knife and tapped Bria's wrist with the flat of it. He was not surprised when she recoiled as if he had cut her. "Think twice about letting Mr. Kincaid go," he said. "Once about how disappointed I would be and once about your mother."

Bria sat very still, her eyes fixed on Orrin. Her voice was barely a whisper. "I understand."

Orrin nodded, satisfied that she did. He leaned back in his chair and twirled the wineglass between his fingers. "You can find me in the Battery, Kincaid, should it come to that. I don't expect to return until November but be assured you may apply to me for help before then."

Luke couldn't imagine that he would apply to Orrin Foster for anything. "Yes, sir. Thank you." He speared some meat and potatoes. "What is it precisely that you're hiring me to do?"

Bria spoke again. "I already told him you wouldn't approve a new stable."

Orrin ignored her. "Do *you* think Concord needs a new stable, Kincaid?"

"Yes. If it's your desire to expand the stud. What you have now is rotting. It looks as if it must be the original structure. It's been enlarged, shored, and painted, but the wear at the foundation is visible. The roof leaks. You want to keep valuable horses dry. It could be patched, of course, in the same manner that was done to this house, but in a few more years it would be all patchwork."

When Orrin cleared his throat it sounded as if he were moving gravel. "You noticed the roof, eh?"

"Among other things."

"Go on."

"Well, I didn't tour your home but there are some structural features in the study I would change. The shelves, for instance, before they collapse, and at least one of the windows before the draperies are ruined."

"You think I was taken by the locals when I was restoring this house?" Orrin demanded.

"I think you were given some poor advice about what it would take to properly restore Concord."

"Hah!" He pointed to Bria. "What did I always tell you about the men I was forced to deal with? Cheats. All of them. They saw my good Yankee greenbacks and lined their pockets with them. And now Kincaid here tells me the work is already deteriorating. That's right, isn't it, Kincaid? That's what you're telling me."

"Yes."

"What do you make of that, Bria?"

"I suppose it means you were taken, Orrin," she said levelly.

"Taken by everyone who sold you lumber, nails, paint, and plaster. Taken by the carpenters, painters, and roofers. I don't know about the drapers and furniture craftsmen. Your new friend has made no assessment of their worth."

Orrin raised an eyebrow at Lucas. "Well?"

"The furnishings seem to be of quality," he said. "But I admit to no expertise in that area."

"What is your expertise?" Orrin asked, nursing his drink.

Lucas shrugged. He glanced at Bria but did not catch her eye. He gave his crooked, self-effacing smile to the boor instead. "I suppose you'd call me a handyman."

Orrin's own smile was a trifle lopsided. "Is that right? And where else have you worked?"

The dinner continued through another course, lighter fare this time, and ended with thick slabs of warm apple pie. Orrin finished off the first bottle of wine between bites and ordered Addie to open another. He listened to Luke discuss his travels across the south and west and the work he did in the cities. Bria contributed little to the discussion, which suited him just fine. It had been a long time since Orrin had anyone of his own northern persuasion to talk to. His presence in these parts was tolerated, not accepted. He told himself sometimes that if he hadn't liked liquor before coming to Concord, he certainly would have developed a taste for it by now.

Orrin patted his stomach at the meal's end. "I suppose you would get a lot of work in these parts, what with the rebuilding and all, but damn me if it don't seem like you're a lost pup looking for his mother. You move around like some desert nomad."

Luke would not have suspected that Orrin Foster could be so perceptive. There was an element of truth to what he'd said. "I have references," Luke said. He saw Bria look up at this and her expression was faintly accusing. She was wondering why he hadn't offered references to her. "You're not the first person to wonder why I don't stay in one place long."

"Well? What's the answer?" asked Orrin. "Are you running

from something?'' He glanced at Bria. ''What think you, Bria?
Is he a felon? You may have been hasty with your invitation
to dine.''

Bria let Orrin snort and chuckle at his own humor before
she answered. ''I agree it's a possibility. Shall you let him go
now?''

''We haven't heard his explanation yet. And the man says
he has references.''

''A felon can be expected to lie,'' she pointed out. ''And
his references could be worth no more than the paper they're
written on.''

Orrin nodded sagely. ''You accepted Confederate money
when the same could be said of it.'' He studied Lucas over the
rim of his wineglass. ''Well, what do you have to say for
yourself? Are you eluding the law or of a peripatetic nature?''

''The latter, sir. I have a bit of the wanderlust in me. I enjoy
seeing new places.''

''Seems to me that urge to move on must come from somewhere,'' mused Orrin. ''Your father a rover?''

''I don't know. Perhaps. He was gone before I was born.''

''Hah!'' Orrin smiled deeply. ''Then we've got to the bottom
of it. A rover. Just like your papa. I suspect there are worse
natures one could inherit.''

''I've always thought so,'' Luke said.

Orrin finished his glass and poured another. He offered the
same to Luke. He chuckled when Luke hastily placed his hand
over his glass. ''Not to your liking, is that it? Shall I have
Addie open another bottle? Something sweeter?'' He turned to
look at the housekeeper standing at the sideboard. ''Addie! Our
guest wants something sweeter. Open another bottle.''

''No,'' Luke protested. ''I'm fine. I find I have no—''

''Nonsense. Another bottle, Addie. Bria. Help her pick out
something sweeter than your disposition.'' He nodded, pleased
with himself as Bria quietly removed herself from the table and
went to assist the housekeeper. After examining the contents of
the sideboard cupboards they both left the room. ''Good,''

Orrin said, leaning forward in his chair. He set his glass down. "We have a few moments alone."

Luke realized then that Orrin Foster was not a sloppy, stumbling drunk, but a steady and serious one. He could probably consume a quarter of his own stock before his wits were noticeably addled. The man might be a boor but he was no buffoon except that it aided his own purpose. Luke found himself leaning a little forward also.

"I don't hold with leaving bastards behind," Orrin said. "Now maybe that was what was done to you, and maybe not, but if it was, that's one part of your daddy's legacy that will *not* be repeated here."

Luke's brows lifted. "Sir?"

"Oh, don't 'sir' me now," Orrin said impatiently. "I'll expect you to marry her if you put something in her belly besides your wick. I'll insist on it. So will her mother. The girl's a slut, plain and simple, else she'd be married by now. No one around here will have her. Used goods and everyone knows it. From time to time Austin Tipping from over at High Point comes sniffing. He's heard the same lecture as you, so don't think I singled you out. She'd have you both, probably together, but she doesn't want marriage. There'd be hell to pay everywhere you turned should it come to that."

Orrin resumed his earlier position in his chair, stretching his legs under the table. "Just laying it out for you. She's a tempting piece. Always has been. She knows it, too. Of course butter wouldn't melt in her mouth." One corner of Orrin's lips lifted slyly and his eyes narrowed on Luke's face. "But then there's other places to stick your wick without it shriveling from the cold. One in particular if you don't want bastards."

Lucas had a vision of himself grinding Orrin Foster's face into what was left of his apple pie. It hardly satisfied him. In his mind's eye he had Foster's neck under his foot and was pressing slowly on the man's windpipe. Foster's eyes were bulging and his color was changing from bright red to a deeper, more interesting shade of plum.

"You understand me, Kincaid?" Orrin jabbed at the edge of the table with his forefinger to garner Luke's attention. "Seemed to me that you weren't rightly listening there for a moment."

"I heard you, sir," Luke said calmly. "And I understood."

"Good." He jerked a thumb toward the hallway where the light footfalls of Bria and Addie could be heard approaching. "Just in time." As they entered the room Orrin was pursuing another line of questioning. "So where are these references? I'd like to review them before I leave for Charleston."

They were in his other jacket. Luke found himself unwilling to tell Orrin that. If Bria's stepfather knew that she had given him fresh clothes there would be more accusations heaped on her head. "I don't have them with me just now."

"Well, where do you have them?"

Bria saved Lucas from answering. "They're probably in his room."

"His room?" Orrin said. "You gave the man a room?"

"I had Jeb show him to the old overseer's cabin. It was just for the night. Or at least I thought that's all it was. Now that you've hired him, I suppose he'll be taking up more permanent residence there."

The look Orrin passed to Lucas was knowing. *Do you see? Her hospitality was meant to get you to herself away from the house.* "I want to see those letters of reference," was all he said.

Luke pushed away from the table. "I'll get them. Excuse me." He managed not to run from the room, but only just. He paused once he was outside the house. The breeze from the river was stronger now. It felt refreshing, even cleansing. Luke had a notion to go to his cabin by way of the river. He felt as if he'd been wallowing in a sty since the first course was served. Better that Addie should throw slops in a trough and let Orrin serve himself.

Luke started across the verandah slowly. What the hell had he gotten himself into? He thought of his mother. "This is your fault," he said under his breath. His aunts came immediately to mind. "And *yours,* too."

Bria was sitting quietly at the table when Luke returned. Orrin had roused himself to leave his chair and go to the sideboard in search of the perfect cigar. The table was cleared and Addie had been dismissed. Candlelight gave the room an illusion of warmth. Reflected flames from the candelabra flickered in the windows. The first inkling that night was approaching came in the guise of blue-grey shadows settling between the cottonwood and hickories. Somewhere distant a barn owl was playing the role of an early bird, cruising the fields for mice. Its shrill hiss could be heard: *kschh, kschh.*

Luke held out the envelope he carried to Orrin.

"Put it on the table. I'll read it in a moment." He continued to root through his box for a cigar that would satisfy him.

Luke returned to his chair and placed the envelope where Orrin's plate had been. He saw Bria's eyes glance in that direction but she made no move to take it. Orrin would have probably slapped her hand.

Bria spoke quietly, a familiar coolness in her tone. "My stepfather has suggested a tour of our home this evening before you retire."

"As you wish."

"This has nothing to do with *my* wishes, Mr. Kincaid. I thought I'd made that clear."

Orrin shut the lid to the cigar box loudly. "Oh, you have, my dear." He sniffed the length of his cigar again, taking obvious pleasure in the heady aroma. "Perfect." He pulled a small pair of scissors attached to a fob from his waistcoat pocket and snipped one end. "Can I offer you one, Kincaid?"

"Yes. I'd like that." Luke accepted the box and chose one with little of the care that Orrin had shown. Orrin snipped the end for him and shared his match. The tobacco was strong and Luke almost choked on his first draw.

"Careful," Orrin said, puffing more gently. "These are specially made for me. My own blend. Most people find they take some getting used to.''

Luke counted himself among that group. Through the fog bank of smoke he saw that Bria was barely holding her smile in check. He wondered if it was the green pallor of his complexion that amused her. She was a cruel woman. He could break her, he thought, make her give in to one of those rare beacon-like smiles, if he was willing to make more of a fool of himself. It did not bode well for him that he was tempted.

Orrin placed a glass ashtray on the table and sat down. He kept the cigar between his teeth as he picked up the envelope. ''You're showing your hand, Bria,'' he mumbled, extracting the letters. He told Lucas, ''She hates cigar smoke. Usually leaves the room with her mother as soon as I open the box. Elizabeth can't abide them, either. Must be these references that are keeping her in her seat. That, or she's waiting for you to be sick.''

It was all Luke could do to keep from choking.

''Do you need a pat on the back, Kincaid?'' Orrin asked absently. He had unfolded the first letter and his eyes were sweeping the contents. ''This looks in order. You didn't write this yourself, did you?''

''No, sir.''

Orrin grunted softly and made no other comments until he finished with the entire packet. He returned the last one to the envelope and handed it back to Luke. ''Seems in order,'' he said. ''Pass it to Bria if you wish. She may know some of the families. She can read them while I take you through the house. I'd like to hear your opinions myself.'' He gave Bria a quelling glance as she started to rise. ''I know my way around,'' he told her coldly. ''You are not invited.''

''I mean to read Mr. Kincaid's references in the drawing room,'' she said, accepting the envelope from Lucas. ''Does that meet with your approval?''

''Very well. Give us a moment. I'll begin Kincaid's tour there. You can come in when we're gone.''

Luke saw that Bria wanted to protest this edict but she bit back her request and acquiesced with more grace than he would have shown in the same circumstances.

Orrin's tour was thorough although his knowledge of the house itself had no breadth. Luke suspected Foster's initial interest had been in the plantation's undeniable grandeur. The first time Foster had seen Henley—as it had then been named— the house would have shown the ravages of war. The Yankees who plundered it had done considerable damage, but ultimately spared it from being burnt to the ground. That Orrin was able to acquire the house and the property for the price of the taxes owed was no more than stealing from the Hamiltons. Their tenuous claim to their former home came through Elizabeth's marriage to Orrin. The fact that Foster's purchase was legal and even sanctioned by the government somehow made the theft more grievous, not less.

Looking around, studying the care of construction that had gone into first building the house, then maintaining it for most of its years, Luke understood why the Hamiltons wanted it back. Orrin could admire the beauty of the house, but he had no appreciation for its roots.

"Concord is like a woman with good bone structure," Luke told him, thinking Orrin might understand this particular analogy. They were in the attic and Luke was pointing out the rafters and ceiling joists below the mansard roof. "When she's older, she will still be beautiful. She won't be ageless but her age will make her interesting and fine lines will lend her character. Some would even say she's lovelier than she was in her youth."

Orrin frowned. "Who the hell would say that? Someone who's forgotten what firm flesh feels like under these." He held up both hands, palms out, and made a squeezing motion with his fingers. "I don't want a house with sagging teats."

Luke tempered his sigh with a small cough and pretended more interest in the ceiling joist construction. Thank you, Mother, he thought. Nancy. Lyssa. Maggie. Laura. Livia. Madelyn. Thank all of you, too. "Well, sagging teats is precisely what you will have if you keep authorizing repairs without a care for the deep structure. With proper attention this house will outlast us both and never show her age again except in a way that makes her more valuable."

Orrin understood value. "You mean she'll be worth more in ten years than when I bought her."

"Considering the bargain you must have gotten when you purchased her, I'd say she could be made to be worth ten times your initial investment."

Orrin rubbed the underside of his chin with his knuckles. His eyes narrowed shrewdly. "My initial investment, eh? And what of the money I've sunk into her since? What about the money you want me to sink into her now?"

"If you never spent another cent from this day forward, I'd say the funds you used for improvements are already lost to you. However, if you're willing to see the restoration through properly, then it will not be a loss in the end, but a considerable gain."

Orrin was silent, taking this in. "You do this for a living, do you? Reach into a man's pockets and extract his wallet? Is this what you did in Philadelphia and Richmond and Atlanta? Isn't anyone hanged for thievery any longer?"

Luke thought this last question a particularly interesting one coming from Orrin Foster. "You read my references. The people I worked for were very well pleased."

"Too pleased, I'm thinking." He waved his hand in a dismissive gesture. "I'm not saying you're a liar, Kincaid. I'm just exercising my right to be cautious. You're telling me I've already been taken once by the locals. There are only two reasons I'm half-willing to trust you. One is that you're a Yankee and the other is that it sticks in the neck of my stepdaughter like a chicken bone. Now, I'm going to authorize the release of some funds to put at your disposal and I'll arrange credit at the lumberyard and the like in Charleston, but you should know that I'll be keeping an eye myself on expenditures and I'll be checking some of those references. If there's something I should know about them, then tell me now. Don't waste my time or my money. You don't want to be running from the law if you're not already.''

Luke had one hand braced on a rafter. It kept him from placing it around Orrin Foster's throat. ''That's clear enough, Mr. Foster.''

''What makes you think you can deal any better with the locals than I could?'' he asked. ''They'll take the same amount of pleasure cheating you as they did me.''

''Let's see how it goes,'' Luke said. He did not want to say that he had never had the problem before. Given Orrin Foster's manner, Luke imagined the merchants and laborers had gone out of their way to lighten his pockets. ''You did a lot of the repairs here shortly after the war. Supplies were scarce then and prices were running as high as the emotions. Things have changed some since then.''

Orrin grunted. ''You haven't spent enough time in the South if you believe that.''

''What brought you here?'' asked Luke.

''Opportunity and circumstance.''

''And what keeps you here?''

Orrin spread his hands. ''The Hamiltons aren't the only ones attached to this land. It's Concord now.'' He walked over to one of the dormer windows and tapped the glass to point out the land beyond. ''It's mine for as far as the eye can see from here. I'm not leaving it behind.''

Luke had nothing to say to that. The house had cast something of a spell over him. Henley Hamilton had used bricks from ships' ballasts to build his home. The brick was so closely matched that Luke knew there had never been enough of it in one ship's hold to construct the home. It would have taken half a dozen or more ships before Henley would have had enough to begin construction. In the early 1600s it was quite a feat. This home was more than a sanctuary for Henley Hamilton and his family. It was a labor of love.

"How much?" Orrin asked.

Luke shook his head slightly, sliding back to the present. He ducked and stepped out from under the rafters to where he could straighten easily. "Pardon?"

"How damned much is it going to cost me?"

Luke didn't hesitate in naming the price. He had been making calculations in his head since Orrin began the tour. It was a fair estimate, he knew, and it took into account problems he might encounter that weren't easily visible. If there were no unexpected expenses, Orrin would never have to spend the entire amount.

Orrin rocked back on his heels as if warding off a blow. "That much, eh?"

"To do it right," Luke said. "And I won't do it any other way."

"Easy for you to be a man of principle with *my* money," Orrin grumbled.

Luke found himself smiling at that. "Yes, sir."

"Very well. You shall have it. In my accounts, of course. Don't think you can simply help yourself to the whole of it and no one will be the wiser." Orrin started for the steep attic stairs. He braced one hand on the banister and took the first step cautiously. "And remember what I said about my stepdaughter. She'll try to wheedle my money out of you if you give her cause to think she can do it. Always needing money for something, that one is. It'll only get worse if she spreads her legs for you, Kincaid. Mark my words. Bend her over a table and have at her if you must, but don't let her entice you into her bed. A woman shouldn't have that much power."

Luke was relieved when Orrin continued down the stairs at a quicker pace. The temptation to assist his descent with a swift kick in the arse was almost too much to resist.

Bria lay in her bed and stared at the ceiling. The window to her room was thrown open and the long, lightweight curtains billowed and fluttered like sails. The oil lamp on the bedside table cast a wavering light in spite of the glass globe that protected its flame. In the shadows that flickered across her ceiling Bria could make out no friendly shapes. They were ominous to a fault.

"Ridiculous," she whispered, watching another amorphous shadow slip from the ceiling and run down the wall. Like a spill of ink it collected in cracks and crevices. It was alternately the spider, then the spider's web. She closed her eyes again and this time turned on her side. As she had on a number of earlier occasions, Bria sought more pleasant thoughts to lull her into slumber.

They didn't come.

She rose from the bed and padded to the window seat where she secured the curtains. Her view was of the gardens and the woodland that lined the river. Pines and willows were easy to distinguish. She knew the cottonwood, sweet bay, and laurelcherry trees by the shape and height of their crowns. Bria leaned farther out the window. From this new vantage she could see the stables and some of the outbuildings. Beyond them, barely visible except for their roofs shining like ghostly palm prints in the moonlight, were what was left of the slave quarters.

Most of the houses were unoccupied, long in need of being torn down so the lumber could be salvaged and used where it was most needed. Orrin wouldn't let her do it. The fact that they were there and the fact that they were largely empty was Orrin's way of reminding Bria and Elizabeth of northern triumphs. *His* triumph, too, though he had never put on a uniform or taken part in any of the campaigns. His fortune had been made supplying the weapons and machinery of war and in that manner he had been more effective than any company of soldiers.

There were still over a hundred laborers on the plantation, most of them black. Half of them lived at Henley before the war; the remainder came later, many from surrounding farms and plantations, free to choose their work this time. In exchange for a parcel of land and a small wage, they also worked the wetlands at Concord. They kept back some of the rice and cotton for themselves and sold the rest to Bria. They were always free to market it themselves but the price she paid them was fair and she bore the expense of getting the crop to the city.

The houses that were erected on the parcels were in some cases no better than shanties. Although conditions had slowly improved, most of them still could not match the slave quarters at Henley for size or comfort. Bria had suggested to Orrin that he allow the hands to use the lumber from the quarters to build better homes for themselves on the individual parcels. He surprised her by agreeing immediately, then made her remember who she was dealing with by naming a price that no family among them could afford to pay. The quarters stood as they were.

Occasionally Bria noticed boards missing from the back side of one or the interior floor of another. Windowpanes never seemed to break or crack, they just disappeared. She never mentioned these losses to Orrin. Bria had no evidence to support her belief, but she suspected her stepfather had his own way of exacting retribution against the men and women who worked for him. For all that Orrin professed abolitionist views, he had no real desire to change the status quo. Reform was left for the conquered to figure out.

It was not going well.

Bria slipped back inside the window. There was no light in Lucas Kincaid's quarters. She'd heard Orrin's heavy tread on his way to his room a while ago. Lucas must have retired at the same time. Bria wished she had looked for him then. She wanted to know what had been decided. Orrin and Luke had been close-mouthed when they returned from the tour. When that mood was upon Orrin, Bria knew better than to challenge him. She'd bid them both good night at the point when Orrin suggested a friendly little card game.

Bria knew there was no such thing.

A noise in the hall caught Bria's attention. Her head cocked to one side as she listened again, harder this time. She heard footsteps but they were not familiar. Orrin's tread was particularly distinctive and she knew Addie's shuffle and Jeb's loping stride.

Bria slipped into a cotton wrapper and belted it loosely. She pulled the lapels together over the low, scooped neckline of her nightshift, then opened the door cautiously. She pressed her face into the opening and looked first to her right, then her left.

Lucas Kincaid caught her eyes on the return sweep. He placed a finger to his lips.

"I'm not going to scream," she said, offended. Did he think she was fainthearted or lacking in good sense? "Where are you going?"

"For a swim."

"The river's that way." She opened the door wider and pointed over her shoulder.

"I know where the river is. I could see it from my window."

Bria knew that wasn't possible from the overseer's house. A small vertical crease appeared between her brows as she frowned. "Where exactly *is* your window?"

He pointed one door down. The room adjoined Bria's. "Your stepfather insisted," he said. There was no amusement in his tone. "Would you like to accompany me to the river?"

Chapter Four

"Accompany you?" Bria asked, her brows lifting. "For a swim?"

"Well, I'm not going to drown myself," said Luke. "You may join me in the water or not as is your pleasure."

"I think not."

He shrugged. "Very well." Luke continued down the hallway.

"Wait!"

He stopped obediently and turned slightly on his heel. "Yes?"

"Are you truly going swimming?"

Luke nodded.

"But it's so late."

Feeling no need to explain himself to her, Luke simply shrugged again. He turned once more and started off. This time when her plea to wait came, he ignored it. The desire for a cleansing dip in the river had been with him since dinner and he knew he wasn't going to sleep without it. Playing a few hours of poker with Orrin had only intensified that feeling, not lessened it.

When Luke reached the landing for the stairs, he glanced

back. Bria was no longer in the hall and her door was shut. He felt a vague sense of disappointment that she had retreated. He considered this, absently raking back his hair. It was probably just as well that they would talk tomorrow. Cleansing himself of Orrin Foster's influence was only one of the reasons he was seeking a cool dip in the river.

Luke hurried down the stairs.

In her room Bria had returned to the window seat. She sat there, her long legs drawn toward her knees, waiting to see if what Luke had said could possibly be true. On warm summer nights her brothers used to slip from the house when they thought everyone was abed. Their usual destination was the river. If she listened carefully she could hear them splashing and calling to each other. Mammy Komati knew about these late-night escapades. She warned Bria to stay away. *'Sometimes boys get to having a fever in their blood. Like as not the river's churning white trying to cool it. You leave 'em be, Miss Bree. Some day the fever will come on you and you'll find yourself at the river same as your brothers.'*

Bria didn't know why she had heeded Mammy on this occasion when she defied her on so many others. She was older by then, that was true. David was nearly a man full grown, sweet on Emily Tipping now, not her governess. Rand and Shelby's affections changed every Sunday depending on which girl had the prettiest bonnet. Their antics to draw attention to themselves amused Bria. Usually they drew the attention of the minister and were forced to listen to a lecture on their way out of the service. While they stood on the steps being chastised, the real objects of their affection were being escorted to their carriages by less fevered young men.

Bria realized she had been smiling at the memory only as it was fading. Luke's sudden appearance below caught her eye. She could make out his easy, untroubled gait as he walked through the gardens. He never stopped but he also gave no appearance of being hurried. He certainly was headed in the direction of the river.

Bria jumped up from her perch and threw off her robe. She pulled a navy blue gingham dress from a peg in her armoire and slipped it on over her nightshift. She found the stockings she had worn earlier and sat on the edge of the bed to put them on. At her vanity she added shoes and quickly brushed out, then rebraided her hair.

It was not a fever in her blood that brought Bria to the river's edge, but curiosity. Mammy would have been disappointed.

Bria slowly walked the precipice of the riverbank, looking for Lucas Kincaid. There was sufficient moonlight, and her eyes had adjusted well enough to the dark that Bria supposed he would be easy to see. "Mr. Kincaid," she called softly. "Are you there?"

There was no answer. When she would pivot quickly at the occasional splash it was always a fish that had caught her attention. Had he drowned himself after all? she wondered. "Mr. Kincaid?" She made several more passes along the bank, calling his name. Surely he would have heard her, she thought, and made some reply if all was well. She cupped her hands around her mouth. "Mr. Kincaid!"

"You're going to wake everyone at Concord."

Startled by the voice at her back, Bria almost pitched headfirst into the Cooper River. A pair of hard, masculine hands gripped her waist from behind and saved her. Luke pulled her toward him. For the space of a heartbeat Bria was speechless. When she found her voice it had the keening pitch of a wounded animal.

Luke's hands dropped away immediately but he wasn't fast enough to duck her blow. She spun, her hands folded together in a single fist, and threw her body into the movement as if she were swinging a hammer. The momentum of her stiff-armed spin kept her going in the same direction and away from Lucas, while he staggered back under the power of it.

Bria's punch sent Luke away from the riverbank while she was precariously balanced on the edge again. This time Luke didn't try to save her. He was massaging the ache in his jaw when she disappeared over the side.

Luke sat down in the grass and drew his legs up tailor fashion. At this angle he could not observe Bria's rolling descent into the water. He had to be satisfied with the sound of some stones being dislodged and a few muffled squeals. He found it was enough. The hard thump as she hit the water was particularly good.

Luke ran his tongue along the edge of his teeth. They were all accounted for and none seemed to be loose. He was certain he would have a bruise on his chin in the morning and it bore thinking about how he was going to explain it to Orrin Foster. He was still considering his problem, his chin resting thoughtfully in his hand, when Bria pulled herself up over the bank.

Her garments were sodden and her shoes made a small squishing sound that could be heard over the steady dripping from her dress and hair as she approached him. He sat up straight and held out one hand to halt her progress. "That's close enough. I already have one injury I'll have difficulty explaining away. I cannot rouse myself at this hour to come up with a second."

Bria gathered great bunches of her gingham skirt in her hands and began to wring water from the fabric. The grass at her feet was drenched when she was finished. She glanced around her and spied a fallen log not a great distance away. Gamely, she trudged over and sat down, giving Luke her back. Reaching below her gown, she took off her sodden shoes. She held them upside down and let them drip water for a few moments before she rolled down her stockings and stuffed them inside the shoes.

Bria stood up long enough to change her position on the log so that she was facing Luke. He was no longer sitting with his legs folded in front of him. He was half-reclining on the ground, supporting his upper body on his elbows. He was not looking at her, but staring out across the river. She could not see his expression clearly enough to know that he was angry with her but she felt certain he was out of patience.

She twisted her braid. Cold water dripped onto the bodice of her gown. She tried again, this time holding it away from her as best she could. "That's Beau Rivage across the way," she said quietly. "There was a scandal there years ago. One of the sons took up with the Underground Railroad and escorted slaves north. This was long before there was any notion that it would take a war to settle differences. Mammy Komati says that Graham Denison was all anyone talked about for months when the truth came out. The Denisons couldn't show their face in town or at church. Graham never did show his. He up and disappeared."

Luke's reply was a soft grunt at the back of his throat. He didn't glance in Bria's direction.

Bria's shoulders sagged a little. She let go of her braid and let her hands rest at her sides. Her fingers found a hold in the irregularly furrowed bark of the fallen swamp oak. "I'm sorry, Mr. Kincaid. About hitting you, I mean. I didn't do it because I thought about it. It just . . ." She hesitated. No explanation that she wanted to share came immediately to mind. "It just happened."

Luke believed her. She hadn't had time to think about her response. If it had been planned he would have easily had a few seconds to get out of the way. No, this had been something else entirely. She had reacted out of panic. Out of terror.

"It was not my intention to startle you. I thought you would have heard me crashing through the trees."

Bria shook her head. She remembered his light, almost soundless tread in the hallway outside her room. He had not crashed through the woods but she didn't believe he had purposely set about to sneak up on her, either. "I didn't hear you," she said. "Not until you were just behind me. I thought you had been swept downriver or drowned."

His head swiveled in her direction. She was serious. She had been worried that something had happened to him. It explained her preoccupation and inability to hear his approach. "I was changing back into my clothes," he told her. "I needed some privacy."

"Oh." So he had been swimming in the altogether. She knew her brothers had. It was one of the things they laughed about conspiratorially, as if she were not yet old enough to grasp their meaning. "You might have answered my calls."

"And have you charge through the trees after me? I think not."

Bria had to concede the point. "You're right. I might have done that."

One of Luke's dark brows kicked up. He hadn't expected her admission. "I thought you were going to remain in your room."

"I changed my mind."

That was clear enough. The why of it was still a bit murky. "You may as well come over here," he said. "There is no sense in calling attention to ourselves by talking more loudly than we have to."

Bria looked down at herself. Beneath her wet gown her skin was cold and clammy. Her shift clung to her like a tight and wrinkled skin.

Luke looked around. "I have a blanket somewhere. I took it from the cabin before I came down here."

So that was what had taken him so long to appear in the gardens. Bria's eyes skimmed the ground as she joined the search for the blanket.

Luke spied it first. The grey woolen material had not looked so different from a pile of stones nearby. He scrambled to his feet and retrieved it. He noticed that in spite of Bria's shivering, she came forward a little reluctantly to accept it. He continued to hold it out patiently when she hesitated a few feet from him. "Take it." He gave his hand a small shake to emphasize his words.

"Don't you want to sit on it?" she asked. Her teeth were chattering to such a degree that she almost bit her tongue.

In answer, he snapped it open and held it across his outstretched arms. "Come here," he said. "Let me put it around you." The offer had the desired effect. Rather than let him do it, Bria removed it from his hands and draped it around her own shoulders. Luke watched her hug it close. "Do you really want to return to the house?"

She shook her head. "I—I hav-v-ve s-s-some questions."

"I thought you might." He pointed to the darker edge of the woods. "Go over there and get out of your dress. Toss it to me and I'll hang it from a branch. It will dry some. Wring out your undergarments better this time around, then make that blanket more secure. Shall I start a small fire?"

"Oh, no," she reminded him hastily. "Someone might see."

Luke did not ask who. Perhaps Bria knew Orrin did not sleep as soundly as he would have Luke believe. "Go on. Unless you want me to escort you back to the house?"

"N-no." She did not want to track water into the house. Unless she cleaned it up tonight the trail would inevitably raise questions. Orrin planned an early start for Charleston so he would be clear-headed enough to ask questions. If he somehow came to learn that she had been at the river tonight he would never stop needling her. "I'll d-do it."

Bria ducked her head as she turned and fled into the woods. She did not toss her dress out to Lucas as he had instructed, but carried it out over her arm when she was done. She handed it to him, close enough now not to miss his faint smile.

Luke took the dress from her outstretched hand and draped the sleeves over two sturdy, parallel branches he had found for just such a purpose. "There," he said, stepping back to admire his handiwork. Water began to slowly drip from the hem. He nodded, satisfied, then turned around. "Where do you want to sit?" He saw that Bria had already found a spot on the ground that was cushioned by a thick spread of pine needles. "There is just fine."

Luke joined her, judging the distance from her at a good arm's length before he sat down. Out of the corner of his eye he saw her scoot away only a few inches. "Are you warming?"

Bria nodded, surprised to find that it was true. Her teeth had stopped chattering and her skin was no longer prickly with cold. "I really am sorry, you know," she said quietly.

"It's all right. I think you got the worst of it."

"My clothes will dry easily enough. I believe you're going to have a bruise."

Luke stretched his jaw and touched the spot where she had hit him. It was most definitely tender. "You're right."

"What will you say?"

He shrugged. "Probably that it happened this afternoon and is only now starting to bruise. Something will occur to me."

Bria remembered the way Orrin had almost gotten the best of him. "You're not much of a fighter, are you?"

Luke tempered his grin. She could have posed that question to most anyone in the Five Points neighborhood where he grew up and received a very different answer. "No," he said. "I'm not."

"Do you have any brothers?"

"No."

Bria nodded. It was as she expected. "That it explains it, then. You're an only child."

"And that's why I'm not much of a fighter?" He considered this, amused. "How do you draw that conclusion?"

"My brothers fought a lot. Oh, they liked each other well enough, but there were times they went at it something fierce. On hot summer days dust would fly when they got to grappling and throwing each other to the ground. Mammy Komati would toss a bucket of water on them, sometimes two, to cool them off. They'd wallow in the mud a bit after that but you could tell their hearts weren't in it. I suppose having brothers gives you plenty of reasons to learn how to fight and lots of excuses to use what you learn."

In the dark Luke's smile deepened. "I expect you're right, Miss Hamilton."

Bria drew her knees toward her chest and smoothed the

blanket over them. She hugged her calves. "What decision did you and Orrin come to after the tour?"

Luke didn't think it was possible for Bria Hamilton to look less business-like than she did now, but there was no mistaking that she meant to conduct it. Her voice had lost its trace of pensiveness. The cadence was clipped now and the full measure of her self-confidence had returned. "I gave him a price for renovation of Concord and he agreed."

Bria's head snapped up. "You mean it?"

Luke nodded.

Her eyes narrowed suspiciously. "What price?" If Orrin had agreed to an impossibly low estimate then nothing worth doing would be done.

Luke told her. He had the satisfaction of watching her eyes widen. She simply stared at him. It was not that he thought she didn't believe him, but more that she seemed afraid to.

"Can that be true?" she whispered huskily.

This time Luke made the sign of the cross on his chest. "I swear."

She smiled then, oblivious to the effect it had on her companion. She did not see Luke's eyes darken nor could she feel his heart slam against his chest. She did not know that his mouth was suddenly dry or that there was a faint roaring in his ears. Bria closed her eyes briefly. This news was surpassingly wonderful. When she opened her eyes it was to find Lucas sitting in much the same position she was. She imagined that from a distance they looked a little like a matched pair of bookends holding up the pond pine between them.

"It's wonderful," she said.

Luke said nothing for a moment, not trusting the timbre of his voice. When he finally spoke, his tone was almost as dry as his mouth. "As if this was not done by your design," he said. "Your fingerprints are all over it, Miss Hamilton. But you're clever. I'll give you that."

"Normally I would be flattered by some acknowledgement

of my intelligence, Mr. Kincaid, but I'm not entirely sure you mean to be complimentary.''

He chuckled and shot her a wry glance. "I do. Your performance at dinner this evening was masterful. I enjoy the theater and make a point to attend in whatever city I'm working. I vow there is no actress equal to you on the stage from Atlanta to New York.''

"Then you do flatter me.''

"I speak the truth.''

"Then it is good to know that I can have a career in the footlights if it comes to that. And, Mr. Kincaid, if my stepfather suspects my fine hand in what was done tonight, it *will* come to that.''

"I have no reason to tell him. I have a job, after all.''

Bria drew in her lower lip to dampen her smile. "You do, don't you?''

"I certainly do. Did you know at the outset you would be so successful?''

"Of course not. If I had do you think I would have followed you here? I thought there was a fair chance that I could get him to hire you, but that he would accept your assessment of Concord, well, that was rather more than I hoped for. Until I heard you speak tonight, I wasn't completely certain what your assessment was.''

"You did an excellent job of not placing any faith in it.''

"I don't have any faith in it now,'' she told him. "Orrin has faith in it. I have the soundness of my own judgment. I know most of what needs to be done here at Concord, Mr. Kincaid. Your assessment agreed with mine. Orrin trusts you because he has no choice. I trust you because I do. Ask yourself whose trust you would prefer.''

Lucas already knew. He asked a question he didn't know the answer to. "Why does your stepfather hate you?''

"He doesn't hate me.''

"No?''

"No,'' she repeated.

"Then—"

"He's afraid of me. There's a difference."

Luke remembered the threat she made at dinner when Foster threatened to put down her horse. He could think of other exchanges when Bria had accepted Orrin's rebukes or directives with no retorts and once when she had admitted understanding his thinly veiled threat. *'Think twice about letting Mr. Kincaid go,'* he had said. *'Once about how disappointed I would be and once about your mother.'* "What does he imagine you'll do to him?" Luke asked.

"He told you this evening."

"He did?"

"He said I was trying to kill him."

"You mean he was serious?"

"I believe he was. At least he has always seemed so to me."

"But that's—"

Bria turned an enigmatic smile on him. Her dark sapphire eyes gave nothing away. "Absurd?" she finished for him. A single brow arched. "Is it?"

Realizing he was on the verge of taking her bait again, Luke kept his mouth closed. Hadn't he thought of doing some things to Orrin Foster himself this evening? Pushing his face in a plate of apple pie. Pressing his windpipe closed with the heel of his shoe. Kicking him down the stairs. But when real action was needed, it was Bria who had laid him out cold with a stone the size of her fist.

Perhaps Orrin was a better judge of his stepdaughter's intent than Lucas was. He had known her longer. More to the point, she had known *him* longer.

"How is Orrin going to release the money?" Bria asked.

It was as if their last exchange had never taken place, Lucas thought. "He says he will have a separate account drawn up and arrange credit with suppliers in Charleston. He intends to oversee the expenditures himself."

Bria nodded. It was as she expected. "That will make it more difficult," she mused.

"What?"

It was only then that she realized she had spoken aloud. What would he think if he knew what she had planned? She said carefully, "There are things that need to be done at Concord besides the house proper."

"The price I gave Orrin included new stables."

She certainly hoped so. The sum Lucas had named was enormous. "Improvements," she said vaguely. Things her stepfather would *never* approve, even with the sanction of another Yankee.

"What improvements?"

"They're really none of your concern."

"None of my concern? But then how am I to—"

"They will not be your responsibility." Bria could feel the conversation giving rise to her impatience. "They'll be mine." Luke's tension had become a tangible thing, as had her own. She could feel them both repelling it as though they were the like ends of two magnets. "What is it?" she asked when his silence grew beyond bearing.

"I won't let you compromise what I've agreed to deliver. My arrangement is with your stepfather, not you."

"As you pointed out earlier, the fact that you have an arrangement at all is due in no small measure to me."

"And I thank you. But it doesn't mean I'll look the other way while you undermine me." For the first time he saw real panic in Bria's expression. He did not lessen his stance. "Your stepfather already warned me you would want money. That's what this is about, isn't it?"

Bria said nothing.

"He expects something like this, Miss Hamilton. You would do well to reconsider whatever scheme you're hatching."

Bria could simply sit no longer. She jumped to her feet. In her haste she stepped on one straggling corner of the blanket. The knot under her arm loosened, and before she could pull it tight the blanket fell to the level of her waist.

Luke's eyes had followed Bria as she rose to her feet. Now

they were fixed on the perfect roundness of her breasts visible through the damp, clinging fabric of her shift. There was a slant of shadow that deepened the valley between them and a silvery cascade of light that fell across one shoulder. He didn't blink. Didn't move.

Neither did Bria.

She stared at him, frozen. Her stillness was so profound that it seemed she had stopped breathing. In moments her heartbeat would come to the same end.

Lucas stood slowly and approached her just as cautiously. His watchful, predatory advance kept Bria just as she was. When he closed the distance between them he placed his hands, not on hers, but on the curling edge of the blanket. Keeping his eyes on Bria's impossibly wide ones, Luke unfolded what was left of the knot then lifted the blanket until it covered even the high curve of her breasts. He refastened the knot, pulling it tight, his knuckles passing lightly across the damp lawn fabric only once.

"I have no intention of saying anything to Foster," he said quietly. Luke's hands fell to his sides. "I can keep that promise as long as you don't make it impossible for me. Do you understand?"

Bria took a shallow breath and nodded.

Luke stepped back. "Good."

I shall just have to make certain you don't catch me.

Orrin left early the next morning. Bria was not dismayed in the least when Lucas went with him. Hadn't she informed Luke he would be returning to Charleston? He hadn't seemed pleased then, but he didn't object when Orrin suggested it. He would have had to make the trip himself inside of a week in any event. There were suppliers and merchants to meet and contracts to be drawn up. He had to make arrangements for materials to be delivered to Concord at the time he anticipated needing them.

Within minutes of his departure, Bria cornered Luke in the entrance hall while Orrin was walking ahead to the carriage. "Don't forget your carpetbag," she whispered with a touch of sarcasm.

He blinked. She hadn't spoken but a word of greeting to him this morning. Not for a moment did he think it was all a performance for her stepfather. "What are you talking about?" he asked with credible patience.

"Your clothes. I don't know why you saw fit to arrive here yesterday in those rags, but you should return with a better wardrobe. I will not continue to supply you with my brothers' leavings."

Luke was still wearing the tan broadcloth suit she had given him to impress Orrin yesterday. Bria was right that he had other clothes in Charleston. They were in the room he had let while he made inquiries and worked out the best manner in which to arrive at Concord. A few days ago it had seemed that Bria Hamilton was the key. Everything he had learned about her said she would be more likely not to throw him out if he appeared in need of help. That was not to say she would take him in, only that she wouldn't show him the door upon their initial acquaintance. Orrin, on the other hand, was considered unapproachable and unlikely to make the final decisions regarding Concord anyway. That left Elizabeth Hamilton Foster, and Lucas had found that anyone he'd talked who knew her was particularly tight-lipped. The widow of Andrew Hamilton was still accorded great respect. She was not fodder for gossip, at least not in the presence of a Yankee.

"I'll see what I can do," Luke said. "But ask yourself if you would have given me any time yesterday if I had arrived looking like I didn't need the work."

That rocked Bria back on her heels. She almost didn't catch Luke as he spun and headed for the door. Orrin was calling him impatiently from the carriage. "Wait!" She had a hand extended to tug on his jacket but it didn't come to that. On the threshold, Luke stopped and looked over his shoulder. He glanced down at her hand and one corner of his mouth curled derisively. It was enough to make Bria withdraw her outstretched hand.

"What is it?" he asked.

"Then you're not a gambler?" Bria was not entirely successful in quelling the note of despair in her voice. She heard it and knew that Lucas Kincaid would not miss it, either.

He did not answer immediately but held her eyes, his own features set gravely. "I gamble, Miss Hamilton. All the time." He left then.

Bria took his place in the doorway and watched him go, unable to call him back with her stepfather watching even had she been willing to do so. It was finally Addie's approach that had pulled her away from watching the carriage go.

Bria stepped inside and shut the door, leaving the dust to settle on the steps and in the drive. "What is it, Addie?"

Addie's hands had always been out of proportion to the rest of her, large and strong in a frame that was otherwise petite, even fragile. She was making a pretense of wiping those hands in her apron now, but Bria knew she was actually wringing them. "You looked worried, Miss Bree. Is something wrong?"

Bria placed one hand lightly on Addie's shoulder. She shook her head. "No, Addie," she said quietly. "I shall just have to have a better plan."

Devising one, however, was not such an easy thing. There were distractions enough over the course of the next week to keep Bria's mind firmly in the present. Three field hands and one child were struck by malaria. Bria went to their homes herself with medicine and food but she knew that neither might be of any help. Some people died whether they were attended to or not; others lived in similarly mysterious circumstances. Bria was the first to acknowledge that attending to a problem made *her* feel better. She had to do something.

There was hardly an inch of Bria's skin exposed when she rode out across the lower wetlands to deliver supplies to the families. Even on the hottest days she wore riding gloves and a long-sleeved jacket over her blouse. Her riding skirt fell to mid-calf while her boots reached her knees. She wore a straw hat, usually secured with a black grosgrain ribbon. The hat's wide brim shaded her face from the relentless rays of the sun.

Men in the fields often took an opposite approach. They stripped down to their britches so their backs gleamed liked polished obsidian as they bent over their work. Most of them went bare-headed in defiance of the sun and the sweat on their brows made their foreheads glisten. Invariably they stopped working long enough to lift a hand in Bria's direction as she passed on the edge of the flooded rice fields. She could not help but wonder as she returned her greeting which among them would be struck down the next day or the day after that.

At the hottest point of the day, when even the mosquitoes seemed too hampered by the heat to flit around her, Bria found herself wishing she was in Charleston with her mother, enjoying cooling sea breezes and lemon ices. She didn't dwell on it long. Orrin was there, and so for a time was Lucas Kincaid. Bria knew she had made the right decision by staying back.

It wasn't only the malaria that kept her occupied. Lightning struck an ancient oak during a nighttime thunderstorm. The tree had been on the land long before the first European settlers came to the Carolina shores. At its crown the red oak topped one hundred feet and spread shade during some parts of the day nearly twice that distance. Its ridged gray trunk was five feet thick. The sharp cracking sound of it being torn asunder had brought Bria upright in bed. There was no mistaking that sound for thunder.

She went to the verandah and was soon joined by Addie and Jeb. They sat there for what was left of the night, listening to the rain and silently mourning their ancient friend. At first light the extent of the damage was clear. The red oak's trunk had been split cleanly and the half still standing could not possibly survive—at least not with the dignity of its former self. Reluctantly she ordered it taken down.

The small curing shed had been destroyed by the tree's fall.

After the debris was cleared the salvaged meat and equipment was temporarily moved to the summer kitchen. The overseer's quarters were damaged by the red oak's sweeping crown. Smaller branches had crashed through the windows, but a large one had pierced the wall just above Lucas Kincaid's bed.

"Like a knife through butter," Jeb said, surveying the damage with something like admiration in his eyes. "Don' that beat all. Why, if Mr. Kincaid had been here . . ." His voice trailed off when he saw Bria's perfect stillness.

"Yes," she said quietly. "Why, if *only* Mr. Kincaid had been here."

The lay-by flow had been added gradually to the rice fields until the plants were completely submerged. Just before she ordered it done, leaffolder larvae had been found on the tender shoots of the rice plants. Some of them could be picked off by hand but mostly the rice plant's survival depended on natural predators like ground beetles and waterbugs, earwigs and damselflies.

Bria inspected the growth of the seedlings daily, in her mind comparing it to other successful harvests. She randomly selected plants to judge them for growth and color and root extension. She often worked in the small greenhouse that Rand had constructed for her. Not visible from the house, it was tucked away in a clearing beyond the stand of trees to the south. Designed to be part greenhouse, part laboratory, Rand had given Bria some of his scientific equipment to aid her in raising Concord's lifeblood crop. He had shown her how to use a microscope and make comprehensive notes that would mean something to her in successive experiments. He had also shown her how to control growth and cross-pollinate in the laboratory. Bria did not share Rand's broad naturalist interests, but she did care deeply about her rice plants. Since she began experimenting, she had developed two new varieties, both of them heartier and less tasty to caterpillars. Leaffolder larvae, however, still feasted on them.

Lucas Kincaid returned on Saturday, a full ten days after his departure. Bria didn't know he had arrived until she saw him standing outside the overseer's house, inspecting the storm's damage. She reined in Apollo but didn't dismount. She let the horse nudge Luke's shoulder.

"Hey," he said, digging in his heels when Apollo would have pushed him along. He dropped his hat and turned, holding his palms out in surrender. "I don't have anything for you." To prove his point, Luke put his hands in his pockets and pulled them out empty. He looked up at Bria. "Do you think he understands?"

"Probably not. He's spoiled. He thinks everyone has a treat for him." She reached in the pocket of her jacket and showed him the small apple she was saving for later. Repocketing the apple, she said, "He likes to have his nose rubbed."

Chuckling, Luke obligingly scratched the gelding's nose. "It looks as if you had quite a storm here," Luke said to Bria. "How long ago?"

She thought back. The days seemed to have blended of late. "Four . . . no, five days ago."

Luke nodded. He looked around, not able to put his finger on what was different in the immediate landscape.

"It was the old red oak," Bria said at last. "Lightning struck it." Off and on for the length of his absence Bria had wondered what Lucas Kincaid meant by one of the last things he'd said her. *But ask yourself if you would have given me any time yesterday if I had arrived looking like I didn't need the work.* Looking at him now, nattily turned out in long black frock coat and deep red cravat, Bria knew she would have had Addie point him back to the road. His trousers were still tucked in his riding boots. The boots and his coat showed a surprising lack of dust for having made the journey from Charleston. It made Bria wonder if he was simply fastidious about his appearance or if Orrin had actually let him bring back the carriage. She hoped it was the latter. The thought that he would turn out to be overly conscious of his appearance annoyed her.

"What's wrong?" he asked. Luke was very much aware

that he had become the target of her disapproval. She was staring at the turned-down collar of his white shirt. He resisted the urge to pull it away from his neck when it began to feel tight.

"How did you get back here?" she asked.

"The carriage. Your stepfather said he would rent one when he and Elizabeth were ready to return."

"Oh."

For reasons that Luke could not fathom, Bria's irritation with him seemed to vanish. Had she thought he'd *stolen* the carriage? Luke scooped up his low-crowned, wide-brimmed felt hat from the ground where he'd dropped it. He threaded his fingers through his hair once before he returned it to his head. "Was anything else damaged?" he asked.

Now he looked like the gambler he professed to be, Bria thought. Or what *she* imagined a gambler looked like. She had no trouble envisioning him at a card table now, dealing himself the winning hand from somewhere in the deck. She would have definitely had Addie show him the road because the thought that he could help her would never have crossed her mind.

Bria shook her head, not in answer to Luke's question but as a way of clearing her thoughts. Beneath her, Apollo shuffled at her inattention. Bria steadied him. "What?" she asked Luke. "I'm sorry . . . I didn't . . ."

"Damage," he repeated. "I was inquiring about the extent of it."

"The curing shed was destroyed. There are dikes and floodgates in need of repair but that had nothing to do with the storm. I had to have the oak felled."

"You did?" He looked past Bria to where the old oak had stood. He wondered how he had not immediately missed its wide-spreading crown against the sky. Now that she'd told him, its absence seemed obvious. He wondered if she had experienced any sense of loss for the ancient tree. There was no emotion in her voice when she spoke of having it felled. "I'm sorry about the tree," he said.

Bria shrugged.

Luke stared at her a moment longer. Was it lack of emotion or too much of it that made her respond in that manner? When no answer occurred to him, he asked, "What about the wood?"

"Taken to the sawmill. There was lumber to be salvaged."

He nodded. "Good. Then I can use—"

"I'm afraid not," she said coolly. "I already have plans for it."

Luke didn't ask about her plans. He did not think she would tell him. He supposed this was the kind of decision Orrin placed in her hands anyway. "What about the damage to this place?" he asked, pointing over his shoulder to the overseer's house. "Do you intend that it should be repaired?"

"Not with my lumber."

"Then you won't mind if I continue to sleep in the big house?"

"I'll mind," she said. "I just won't be able to stop you." Her smile was tight, without humor. "Didn't Orrin extend an invitation for you to do that very thing?"

"He did, but I wasn't going to take him up on it." He looked back at the shattered windows of his quarters, then to Bria. "Now I will."

"I do have some say over what room you'll occupy," she told him. "It will no longer be the one that adjoins mine. You can have Rand's former room. You'll find it larger and more comfortable."

"And on the other side of house."

"Exactly." Bria pulled on Apollo's reins and brought him around. Before she nudged him in the direction of the stable-yards, she asked Luke, "Will you be joining me at dinner?"

"I didn't know I was invited."

"You just were."

Dinner turned out to be a quiet, occasionally tense affair and it remained so over the course of the next three weeks. Luke's conversational overtures were politely rebuffed. Bria was never uncivil to him but she was also never encouraging. When Luke asked if she wanted to play cards one evening she looked at him as if he'd left his good sense in Charleston. Luke found himself eyeing Orrin Foster's liquor cabinet with considerably more interest as time went on.

During the day Luke had much to occupy him. He had access to the entire house and he made good use of the opportunities available to him. Bria was often gone to the fields and on the occasions when she could have easily surprised him he was always hard at work. She and Apollo were not difficult to spot from any of the eight dormer windows in the attic.

To date his searching had been futile. Orrin Foster had left too few clues for him. Far more successful and satisfying was the restoration of Concord. Luke had a small crew of men working for him, selected from among a score of hands working elsewhere on the plantation. All of them were recommended by Bria, and Luke had no reason to think she would sabotage his work by suggesting unskilled or belligerent laborers.

To a man they were hard workers. They had no complaints, rising several hours before dawn so they could work in the attic before the temperatures became intolerable. Under Luke's supervision they literally raised the roof on the old house so they could replace the rotting understructure without it crashing on their heads. They had one day of rest after lowering it again while they waited for the delivery of the red roof tiles. The delivery was not late; it was Luke and the men who were ahead of schedule.

Some days Bria did not know what to make of what was happening at Concord. On the day the roof was raised she sat on Apollo in a distant orchard and watched the progress. She alternately prayed that no disaster would strike and prepared herself for what she would do when it happened. It was not that she didn't think Lucas Kincaid could do it; it was just that she did not think it could be done.

She most often observed him from a distance, working along-side the men on the roof or unloading lumber from the wagons when they arrived. Sometimes she would see him removing his hat and wiping his brow with the sleeve of his shirt. When he wasn't wearing a shirt he used a kerchief in the back pocket of his trousers. At first his skin had gleamed whitely in the summer sun. Gradually it developed a bronze patina, as though the taut muscles of his back and chest and arms were meant to be preserved by the sun, not destroyed by it. Where he had simply stood out before, as a bleached shell might against the darker sand, now he had his own radiance and light shimmered across his neck and shoulders when he stood and stretched.

In the light of day his hair was no longer that same dark coffee color it had been at their first meeting. Bria observed shades of fiery autumn red in the strands when he raked back his hair. He made the gesture with some frequency: when he was thinking, when he was hot, when he was frustrated, and often, with her, when he was confused.

Bria understood all of that. Especially the confusion. She was experiencing it herself. The discomfort of that emotion, or any of the emotions he engendered in her, made Bria more wary. In turn, she kept her distance, not just from him, but from herself as well. She was ruthless in suppressing whatever feeling came to the forefront of her mind. It was as if she were holding her own head under water. There were moments when she could not breathe.

Most of those moments were preceded by a pair of implacable grey eyes turned in her direction or a smile that was at once questioning and knowing. Bria began to think of going to Charleston for a reprieve.

Lucas Kincaid confused her in ways that had nothing to do with his face or his form. He had shown her detailed plans for the stable and layout of the yards. He unrolled them across the desk in the study for her to look at. Another man might have presented them with a flourish and a surfeit of pride in his accomplishment. Luke showed them to her for her approval.

"Hasn't Orrin already approved them?" she had asked.

"I don't want Orrin's approval. I want yours."

He was not flattering her, she realized with a small shock.

He meant it sincerely. He knew she was the one who cared about the stables and this was his way of telling her. Bria had given her approval, of course. What he had proposed was everything she had wanted. She had small suggestions and he accepted the ones that improved his design and explained to her why the others wouldn't work. She had thanked him, not for the design itself, but for sharing it with her, though she never made the distinction clear to him.

There were other plans, she'd discovered later. Curiosity piqued by the first set she'd been shown, Bria went looking for more of the same. While Luke was occupied on the roof, Bria let herself into his room. She was not at ease conducting the search but she reasoned that since she knew the size of the objects she was looking for, it was not as if she needed to go through all his belongings. As it turned out, they were in the second place she looked: under his bed.

Bria sat on the floor, examining the detailed drawings of the stable again. She slid it carefully to one side and stared at the one beneath it. It was not a design for a structure this time, but the layout of an expansive landscaped garden. She recognized what she saw as an extension of the existing gardens at Concord. He had guessed all along that what he had toured was a smaller and less-well-thought-out version of what had been there before the war.

Lucas's plan had the perfect symmetry and classic proportions of ornamental gardens that ringed European palaces. Locally, only Middleton Place had ever boasted such spectacular gardens. What Lucas proposed did not cover sixty-five acres as antebellum Middleton gardens had, but he made use of the acreage on all sides of the crumbling foundation for as far as the eye could see. There would be mazes to walk through and pools that would reflect the color of the sky. In the springtime it would be as if a fireworks display had run aground. Azaleas and camellias, in all their glorious variety of color, would be in bloom. There were paths that led into the woodland where Luke had marked places for planting rhododendron, holly, and wisteria. Bordering the woods in the area of the slave quarters were fields given over to wildflowers. He had sketched tiny pictures of plants that had come to his mind. Bria recognized wild geraniums and hyacinths, bluebells, hepatica, purple coneflowers, and bee balm.

She shook her head, awed by the intricacies and thoughtfulness of the design. He had not chosen the wildflowers at random, but as someone who knew their blooms would give the fields color from springtime to autumn.

There was another detail which did not elude Bria's eye. Nowhere in Luke's plans did the slave quarters or overseer's house exist.

Bria had looked through other plans. They consisted mostly of more complete renderings of some of the house restoration. There were details of the crown moldings and tiles in the various fireplaces. He had sketched certain aspects of the construction so the men working with him could follow his plan.

It was thoroughly remarkable. And unsettling.

Who *was* Lucas Kincaid?

Bria had determined then that she might never know if she continually held herself at a distance. The problem was that she had no clear idea of how to go about anything differently. It took her three days to decide that she would begin by inviting him to her greenhouse.

Luke did not bother to mask his surprise. Bria had to expect that he would wonder at the invitation. She had not extended herself in any way toward him in the three weeks since his return. Even though he suspected she had been pleased when he showed her the plans for the stables, her thank-you had been cursory and emotionless. She may as well have been thanking him for passing the sugar. He had shared enough meals with her to be more than a little familiar with that tone.

"I'd like that," he said. "I've only seen the building from the outside." He had attempted to enter it once. It was unlikely that he would have found anything there but it was one of the

few places he had never explored. As it turned out, Bria kept
it locked.

"I keep it locked," she said. "Some of the equipment is
valuable, but only to me. I worry about animals getting in and
destroying my experiments."

Now Luke was intrigued. "You have experiments?"

"Mm-hm. With the rice plants. I've never had much success
with the cotton." She stepped lightly down the stairs leading
from the verandah and paused at the bottom, waiting for Luke
to join her. He seemed to be hesitating. "This way," she said
pleasantly.

Luke absently raked back his hair. He saw her smile as she
watched him but couldn't divine the reason. He fell in step
beside her. "Does this mean you've forgiven me?" he asked.

"Forgiven you?"

"For that first night at the river . . ." He didn't finish. For
a moment he thought she was going to be sick. "Miss Hamilton?"

Bria had a vision of herself as she had been that night, frozen
still with fear, all but naked in her damp shift, exposed in a
thin veil of moonlight and gossamer shadows. She could still
feel the pass of his thumb across her skin as he adjusted the
blanket around her. For days it was like a brand on her flesh.

"Don't speak of it again," Bria said. She ruthlessly sup-
pressed the feelings clawing at her. It was happening again,
that sense of resolutely holding her own head under water. The
nausea of the powerful emotions passed when she couldn't
breathe. Then she walked on.

Chapter Five

Luke was quiet the remainder of the way to the greenhouse. Bria either did not care or she did not notice. He wondered at her ability to dismiss unpleasantness from her life. Where did she put it and how did she keep it there? He had never built a house that did not have some place for storing the odds and ends collected throughout a person's life. It might be in the attic or behind paneled doors under the stairs. People filled the space with things they no longer wanted to look at or no longer needed. Sometimes items were placed there for the value of their sentiment.

And then there were the things no one else was meant to see.

Luke came out of his reverie as Bria unlocked the greenhouse. When she opened the door she stood back and gestured for him to precede her. He was keenly aware of the honor she was according him. This place was her sanctuary. He did not think many people had been invited inside.

The air was thick with humidity and redolent of the fragrance peculiar to growing plants. Luke could smell the richness of the earth in the pots crowding a wooden bench on the opposite wall. The greenhouse was not a large structure, but then it didn't have to be for Bria's purposes. Luke's practiced eye measured it ten feet by twelve. Above him the sky shimmered through mist-covered panes of glass. On all sides of him, but not dangerously close, were bayberry and magnolia trees.

Bria moved around Luke and worked her way down the center aisle to prop open more windows. When the panes were too high for her to reach she used a wooden rod fashioned for just such a purpose. "I'm glad I came," she said. "One of the difficult things is managing the temperature. If I'm not careful I can burn the seedlings."

"What is it that you're doing here?" In addition to the pots on the bench there were shallow trays filled with water and sediment from which tender green shoots were emerging. The worktable had a microscope and was otherwise crowded with beakers, potting tools, and a stack of papers that were curling from the humidity.

"Just some things that Rand showed me how to do. My brother is a naturalist. You knew that, didn't you?"

Luke shook his head. "I thought he was looking for the Hamilton-Waterstone treasure."

Bria could detect no derision in Luke's tone. That was not so usual when people outside the family spoke of the treasure or Rand's search for it. "He is," she said, "but that's not what he had planned to do with his life. Solving the riddles and treasure hunting was always Shelby's notion of a good adventure. David would have inherited and managed this plantation. But Rand meant to be a naturalist. He studied two years at Oxford. Where did you study, Mr. Kincaid?"

Luke was bent over the microscope, adjusting the mirror and fiddling with the dials so he could see the specimen on the slide. He answered without thinking. "Princeton." His hand stilled as soon as he heard himself. He straightened slowly and looked at Bria. "There's no reason for you to look quite so pleased with yourself. You could have asked anytime."

"I just did."

"And I answered. With no thumbscrews applied. What else would you like to know?"

A little of Bria's bravado faded. She sounded almost weary when she spoke. "Why are you here, Mr. Kincaid?"

"I thought my work would speak for itself."

"It speaks about the work. It doesn't tell me anything about you."

"Doesn't it? That's odd." He looked around the greenhouse, taking his time before his grey eyes speared Bria's again. "Your work tells me some things about you." He didn't wait for her to ask what he meant. In truth, he wasn't certain she would. "It speaks to what is important in your life. Your family. This land. Your privacy." He observed Bria's weight shift slightly. Otherwise she remained still, her chin barely raised and her arms at her side. "You are intelligent. More than that, you are clever. It is not enough for you to do good work. You want to do it better. You care about improving things, even if it means changing their nature. The people who work for you are not above your notice and you do not suffer fools." He paused and a faint smile played on his mouth. "Except perhaps for your stepfather."

"And you," Bria said. She was not smiling.

"And me," Luke said easily, not taking offense. "Shall I go on?"

"Whatever is your pleasure."

"You do not avoid responsibility and can make difficult decisions. More to the point, you are able to make decisions in difficult circumstances. The fact that you remain here at Concord during the malarial season suggests you are dedicated or fearless or simply hiding. One might say—"

"Nothing more," she interrupted. "I've heard enough."

Luke did not try to finish his thought aloud. Bria's face was devoid of color. The edge of her lower lip had been drawn in as if she was holding it between her teeth to stop it from trembling. Her eyes, though, remained untouched by her thoughts. If they were windows to the soul, then Bria Hamilton had none.

Luke turned away from her, breaking the thin thread of tension between them and threw her a lifeline instead. "Tell me about these experiments of yours."

It was a moment before Bria found her voice. "I'm trying to develop heartier strains of rice. Rand said that such a thing is possible. Have you heard of Gregor Mendel?"

"No."

"About ten years ago he published his work on the laws of heredity. He spent years experimenting with the cross-pollination of certain flowers to arrive at his conclusions. I have it in the library if you would be interested." Bria shook her head, her lips set a trifle self-mockingly. "No, of course you wouldn't be interested. It's dry reading, really, and not to everyone's tastes."

"I'm sure you're right," he said. "And it's kind of you not to point out that I wouldn't understand a word of it."

"Oh, I didn't mean—"

"I know you didn't. I just said so, didn't I? Go on, tell me more."

Bria approached the table holding the trays of rice seedlings. "I'm not certain that rice culture can survive much longer in this area, not unless each plant can be made to be more productive. It takes too many workers to harvest the crop. If we can agree not to argue about the practice of slavery, permit me to say that at least for the growing and harvesting of rice it provided the necessary labor. Since the war ended every plantation has difficulty finding enough workers for the rice fields."

"That's not surprising. The conditions are terrible. Water rising above the ankles. Snakes. Spiders. Swarms of mosquitoes. And then there's the malaria."

"Do you think I don't know these things?" Bria felt her voice rising and she resolutely pushed her irritation down. "There is also increased competition from the western states. They can use machinery on the plains that is not suited to this soil and topography. That, more than anything, may prove to be the end of this Carolina gold.

"This is not the first time my family has had to respond to changes in the market. This plantation used to raise a fortune in indigo. There hasn't been money in that crop since after the Revolutionary War when British subsidies ended. I am gradually turning more of the land over to cotton production and expanding the peach orchards. I hope one day Concord will also be known for its thoroughbred horses. In the meantime I'm studying ways to improve the rice crop. I think you were right about me in one respect: I want to change the nature of things. If I can develop an aromatic strain that requires fewer workers to tend or harvest it, then we can continue to grow it. If not . . ." Bria shrugged. "Then we can't."

Luke did not have to pretend to be impressed. He was. "How long have you been doing this?"

"I suppose it's been six years now. That's how long ago Rand built the greenhouse for me. It was not long after I began to take more responsibility for the running of the plantation. Before the war we had an overseer and a driver who tended to things. My father and David knew every inch of Henley, but they were all gone by the time Orrin arrived. He tried his hand at managing for a few years. We were fortunate when he lost interest."

Luke noticed there was no bitterness in Bria's tone. It was simply a statement of fact. She could have only been eighteen or nineteen when she took over for Orrin. He picked up one of the terra cotta pots on the bench and passed his finger across the feather spikes of the light green sprouts. They were like velvet under his touch. "This isn't rice," he said, raising it to his nose. "It smells like dill."

"It is. I grow herbs. Mammy Komati always had an herb garden for poultices and potions and the like. I keep a little of it here." She picked up a pot of mint and raised it to her nose as Luke had. "I don't really use them for anything. We still have an herb garden that one of Jeb's daughters tends. I just keep growing these for the fragrance and the pleasure of fussing with them. It keeps her close." She hadn't realized she was going to express that sentiment until the words were too far gone to call back. Aware of Luke's eyes on her, Bria returned the pot to its place. She busied herself sweeping crumbs of dirt away with the side of her hand. "It sounds rather foolish, doesn't it?"

"Tender," he said. "It sounds tender."

Bria looked up suddenly. Luke was very close to her now and she had no clear recollection of how that had come to pass. He was no longer holding the pot of dill. One hand rested lightly on the edge of the table while the other remained at his side. He did not threaten her in any way, yet Bria could feel her heart trip over its own beat. She stared at him, unable to look anywhere else.

"May I kiss you, Miss Hamilton?"

Bria's eyes widened fractionally. She didn't say yes. She didn't say no. What she said was, "Why would you want to?"

The center of Luke's eyes darkened. "Because I find that I am like you in one respect. I also want to change the nature of things."

Luke waited for Bria to back away or turn her head. When she did neither, he lowered his. Her lips were soft and dry. In spite of the heat of the greenhouse, they were cool. Beneath him, they were parted by the narrowest margin. His mouth gently touched her upper lip, then the bottom one. He lingered only a moment. When he drew back, his lips gave the softest tug on hers.

Standing as if outside of herself, Bria watched as she leaned toward Luke when he straightened. It was only a few degrees, almost imperceptible. Her heels never left the ground and she didn't raise her arms. She did not throw herself at him. She had only wavered, and only for a moment.

Yet there was no denying it had been deep and abiding shame that she felt. Bria swallowed it back like gorge rising in her throat. It burned and almost made her gasp, but its acid heat was preferable to the other. She would *not* feel this way. She would *not* feel anything.

"You won't do that again, will you?" she asked.

He wondered what promise he was willing to give her. "Not soon," he said at last. *Not soon enough* was what he thought.

Bria fingered the key in the pocket of her apron. As soon as she realized Luke noticed the movement she stopped.

"I should be going," Luke said. "This has been a rather long break from my work. The others will be wondering where I've been." He smiled and took out the handkerchief in his back pocket to wipe a bit of dirt from his hands. "I can find my way back."

Bria nodded. She watched him leave. When she was sure he wasn't going to return, Bria sank to the floor and buried her face in her hands. Her shoulders heaved once but her eyes remained clear and dry. Tears would have been a relief.

She did not see him again until dinner. He had washed and changed out of his work clothes. His hair curled slightly at the collar where it was still damp. The day's hard work did not show on him except for a certain air of satisfaction that could not be washed away. As he eased his whipcord-lean frame into his chair at the table, Bria looked down at herself. She had only bothered to take off her apron.

Trying not to call attention to herself, Bria tugged on the sleeves of her gown. Where they had been folded back to the level of her elbows, she now brought them down to her wrist. While Luke was helping himself to the platter Addie lifted in front of him, Bria flattened a few wayward strands of hair and surreptitiously smoothed the neckline of her gown.

Her hands stilled when she noticed Luke's faint smile. Bria's hands dropped, her chin came up, and her eyes fairly dared him to say something.

So he did. "Are you finished preening?"

Bria's mouth parted in surprise. No retort except a denial

occurred to her and offering that poor defense was unwise. She imagined she looked rather like a fledgling bird, her mouth agape. Luke must have thought so, too.

"Shall Addie feed you directly from the platter?" he asked. "Or will you put it on your plate first?"

Bria's mouth snapped shut. She gave Addie a sour look as the housekeeper chuckled. She also noticed the look had no effect. Addie did not even try to hide her broad smile as she brought the platter around.

Bria sighed. "Must you always give voice to your thoughts, Mr. Kincaid?"

"You make it difficult for me to resist," he said. "I'm afraid I have little self-control and you goad me so prettily."

That brought Bria's head up. It was all she could do not to snort her derision. "So the fault is mine."

Luke shrugged and began to apply himself to his meal. "If you choose. That is not what I meant, however. I believe I said I am the one lacking discipline. Whether you tempt me or not really has no bearing."

His response was unexpected. Bria did not know what to make of it or even if she believed he meant it. She picked up her fork and speared a few carrot medallions. They dripped butter. Unaware that she was frowning or that her brow was puckered, Bria lifted them slowly to her mouth. Her food hovered a few moments, halfway to its destination, before Bria suddenly set it down again. She raised her eyes only to find that Luke was watching her. He seemed to be waiting though Bria could not have said there was anything expectant in his expression.

Her fingers closed around her water glass and she lifted it to her lips. Her mouth was so dry she could not have moved words over her tongue. She drank deeply, very much aware of Luke's eyes on her mouth, then her throat. He held her glance when she finished and set her glass down.

Unnerved by his patience, Bria asked, "Do you think I mean to say something?"

"Don't you?"

"Not all of us are compelled to express our every wayward thought."

One of Luke's brows arched. "Wayward?"

"Do not be disagreeable, Mr. Kincaid. I simply meant—"

"Luke," he said.

"What?"

"My name is Luke. I find this formality wearing and if you're going to dress me down it would be more effective if you used my Christian name. Nana Dearborn did."

His grandmother again, Bria thought. Her mouth twitched a little. She suspected Nana Dearborn had been a stickler for formality even with her grandson. "I'd wager she called you Lucas."

"She did."

Bria hesitated, expecting that he would ask her not to. When he said nothing she realized the choice was hers. She bowed her head slightly in his direction, making the concession. "Very well . . . *Luke*."

He grinned. "Regally conferred, Miss Hamilton. It frightens me what you might have done with a scepter and a throne at your disposal."

"Now you're mocking me."

Luke's grin merely deepened. "Yes," he said, unrepentant. "I am."

Completely disarmed by his easy admission and his quiet good humor, Bria returned to her meal. She also could not remember why she had been thinking it was necessary to take him to task. It seemed now that anything she had been about to say was better left unsaid.

It was not until Addie was serving dessert that Bria realized the meal had passed in comfortable silence. She could not have imagined that happening three weeks ago or even yesterday. It was simply more than she could have wished for, more than she had known she wanted.

"Addie." Luke motioned to the housekeeper, then indicated

his slice of peach cobbler. "This is delicious. Did you make it?"

"That's Elsie Brown's doing," Addie said. "She's prideful about her cobbler."

"And she should be. I'll tell her myself later."

"She'd like that. Master Andrew always made a point of complimentin' her. And the boys, well, they'd try to steal it out from under her nose, so she knew they liked it. But it seems lately no one appreciates a good cobbler anymore." The dark brows she lifted in Bria's direction communicated everything she left unsaid.

When Addie was gone from the dining room Bria felt compelled to explain. "I suppose I forget the niceties from time to time. My father was considerate to a fault. He made a point to let people know he appreciated their contributions. Orrin, of course, makes no effort, but I was taught better than that. I suppose I'm fortunate to have Addie to remind me."

Luke wondered about Elizabeth Foster and what role she occupied at Concord these days. Bria had never voluntarily talked about her mother and Luke had never broached the subject. For reasons he did not entirely understand, Elizabeth was not a topic for discussion.

Luke took another bite of the warm cobbler. The sweet peaches seemed to dissolve in his mouth. "Has Addie always been with you?"

"For as long as I can remember. She was born here. Her husband went north after the war. He had some idea about making money and sending for her. He's been gone six years now and she hasn't heard a word."

"Why didn't she go with him?"

"It's not so easy to leave what's familiar," Bria said. "At least that's what I suspect Addie would say. I know she loves Durrel. I think there was part of her that wanted to go."

"So he's deserted her?"

"She doesn't believe that." Bria was quiet a moment, her gaze reflective and vaguely troubled. "Neither do I," she said finally. She looked at Luke suddenly, a little startled by her admission. "I've never said that to anyone before, not even Addie."

"What is it that you suspect?" asked Luke.

She supposed she could have expected that Luke would force her to say the words. It was not in his nature to talk around unpleasantness. "I suspect Durrel's dead."

"Dead?"

"Is it that you don't understand the word?" she asked. "Or that you wish me to elaborate?" She was immediately sorry for her tartness. It was her own discomfort with the subject that made her quick to reproach Luke. "I apologize," she said with rather more stiffness than she wished. "I was not—"

Luke held up one hand, stopping her. "No, I gave no thought to the objectionable nature of this topic. Forgive me for pursuing it."

Bria had no reason to doubt his sincerity. She acknowledged that it was her own perverse nature that made her want to continue. "You will think it passing strange, but I find I would like to finish this."

"Very well."

"What do you know of the Klan?"

"Not much. Is it active here?"

Bria nodded. "I understand there is a chapter up in Georgetown County. All over the Carolinas, for that matter. Whites are scared of the freedmen. Someone loots or makes a commotion and then someone else is blamed and then there's a call for retaliation and before you know it someone's dead. It doesn't matter who started it or who kept it going, but usually when someone's dead the color of his skin is black."

"You think something like that happened to Addie's husband?"

"It's possible," she said quietly. Bria's eyes slipped away from Luke's and her voice was barely audible now. "It's likely."

Luke wondered what Bria knew, or thought she knew. He

said nothing, waiting her out. She was silent so long that he considered she may have nothing to add after all. Still, he made himself wait a beat longer.

"Orrin," Bria said, rewarding Luke's patience. "He was not happy about Durrel's leaving."

"Why was that?"

"Durrel was master of the stables." Her voice became clearer as she explained. "It was acknowledged that he knew more about breeding horses than anyone in the Carolinas. His choices were trusted by my father and other planters sought out his advice at auction. You have to understand that when Orrin married my mother the stables at Henley were almost barren of cattle. There were some draft horses and mules but the good riding stock had been confiscated by troops from both sides. I had managed to save Apollo, but—"

Luke grinned crookedly. "But he's a gelding."

"Exactly." Bria found she was returning his smile. "Orrin had more interest in horseflesh than he did in the management of other aspects of the plantation. He recognized Durrel's skill in part because other planters in similar straits tried to hire Durrel to work for them. This placed my stepfather in a difficult position. Orrin had to keep raising Durrel's wages—which he didn't like—and he also had to defer to Durrel's judgment—which he liked even less. When Durrel decided to leave Concord, probably at the encouragement of a northerner he met at auction, Orrin felt betrayed."

"He said as much?"

Bria shook her head. "No. Never. He grumbled for a while, drank even more than was his habit, then suddenly accepted it. In the days prior to Durrel's departure he was almost cheerful. I remember my mother asked him if he had found someone to hire in place of Durrel. He said that he hadn't. It struck me then as odd. Good-naturedness was out of character for Orrin."

Bria pushed away the uneaten portion of her cobbler. "I'm afraid I did not give it full consideration then. Frankly, I did not know what to make of it. In the intervening six years, however, I've had ample time to think about what happened.''

''And no evidence to support your conclusions,'' Luke ventured.

''Naturally. Orrin may or may not be a member of the Klan. It's likely that he is, even understandable.'' She caught Luke's questioning look. ''My stepfather wants to be like the other landowners. He wants to belong. He would join the Klan to be part of this New South if it meant going against his personal beliefs. The truth is, it doesn't. At the same time, he would hide his involvement from my mother and me because it also serves his purpose to pontificate on the evils of slavery. He enjoys reminding us how Henley was brought to the point where he could take it over.''

''Then you think he initiated some action against Addie's husband.''

''Yes. Initiate is the right word. Orrin may have done nothing himself except set it in motion. I doubt Durrel made it as far north as the Pee Dee River.''

They both fell silent as the doors to the dining room parted and Addie entered. She inquired if they wanted coffee. When they declined she cleared away the dishes in short order and left them.

''Does she never talk about it?'' Luke asked when Addie's footsteps could no longer be heard.

''No. It may be preferable to her to believe Durrel has abandoned her. If she accepted my thinking on the matter she'd have to admit she is working for his murderer.'' Bria scooted her chair back. ''In any event, I'm not eager to discuss it with her. I hope you will consider my wishes and remain silent as well. As you noted, I have no proof and am unlikely to come by any. The sad truth is that even if I had Orrin's signed confession it would come to nothing.''

Luke believed her. He simply nodded, taking it in. ''I thought I might take a walk. Would you care to join me?''

"No, thank you. I have accounts to review and I must develop my list of things to accomplish tomorrow."

"Two very good excuses for not being alone with me."

"Yes. They are."

Laughing, Luke stood. He came around the table and held Bria's chair while she came to her feet. "I'm only surprised that you admit it so easily."

Bria paused. "So am I," she said softly. Before he could comment, Bria fled the room for the relative safety of the study.

Luke watched her go and made no move to follow. He recognized that Bria was finished making overtures this evening. He could easily imagine that she would ruminate for the rest of the night on what she had already said. Luke would rather that she thought about the kiss. He knew he would.

His walk took him past the rice mill and ice house and eventually he meandered to the river. For more than an hour he sat on the bank, drinking in the cooling breeze and watching lights flicker in the plantation house across the way. Occasionally he let a stone fly and listened for the sound of it skipping across the surface of the water.

He didn't know if he was in the right place, yet there was an undeniable sense of coming home. Since beginning the work at Concord he had allowed himself the luxury of imagining that he was working for himself, not an employer. He thought about the construction and restoration not only in terms of what was good and proper for the house, but in terms of what *he* wanted. He had never done that before. Luke was not certain he should be doing it now.

He considered what Bria had said about Orrin Foster, then he considered what he knew about the man from his own experience. Luke thought about his mother, all six of his aunts, and everyone else he had talked to that had brought him to this point, this place. Would they recognize Orrin Foster? And if they didn't, how could he?

He carried the question back to the house. It occurred to him that another search of the study might be in order but when he reached the hallway he saw light coming out from under the doors. Bria was still there.

Luke retraced his steps a few feet and slipped into the music room instead. It was not a room that he visited often, and from what he could tell it was a room that Bria never used. Occasionally he saw Addie or one of her helpers polishing the grand piano or gliding a feather duster along the keys. The room was furnished with two sofas and several Queen Anne chairs. There was considerable space available to add chairs for a concert or to move the existing ones aside to make room for dancing. The acoustics could bear improving but it was not a bad room for a small musicale.

Luke pulled out the piano bench and sat down. He lifted the lid and ran his fingers lightly over the keys. They were stiff and did not respond easily to his touch. It had been a long time since the instrument was played.

Luke stretched his fingers, then played a C scale. He winced at the flat tones from some of the keys. Gamely, he went at it again, this time continuing past C and adding more complicated scales. His fingers became limber with the exercise and the ivories responded with less pressure. Nothing changed about the instrument's occasionally dull or off-key responses, but Luke did not let it stop him. When he felt sufficiently prepared for the challenge, he let the last notes fade from his exercises and attempted one of Chopin's simpler etudes. His fingers were still clumsy in places and he stumbled trying to remember the exact phrasing of the music. When he closed his eyes it came more easily to him.

The notes lifted and on some occasions soared. He was not bothered that the wrong notes were hit just as confidently as the right ones. His fingers always found the melody and music swirled around him.

"Who gave you permission to be here?"

Luke's fingers stilled. He hadn't heard the door open but it would have been impossible to miss Bria's tight, furious voice. He opened his eyes and turned his head in inquiry. How long had she been there? Had she announced herself immediately upon opening the doors, or had she stood there a while watching him?

"I didn't realize I required permission," Luke said calmly. "If that is indeed the case, then I suppose it was given to me by your stepfather who said I may go anywhere."

Bria could feel her face flushing. Her fingers tightened on the door handle. "But not *use* anything as you like," she said. "That's mine. The piano's mine. You can't touch it. I forbid it."

Luke's fingers slipped from the keys to lie in his lap. He was struck by her white-knuckled grip on the door. *She's steadying herself,* he thought. *She's actually trembling with anger.* He paid no attention to her words. They were merely the sentiments of a spoiled child with no capacity for sharing. The tone, though, was raw and pained and hinted at some grievous injury.

Luke stood and pushed the bench beneath the piano. He closed the lid over the keys, then lowered the case. He did not let his fingers linger over the rich ebony wood. He stepped away from the piano's graceful curve and faced Bria directly. "I beg your pardon," he said gravely.

Bria tried to accept his apology and give ground but the words were clogged in her throat and her feet stayed the spot as if nailed there.

Luke started toward the entrance and found his way blocked. "Your stepfather did give me permission to make use of one thing in his home," he said without inflection.

"Not my piano," Bria said.

"No, not your piano. You." Luke saw Bria suck in her breath and knew she understood the import of his statement. This time when he took a step forward her hand twisted on the handle and the door flew open. She pressed herself against it until he passed. "Good night, Bree."

It was hours later that Luke heard the discordant crash of keys being struck at random. In the music room the sound of it must have been shattering. In his bedroom it was barely audible. Luke knew he might not have heard it at all had he been sleeping.

He sat up. It would be Bria, of course. No one else would be touching the instrument. The staff would know the rules, even if he hadn't.

Luke found his trousers where he had thrown them over the back of a chair. He pulled them on swiftly and tucked most of the tail of his nightshirt inside. Extra material ballooned a little around the waist. A sideways glance in the mirror as he passed assured him that he looked vaguely disreputable. He thrust one hand through his hair, flattening spiked strands. It was only marginally helpful. Shrugging, he moved on.

It was not until he was in the hallway outside the music room that he asked himself why he had come. Contrary to his nature, he hadn't considered his actions before he found himself in the middle of them. Bria did that to him, he realized. Or perhaps it was what he did to himself. Luke wasn't certain. He only knew that he reacted strongly to her and often in an ill-considered manner.

The door was open and Luke moved to step into the threshold. The sight of Bria on her knees beside the piano bench brought him up short.

She held a corner of the bench in one hand to steady it and herself. In the other she had a thick polishing cloth. She was rubbing the dark wooden bench legs with more determination than she used to rub down Apollo. The wood gleamed under her care.

When she finished all four legs and the top of the bench Luke watched her sit back and survey her work. From where he stood he could not see that anything had been left undone, but evidently Bria was not satisfied. She started polishing the top of the bench again, this time with harder, punishing strokes.

When she completed the bench to her own exacting standards Luke thought she would be done. The piano was already polished to a high, reflective gloss. Lamplight shimmered along the surface of the ebony case like moonlight on a dark pond.

The keys, Luke knew, had been rubbed down. That was what had created the cacophony of sound that alerted him in the first place.

In anticipation of Bria setting aside the cloth and pronouncing herself finished, at least in her own mind, Luke stayed his place on the threshold. What he saw made it impossible for him to move for a moment longer.

Bria began polishing again. She started with the case and used the cloth in wide, sweeping circles. She stood on tiptoe to reach the center of it, then slowly worked her way around so that if she had ever looked up from her task she would have seen Lucas in the doorway.

When she was finished with the case she did the same with the sides and the legs. She polished the music stand and rubbed down the lid. Afterward she raised the lid and used a cloth with no polish on it to clean the keys again. From Luke's perspective it seemed she was oblivious to the harsh, jarring sounds she created. He let her go until she knelt on the floor just as she had been kneeling when he first came upon her. When she began rubbing the lid of the bench he moved forward to stop her.

Though his passage across the room was not silent, Luke did not expect Bria to hear him. Even when he hunkered down beside her she did not acknowledge his presence. She continued to rub the bench. Beneath the thin material of her nightdress Luke could make out the taut muscles in her forearm and shoulder driving the action.

Except for the flush of exertion in her cheeks, Bria's face was pale. Her features were set unnaturally hard. The clench in her jaw was so tight that Luke wondered if it was possible for her to crack her teeth.

"Miss Hamilton," Luke said quietly.

She didn't stir from her task. She didn't blink. It was not that her eyes had lost focus but that they only had one focus.

Luke spoke more firmly this time. "Bree."

She didn't so much as pause.

Luke laid a hand over her wrist at the same time he said her name. ''Bree!''

He was not entirely taken off guard when she launched herself at him. It was because he expected something of this nature that he had hesitated in touching her at all. Still, Bria's strength was a force to be reckoned with.

Her initial onslaught was powerful enough to throw Luke off balance, no matter that he was prepared for it. He was able to break her short fall to the floor with his own body and fended off her first frenzied blows by blocking them with his arms.

Bria fingers curled like talons. She clawed at Luke. It was only because work kept her nails short that she was unable to inflict damage to his face. She still managed to draw blood at the curve of his neck and shoulder.

Except for a pained grunt, Luke had no time to acknowledge the scratch. Bria's knee was grinding into the fleshy part of his thigh and the thought that she would jerk it upward and do the same to his groin spurred him to take control. It was no simple thing to accomplish even when he put all his strength behind it. Bria was all arms and legs and frenzied energy.

She kicked and twisted and struck blows with her fists. She used her head like a battering ram and caught him on the underside of the chin, hard enough to make his teeth rattle. He tasted blood on the inside of his mouth.

Luke turned, first only on his side to see if he could hold her there. He tried pinning her with one arm and leg but she managed enough wriggling room to sink her teeth deeply into his shoulder.

Luke did more than grunt this time. Pain made his eyes water. He swore harshly under his breath, then more loudly as she tried to bite him again. It was all he could do not to strike her.

When Luke twisted again it was to put Bria under him. He felt her hot breath on his face as air was forced from her lungs. He gave no quarter. She pushed at his shoulders and tried to heave him off. He was immovable. Bria sucked in a breath and heaved again, this time trying to squirm out from under Luke. He covered her like six fathoms of dark water. He held her on all sides, exerting an unrelenting pressure instead of weight. She seemed to lose sense of up and down and simply fought because it was not in her nature to surrender.

Toward the end her breath came harshly and unevenly. Her struggles were sporadic and without real strength. Luke had a vision of himself pinning back a butterfly's wings and it was not an image he relished. There was no pleasure in holding Bria down and no thought of revenge for the wounds she had already inflicted.

He had felt compelled to stop her. He also believed that she wanted to be stopped. There had been one moment, no more than a heartbeat, when she had looked at him with real emotion in her eyes and begged him to stop her. Then, as if she couldn't admit it to herself, she turned all her fury on him.

So Luke held her now, his grip firm and unrelenting. And although Bria could not appreciate it, it was also security and reassurance. It was all those things until Luke felt her body go slack under him.

He rolled off Bria and lay on the floor beside her for several minutes. He half expected to find Addie or Jeb or one of the house servants gawking at him from the doorway. There was no one. Apparently they were all sound sleepers or they had been cautioned against interfering.

"Bree?" There was a light film of perspiration on her forehead. Her cheeks were still flushed. Luke sat up and moved closer. He took one of the tails from his nightshirt out of his trousers and used it to wipe her face. Bria's dark lashes fluttered once, then were still again.

She was an awkward bundle to pick up but once Luke had Bria in his arms it required little effort to move with her. With some concern that she might wake and fly at him again, Luke managed the stairs almost as quickly as he would have alone. The door to her room was slightly ajar and he nudged it open with his bare foot. There were no lamps burning but there was sufficient moonlight at the window to permit him to find Bria's bed easily.

He laid her on the rumpled sheets and blankets and backed away from the bed. That was when he noticed the hem of Bria's nightgown had ridden up her thighs and that her skin had a blue and silver luster in the moonlight. The sound that came from the back of his throat was part groan, part sigh. Luke pulled the hem down over her knees. It would have to be enough that he remembered what the curve at the back of her legs felt like over his arm.

Luke lighted the oil lamp on Bria's bedside table and adjusted the wick so the flame would not disturb her. He had noticed on his occasional wanderings through the house late at night that there was often light coming from under her door. At first it made him especially cautious because he assumed she was up reading or working at her desk. He asked Addie about it once, offhandedly remarking on Bria's odd work hours so there would be nothing suspicious about his interest. Addie told him that Bria always went to sleep with a lamp burning. *She likes a night light. Has for years.*

Luke didn't ask more though he'd wondered how long *years* had been. Since childhood? Since the war? Since Orrin Foster had come to Henley? He couldn't ask Addie then and he couldn't ask Bria now, but he left the lamp burning out of respect for her comfort.

He backed out of the room quietly, pulled the door until he felt the latch click in place, then went to tend to his own wounds.

Bria did not have to go out of her way to avoid Luke over the next week. It was surprisingly easy. She was in the fields at dawn in preparation for the September harvest. She checked the plants at random, judging their ripeness, and went over the field assignments. Itinerant laborers arrived almost daily to hire on to help with harvesting the rice and Bria still wondered if she would have enough men and women to do the work.

Although she did not share her concern with Luke, she suspected his workers did. One by one they came to her and announced they were released from their labors at the house in order to help in the fields.

With work fully occupying her outdoors, Bria sometimes did not arrive at the house until dusk. She did not seek Luke out then, even if he was having dinner at that time. She chose to retire immediately to her room where Addie had a hot bath waiting or a tub ready to be filled. Sometimes she ate while she soaked. Sometimes she fell asleep before she ate.

She slept hard and dreamlessly and for both of those things she was grateful. During the course of her day she discovered that while she could easily avoid Lucas Kincaid, keeping him out of her thoughts was not accomplished by wishing it so.

Her memory of what had happened in the music room was not entirely clear. What she could remember was a series of disjointed images, like a photographic album where the pictures had been mounted at random.

In one she was lying fully across Luke's lean frame. In another she was kneeling at the piano. In yet another she was straining to reach the center of the piano case. Her reflection came back to her as she polished the gleaming surface. She had an image of herself trapped under Luke's body. One with her face buried in his shoulder. The sensation this evoked was powerful enough to make Bria gag. She could taste his cotton nightshirt in her mouth. In the last she saw her fingers on the keyboard and heard the harsh accompanying chords.

More than once Bria found herself far from the main house, sitting on Apollo's back and holding her hands over her ears. The sounds from the music room that night would not be silenced.

Work dulled the roar. Just before the plants were fully ripe Bria ordered the lay-by flow withdrawn. Water that had protected and supported the rice plants was now removed from the fields by the same series of canals and trunks that brought it. In the last harvest before there were guns fired at Fort Sumter,

Henley's yield had been almost 500,000 pounds of rice. Bria hoped for half that harvest now. It would be a victory of sorts over every obstacle that been placed in her path.

On the morning of September 5 Bria announced the rice was ready for harvesting. Men and women, armed with large sickles called rice hooks, began cutting a swath through the fields. They moved with precision and a certain uniformity, swinging the rice hooks in a wide arc like the arm of a pendulum. From a distance it looked like an army was on the march.

The cut rice was laid on the stubble to dry overnight. In the morning women moved across the fields collecting the plants into sheaves while the men continued to cut acres ahead of them. Wagons moved slowly across the cut fields to be loaded with the sheaves. They were then driven down the dirt road to the rice mill. When one of her drivers became sick, Bria took over, hauling sheaves to the mill herself.

Had Bria known this was what would tear Luke away from his own work, she would have thought better of assuming the responsibility.

For Luke, watching from one of the upstairs bedrooms, it was enough. He literally spit nails. They fell on the sill where he was working. He laid his hammer beside them. By the time he reached the rice mill Bria had stepped down from the wagon and was helping unload the sheaves.

He blocked her path. When she ran into him because she couldn't see over the top of her armload, he took the sheaves from her and carried them into the mill himself.

The threshing and pounding mill was operated by a steam engine. Fires for producing the steam necessitated a chimney. This independent structure was taller than the two-story mill. It stood some ten feet behind the mill and was connected by an underground system. Smoke curled from its opening and the smell of burning wood permeated the air.

Luke dropped his load where he saw others drop theirs. When he stepped outside the mill it was in time to see Bria gathering up another armload. This time when he took it away from her he didn't turn immediately.

"Sit over there," he said, jerking his head to indicate a shade oak. "And stay there until this wagon is empty. I'll take you to wherever you left Apollo and then I'll drive this wagon to pick up the next load." He saw her mouth part to begin an argument. Luke's grey eyes narrowed and he pinned her back with his glance. He knew there was a possibility she would take this as a challenge but he counted on the workers in their midst to help her think through her response. He watched the stubborn set of her features reflect frustration, then soften briefly as she reckoned with surrender.

"Very well," she said finally. Bria turned and walked in the direction of the sheltering oak. And she kept on walking.

Between trips from the wagon to the mill, Luke saw Bria disappear into the house. How like her to define the terms of her surrender. He merely shook his head when she appeared later with Addie and Martha carrying sandwiches for the workers. While Addie set out the food on the portion of the wagon that was cleared, Bree and Martha carried pitchers of cool water from the pump for refreshment.

When the wagon was empty save for a basket of sandwiches and a keg of water to carry to the field, Bria climbed into the seat. Luke was already there holding the reins. He snapped them smartly and the team began their wide turn in the yard. They knew the direction without much in the way of guidance from him.

The day was clear and bright. Sunlight lent the tops of trees a vivid green hue and made the underside of their canopies appear like dark emerald velvet in contrast. Bria's face was shaded by a wide-brimmed straw hat that made no claim to fashion. The band was darkened with sweat and it was held in place by a black grosgrain ribbon. When she saw a rut in the road ahead she clamped down on the crown to keep it in place.

Luke glanced over at her. "When you grow weary of hitting yourself on the head, you can always tie that ribbon more tightly."

Bria's mouth flattened and she swallowed the words that came immediately to her mind.

Luke simply shrugged. "As you wish."

The wagon jounced along. Bria's arm brushed Luke's but there was no way she could avoid the contact. When she wasn't holding down her hat her fingers were curled around the edge of her seat. He seemed perfectly comfortable with the silence between them. Bria was not.

"You didn't have to stop what you were doing to come out here," she said.

"It would be rather difficult to continue working there *and* be here, don't you think?

"I *meant*," she said more firmly, "that you didn't have to come here at all."

Luke pretended to think about that. "No, I suppose I didn't."

"Then why—"

He interrupted her. "That should be obvious, even to you. I came to help because I wanted to. With the harvesting going on I have no workers left in the house and you're still out here completing the twelve labors of Hercules. I thought you would welcome the assistance if not the company. If you meant to go on as you have this past week, working yourself into a collapse to avoid me, consider it ended now."

"It's harvest," she explained. "Everyone works hard."

Luke yanked on the reins and applied the brake, bringing the team to a halt. Dust settled under their hooves. He turned on the seat, for once making no effort to hide his impatience. When Bria shied away it only made the set of his jaw more rigid. Dropping the reins, Luke's left hand shot out and he gripped Bria's stubborn chin between his thumb and forefinger. He lifted it a few degrees to see her eyes clearly.

"Everyone is *not* who I care about." His eyes dropped away from hers and fell to the level of her mouth. "Oh hell," he said softly. "Why explain at all?"

He kissed her.

Chapter Six

Bria did not blink. She did not move. The touch of his mouth on hers was light at first. His fingers exerted more pressure on her chin than the lips that covered hers. It was not a compelling, insistent kiss. Not in the beginning. Bria stayed just as she was, her fingertips pressing whitely against the wagon seat, holding it for purchase when everything around her seemed to tilt on end.

His mouth parted a fraction. He tugged on her upper lip, then her lower one as his position changed. His fingers relaxed and fell away entirely. His lips slanted lightly across hers. He nudged her. Once. Twice. Bria's mouth opened under this gentle persuasion.

Luke held himself still. With the part of his mind that was thinking clearly, he knew he should not press this small gain. Bria was not so much responding to the kiss as she was simply allowing him to do it to her. He drew back, afraid she would feel the imprint of his rather sad smile and know somehow that he ached for her.

When he opened his eyes he saw that she was staring at him. "Do you never close your eyes?" he asked quietly.

"When I sleep."

Luke's grin slowly surfaced and his voice teased her gently. "But not when you kiss."

Bria did not know what to say, and though she would rather have looked away, she found it was not so easily accomplished. Without benefit of his hands, his arms, or his mouth, Luke held her. Bria simply shook her head.

A small crease appeared between Luke's dark brows. His fingers absently threaded through his hair. "Bria?"

Her head tilted slightly in response to his question. Sunlight was stopped by the wide brim of her hat and a shadow slanted across her features.

"You've been kissed before, haven't you?"

"Of course."

Luke did not believe there was any *of course* about it. Nothing about Bria Hamilton was quite as it seemed. "Sometime other than at the greenhouse."

"You are not the only man Orrin has invited to make use of me," she said curtly. "Did you think you were?"

Now it was Luke who was struck mute. The gentle, crooked grin vanished.

Bria felt as if she could breathe again. Her chin came up and there was a quiet defiance in the lift of her head. "What surprises you, Mr. Kincaid? The fact that my stepfather does it or that I admit it? You said it yourself a week ago. It was your parting shot as you left the music room. Had you forgotten?"

"No," Luke said. "I hadn't forgotten."

"Then perhaps you thought I had. Or perhaps you thought good manners would dictate that I never speak of it again." Bria shrugged. "Forgive me, but I am not so interested in your comfort that I will forgo my own."

Luke steadied the horses as they shifted restlessly. He was glad for the momentary distraction. "You must know that I regret having said those words."

"Must I?" she asked. "Weren't they the truth? Didn't my stepfather make such an offer?"

"It doesn't matter."

"You're coming rather late to an apology."

"You've made certain of it by avoiding me."

"Do not lay that at my doorstep," Bria said. "If your conscience had bothered you overmuch you would have found a way to make your regret known."

It did not ease Luke's mind to admit that she was right. The horses shuffled again. He eased off the brake and snapped the reins. The wagon slowly rolled forward. Out of the corner of his eye he had a glimpse of Bria's satisfied smile. She knew she had made her point.

The wagon creaked and rattled over the rutted road. Luke concentrated on avoiding the deepest creases. Ahead of them and off to the right he could see where sheaves of rice had been laid down across the stubble. Ahead of that he could make out the colorful kerchiefs of the women gatherers as they rose from binding one sheaf and bent again to take another.

Luke looked around him. He didn't see Bria's horse tied in any stand of trees. "Where did you leave Apollo?"

"John Whitney took him home."

"You mean he's back at the stable?" asked Luke.

"No," Bria said. "I mean John took Apollo to *his* home. John was too ill to walk. I can get Apollo later, when we've finished with this field."

Luke decided that arguing with her would serve no purpose and keeping her in sight was the best means of assuring she didn't work herself into exhaustion.

At dusk Luke admitted that he was closer to collapse than Bria was. The small of his back ached from bending to pick up the sheaves and toss them into the wagon. The women who worked beside him and around him chattered and sang through their labors. Luke soon lost the enthusiasm to join them.

Bria drove the wagon slowly up and down the rows. Knowing full well the difficulty of the gathering, she offered twice to exchange places with Luke. He refused both times. On each return to the rice mill he made Bria relinquish the reins. When they arrived he would not allow her to carry in the sheaves.

On one trip she went into the house and found him gloves for his blistering hands. On another she served him Elsie's warm cobbler to revive his flagging energy. On the third return she asked Addie to make certain there was a hot bath waiting for Luke when they came back with Apollo.

They had to leave the wagon by the edge of the road and make the last mile to John's house on foot. Bria insisted that she could go alone and Luke ignored her. Shrugging, she set out at a brisk pace. The path was familiar to her and the approaching darkness was no real impediment. Even when the trail narrowed so that she and Luke could no longer walk abreast, Bria's steps did not falter. She slowed imperceptibly, shortening her stride when she heard Luke fall back.

"John Whitney used to work in the main house," she told Luke. "Orrin thought he was uppity so he banished him. For a long time Addie sent me out here with food. I think she was afraid John wouldn't be able to fend for himself." Bria glanced over her shoulder at Luke. She could hear, more than see, his uneven gait. She paused a beat so that he could narrow the gap between them and then went on. "As it turned out, John was quite good at doing for himself. We agreed never to share this with Addie as it gave her pleasure to fuss. And I also liked coming out to see him."

John's house was situated in the middle of several acres of cleared land. It was no bigger than the old overseer's home but it was tended with care. The whitewashed exterior made it less inviting at night than it did during the day. The warmth was bleached out of it and it seemed more an apparition than anything of substance. Dark tendrils of ivy crept along the sides, across the windows, and up the chimney like runnels of blood from an open wound.

Lamplight shone through the unshuttered windows. Except for the flickering light there was no movement inside.

"Does John live alone?" Luke asked.

Bria nodded. Ahead she could see Apollo tethered to a post outside the door. "You should stay here," she said, holding her hand to halt Luke's approach. "It may be malaria. It would be better if you didn't expose yourself to the sickness."

Luke snorted softly. "What about you?"

"I've been around it all my life and haven't contracted it yet. There's no telling what it would do to your Yankee blue blood."

"Aaah. My Yankee blue blood. Of course. I'll wait here." He stood behind her on the small stoop while she knocked and followed her right in when she entered. He merely shrugged when she shot him a sour glance over her shoulder. There might have been a complaint to follow but a moan from the adjoining room distracted her.

John was lying sprawled on his back on the bed. A tangle of sheets gleamed whitely around him and defined the dark contours of his body. He was still save for the slow, rolling movement of his head. It lolled from side to side as if nudged by an invisible hand. When Luke and Bria moved from the doorway and light from the other room filtered in, it was possible to see that John's face and chest were shiny with sweat.

"There's a pump out back, Luke. Get me a pitcher of water." Bria did not give any thought to her order except to expect that it would be followed. She moved toward John's bedside as Luke moved away. When he returned with the pitcher she had straightened the bedclothes and found cloths to wipe down John's skin. "There are medicines at the house," she told Luke. "Addie will know what to give you. Take Apollo and go back for them. You needn't return yourself. Jeb will come out. Or send one of the grooms."

"I'll come," he said firmly. "Will you be all right?"

Bria merely raised one brow and gave him an arch look. She managed to communicate clearly that she was much safer with John than she had ever been with Luke.

"Point taken," Luke said dryly. "I won't be long."

He was not. He returned within the hour with medicines *and* Addie. "Could you have stopped her?" he asked Bria when she looked as if she meant to take him to task.

Since Bria was already having to give ground for Addie at John's bedside, she did not answer his question.

Addie shooed her away as she bent over John. "He's just a shadow of himself," she clucked softly. "Does he eat anything I send to him?"

Luke and Bria exchanged glances. John was ill, certainly, but the only thing shadow-like about him was the dark hue of his skin. He was of a robust build, thick-necked and broad across the shoulders. He looked as if he ate everything Addie sent and more besides.

Addie placed the basket of medicine, broth, and more substantial foodstuffs on the floor beside her. She plucked the cloth lying on John's forehead and dipped in the pitcher. She didn't spare a glance for either Bria or Luke as she wrung it out. "Go on," she told them. "Both of you. I'll take care of him now. Miss Bree, you'll find Martha able to manage well enough. Don' let her upset the way I do things, d'you hear?"

"Everything will be exactly as you want it," Bria said gently. "I'll send someone out to check on you both in the morning."

"That'd be a kindness." Addie wiped John's face and neck. "Go on," she said again. "I expect Mr. Kincaid's bath is getting cold."

Luke gave Bria an inquiring look and chuckled to himself when she resolutely ignored him. He followed her outside. Apollo stood beside the mare that Addie had ridden. He automatically went toward her so Bria could have her own mount.

Bria hesitated as Luke began to release the reins. "I think we should leave Dulcie here for Addie. She may have need to reach us during the night."

"Very well." He refastened the reins and went to Apollo. Before Bria could gainsay him he was in the saddle. "I'm not walking," he told her. "And neither are you." He held out his hand. "Come on. We can both ride."

"That's ridiculous. I'll walk as far as the wagon and drive it back to the main house."

"The wagon is already back there. I had one of the grooms

get it.'' He kept his hand out. His fingers curled lightly. ''Come on.''

Because it seemed as if it were a matter of complete indifference to him, Bria relented. She put her hand in his and was pulled with very little effort into position behind him.

''You have to hold onto me,'' he said. His tone did not betray the smile that had come to his lips. Luke felt Bria adjust her seat slightly and take a tentative hold of his jacket. ''Wouldn't you be more comfortable astride?''

Bria knew she would be more secure but she didn't know about comfortable. ''I will need some help,'' she said at last. Luke's arm was immediately there, reaching behind him to support her while she brought one leg up and across Apollo's back. Her split riding skirt accommodated this change easily. She eased closer to the back of the saddle. ''I'm ready.''

Luke didn't urge Apollo forward. ''You still need to hold on,'' Luke said. When her fingers only curled in the material of his jacket, Luke reached behind him again and grasped her wrists. ''Like this.'' He brought her hands around his waist and held them there momentarily. ''Can you do that?''

Impatient with herself, Bria had an urge to snap at him. She held it back and simply said, ''Yes. I can do that.''

Luke pushed his heels against Apollo and brought the horse around. After they passed the clearing the gelding picked his way through the woods as easily as his mistress had earlier. When they reached the open road again Luke let Apollo find his own comfortable pace.

''Is there really a bath waiting for me?'' Luke asked Bria.

Behind his back she scowled. ''An icy cold one.''

He grinned, imagining the look she was giving him. ''I won't think any less of you for your occasional acts of kindness,'' he said. ''And since it gives you so little pleasure to do these kind turns, I won't think any more of you, either.''

''I wish you would not think of me at all.''

Luke did not answer for a moment, then said, ''I'm afraid that's not possible.''

Bria had been on the point of leaning into Luke's back. Now her arms loosened their grip around his waist and she straightened. "Is it because of what Orrin said?" she asked. Before Luke could answer she went on. "I know you heard him call me a whore. That was to my face. I can imagine the kind of things he's said behind my back."

"Bria." Luke said her name in a tone that was meant to stop her. Instead it was Apollo who came to a halt while Bria went on as if he'd said nothing.

"You've already confirmed that such a conversation took place," she said. "That he offered you use of me is proof enough of that."

"Bria." Luke said her name more firmly this time. "Can you not dismiss it from—"

"Dismiss it from my mind?" she interrupted. "As if it never happened? I'm sure I could." She laughed shortly, without humor. "My mother would very much approve of your suggestion. Did you meet her in Charleston perhaps? She would rather there be no unpleasantness." Again, Bria did not wait for Luke's reply. "It was much the same when Macauley Stuart visited. He was the doctor charged with keeping Claire Bancroft in good health. Rand was forced to accept him on the voyage in order to secure the funds he needed. Claire's godfather insisted. When *Cerberus* docked in Charleston, Rand really had no choice but to allow the doctor to accompany Claire to Concord.

"I did what I could to stay out of Stuart's way and I was successful for a day or so. I know almost exactly when Orrin drew the good doctor into his confidence. Dr. Stuart's manner did not change in the public eye, but privately he did and said things that let me know he had accepted Orrin's opinion of me. He caught me alone in the stand of cottonwoods not far from the gazebo. When I made to leave him he called me a whore and a slut with the same vehemence as my stepfather. I realized then how convincingly Orrin paints the picture."

Bria was not unaware that Luke was sitting almost as rigidly as she was. Even though her embrace had loosened, she could feel the tension in the muscles of his abdomen and back. "What?" she asked, her voice softly challenging him. "Do you deny that it's so? How can you when Orrin made you a similar offer?"

"What happened?" Luke asked instead. "That night. Did Stuart attack you?"

"No. I would not characterize it as an attack. No more than your kisses are an attack." Bria felt Luke's entire body wince at this verbal jab. Beneath them both Apollo stirred restlessly. "I screamed and Rand came to my defense. Stuart didn't bother me after that."

"I can imagine," Luke said dryly.

"Good. Then you know what Rand will do to you."

Luke could almost feel his nose being flattened against his face. "What did you tell Rand about what happened?"

Bria shrugged. "I told him Stuart kissed me."

Luke considered that a moment. "But not that he called you a whore or that your stepfather as good as sent him after you."

"No," Bria admitted. "I didn't tell him that."

"Why not?"

"He would have killed Stuart and then gone after Orrin."

Luke nodded. It explained why Orrin Foster was still alive. Bria had acted to protect her brother, not Foster or the doctor. "And you never mentioned any of this to your mother?"

"No," she said softly.

Luke realized the conversation had come full circle. "Because she would rather there be no unpleasantness," he said.

Upon hearing her own words spoken back to her, Bria felt a certain weariness settle on her shoulders. "I shouldn't have said that. It isn't entirely true."

"Then what *is* true?" asked Luke.

Bria tightened her hold on Luke's middle, then gave Apollo a firm kick herself. "I want to go home," she said. "That's what is true."

* * *

Luke rested in the bath water that had been drawn and heated for him. Contrary to Bria's predictions, the water was still hot enough for him to enjoy a leisurely soak. Every one of his muscles ached. The feeling was not entirely unpleasant. He had never shirked hard work before but the nature of what he had experienced in the rice fields today was beyond anything he had known. It was going to be difficult to present himself at breakfast tomorrow morning without limping as he crossed to the table or groaning as he eased himself into his chair.

His hands rested lightly on the edge of the copper bath. He turned them over lazily and examined his palms. The skin was red and chafed. When he closed them into fists he could feel his fingertips pressing against the tender beginnings of blisters. It would be much worse, he knew, if Bria had not given him gloves.

His stomach growled. Too many hours had passed since Bria had brought him that warm slab of peach cobbler.

Luke let his hands fall. Water lapped at his chest. He sunk lower, closing his eyes.

Bria used the toe of her boot to rap on Luke's door. When there was no response she balanced the tray she was carrying awkwardly in one hand and turned the handle with the other. She nudged the door open and stepped inside. An oil lamp burned on the bedside table. It provided sufficient light for Bria to see that Luke was indeed sleeping.

She had expected to find him in bed, not in his bath. Resolutely averting her eyes, Bria's hands tightened on the tray and she carried it to the foot of the bed. She set it down and backed away.

"You're staring." Luke opened one eye fully and gave her an arch look. The lid of his other eye lifted slowly. He noticed that Bria did not move. She was still dressed in her lightweight jacket and riding skirt. Her blouse was unbuttoned at the throat.

Her only other concession to comfort was to loosen the coil of honeyed hair at the back of her head. The plait was softened by the dark green ribbon woven through it. "You're still staring," he said. "I'm not above telling your brother and having him flatten *your* nose."

She blinked then but when she spoke it was not as if she had heard him. "You were smiling," she said, her tone faintly awed.

"Yes?"

"In your sleep."

At another time he might have laughed outright at her puzzlement. It was the very gravity of her tone that stayed this reaction. "I suppose I might have been."

"You *were*."

"Then I was." Luke thought back to what he remembered. "Aaah," he said softly, the smile returning. "I was thinking about peach cobbler." It was not the entire truth. Bria figured largely in that memory. He hadn't been thinking about eating cobbler. He'd been thinking about her *bringing* it to him.

"Cobbler," she said. "Really?"

The surface of the water rippled as Luke patted his stomach. "Really."

A glimmer of a smile touched Bria's mouth. "Imagine that. I don't think I've ever dreamed about Elsie's cobbler, although I like it well enough." Bria remembered suddenly one of the reasons she had come. She pointed to the tray on the bed. "I brought you dinner."

"Thank you."

Bria's weight shifted. Her lips parted.

Luke watched her. "Was there something else?"

There was but she found she was not yet prepared to act on it. Bria's gaze faltered, slipping away from Luke's face. It moved past his cheek then fell lower until it came to rest on his shoulder. With no indication of what she intended, and no clear idea herself, Bria approached Luke's bath.

"Bria?" Luke did not think she even heard him. He drew

his knees toward his chest as he sat up straighter. "Wish me pleasant dreams and go," he told her. The water was growing cold but not nearly fast enough to suit Luke.

Bria sank to her knees beside the tub. "Where is your sponge?" she asked quietly. "Never mind. I see it." She picked it up off the nearby stool. "And the soap?"

Luke felt the bar under his right foot. He was not entirely sure that she wouldn't search for it. His hand plunged under the water. He found it and handed it to her.

Dipping the sponge, Bria sidled on her knees toward the back of the tub. "Lean forward." She prodded Luke gently with the wet sponge when he was slow to obey. Water ran in cool rivulets down his back. "That's better. You cannot reach here."

Luke didn't argue with her but it was only because he couldn't formulate a coherent thought. Every muscle in his back tightened when she applied the lathered sponge to it. He was not so dumbstruck that he couldn't manage a strangled sound at the back of his throat.

Bria soaped Luke's shoulders and applied the sponge from side to side. When his head drooped forward slightly she ran it along the length of his exposed nape, then lower, along his spine, until her hand would have had to dip under the water. His skin was taut beneath her touch. She felt the ripple of smooth muscle across his back.

Luke lifted his head slowly and flexed his shoulders, working the soreness out in small waves. His eyes caught his reflection in the cheval glass across the room. His glance lifted to Bria's face just past his own shoulder. He smiled to himself. Her eyes were squeezed almost as tightly as the fist she had around the sponge. Far from being at her ease, he doubted she was enjoying any part of what she was doing to him. *So why the hell was she doing it?*

"I'll take it now," he said, reaching behind him for the sponge. His hand brushed her fingertips and her movements ceased immediately. "You've done enough." More than enough, he thought. If he was going to sleep at all tonight he would have to relieve himself in the sheets.

Bria came jerkily to her feet. She wiped her damp hands on her riding skirt. The water and dust left a trail of muddy fingerprints. "I'm not a whore," she said suddenly.

Luke was still reeling from this announcement when she fled the room.

They did not work together the following day or the day after that. Luke knew it was by Bria's intention. He was beginning to understand that any confrontation with him would make her disappear for days. It was not that she went anywhere, just that she became unapproachable or unavailable. She never left Concord but it was as if she had vanished.

John's condition did not worsen. When Luke visited he saw that Addie was encouraged but afraid to make too much of it.

"You're comin' on the heels of Miss Bree," Addie told him as she emptied the basket he brought. "Can't be that she sent you out here, not with her comin' out herself."

"No," said Luke. "I wanted to see John's progress."

Addie's dark eyes crinkled at the corners as she chuckled. "Drivin' that wagon is powerful hard work."

Luke shrugged, then he ruined the effect by wincing at the effort it took to appear careless. All along his back and shoulders he could still feel the strain in his muscles. "Powerful hard," he was forced to agree. "But I didn't really come about that."

Addie paused in her work and looked up. Her expression was curious yet somehow knowing and when she spoke her tone had the quality of both a statement and a question. "You and Miss Bree been fighting again."

Luke answered honestly. "I don't know."

Addie chuckled again. "Could be Miss Bree's argument is with herself."

"Does she do that often?"

Shrugging, Addie went back to unpacking the basket. "No

more or less than any of us do, I expect. Best you stay out of the way.''

"She makes that easy enough." Luke pulled a chair away from the table, spun it around, and sat down so that he straddled it. He rested his forearms across the top rung of the ladderback. "Was she really just here?"

Addie nodded. "You should have passed her in the woods."

"I didn't. She must have seen me first."

That information made Addie pause again. She opened her mouth to speak, then thought better of it. She bent her head to her task and busied her fingers instead.

"Addie," Luke said quietly. "I really came to see you. Tell me why Bree does this."

"Ain't for me to say."

"Then who will?"

"Nobody, I reckon."

Impatience and frustration got the better of him and Luke's sigh was audible. He tried a different tack. "Does she hide from people besides me?"

"You tell me," Addie said. "You ever know her to leave Concord?"

"Not since I've been here."

Addie turned her hands palm side out. "That surely must say something to you."

"Do you mean that she *never* leaves this plantation?"

"Not since she's had a choice in the matter." Addie ducked her head again and she pressed her full lips together as if she'd already said too much.

"Who is she avoiding in Charleston?"

Addie turned away from the table and went to the wood stove where she was heating chicken broth. She lifted the lid on the pot, sniffed, and stirred.

"Addie," Luke said.

She was not proof against the pleading she heard in his tone. Her skirts swayed as she swung around to face him, hands on hips. "Now you listen to me, Mr. Kincaid. I like you just fine and from what I can tell so do most of the folk who work here, but that don' mean I'm about to tell you what Miss Bree can say for herself. Ain't no one here goin' to do it, so save your breath. If it's things you want to know, then ask her.'' Addie held up one hand to stave off his next question. ''Forget whatever Mr. Foster's already told you about her. I could get in a lot of trouble for saying so, but I don't recollect ever hearin' one true thing come out of that man's mouth. The last man that listened to him had a passel of bruises to reckon with.''

''You're referring to Dr. Stuart,'' said Luke.

All of Addie's surprise registered on her face. ''Who told you that name?''

''Bria did.''

Addie considered this for several long moments. She said softly, thoughtfully, ''Then could be she's fixin' to tell you what you're never going to hear from these lips.'' She stopped avoiding Luke's gaze and held it instead. ''If she does, you go gentle with her.''

Luke saw Addie's mouth clamp tightly again. He stood up slowly, wondering if he could possibly get a few more words from her. ''One more thing, Addie,'' he said, picking up the empty basket. ''About the piano.'' He didn't go on because Addie was already shaking her head.

''You shouldn't play it,'' she said quickly. ''Miss Bree won't like it.''

Luke realized then that no one sleeping in the house that night overheard him at the piano. It followed that they knew nothing of Bria's odd behavior afterwards. ''Yes,'' he said. ''But why?''

Addie's features relaxed. The furrow in her brow disappeared and her expression became almost wistful. ''Bria and her daddy used to play all the time. I don't expect there's any harm in you knowin' that. She loved her daddy. They'd play for hours after dinner. Seemed like music filled the house in those days. With Miss Bree up to every trick with those rapscallion brothers of hers, it was music that brought her inside.'' Addie shook her head and her pensive air faded. Behind her she could hear the broth simmering. She turned and took the pot off the stove. "There's no joy for her in it any longer. That's why you shouldn't play."

"I'll remember that," Luke said. "Thank you, Addie."

She shrugged and kept her face averted. It was not until she heard the door close that she pressed one corner of her apron to her damp eyes.

"Would you like to play a few hands of poker?"

Luke looked up from the book he was reading. He simply stared at Bria. She was holding a deck of cards, shuffling them idly as she stood in the doorway of the study.

"You needn't look so astonished," she said. "I *do* play, you know."

"What astonishes me is that you're speaking again."

Bria's head tilted to one side and her brow puckered. "What an odd thing to say," she said. "I was not aware I had stopped."

"You stopped speaking to *me*."

"I haven't seen you."

"And why is that?"

"I thought it was because you were busy. Do you mean to say you've been intentionally avoiding me?"

Luke set his book aside and came to his feet. "I can see that I'm hopelessly outmatched by your superior intellect and reasoning."

"Nicely conceded," Bria said. She stopped shuffling and held up the cards again. Her smile was gently mocking. "You told me you were a gambler. Shall we?"

"What stakes did you have in mind?"

"Pennies."

"That doesn't make for a very interesting game."

"I can't afford to lose anything else."

"But you're risking your chance of winning as well." Luke held out a chair for her at the card table. Although the dark wood had been faithfully polished, the surface was scarred by hot cigar ash and marred by the damp rings from Orrin's bourbon glasses. "Have you considered that?" he asked, taking his own seat across from her.

"Mr. Kincaid," she said pointedly. "If I win, then you're no player at all."

"You think I'm that good?"

"I have no idea. I only know how bad I am." She dealt them each five cards. "Nothing wild," she said. "Jacks or better to open. The chips are in that drawer behind you."

Luke swiveled in his chair and found them in the middle drawer of the stand at his back. He distributed five dollars worth to each of them. He tossed one chip into the middle of the table and waited for Bria to do the same. "You have to put something in the pot to begin," he reminded her after a moment.

"What?" She looked up from studying her cards. "Oh. Yes. Of course." She used her forefinger to push one chip toward his.

"You have to let go of it," he chided her.

"Hmmm." Bria took her hand away slowly.

Luke grinned to himself. He understood why Bria only wanted to play for pennies. She would never have been able to part with higher stakes. Luke tossed in another chip. "Two cards, please."

Bria gave him two and took three for herself.

"That will cost you a chip," Luke told her. He watched her reluctantly part with another one and resigned himself to a very long game.

He won the first six hands. Luke pointed to her dwindling pile of chips. "Are you certain you want to continue?" he asked. "I shouldn't like to break you."

Bria merely passed him the deck. "Deal."

Luke leaned back in his chair, stretching his legs under the table, and shuffled. "Who taught you to play poker?" he asked.

"My brothers."

He chuckled, shaking his head. "Are you certain they taught you correctly? I mean, did you *ever* win a hand playing with them?"

Bria's entire body snapped to attention as if Luke had shaken her. "They wouldn't have . . ." Her voice trailed off as she gave his question full consideration.

"Bree," Luke said gently. "They tied you up to play Captured Indian Princess."

She nodded slowly, her brilliant sapphire eyes widening. "They did, didn't they?" Bria had to laugh at her own naivete. "All these years, I never suspected. I just thought I had no talent or luck for the game. Rand will have to answer for this."

"The best way to make him pay is to learn the game yourself." He watched her absorb this information. Her features became thoughtful. "I'll teach you if you like."

Bria nodded with a certain finality. "I do like," she said. "In fact, it's indecent how much pleasure I shall take in beating Rand."

"Good." He was strangely relieved to find she could take pleasure in something. "We'll play a few open hands to begin with."

Luke proved himself to be a patient teacher. Bria's brothers had not neglected to give her rules of the game but they had misled her about the chances of winning any particular hand. She was more likely to try to draw for straights and flushes than she was to stand pat with three of a kind or even two pair. She gave up what might have been winning hands to take chances on less likely combinations of cards.

They had taught her nothing about bluffing. As Luke suspected, once she understood the role it played in the game it came as naturally to her as breathing.

"What word do you hear about John?" he asked.

Bria kept her eyes on her cards. "Do you mean to distract me?"

"Actually, yes. If I can. It would be better if you could learn to make conversation as part of the game. It will certainly impress your brother.''

She glanced at him suspiciously. ''Really?''

Luke nodded.

''Oh, very well. I spoke to Jebediah when he returned from taking dinner out to Addie. One card, please.'' Bria plucked one card from her hand and put it aside. She replaced it with the one Luke slid in her direction. Without rearranging her cards, she looked up at him. Her features gave nothing away. ''He says that John's fever broke late this afternoon. He's been sleeping comfortably since then.'' She frowned a little. ''You mustn't think you have to keep working in his place until John returns.''

''I don't think that,'' Luke said. ''I'm still doing it because I want to.''

She nodded faintly and glanced at her cards again. ''Have I said that I've appreciated your help?''

''Not in so many words. But then I don't think you offer to scrub the back of every one of the men who work for you.'' Luke watched some of the color leave Bria's face. ''Did you think I would never mention it?'' he asked.

''I hoped that you would dismiss it.''

He remembered saying much the same thing to her. ''I should never have suggested you do that.'' He would not let her use his own words against him. ''It was wrong. *I* was wrong.''

Bria matched Luke's last raise, dropping a short stack of five chips into the kitty. ''You find it easy, don't you? To admit that you're wrong.''

''Not especially easy,'' he corrected her. ''But important and necessary.'' He paused a beat, a self-mocking smile tugging at the corners of his mouth. ''On those few occasions when it's true.''

Bria gave him a small nod, acknowledging that he was not admitting to many mistakes. ''Your grandmother's teaching?''

''God, no.'' Luke was surprised at his own vehemence. ''Nana Dearborn was *never* wrong.''

"I see."

"My mother taught me there was more trespass in not owning an error in judgment than there was in misjudging in the first place."

"I like that."

"I think you'd like her." He pointed to her hand. "Show me your cards."

"I paid to see yours first."

Luke spread out his hand. "Three ladies."

Bria laid down three of her cards. "I have jacks," she said.

"Sorry." Luke reached for the pile of chips in the middle of the table and started sweeping them to his side.

"Not so quickly," she told him. "I also have this pair of threes. That's a full house, I believe."

Luke pushed the chips in her direction and watched Bria gather them up. Her gleeful smile was positively wicked. "I feel a little sorry for Rand," he said.

"You should feel sorry for yourself. He won't blame me. He'll blame you for teaching me."

If anything, her smile became more wicked. She was enjoying herself, Luke realized. He won the next hand, then one went to her. He won four more before they agreed it was enough. "I can give you an opportunity to win your money back tomorrow evening," he said.

Bria stood and went to the desk. "I think I should point out that you haven't seen my money yet. Thus far I've only lost chips." She opened the middle drawer and withdrew a small leather pouch. When she looked up it was to find Lucas watching intently. "Did you think I meant to renege on my debts?"

"I had more concerns about the letter opener you keep there."

His tone was so arid that Bria could not tell if he was entirely joking. "I wouldn't do that," she said finally.

Luke grinned crookedly, then laughed and ducked as she threw the pouch at him. It sailed harmlessly over his head.

"A smarter man would have caught it, Mr. Kincaid." Bria

managed to reach it before Luke. She half-turned and held it out of his reach while she withdrew the right amount of currency and coin. "There," she said, placing it on the table before him. "All debts paid in full."

Luke was tempted to take her by the wrist and pull her onto his lap. She would have fit snugly there, all rounded bottom and nicely curved thighs. Other women he had known would have not only welcomed it, they would have expected it. Only a fool would have thought the same of Bria Hamilton. He let his fingers curl around the money instead. He slipped it into his pocket.

Bria sat down again, this time in the chair beside him. "Do you think my stepfather is a good poker player?" she asked.

Luke was not distracted by her air of casual interest. "He's better than you."

"That is hardly any gauge of his skill."

"True." He arched one brow as he studied her reaction. "There's no need to look affronted. I was agreeing with you. Very well, since you are serious about this, then I would say he's better than a fair to middlin' player. I have not had much opportunity to test his skill. There were the few hands we played here at Concord and perhaps a dozen others in Charleston. I did not have the means to sit at the same table with Orrin and his friends. I was only engaged when he was bored."

"Did you observe him playing with his friends?"

"Only once. I brought a purchase order around for him to sign and I was invited into the room where he was playing. There was a lot of money on that table and before I left it went into the pile in front of your stepfather."

"Did he cheat?"

"Not that I could see."

"Was he drunk?"

"He was drinking. I couldn't say if he was drunk. Orrin's tolerance for liquor is frankly astonishing."

"Could you win against him?"

Luke's eyes narrowed. Although Bria had not moved and her eyes remained shuttered, in Luke's mind she had suddenly leaned forward and the sapphire eyes sparkled with icy brilliance. He answered carefully, aware of the potential for a trap. "Perhaps," he said.

"Perhaps?" Bria frowned. "That means nothing."

"It's honest. If you're looking for some assurance that I can win any one hand against your stepfather, then the answer can only be 'perhaps.' Can I win *every* hand against him? No. Can I win the majority in any given match? Yes. But can I guarantee that I will win a single hand? No."

"I thought you said you were good."

"I did. And I am. But I also know that sometimes skill is no match for Dame Fortune. If she is consistently sitting at Orrin's side I would be hard-pressed to emerge from the table still wearing my shirt. Do you understand what I'm saying? It would not be called gambling if the outcome were known." He studied Bria's perfect oval face. The only sign that she was experiencing any distress was the uneven line of her lower lip. She had drawn it into her mouth and was worrying it gently between her teeth.

"Suppose you tell me the purpose of these questions," Luke prompted. "You have something in mind, I take it."

Bria released her lower lip. "I do. I don't think I'm prepared to share it." She stood. "Would you like a drink, Mr. Kincaid?"

"Yes. And I thought we agreed you would call me Luke."

"I believe you're right." Bria went to the walnut cabinet where Orrin kept his liquor. She opened it and ran her index finger across the selections. "Is bourbon to your liking?"

"Bourbon's fine."

She nodded and pulled the decanter out. "What I don't recall is that I agreed to permit you to call me Bria. Most especially not Bree."

"I believe you're right, Bree."

For once Bria was not entirely successful in schooling her

features. The remnant of her smile was still visible to Luke as she turned with the decanter of bourbon and two glasses. "You must have been the bane of your grandmother's existence," she said lightly.

"I was."

Bria blinked. Humor had been noticeably absent from Luke's tone. "I'm sorry. I didn't mean—"

He waved her apology aside. "It's all right. It's true enough."

Bria poured three fingers of bourbon for him and two for herself. "Why did you live with her?"

"My mother sent me to her. Nana Dearborn convinced her it was better for me."

"Did you want to go?"

"Not remotely." He picked up his glass and took a sip. The bourbon went down smoothly and kicked up just the right amount of heat in its wake. "My mother couldn't be talked out of it. When I saw that none of my aunts could sway her, I knew she wouldn't listen to me. So I went. It was hardly the horror I imagined it would be. I learned how to step lightly around Nana Dearborn. I stayed for eight years, until I was sixteen. When I went back to my mother she let me stay until I went to college." Luke anticipated her question. "Yes, I wanted to go this time. Mother had been saving for my education for years."

"How?" Bria asked. She sat down again and raised her glass. She studied him over the rim for a moment. "Forgive me—it's really none of my business, is it?"

"I don't know," Luke said frankly. "I'm not quite certain what your business is. I suppose as a guest in your home you have some right to know the particulars of my life."

Bria knew that wasn't true. Her mother would be appalled by her manners. Luke was simply being gracious, though why he should extend himself to her was outside Bria's understanding. "It's just that I remember you said to Orrin that your father was gone. Did your mother remarry?"

"No. She runs a boarding house in the city. My aunts live with her."

"It must be a large house to accommodate all six of your aunts and guests besides."

"Large enough."

Bria sighed. She sipped her drink. "Do you know, I think I pity your grandmother. Seven daughters and not one of them wanting to live with her."

Luke eyed Bria's glass. She hadn't drunk enough to feel the effects of the alcohol. Luke decided not to correct her thinking or tell her not to squander her few emotions on Nana Dearborn. He set his drink down and picked up the cards. He shuffled them a few times and dealt out five apiece.

"What's this?" she asked. "I thought we were done."

"With money stakes," he said. "I have something else in mind."

Bria did not pick up her cards. "I'm afraid I won't play without knowing what I'm risking."

"If I win you have to tell me why you really came into my room a few nights ago. If you win you may have the answer to any question you want to ask me." He expected her to take time to consider the consequences fully. What she did was finish her drink in a single swallow, set the glass down, and pick up the cards. She fanned them out and held them up so that only her unfathomable eyes were visible as she gave her reply.

"I accept the wager," she said.

Luke could not tell if she was smiling. When she lowered her cards she certainly wasn't.

"Two cards," she said.

He dealt them to her and took none for himself.

"You must be certain of your hand," Bria said.

"I am." He laid down a full house, tens over fours.

"Very good." She turned her fanned cards over so that Luke could see they were all clubs. "But this is better." Bria picked up the decanter and poured herself two fingers of bourbon this time.

"Dutch courage?" Luke chided her. "You won the wager."

Bria ignored him and took a large swallow. She felt the unnatural heat flush her cheeks almost immediately. "Didn't you say that when you know the outcome it isn't really gambling?"

"You knew that you were going to win?"

"No, I knew that you were. The reason I came into your room the other night was to pose the same question I'm going to ask you now."

Luke was intrigued. He prompted her quietly, "And?"

"And ..." Bria finished her drink. Her fingertips were pressed whitely against the empty glass. "And I was wondering if you would agree to marry me."

Chapter Seven

Bria rolled the empty tumbler between her damp palms. "I'm willing to pay you for your trouble. I would be hiring you, really. You came to Concord looking for work. This is the job I am offering."

"Marriage," Luke said flatly. "Marriage to you."

"Well, yes. It's no help if you marry someone else." Bria was struck by a thought that had simply not occurred to her before. "*Is* there someone else?" she asked. "You told me once you weren't married, but I never thought to inquire if there was a fiancée or a sweetheart."

She had offered him a simple enough escape route. Even pointed the way. He only had to lie. "No," he said. "There's no one." Luke eyed the tumbler between her palms, then his gaze moved pointedly to the crystal decanter.

Bria watched the shift in his grey eyes. "I'm not drunk," she said. "I've been considering this for some time so you mustn't think it's the bourbon. True, I needed reinforcement to pose the question, but that's all. My brain is not addled."

"You'll understand if I reserve judgment."

"As you like." Bria set down her tumbler and folded her

hands in her lap to keep them still. "Is it especially warm in here? Shall I open a window?"

"That would be the bourbon," Luke said dryly.

"Oh." Her smile was a trifle wan. "I don't have much experience with liquor. For myself, I mean. I know what it does to Orrin." She picked up her winning cards, spread them into a fan, and waved them in front of her face. "Am I every bit as flushed as I think I am?"

"Every bit."

"This is not going well, is it? You haven't answered my proposal."

Luke stood. "I think we should go to the verandah. Fresh air is in order." He stepped behind Bria's chair and steadied it while she came to her feet. Then he offered his arm to steady her. When she accepted it without hesitation, Luke suspected she was feeling the full effect of her reckless drinking.

Luke escorted Bria to one of the wide wicker chairs before he retracted his arm. She had an air of grave dignity about her as she lowered herself into the chair.

"Why are you smiling?" Bria asked. "It's no good pretending you weren't. My eyes are not so far crossed that I can't see what I see."

Luke didn't try to deny his amusement at all. His grin actually deepened so that creases appeared at the corners of his eyes. "I'm certain that made sense to you."

"Of course it did," she said tartly. "I wouldn't have said it otherwise."

He nodded. "I was smiling because you take to that chair like a sultana to her throne and if your tone becomes any more imperious with me, I'm afraid I shall start bowing and scraping at your dainty feet."

Bria considered that. "I don't think you should notice that the sultana has dainty feet," she said. "Or perhaps it's just that you shouldn't mention it. I am not clear on all the particulars. Should I permit you to sit now?"

"That would be welcomed."

With regal economy of motion, Bria used her chin to indicate the chair at her side. She nodded approvingly when Luke took it. "I should be the sultana," she said.

"I've always thought so." He stretched casually in his chair. His elbows rested lightly on the wide arms and his fingers were clasped over his abdomen. He tapped his thumbs together as he stared out over the gardens. Fireflies flittered over and through the hedgerows, winking in and out like distant stars.

"You haven't forgotten our wager, have you?" asked Bria. She had abandoned her regal posture and imperious tone. Her voice had the earnestness of a young girl.

"I haven't forgotten." He'd hoped she had. "Do I have to answer it tonight?"

"Don't you expect debts to be paid immediately?"

"Sometimes I accept a marker. When I know the person is as good as his word." Luke's attention swiveled from the gardens to Bria. "Will you permit me to think about it tonight?"

She nodded. He could have said no outright, she reasoned. The fact that he was willing to consider it at all gave her hope. "You haven't asked how much I'd pay you. I have some money set aside but you may find it a paltry sum for what I'm asking of you."

"I'm not interested in your money, Bria."

"Oh, but you must be. I want you to consider this a job."

"I'm sure you do. Then you would be justified ordering me around like any of your other hired hands."

"Well, yes," she said slowly. "I confess I find your objection bewildering, Mr. Kincaid . . . *Luke* . . . I mean. You don't expect a *marriage*, do you? That's not what I was proposing."

It occurred to Luke that he should have carried the bourbon with him. A stiff drink was certainly in order. "I thought you asked me if I would agree to marry you?"

Bree was instantly relieved. "Yes, you remember it exactly. For a moment I wondered if you'd heard something else. We can be husband and wife without having a marriage. People do it all the time."

"I don't think their approach is quite so cold-blooded. They arrive at the altar with some expectation that there will be a union of hearts and minds."

Bree's deep blue eyes lost their soft focus as she studied Luke. "I think you must be a romantic," she said finally.

"I suppose so."

"I'm not."

"I've reached the same conclusion."

"Then you understand what I want," Bria said.

"Not remotely."

She sighed. "Are you being difficult or is it the drink that makes it seem so?"

"A little of both. Tell me again what you want."

"Marry me," she said. "It will be of a temporary nature. We will draw up a private contract to that effect. You may divorce me. I'll give you that satisfaction. You may choose the grounds. I have no care for my reputation and people will believe whatever you say."

"Why would they do that?" he asked. "I'm a stranger to this area."

"Exactly. People know me. Or at least they think they do. I endeavor not to disappoint them." She waved one hand in a small dismissive gesture. "No matter. I will divorce if you haven't the taste for it."

"If it's to end in divorce, then why marry at all?"

"Because as my husband you can secure Concord."

Luke's eyes narrowed. "And how would I do that?"

"You would win it away from Orrin at the card table."

The fact that she was absolutely serious didn't stop Luke from laughing with real humor.

Bria was undaunted by this reaction. "I mean it," she said, preparing to convince him. "You could do it. It's only a matter of manipulating him into the wager."

"There's not that much bourbon in the Carolinas. He won't do it."

"He will. I can make it happen."

Luke conceded the point to move the argument along. "Very well. Then how do you propose that I win? We had this conversation earlier. There can be no assurances, Bree. You won a hand from me yourself."

"I don't mind if you cheat Orrin."

"Thank you for your permission, but I thought you Southerners prided yourself on a code of honor."

"That was the Old South."

Luke found himself chuckling again. "Indeed," he said softly. "And after I win Concord? What happens then?"

"You make a wildly romantic gesture and sign the deed over to me."

Closing his eyes, Luke let his head fall back against the chair. "Yes," he said. "I can picture it. The deed is lying on the table beside my winning hand. The ink on our signatures is not yet quite dry. Overcome by my wildly romantic gesture, you're throwing your arms around me and kissing me full on the mouth." He raised the lid of one eye to observe Bria's reaction. The smile on her lips was frankly skeptical. "It's a very nice kiss," he went on. "You've learned a great deal in the fifteen years we've been married."

Luke watched Bria snap at his bait. Her slender frame stiffened to such a degree that the chair was no longer really supporting her. He relented slightly. "Twelve years, then."

"There is not enough bourbon in the Carolinas," she quoted him. "I was thinking it could be managed within a year."

Luke whistled softly. "Why not just wait and see if your brother returns with the treasure?"

"I have waited. I've waited years now. It's time I did something myself."

"You believe he'll find it, don't you?"

"Yes. Someday. I don't want to be dependent on him."

"You'd rather be dependent on me?"

"I won't be," she said. "It will be a job for you."

"Save your money for the stake you're going to need to pull Orrin into the game."

"I have money for that."

"So you've been planning this for some time."

Bria shook her head. "No. The money was saved from last season's profits. It was marked for improvements with the mill and barn. There are floodgates that need to be repaired. Orrin doesn't know I have the money. He would want to make all the decisions if I told him about it."

"So you'll use his money against him."

"It's *my* money. The profits are the result of my oversight. Orrin doesn't pay me a wage for my work and I've never asked him for one." Bria placed one hand to her temple and rubbed it. She could feel the beginnings of a headache. "If you wish to think I'm stealing from him, then you may do so. I find I can live with these moral lapses."

Luke shrugged. "I was not passing judgment." He watched her massage her temple for a few moments. "Come here."

Her fingers stilled. "Pardon?"

"Come here. Bring the cushion and sit here." He sat up straight and pointed between his splayed legs. "I'll take away your headache. It seems only fair since I probably gave it to you in the first place."

"No," she said honestly. "I think it was the bourbon."

Luke smiled and tapped the front of his chair. "Here. I promise you won't regret it."

Bria regretted it as soon as she stood. Her legs were no longer steady under her. With exaggerated care she crossed the short distance to Luke. He took the cushion from her hand and dropped it in front of his chair. Bria turned and her legs folded with surprising ease. Her skirt billowed around her.

"Lean back," Luke said.

She did as she was told.

"Close your eyes."

"They already are."

Luke bent forward and saw for himself that it was true. It was definitely the bourbon that made her this pliable. "I'm going to put my hands on your shoulders."

"All right." She braced herself for his touch. "In some small way this must be what it was like for Claire."

"Claire?" Luke rested his palms lightly on her shoulders. His thumbs made two circular paths at the base of her neck.

"Rand's passenger," she said. "Claire Bancroft. I've mentioned her before."

It was in connection with something she'd said about Dr. Macauley Stuart that Rand finally remembered. "You spoke of her health. Does she often have headaches?"

"I don't know about that. Perhaps. I thought of her because I had my eyes closed and you told me what you were going to do. Rand had to do that all the time for Claire. He was quite good at it, actually. Even Cutch was not so reliable as Rand. It certainly never became second nature to Dr. Stuart."

"Claire is blind?"

Bria nodded. "Didn't I say that? No, I suppose I didn't. It's really not the first thing one thinks of when Claire comes to mind. If Rand is at least half as smart as I think he is, he'll marry her. I'm sure he's in love with her."

"Imagine that," Luke said softly. His thumbs moved higher on Bria's nape. In response to the pressure, her head lolled forward a few degrees. He felt her taut muscles ease for the first time.

"Imagine what?"

"That you would acknowledge some link between love, marriage, and intelligence."

"Do not make too much of it. I was speaking of Rand. It would be right for him."

"He's wildly romantic, then."

Bria laughed softly. Luke's fingers felt surprisingly good against her scalp. "Can you doubt it? He's in the South Seas solving a riddle and hunting a treasure. Naturally he's convinced himself that it is an eminently practical pursuit—he has his research to assist him in that view—but I would say that my brother is most assuredly a romantic."

Luke's fingers stilled. "It's the quest," he told her. "All true romantics have a quest."

Bria felt him begin to knead her scalp again. The pins that anchored her coil of hair were being plucked one by one. She leaned forward, out of his reach, and twisted so she could see him. There was a small vertical crease between her brows. "You sounded as if you might know something about it."

Luke placed his palms on either side of her head and turned her back around. His fingers delved into her hair again. "I read *Don Quixote*."

Bria believed him, but she wasn't sure that was where the answer to her question lay.

"Have you considered at all that you don't know very much about me?" Luke asked.

It was a little startling to realize their thoughts were traveling similar paths. "I'm gambling," Bria said. "I know that. It's what my mother did when she married Orrin."

Luke did not ask if Elizabeth Hamilton had won or lost. Assessing that was not so easy with the kind of gambling she had done. She'd gained the right to stay at Henley but could all these years with Foster be considered a victory? "I've seen the photographs of your mother in the drawing room," Luke said. His fingers continued to sift idly through her hair. "And there's her portrait in the music room. She's a lovely woman. She could have chosen anyone, I imagine, yet she chose Foster."

"She's beautiful," Bria said. "And there were fewer choices than you think. In any event, you're right: she chose Orrin. Who can say that some other choice might have been better? It certainly could have been worse. She made the best decision she could with the information she had."

"As you think you're doing."

Bria nodded heavily. "Yes. Just as I'm doing." Her head drooped forward and remained there. When Luke's hands came to rest on her shoulders again she didn't tense.

Luke realized he couldn't change her mind. He changed the

subject instead. "I couldn't help but notice that among all the photographs in the drawing room, there are none of your stepfather."

"His choice. He would not sit for a wedding photograph with my mother."

"There's no portrait, either."

"From time to time he talks about getting one done but he never hires an artist. It should have been painted long ago. He was never so handsome as my father but he used to be tolerable to the eyes."

Luke's chuckle rumbled deep in his chest. "Don't mince your words."

Bria's smile was relaxed and a trifle sleepy. "I think my headache's gone."

"If you only think it, then you're not ready to get up."

She would never be ready to get up. She'd lost all feeling in her legs. Even the nerve endings across her back were dulled. Luke had done that to her. Because no protest came immediately to mind, Bria let him continue.

She woke as he was carrying her up the stairs. Through heavy lashes raised only a fraction, she stared at the clean sweep of his jaw and the set of his mouth. "You've done this before," she murmured.

"Just once."

"Mmmm." Bria closed her eyes and her head fell back into the curve of his shoulder. She did not stir again until morning.

"Why didn't you wake me?" Bria threw back the covers on her bed and scrambled out.

"I'm waking you now," Martha said practically. "Mr. Luke said if I didn't see you before ten I should come for you."

Bria glanced at the clock over the mantel. With a disheartened little cry she confirmed the time. "You know I rise hours before this."

Martha nodded. There were many days when Bria was the first one up. "He said you were feeling a bit under the weather."

Under the influence, Bria translated to herself.

"Pardon, Miss Bree?"

"Nothing." She hadn't been aware of speaking aloud. Bria looked longingly at the screened area of her bedroom. There was a bath waiting for her and no time to take it. "Put my riding things out on the bed, Martha. I'll wash at the basin."

Bria dismissed Jeb's daughter as soon as her clothes were laid out. She knew she was going to wash and dress with unseemly haste and wanted no one to answer to. Downstairs she waved off a reminder that breakfast was waiting for her in the dining room. She paused long enough to inquire about John's health when she glimpsed Addie walking toward the kitchen.

"I'm just on my way to prepare some real food for that man," she announced. "He's going to be fiddle fit before a week's gone. If you're looking for Mr. Luke, it's him that's spelling me."

Bria's shoulders sank a little with this information. She couldn't very well ride out to John's house and demand her answer.

"Everything all right, Miss Bree?" Addie asked. "Mr. Luke said you might be feelin' a trifle off this morning."

Off color, she translated again. Or just plain awful.

"Pardon?"

"Nothing, Addie. I'm not looking for Mr. Kincaid at all." Bria slipped away before Addie could make a better assessment and decide she was lying.

Apollo was happy to oblige his mistress by taking to the road at a full gallop. A transparent cloud of dust marked their passage. Bria reached the far fields where the rice was still being cut and gathered before she slowed Apollo to a walk. She monitored the progress of the workers and determined that it would be another two days before all the rice was harvested. She examined samples of the uncut plants and saw that they were not yet overripe. Afterward she made a tour of the gates and canals and looked for wear that would signal repairs needed to be made sooner rather than later.

She wended her way through her orchards and cotton fields, then along the river bank before she returned to the house. She never once caught sight of Luke though she had seen Addie on her way back to John's.

Bria parted the doors to the study with more force than was strictly necessary. She stepped inside and concentrated on removing her riding gloves. Agitation made her clumsy and she almost stamped her foot in frustration. *He's avoiding me.*

"Pardon?"

Bria's head snapped up. Luke was standing behind the desk. He was leaning forward, his arms braced. His drawings were rolled out across the top. He had been studying them until she interrupted. "You've been avoiding me."

"Was I? I've been right here."

"You were at John Whitney's this morning."

"That was very late this morning," he said. "I waited at breakfast for you. When you didn't come down I realized you—"

"You told Martha to let me sleep."

"Are you accusing me of something? Perhaps you'd better come in." He politely motioned her forward.

Bria finished removing her gloves and tossed them on a table. She closed the doors, took a deep breath, then let it out slowly. She forced herself not to react to the smile hovering about Luke's mouth. "I wish you had not interfered," she said quietly. "Martha would have come for me otherwise."

"Then I apologize." He saw that Bria was looking at him expectantly. "Should I say something more? Was I not contrite enough?"

A muscle worked along Bria's jaw. She saw Luke's attention drop to it and stopped grinding her teeth. After years of feeling so little, sometimes nothing at all, being around Lucas Kincaid was like falling into a garden of nettles. She was constantly being stung in small ways. It was difficult to ignore her own vulnerability. "You were infinitely contrite," she said.

"And infinitely obtuse. I'm afraid I don't know what else you're expecting."

"Do you mean to tell me you've forgotten our wager?"

Luke sat down and regarded Bria consideringly. "No, not at all. But I wasn't certain about you. I had to hear you say it. In fact, I'd like to hear a bit more."

"What? You want me to repeat it?"

"Yes. Without the bourbon this time." He made a steeple with his hands and rested his chin on the point of it. "I have to be certain this is what you want, Bree."

"If it pleases you," she said after a moment. She crossed the floor and came to stand on the opposite side of the desk. Her arms hung at her sides, her palms turned slightly outward. "I asked if you would agree to marry me."

This time Luke saw no expectancy in her expression. The remoteness had returned to her deep sapphire eyes. "Then my answer is yes," Luke said. "Yes, I'll marry you."

Bria's head dipped once in slow assent.

"Perhaps you should sit down."

"I'm fine." Her hands found the arms of the chair behind her and she sat down anyway. "You understand it will be legal, don't you?"

"I gathered that. Legal but not real."

"Yes. Exactly. Legal but not real."

Luke noticed she seemed pleased that he'd made the distinction. She would be less pleased if she realized he didn't fully understand it. "Are you breathing?" he asked.

Bria's brows went up as she sucked in a little air through her nose. "Yes."

"You have to let it out again."

"Yes. Yes, I know." But he was right. For a few moments she had forgotten the mechanics of breathing. "I'm fine."

"Would you like a drink?"

"No!"

Luke's eyes strayed to Bria's riding gloves on the table by the doors. She had come straight from outside to the study with no expectation that she would find him here. He wondered what work she had intended to do. "Am I keeping you from something?"

"It can wait."

Luke realized he was absurdly pleased by her answer. She was not often a body at rest. Some of his most vivid images of Bria were the ones where she was in motion: dashing across the field to catch Apollo; riding at full tilt through the yard; plunging down the river embankment. Yet here she was in front of him, their positions reversed from the day of their first meeting. He occupied the space behind the desk; she was in the uncomfortable position of seeking something from him.

She was extraordinarily lovely. Wisps of radiant, honey-colored hair framed her face like a nimbus. Her skin was clear and creamy and her mouth was pink and lush. She had a slim nose and a beautifully defined arch in her cheeks. The long lashes lent her a certain mystery but did not shutter the implacable sapphire eyes.

Bria unbuttoned her jacket and let it fall open. She plucked at her blouse where it, and the chemise under it, was sticking to her skin. She was very much aware that she was fresh from the fields, covered with a film of dust, sweat trickling down her back. When her chin came up slightly under Luke's quiet scrutiny, it was because she didn't know what else to do.

"You're staring," she said.

Luke was unabashed. "I know. I suspect you'll have to accustom yourself to it. Unless you specifically deny me that pleasure in our contract." He watched her eyes grow a little colder and knew that she was contemplating it. His own eyes narrowed shrewdly. "You don't like it when I compliment you."

"Oh? Were you flattering me?"

He considered her question seriously, as if she weren't trying to needle him. "Perhaps I wasn't. The fact that I experience any pleasure looking at you has much more to do with me than it does you.'' Luke permitted himself a small smile when she had no response. Something would occur to her later when she wasn't so tired and then there would be hell to pay. To delay that moment he asked the thing that had been uppermost in his mind. ''Did you really think I'd say no to your proposal?''

''I don't know,'' she said honestly. A weary little sigh accompanied this admission. Bria tipped her head back a few degrees so it could rest against the chair. Her eyes focused on the row of books above Luke's head. ''I wouldn't let myself think about it.''

''Would you like to take it back? Go on from here as if you never posed the question?''

''No.'' She glanced at him. ''Are you having second thoughts?''

''Always. But I won't change my mind if that's what you're asking.'' He observed something like relief settle on her features. ''When is the wedding?''

''I thought we would marry in December after Mother and Orrin return from Charleston. Traditionally the winter months are when everyone entertains and it gives my mother enough time to make arrangements. She'll enjoy that.''

''Then she won't try to talk you out of it?''

Bria didn't answer immediately. Her mother's reaction was difficult to predict. ''She'll be pleased that I'm finally marrying,'' she said slowly. ''She's wanted that since I was seventeen, and eight years has been a long time for her to wait, but I'm not sure how she will respond to my choice.''

''Because I'm a Yankee.''

''She's in no position to cast stones. She married Orrin, remember? No, I'm thinking about the fact that you have virtually no money. That will be a concern. And she won't be especially pleased by my announcement that we intend to live here.''

Luke had wondered about that. ''Won't Orrin have something to say about us remaining at Concord?''

"He won't make us leave. He likes you and he wants you to finish the house, and while he only tolerates me, he knows he can't manage Concord on his own. This will be the fourth harvest in which we've turned a profit. That's better than anyone else in the county and if nothing else, Orrin Foster wants to retain his bragging rights."

"So he won't object to us living under his roof," Luke said. "But will he object to the marriage?"

"He has no say in it."

"Which is not precisely an answer to my question." Luke didn't add that Orrin seemed oddly possessive of Bria. He offered her up as if it were his right to do so. He made slurs against her, spoke vilely to her, but she was also very much on his mind. It appeared to Luke that Orrin was both frightened and fascinated by his stepdaughter. Neither word was too strong to describe the motivation for Orrin's actions. "Will he try to stop you from marrying me?"

Bria frowned, for the first time uncertain about her plan. "Orrin can be . . . vindictive."

"He's a dog in the manger."

Bria's head snapped forward. "What?"

Luke found her reaction surprising. He was certain she understood the expression. It was the meaning as it applied to her that engaged her full attention. "Surely you know he wants you."

"Yes," she said slowly. "I've told you . . . to manage the plantation. That's why he won't demand that I leave."

Luke shook is head. He realized he needed to tell her his suspicions. "That's not the only reason. He wants you for himself . . . as a man wants a woman."

Bria was on her feet in a single fluid motion. She laid one hand over her roiling stomach. "You're wrong. He's never . . . never . . ." She swallowed the rest of her words along with the bile that rose in her throat.

Luke stood and started around the desk. He stopped when he saw Bria take a step back. "You can't be so naive that you didn't suspect," he said. "Or was this something else you wouldn't let yourself think about?" As soon as he said it, he knew it was the truth. His tone became gently derisive. "And you say your mother is the one who wants no unpleasantness." He thought then that if Bria had not been occupied holding her stomach she would have placed both hands over her ears.

"Did Orrin tell you that?" she asked. Her voice rose a notch. "Did he?"

"Not in so many words." Luke went to the liquor cabinet.

"I don't want a drink."

"Yes, you do. You just don't know it yet." He poured Bria a small measure of whiskey and carried it to her. "Take it. I promise it will help."

"You're not going to try to manage my life, are you?"

"It never occurred to me that such a thing was possible." He held out the tumbler and nudged her fingers with it. When they wrapped around the glass he released it. Luke leaned back against the desk, resting one hip on the edge. He watched Bria slowly raise the glass to her mouth. She barely wet her lips with the whiskey before she withdrew it. "Perhaps you should sit down."

Bria sank into the chair again. Both of her hands wrapped around the tumbler and she stared at the drink in her lap.

"I'm sorry, Bree," Luke said. Some part of him realized he was saying that a lot to her recently. He supposed he should get used to it because he was bound to have cause to express it again. "I didn't really understand how little you knew about Orrin."

She made a short, sad sound that was only faintly reminiscent of laughter. "I thought I understood a great deal." Bria glanced up at Luke. "He hits my mother, you know."

Luke shook his head. "No, I didn't."

But Bria could tell that he wasn't surprised. "It was not so often in the beginning. Months could go by without an incident. In the past few years it's been more frequent. The last time was just before Rand arrived. Mother claimed she fell on the stairs. It was true but it didn't explain Orrin's part in it."

"He pushed her?"

"I didn't witness it. Addie was lurking somewhere close by. She said they were arguing and then my mother fell, but she didn't see it, either. He may have pushed her but I don't think he meant her to fall, at least not down the stairs."

"Did you ask Elizabeth?"

"Yes, but she wouldn't expound beyond her original story. Rand couldn't get anything from her, either. She was still bed bound when he got here. Dr. Stuart even treated her." Bria took another a swallow of whiskey. For just a moment heat pulsed through her body. It radiated from the pit of her stomach and when it was over she realized the unsettling roiling was over as well. "Rand suspected the truth, of course, but there was nothing he could do. It would have gone worse for Mother if he had retaliated. He knew he was leaving soon and couldn't protect her beyond the days that he remained at Concord."

"So he left her protection in your hands."

"I accepted it," she corrected him. "Rand offered to take both Mother and me on board the *Cerberus*. I refused. Mother would never have left and I couldn't leave her behind. And there was the matter of Concord. I *wanted* to manage it. Rand could never quite understand that. He thinks it should be his job and that somehow he's shirking his duty." Bria shrugged and took another sip of her drink. "I left it to Claire to convince him he's wrong. I think she is more persuasive than I am."

Luke found that hard to believe. "What about your brother? Will he accept me?"

"No," she said frankly. "Not until he sees that I'm happy."

"And will you be?"

"I can play at it for the length of his next visit. He will want to be convinced."

"I see," Luke said, watching her carefully. "Have you con-sidered exactly what that will entail? I imagine he'll want more proof than your word and an unflagging smile. I doubt he'll be fooled by either of those.'' He leaned forward and took Bria's empty glass from her. His fingers deliberately brushed hers and she immediately retracted her own hand. He pointed to it. ''That's what I mean. You may not want a marriage but you're going to have to convince people that you have one. You can't keep pulling away from me as if I were a typhus carrier. There's no mistaking your response for shy, maidenly airs or playful flirtation. You should think about your proposal again if you cannot learn to tolerate my touch. No one will be persuaded otherwise, least of all your own family.''

Bria knew he was right. ''I can learn,'' she said.

''My God, Bree. Do you hear yourself? You say that as if I were forcing you to walk the plank. This is *your* idea, not mine.'' When she continued to sit there as if she were screwing her courage to the sticking place, Luke waved a hand dismissively in her direction. ''You can't do it. I'm not challenging you. I'm stating a fact. You'll have to think of some other way to make your scheme work.''

It was only after Luke had taken a few steps toward the doors that Bria realized he was going to leave her. ''No!'' She jumped to her feet. ''No, I can do this. I *can*.''

Luke stopped and turned slowly on his heel. ''It will take more than your word.''

Bria nodded. When she went toward him it was without her usual caution. She hesitated only a fraction of a second before she raised herself on tiptoe and placed her arms around his neck. Her body fell naturally against his. She lifted her face.

''It's a beginning,'' Luke said calmly. He slipped his hands under the open front of her jacket and laid them firmly on her waist. The entire length of her stiffened. Even her lips were pressed tightly together. ''Do you think people won't notice that?'' He settled her more solidly against him. ''Breathe.'' When she did he felt the rise and fall of her breasts against his chest. She must have felt the contact, too. In the next moment she was holding her breath again.

Luke was smiling when he bent his head and touched his

forehead to hers. "Do you know, Bree, that with any other woman I'd accept this breathless state as a compliment. With you, I fear, it's something to be overcome. Now take another breath before you faint."

Bria sucked in a lungful of air. Before she released it, she said quickly, "I'm going to kiss you."

"I was hoping you might."

She closed the short distance between their mouths before she thought of all the reasons she shouldn't. His lips were warm but unresponsive. She touched the upper one, then the lower, just as he had done to her. He didn't move, didn't even follow her by a single degree when she pulled back. "You must act your part, too," she said.

"I'm not an actor. But perhaps I can encourage you. Go on, kiss me again."

When she touched his lips this time Bria felt the shape of Luke's mouth change. It moved under hers, tugging lightly, learning the taste of her ever so gently. She didn't so much lose herself in the kiss as concentrate on it. She studied the nuances: the way his lips parted; the angle of his head; the tenderness of his mouth. She returned those things in kind, and when his tongue swept the underside of her lip she did not rear back.

Luke opened one eye and saw both of hers staring back at him. His chuckle tickled both their mouths. He raised his head. "You might want to close your eyes," he whispered.

"Why? It's harder to think that way."

"That may be true, but it's something people expect when you're engaged in a kiss."

"You don't think we shall have to have a great many public displays of affection, do you?"

"No. Not at all." Then, before she experienced too much in the way of relief, he added, "That would do nothing to advance the cause that you're happy in your marriage."

"It wouldn't?"

He shook his head. "Stolen moments are what's called for."

"Stolen moments," she repeated. Bria's deep blue eyes were suspicious.

"Like this." Luke made a furtive glance to his right and left, then kissed Bria fully on the mouth. "As if we had just ducked into the arbor," he said, raising his head.

Bria's lips were still parted in surprise. She must have closed her eyes, she realized, because she was reeling ever so slightly. "We don't have an arbor," she said, vaguely proud that she was able to make this salient point.

"I'll build one. In the meantime . . ." He looked quickly over his shoulder then kissed her again. "We shall have to slip around the corner of the house when we think no one's watching."

Bria frowned. "Now you're confusing me."

Lord, he hoped so.

"I mean, we'll really be kissing because someone's watching, won't we? We'll only be pretending they aren't."

"Yes," Luke said. She was not nearly as confused as he wanted her to be. "That's the idea. Embracing in the hallway . . ." He lowered his head again and this time she raised her mouth to his. Luke thought he could come to like the taste of whiskey if he could always drink it like this. His tongue nudged her lips apart and swept the ridge of her teeth. He felt a tremor in her arms in the moment before they tightened around this neck. Luke lifted his head a fraction. ". . . behind the stables . . ." He kissed the corners of her mouth. ". . . in the back of a wagon . . ." He deepened the kiss and this time Bria was fully responsive. She arched into him and her body moved lightly, sinuously. She changed positions as he did, her mouth slanting to match his. It required some effort on Luke's part, but when he opened one eye, both of Bria's were closed. ". . . in the corner of the crumbling foundation . . ."

Bria's head snapped back. She pushed at Luke's shoulders and stepped out of his embrace. Her eyes were starkly brilliant in her pale face. "No," she said. There was only the faintest tremor in her voice. "There will be no stolen moments there."

"Bria." Knowing the futility of reaching for her, Luke's hands fell uselessly to his sides. He watched her walk to the table to retrieve her gloves. "Don't ignore me, Bree."

Her over-the-shoulder glance was scornful. "Is there some threat in that?"

Luke's grey eyes reflected only steely indifference. "Think whatever you like, but don't leave this room without making some explanation."

Bria slapped the gloves once against the table top. The staccato snap might as well have been the crack of a whip. She turned on Luke. "What is it that you think you want to know? We were both playing our parts. I'm finished practicing mine for now."

That facile explanation did not satisfy Luke. "It was something else," he said.

"It was nothing."

"It was *not* nothing."

"Leave it be, Luke."

More than anything, it was Bria's use of his name that let Luke know she was trying to placate him. "Was it the kiss?"

"Yes . . . no . . ." Bria saw that either answer was a trap. If she said yes, then she was admitting she had been doing more than playing a part. Answering no would prove there was some other cause. "Can you not just let it pass?"

"Not this time," he said quietly. "What is it about the wall, Bree? That's why you pushed me away, isn't it? Because I said something about the wall. What was that place?"

Staring at a point past his shoulder, Bria answered, "It used to be the icehouse."

Which offered nothing in the way of explaining her behavior. Luke ran a hand through his hair, trying just once to see past her shuttered expression. "How long since it's been used?"

"Ten years."

"Before the end of the war?" he asked. "Or after?"

"Before."

She would have been fifteen then, Luke thought. And it was

very close to the end of the fighting. Beauregard had ordered Charleston evacuated in February of that year. Sherman was on the march again and small forces of Yankee raiders and renegades were foraging the countryside for supplies. Luke knew Bria's father had died at Vicksburg and Shelby had fallen at Manassas. At the end of the war Rand was still in a New York prison. No one spoke of David though. Until now Luke had assumed he'd died somewhere away from Concord. But then who would have been managing the plantation? Not Bria. Not then.

Luke's head tipped to one side. He studied her closely. "How did your brother David die?"

"Yankees."

"Here at Concord?"

"Here at Henley." Her eyes were dry, her voice without inflection. "It was still Henley when he died. This was his home." *As it's been to none of us since,* she thought. None of the survivors. "They came looking for horses and fresh meat. There wasn't much they didn't get. There was no time to hide anything. We didn't know they were about until it was too late."

"Bria?" Her eyes shifted to his and remained there. Luke held her glance. "Was David killed in the icehouse?"

"No. He was murdered upstairs, protecting our mother." Bria's pause was no more than a heartbeat. "The icehouse is where I was raped."

Luke had no immediate, overt reaction to her statement. He didn't wince and make a mockery of her pain. He showed no pity and therefore no expectation that she should feel guilt or shame. Neither did he demonstrate any satisfaction that he finally had the answer he had asked for. He simply accepted it as one of the many things he knew about her, like the color of her eyes or the shape of her mouth or the fact that she liked peach cobbler almost as much as he did.

Bria's brow puckered as she studied him. The fact that he said nothing was maddening, yet it kept her in the room with him. She had fully intended to walk out. Now she recognized that action for what it would have been: dramatic and somehow childish. For forcing that confession from her, Bria had meant to skewer his conscience with her final riposte and leave him pinned to the desk.

Now she was the one firmly in place, held there, it seemed, because he made no judgment and expressed no horror. It was as though he thought it was something she could talk about. "Do you mean me to say something?" she asked at last.

"If you like."

"As if we were talking about the weather?"

Luke's head tipped a little to one side and he made a small shrug. "You say that as if the weather were of no consequence. People get very emotional about it, have you noticed?"

Bria did not want to get emotional. Even as she thought it an unfamiliar ache settled behind her eyes. She blinked. Her lashes felt heavy, damp. Luke's figure blurred at the edges. The sharply defined features of his face softened a little. "I think I want to tell you."

He would not have recognized her voice if he hadn't been watching her speak. It was thick and a bit forced, just rough at the edges like sandpaper worked against the grain. Luke sat back on the desk again and stretched his legs in front of him. His hands rested on the edge on either side. He didn't offer her the chair, but waited patiently for Bria to make her own decision about whether she would sit or stand.

Bria let her gloves fall back on the table but she didn't come forward. She thrust her hands into the pockets of her riding jacket. "There were seven Yankees. Only three ever came to the icehouse. I don't know what they expected to find. It was empty. Like everything else, the Federal blockade made it hard to get ice. Jeb sent me to hide there. I know he thought it was safe.

"They found me crouched behind the door. There was nowhere else for me to go. I don't think I screamed when they grabbed me. I remember a great black wood spider climbing up the inside of the door. I think it would have jumped if I had screamed, don't you?''

Luke nodded slowly. She hadn't screamed because she was afraid someone would come. What could any of them have done against three armed Yankees except lose their lives?

''I fought them, though. I never quit fighting them. I knew it probably wouldn't matter to them, but it mattered terribly to me.'' Tears hovered on the edge of her lashes, then fell. She went on, unaware or uncaring of her wet cheeks. ''The youngest of them went first. The others pushed him to it. I don't think he wanted to. He'd never been with a girl before. They knew that, so they wanted him to be first. They said I was his present.'' A breath shuddered through her and Bria jerkily lifted one hand to her mouth. She pressed her knuckles to her lips and held them there. Her eyes were stark now, haunted and remote. It was as if she had severed some connection with herself.

Without any conscious thought of how it could be done, Bria drifted from the moment.

Chapter Eight

"She's your present, Ohio. Go on. Take her."

Ohio actually took a step back from the girl. She was kicking and clawing like a cat with its tail on fire. He could tell that Daniel and George had no patience for her. They didn't want a fight. They were all tired of fighting.

"Now, you ain't afraid, are you?" Daniel hopped on one foot as the girl lit into him again. "Ow! Jesus, Mary, and Joseph! George, can't you hold her any better than that? By God, I swear she's got another pair of legs under those skirts!"

Inspired by the picture he'd created in his own mind, Daniel yanked her away from his companion, scooped her up, and tossed her over his arm. In another moment she was upended entirely. Her skirt draped down, inside out, over her bodice and down her flailing arms until it covered her face. She wriggled and pushed frantically at it. Without her hands to support her, her head twisted and her cheek scraped the ground. Above her, Daniel confirmed she had only two legs.

She was not wearing a crinoline or petticoats. Those were saved for special occasions, not an ordinary workday. Her shift was already bunched at her waist. Beneath it she wore long-legged cotton drawers. None of the men noticed the hem of *each leg was trimmed with pale blue ribbon. What they couldn't take their eyes from was the copse of fine, dark-honey hair at the juncture of her thighs. Every struggle separated the split in her white drawers a fraction wider.*

"Mother of God," Daniel whispered, staring down at her. "Have you ever seen the like? Pink as a rose petal."

She fought harder, this time to keep her legs together. A heavy hand slipped through the opening in her drawers and cupped her mons. She went rigid as a finger brushed her pubis and then stroked her, spreading her flesh and finally pushing inside her. She bit her lip until she tasted blood in her mouth.

Daniel raised his hand to his nose and sniffed. He closed his eyes. "It's a heady perfume," he told his companions. "I think it must be ambrosia. You'll want some of that, Ohio. She's as untried as you. It's only fitting that you take her first." The girl had renewed her struggles when she felt only one arm holding her. This time Daniel let her drop.

She lost no time scrambling to her hands and knees. A boot in the small of her back pressed her flat to the floor. It wasn't Daniel who restrained her this time. He was closing the door to the icehouse and shutting out the last rays of the late winter sun. The boot belonged to the largest of the three men and he made good use of his weight to keep her under him.

"Go on, Ohio," Daniel said. "What are you waiting for? You need some help with your noodle?"

Ohio was unable to look away from the girl. She was straining against the ground trying to heave off George's weight. She was strong enough to lever herself up a few inches. Her head twisted and she looked back over her shoulder. The last thing Ohio saw before Daniel shut the door was a pair of brilliant and accusing sapphire eyes.

"Well?" Daniel demanded. "I'm thinking George and me aren't going to wait all day. You want some, you take it now. It ain't like you can't find her." To prove his point Daniel pushed away from the door and crossed to where he could hear the girl thrashing. He hunkered down beside her and

pressed one hand on her shoulder. "Let's turn her over. We've got to do something about those legs if our boy's ever going to get his noodle in."

George lifted his boot long enough for Daniel to push her onto her back, then he brought it down squarely on her midriff. They all could hear the breath momentarily being expelled from her lungs. Surprise kept her still long enough for George to kneel opposite his friend. Without any direction passing between them they restrained her arms and shoulders with their knees and one hand, and used their free arm to reach under her legs and draw them back.

"You better get between her thighs now, boy," Daniel said. "If you don't, I'm going to plow this fresh field myself."

Although she kicked, her heels never made contact with anything but air. Every twist seemed to open her wider. She bucked and reared and the effort sapped her strength. Her struggling changed nothing with the men who held her. In the dark it had little impact on the boy who finally knelt between her thighs.

"Pretend it's your bayonet," Daniel instructed. "Do it just like they taught you. Hard and fast and deep. She'll thank you for not making an agony of her first time with fumbling and hesitation."

George adjusted his hold on the back of her knee so she couldn't flail her heels at Ohio. "Dan's right," he said roughly. "And it ain't like you're gonna kill her. Hell, she won't even scream." To make certain she didn't, George moved the hand on her shoulder to her mouth. "Go on. Shouldn't be at all surprised if she likes it."

In an odd way she was glad for the sweaty palm over her mouth. In spite of her best intentions, she would have cried out when the boy plunged into her. It seemed to her that revealing pain would give them more power and somehow make it more real. Still, the urge to scream, to howl, was the instinct she was fighting and her teeth closed over George's hand like it was a leather bit.

He shouted and yanked his hand away. "Goddamn! She took a piece of me." He held his hand up close to his chest, nursing the wound. Blood dampened his shirt.

The entire length of her right arm was numb from the weight of George's knee. It wasn't until she had the sensation of hundreds of pins pricking her skin that she realized his knee had slipped to one side. Her fingers twitched. In moments she had enough feeling return that she could make a loose fist. When sensation passed to her wrist, forearm, then her elbow, she decided she could wait no longer. With enormous effort she swung her arm in the direction of Ohio's bobbing head. Her fist connected solidly with his cheek.

He was as silent receiving pain as she had been. His heaving body collapsed on hers.

"What the hell?" Daniel felt her renewed struggles and managed to dodge a blow as he leaned forward over Ohio. "George! Forget your hand, for God's sake, and get her arm. She's knocked the boy out."

George grunted and found her flailing arm. He secured it by slamming it hard to the ground. "Thought he finished fast," he muttered. "Probably spent himself on her drawers."

Daniel grabbed Ohio by his collar and heaved him off. The boy stirred groggily and finally got to his knees. Daniel growled at him. "Get over here and take your turn holding this rebel she-cat. You're lucky she didn't unman you."

When she realized it was Daniel that was going to crawl between her thighs she found a reserve of strength to renew her struggles and kick out at them all.

If anything, it hurt worse than before. Her back arched once and then she went rigid. She could smell alcohol on his hot breath. The fetid odor of his body clung to his woolen uniform. It mingled with horse sweat and the scent of the earth under them.

He ground his hips against her. Pushing. Pushing. She bit her own lips raw and breathed through her nose. A hand shoved its way under her bodice and mauled her tender breasts.

George's knee slipped again. Once she had become so still under Daniel it was not necessary to hold her tightly. The feel of her breast under his palm was more to his liking than the curve of her shoulder. "Get on with it, Danny. I got what you got for her and three more inches besides."

Red-faced and breathing hard, Daniel snorted. "You got nothing. Count 'em out, George. I'm givin' her twenty, just see if I don't."

Beneath his hand Ohio could feel her jerk in response to every thrust of Daniel's body. As George began his count, Ohio turned his head and was sick.

"Oh, Jesus," Daniel groaned. "Now you've played hell with a man's natural appetites. Get away if you have no stomach for it."

Ohio crawled off and was sick again. He collapsed against the door and sat there unmoving.

The earsplitting report of the Colt surprised them all. In the confines of the icehouse the sound echoed in their heads long after it stopped reverberating off the walls.

"Jesus, Mary, and—" Daniel broke off as he realized he was the one who had been shot. "George—"

The warning came too late for George. The next bullet found its target in the underside of his chin. It traveled upward through his palate and lodged in the soft tissue of his brain. His head was flung back. He was dead before he collapsed on the floor.

She flung the gun away and pushed hard at Daniel's shoulders. His arms had folded under him and he was heavy on top of her. She had to squirm and heave to free herself. Ohio made no move to stop her or assist her. Once the sound of the gunshots became only a mild roar in her ears, she could hear him weeping.

Daniel's voice was weak. "Ohio? You there?" He could not be certain that the crying was not coming from him. There were tears in his own eyes and the taste of blood in his mouth. He rolled over on his back as the girl slipped away and he felt for the wound in his neck. Blood pumped between his fingers with every frantic beat of his heart. "Ohio?"

Bracing himself against the door, the boy pushed to his feet. He fumbled for the handle and pulled it open. Twilight flooded the darkness of the icehouse. He had a glimpse of the dead and dying bodies on the floor and they brought no reaction to his tear-stained face. It was the young girl crouched in the corner that riveted his attention.

She stared at him through eyes that did not quite see him. They were focused and clear, yet it was as if he stood at some great distance from her, or she from him. She did not move or raise her hands to shield herself. It made her both vulnerable and oddly defiant. She was daring him to put this vision from his mind's eye.

They both saw the gun at the same time. It was lying on the floor exactly where she had flung it. She made no attempt to retrieve it. Still watching her, he took a step toward it, bent, and picked it up. He tucked it behind the wide leather belt that closed his jacket, exactly where she had found it in the first place.

"I'll tell the others they ran off," he said quietly. "No one will bother you." He left the icehouse, his face haggard, his eyes as weary as an old man's.

Bria suddenly found that she was sitting in the study again, in the armchair, her legs folded under her. Her hands rested in her lap, her fingers curled in loose fists. She tested her connection to them, spreading them slowly and running them over her skirt to smooth the bunched material. She could feel the dampness of her palms.

Luke was sitting on a padded stool at her feet. It was much too low to the ground for him to be comfortable but he sat there as if he was very much at his ease, waiting for her to continue.

"When the Yankees were gone, Jeb came for me. We dug

up the floor of the icehouse and buried the two bodies there. Afterward we buried David in the cemetery.

"I told Mother what happened to me. She held me close, rocked me back and forth like I was her baby again. She crooned in my ear. Two of them had come at her in the house . . . in her own bedroom. David killed one. The other killed David." Bria's voice was strained, hardly more than a whisper. "She said no one touched her after that. She said she would have killed herself if they had."

Bria looked at Luke. "Is that what I should have done?" Her eyes were haunted now, her expression plaintive. "Was I supposed to kill myself?"

For a moment he couldn't speak. He had listened to her tell her story without comment or question, but it wasn't the fact that he restrained himself from talking that make it hard to use his voice now. It was something closer to anger that strangled his voice and he swallowed it back because it served no purpose.

Luke shook his head first, not trusting himself. "No," he said. "You shouldn't have killed yourself."

"But—"

"No." He cut her off gently. "Your mother spoke as if there was shame, as if she could have borne the assault but not lived with what followed. But there *is* no shame unless you take that burden on yourself. What was done, was done *to* you, Bree. Against your will, not with your consent. You were brave to a fault. You saved yourself. You have nothing—" He stopped and studied her closely when her eyes darted away from his. "Does anyone except Jeb know you killed those soldiers?"

She stared at her hands. "Addie."

"Your mother?"

Bria shook her head.

"Rand?"

"No!"

Luke said softly, "Oh, Bree, I think your brother would have understood. He would have wanted to kill them."

She sucked in her bottom lip and worried it between her teeth.

"You were protecting yourself," Luke said. "That boy practically *put* the gun in your hand. He let you do what he knew he should have done himself and couldn't. In the end, if you had taken up the Colt when it was lying on the floor, he probably wouldn't have stopped you from putting a bullet through his own head. You must have wondered about that."

She had wondered. "So often it seems as if it all happened to someone else; I don't know what I think anymore. In the beginning there were nightmares. I didn't mind them, even when I woke up wet and shaking. When the fear passed I could make myself believe they were just like any other dream, with nothing in common with the realities of my life. Perhaps I did kill the one they called Ohio. There were nightmares where I did exactly that. No one else was in the icehouse with me. Perhaps nothing happened at all. Or perhaps they raped some other girl and I only watched, too frightened to do anything."

She was unaware that tears were coursing down her cheeks again until Luke pressed a handkerchief in her hand. It was wrinkled and damp and she realized he must have done this before. There was something familiar in the motion of crushing it in her fist, then raising it to her face.

Luke watched her use the handkerchief awkwardly, knuckling away the tears first in the manner of a small child, then swiping at her cheeks with it. She hadn't much experience with tears, he realized. This time something in his expression gave away his thoughts.

Bria's uncertain smile was watery and apologetic. "I don't often cry," she whispered. For the first time she noticed that Luke was no longer wearing his jacket. It had been tossed negligently across the desk. His white shirt was as wrinkled and damp at one shoulder as the handkerchief she clutched.

Bria's head lifted suddenly and she stared at him, not seeing Luke as he was now on the stool in front of her, but as he had been earlier, sitting on the edge of the desk. She was standing there with him, her face buried in his shoulder, her fingers curled tightly in shirt. She was sobbing so hard that even the memory of it made it difficult for her to breathe. He held her loosely, his hands at the small of her back, his chin resting in the crown of her hair.

Bria looked down at herself again, then glanced toward the door. Her riding gloves lay on the table. She had been standing there, she remembered, when she had started to speak. She had no clear idea of how she had come to be in the chair.

She held out her hand to return the handkerchief.

Luke smiled. "No. You keep it this time."

This time. So he *had* pressed it into her hand before. Bria drew her hand close to her middle. "I rather think I've said too much."

"You said as much as needed saying. No more, no less."

"You won't . . . you won't repeat what I've—"

He interrupted Bria to save her another moment of panic and uncertainty. "No," he said firmly. "I won't say anything." He watched her closely, wondering if he would be able to tell if she believed him. It only seemed that she wanted to trust him, not that she did. "Do you know that Addie came to the door earlier?"

Bria didn't know that at all. She looked in that direction, half expecting to find Addie still hovering. "I didn't hear her."

"She came to announce dinner was ready. I don't think she expected to find you here." He clearly remembered the astonished expression in Addie's dark eyes when she parted the doors. Bria was on her knees on the floor then, Luke simply hunkered beside her. Addie made to step forward, instantly concerned, but froze when she heard Bria's first tortured sob. Luke waved her off and she backed away quickly. "I think she understood what was happening," he said.

"She couldn't. I don't understand myself. I've never—"

"You haven't cried nearly often enough."

It was true, Bria thought. "I didn't know I could."

Luke came to his feet. He held out a hand for Bria and waited patiently for her to take it. When she was standing beside him, he said, "I'll escort you to your room. You'll wash your face and change your clothes and in a half hour you'll meet me in the dining room."

She lifted her head. His eyes held hers and she nodded slowly, not at all against her will. When she saw one corner of his mouth lift and a smile start to reach his eyes, she felt compelled to warn him. "You mustn't think too much of this. I won't always be so agreeable."

Luke's grin merely deepened. "It never once occurred to me that you would."

It was half past the hour when Luke checked his pocket watch. Bria stepped into the dining room as he was putting it away.

"Am I late?" she asked.

"Not at all. I make it three minutes early."

Bria smiled. It was not as difficult to face him again as she had imagined, and in the time he had allowed her out of his sight, she had imagined a great deal. She suspected he had known that. If he had given her more time it might have been days before she would have been able to sit down with him.

Martha served the meal. Bria discovered her appetite had not entirely deserted her. There were occasions when Luke's eyes on her made it hard to swallow but it was not because he made her uncomfortable. It was because he made her warm.

It was Luke who had trouble concentrating on his meal. The chicken and dumplings could have been paste for all the notice he gave them. When his glance rested on Bria's freshly scrubbed face he did not want to look away.

Except for the slight heaviness of her eyelids and the pink hue in her cheeks, there was no evidence of her earlier tears. She was animated in a way that was unusual for her; her eyes might have been a shade brighter. She caught his glance sometimes and would look away quickly, then risk peeking at him through the curve of her dark lashes. He wondered if she knew his breath caught when she did that.

When they spoke it was of inconsequential things until Martha placed dessert before them.

"I've wanted to talk to you about John Whitney," Luke said casually. He speared a sweetened slice of fresh peach and brought it to his mouth.

Bria looked at him blankly. Of all the things he might have said to her, this was the most surprising. "John? What about him?"

"His house, really."

"Well then, what about his house?"

Now Luke's brows kicked up. He hadn't missed the guardedness in Bria's tone or the way she had immediately braced her shoulders. "Visiting his home during daylight hours gave me an opportunity to look at his house. I couldn't help but notice there have been some recent repairs to his roof."

"Really?"

"With the same materials we were using to repair the roof of this house."

"You must be mistaken. Perhaps it came from what you removed."

"Some of it did. Some of it was new. He couldn't have used the old bent nails. Those were new."

"Nails are nails. You can't tell me you recognize nails."

"I recognize new nails when I see them. And I saw them shining in the sun on John's patched roof."

"But you can't know that they belong to you."

"I know the box that was sitting on John's night table is one of many missing from my inventory in the last few weeks. It didn't always hold the matches that John keeps there now."

"John Whitney is not a thief."

"I didn't think he was. I thought it might be you."

Bria did not try to affect outrage. "Me?"

"It occurred to me when I saw the work done at John's that I should get a better look at some of the other tenant farms at Concord. I can't say that I was terribly surprised to see that all but a few homes I passed showed evidence of repairs. Fresh lumber shoring up some sagging foundations. New bricks and mortar in several chimneys. If I had gone inside I would probably have found paint that matches colors I chose for various rooms in this house.'' Luke's eyes narrowed shrewdly. ''Is that right, Bree? Is that what I would have found?''

She shrugged. ''I wouldn't know. How would I know?''

''Why didn't you tell me you wanted Orrin's money to help them?''

''I'm not helping anyone.''

''Yes, you are. This is what you were referring to the first evening we met. Down at the riverbank. You spoke of improvements. You were never clear, and you were downright close-mouthed once you realized I wouldn't fall in with your plans.''

Bria remained mutinously closed-mouthed now.

''It's dangerous,'' he told her. Luke leaned forward. When he reached for her hand she withdrew it from the tabletop quickly and laid it in her lap. ''Very dangerous. What if Orrin finds out?''

''There's nothing for him to find out.''

''Aren't you afraid it will go badly for them? Worse for you?''

''There's nothing for Orrin to find out,'' she said again.

Luke pushed away his plate. ''I don't care if you deny it to me. It makes no difference. Do you understand? I know what I know. I have the evidence of my own eyes to support me. I don't need to hear it from you.''

''Then why bring it up at all?''

''Because I'm afraid for you.''

She lifted her chin as if to deny her vulnerability. ''Afraid for me? After what you heard today, do you doubt that I can take care of myself?''

''Don't. This isn't the same thing, Bria. Not the same at all.''

''I don't know what you mean.''

''You do,'' he insisted. ''I know you do. Orrin can hurt you by hurting John and Addie and Martha and Jeb and every other tenant you've helped in some way. I won't let myself believe you hadn't thought of that. You might act recklessly in your own behalf but you would not lightly take a risk that could bring harm to others.''

''What does any of this have to do with you?''

''Let me help you, Bree. I can make certain old materials are available by taking more care removing them. I can show your tenants how to make repairs with new lumber and bricks and hide the evidence from an untrained eye.''

''I remember what you said to me at the river. *I won't let you compromise what I've agreed to deliver.* Do you remember saying that, Luke?''

''I remember,'' he said softly.

''You also promised that you wouldn't say anything to Orrin unless I made it impossible for you to do otherwise. Well, have I? Can you take the evidence gathered by your own eyes and pretend you haven't seen it?''

Luke did not hesitate in answering. ''No, I can't. And you should know better than to ask me to do it.'' Some of the rose tint in her cheeks faded as she considered what this meant. Luke went on. ''But I don't know that you've forced my hand just yet.''

''You mean you'll say nothing about this?'' He was silent so long that Bria did not think he meant to respond at all. ''Luke?''

''What would you say to a wedding in one week's time?'' he asked.

Bria merely blinked at him.

''Without the presence of your family or mine. Outside Charleston County, perhaps, where you're not known. Before a justice or in a small church.''

''But why—'' She stopped herself as the why of his proposal was made clear to her. ''Is that the price of your silence?''

Luke said nothing, forcing Bria to draw her own conclusion.

She frowned, turning it over in her mind. ''Do you know,'' she said finally, ''that I can't decide if you're asking too much or far too little. What assurance will I have that you won't demand another boon from me after we're married?''

''None.''

''What do you gain by advancing our wedding a short six or seven weeks?''

''The peace of mind that it's done.''

She simply stared at him, thoughtful now. ''And that's all?''

''That's all.''

''And you won't say anything to Orrin about the other?''

He had never intended to tell Orrin what he knew. ''Not a word.''

''Very well. We can be married as soon as the harvesting is done. Perhaps it's wiser to present my family with the fact of it rather than an announcement that it's meant to be.''

Those were exactly Luke's thoughts.

Bria pushed back her chair and stood. ''You understand, of course, that manipulating me in this fashion does not make me inclined to share a bed with you.''

Luke's shout of laughter rocked Bria back on her heels. Her reaction made him laugh harder. ''Oh, Bree. Not for a moment did I think you meant to share my bed.''

He was still chuckling when she left the room.

Harvesting was complete in two days but it remained for the rice to be threshed and pounded. Once the cleaning and husking process was done the rice was packed in barrels, loaded on a steamer, and shipped to market. Not only did Bria oversee the entire process, she haggled for the best prices from the steamboat captain and the agent who would sell the rice in Charleston. Concord's yield was two hundred thousand pounds. It was not up to pre-1860 production, but certainly respectable and profit-making. The sharecroppers were paid their due for that portion of the yield that was designated as theirs.

On the evening of September 30 the sounds of revelry could be heard wherever one turned at Concord.

Luke found Bria sitting on the steps of the verandah. Her knees were drawn up and her head was tilted to one side. An unopened book lay beside her. In the fading light, the skirt of her red silk gown was like a spill of dark wine.

Luke let the door fall shut with an audible click. Her head swiveled at the sound. When she saw him, her expression did not change. She was neither welcoming nor dismissive.

"I thought you had retired for the evening," she said. "When you went to the study immediately following dinner I did not expect to see you again."

Luke crossed the verandah. He stooped and picked up the discarded book. "*Alice's Adventures in Wonderland*," he read aloud. "Are you enjoying it?"

Bria nodded. "Claire recommended it to me." She held out her hand for it and Luke returned it to her. Bria stretched her legs over the steps and placed the book in her lap. "She had more books than clothes with her on *Cerberus*. At least that's what Rand told me. Cutch and Dr. Stuart read to her."

Luke remained standing. He leaned against one of the large white columns. "Who's Cutch?"

"Rand's second in command. He was a manumitted slave long before the Proclamation. My father gave Cutch his papers after he saved David from drowning."

"And he chose to stay here?"

Bria looked up at him. "You find that strange, don't you? You probably read *Uncle Tom's Cabin*."

"Twice."

"We were not all like Simon LeGree." Bria turned back to look over the gardens. In the distance she could hear the music and raised voices of the revelers. The women had been baking for this celebration. There would be dancing and singing. The men would be bringing in liquor from their hidden stills. No one would be any good for work tomorrow. Bria made certain of it by declaring it a day of rest. "Was there something in particular you wanted?" she asked Luke.

"I thought you should know I've made the arrangements."

He tried to gauge Bria's reaction to this news but could see none. "We can be married tomorrow."

She nodded slowly. "When you never said a word about it since that night, I thought perhaps you wanted to wait after all."

"I have waited," he said. "More than two weeks longer than I meant to. I assumed that you would not be willing to leave Concord in the middle of the negotiations. Was I right?"

"Yes," she admitted. "There were too many details to leave in the hands of others. No one else could have gotten a fair price for the crop. So, what arrangements have you made?"

"We can be married in Summerville. It's not nearly as far as Georgetown and won't require that you be away more than a single day."

The furthest Bria had been away from Concord in recent years was the neighboring plantations. It was unlikely that she would see anyone she knew. Hamilton was a common enough name. It was doubtful it would be recognized as having connections to Concord. "Very well," she said. "What time shall I be ready?"

"We should leave after breakfast. We'll take the carriage." Luke studied Bria's clear and untroubled profile. "Do you want to reconsider this?"

"Reconsider what?" she asked. "Marrying you or marrying you tomorrow?"

"Both. Either."

She turned to him. Her eyes were steady on his. "I haven't changed my mind. Have you?"

"No."

She nodded. It was the answer she expected but she didn't understand it. "I cannot fathom the reasons you would agree to do this."

An enigmatic smile lifted one corner of his mouth. "Can't you?"

The rush of heat to Bria's cheeks made her glad for the onset of night. Her reaction embarrassed her. She stared at her lap

and her fingers traced the outline of the book. "At the risk of
having you laugh at me again, I want you to remember that
we won't be sharing your bed."

"I remember." Luke pushed away from the column and
dropped to the verandah steps beside Bria. He took the book
from her lap and laid it to one side. "But there will be stolen
moments," he reminded her. "I'll live for those."

Bria's hesitant smile surfaced just long enough to make an
inviting target. Luke's head bent and his mouth slanted across
hers. Surprise kept her lips parted. The taste of her was both
tart and sweet. Her hands lifted first to the level of his shoulders,
then came slowly around his neck. She was brought up by the
hand at the small of her back and arched into him. The kiss
deepened. She did not pull away when his tongue engaged
hers.

The faint click of the door behind them was not sufficient
to push them apart. Jebediah had to clear his throat twice.

Luke drew back and looked in the direction of the doors.
He used his shoulder to partly shield Bria. There was nothing
he could do to hide the husky timbre of his voice. "What is
it, Jeb?"

He didn't answer Luke. His head bobbed to get a better
glimpse of Bria. "Everything all right, Miss Bree?" he asked.
"You want I should cut me a switch and send this one off like
I done the others?"

Luke's brows lifted. His eyes darted from Jeb to Bria.

Bria straightened. Her arms dropped to her sides and she
looked over Luke's shoulder. Jeb was studying his fingers as
though contemplating the proper thickness of the switch. "I'm
fine," she told him. "There's no need to run Mr. Kincaid off."

Jeb's head bobbed once and there was a noticeable shifting
of his shoulders as if he were shrugging off a weight. "Just so
you know, Mr. Luke, there would have been no pleasure in
it."

"I suppose I can take some comfort in that," Luke said
dryly. "Who was the last unfortunate you sent off?" Out of

the corner of his eye Luke saw Bria shake her head quickly. Jeb was not so observant.

"That would have been Mr. Austin Tipping."

"He's teasing," Bria said. "Jeb, don't say that. Mr. Kincaid might believe you."

"Mr. Kincaid *does* believe him," Luke said. "Perhaps not the part about the switch."

"Well," Jeb drawled. "I was *thinking* about cutting one for him. I opened the door, though, when Miss Bree showed him to it."

Luke caught Bria's chin with his forefinger and lifted her face. "Is that right? You showed Mr. Tipping the door?"

He wasn't demanding an answer from her because he was upset, Bria realized, but because he was amused. "I did," she admitted. "Several times."

Luke didn't think Bria could know her dark eyes were dancing, or that the icy brilliance had been replaced by something that merely sparkled. "Apparently Mr. Tipping is slow to grasp the meaning of being shown to the door."

Jeb's laughter rumbled in his chest. "Now, that's a fact. Miss Bree. Mr. Luke. I came back to make certain you knew you were invited to join us down at the old docks. That's where we're celebrating the end of the harvest. You can hear those fools the whole way up here. I tol' them that."

"Bree?" Luke searched her face.

She nodded. "Yes, Jeb, we'd like to join you. We have something to celebrate besides the harvest. I'm marrying Mr. Kincaid tomorrow."

Jeb gaped at them both, his expression comically stunned. "Is that a fact?"

"It's a fact," Luke said. "Miss Bree and I are going to Summerville in the morning."

"Summerville?" Jeb was suspicious now. "Miss Bree, you mean to say your mama doesn't know about this? You ain't marryin' in Charleston in front of your family and friends?"

"I know what I'm doing," Bria said. She stood and smoothed

the folds of her gown. Without a backward glance she started off in the direction of the old docks.

Jeb's wide mouth was pulled hard to one side and his brow was deeply furrowed. He scratched the back of his head. "Do you know what *you're* doing?" he asked Luke.

Luke jumped to his feet. "That's a very good question, Jeb. What I'm doing now is going where she leads me."

That did not ease Jebediah's mind. He watched Luke catch up to Bria before he followed them both at a more thoughtful pace.

The celebration lasted until the small hours of the morning. Bria slipped away long before then but Luke walked off arm in arm with the last of the revelers. When she saw him again it did not require much study to conclude that Luke had drunk liberally from the liquor jug that had been passed around.

He denied it. "I didn't drink a lot," he said. "Just often." When she laughed at this absurd subtlety he winced and asked her to be more quietly amused.

A groom was waiting with the carriage when they had finished breakfast. Luke recognized him as the fiddle player from the night before. He looked none the worse for providing the evening's entertainment and sucking back applejack between songs. Luke regarded him enviously.

"Tad will drive," Bria whispered to him when Luke held out a hand for the reins. She steered him toward the carriage step.

"You're enjoying this," he accused. He cast a bleary eye over the crown of Bria's head. Well-wishers had gathered along the circular drive to send them off. They waved back at him when he raised one hand.

"I'm enjoying it immensely," she said. "There's a difference."

Luke grinned reflexively. The effort hurt his face. He rubbed his temple and stepped aside to allow Bria to enter the carriage.

She held out her hand once she was seated and helped steady Luke as he came aboard. He dropped heavily into the seat beside her.

"Smile," she told him. "And wave. Go on, Tad. We're ready to leave."

Once they were beyond the drive, Bria removed the arm she had slipped through Luke's and put some distance between them. "You can sleep if you like. I don't mind. I'll wake you before we reach Summerville."

"I appreciate that you want to be accommodating, but I think I can manage to stay awake, at least until after the ceremony." Ahead of him he saw Tad's shoulder shake. "And you, driver, keep your laughter down. You're rocking the carriage."

In spite of his intentions, Luke had to be awakened before they reached the town. He recovered quickly, throwing off the dregs of sleep and the lingering effects of alcohol at the same time, and gave Tad directions to the Episcopal church where Luke had made arrangements for them to be married.

The minister was waiting for them, along with witnesses. Luke took the license from inside his jacket and handed it over. Out of the corner of his eye he saw Bria's small surprise that he had remembered it. He could have told her it had been in this very same pocket for the better part of a week. He had only to remember which jacket to put on this morning. Jeb helped by laying it out for him.

The ceremony did not take long. The minister was rather pinch-faced and severe in his manner, but his tone was kind and welcoming. He went through the rites of marriage as if it gave him great joy to do so. His phrasing was rich with reverence and meaning.

Bria had given no thought to a ring until the time came for Luke to place one on her finger. Her hand trembled slightly in his larger one. The gold band flashed once in the sunlight. Bria stared at it, holding her breath as he gently pushed it over her knuckles. There was no question that he meant this ring to be hers. The fit was exact.

From somewhere behind Bria she heard the sniffling of the minister's wife and daughter. She looked up at Luke. He was watching her closely, his expression at once expectant and tender. She didn't know she was crying herself until he touched her face. The finger he drew away glistened almost as powerfully in the sunlight as the gold band.

Tad was waiting for them, wreathed in smiles, when they reappeared on the doorstep of the church. He drove them to the Miller House as Luke directed and ate in the carriage while Luke and Bria dined inside.

At the meal's end Bria carefully wrapped the additional slice of cake she'd requested in her napkin. She glanced up when she felt Luke's eyes on her. "For Tad," she said. "I'm not going to sleep with it under my pillow if that's what you're thinking."

"You don't know what I'm thinking," he said. "But I can tell you it has nothing to do with that cake. You can wear it on your head for all I care." For a moment he thought Bria looked tempted. "I was thinking that you're especially lovely this evening."

Bria's eyes darted uncomfortably. "I didn't ask what you were thinking," she said. "I didn't want to know."

"Nevertheless, I want to tell you."

She still could not bring herself to face him squarely. "Then thank you."

Luke stood and held out his hand to her. Her silk dress rustled softly as she came to her feet. Though lacking in a great deal of ornamentation, the simple gown shimmered and reflected the exact sapphire blue of her eyes. She wore small pearl studs in her ears and a cameo brooch at her throat. Nothing about the gown or the accessories was uncommon, except for the way she looked in them. He knew Bria had not wanted to draw attention to herself. He doubted it would have been possible not to.

His suspicion was confirmed when they stepped outside the hotel and saw Tad leaning over the side of the carriage talking to a white man. The man tipped his hat in their direction but turned away and hurried across the street before they reached the carriage.

"Who was that, Tad?" Luke asked once they were under way.

"Just someone I know from the horse auctions. You must have seen him at dinner. He was inside eating."

Luke hadn't noticed him at all. "What did he want?"

"Just askin' about horses. Heard about Miss Bree's plans to expand the stud. Wondered if that was her inside the Miller House." Tad shifted the reins into one hand while he adjusted his hat with the other. "Hope you don' mind me tellin' him it was. Couldn't see the harm in it. Word's bound to get around that there was a wedding."

Luke looked at Bria. Her face was paler than it had been moments before. He sat back in the leather seat and placed his arm along the curved top. "He's right. This was never intended to be a secret."

"I know. It's just that I hoped to be able to tell Mother myself. I don't think I care for her hearing it from a well-meaning friend in Charleston. I should have thought of this." Her eyes were wide as she considered Luke. "Have you told your family?"

He nodded. "I wrote letters to my mother and every one of my aunts. One letter would have done for all of them but they'll enjoy passing these around. I told each of them something different about you. They'll like putting the whole of it together."

Bria's brows puckered as she considered this. "I did not think there was so very much to tell. What did you write?"

"Just little things," he said. "The color of your eyes . . . your hair . . . the way you get that crease between your brows when you're thinking hard." Luke grinned as Bria touched the spot now and realized that it was true. She rubbed it with her forefinger, trying to smooth it out. Luke took her by the wrist and lifted her hand. He kissed the crease. "There. Now it's gone.'' He continued to hold her wrist, drawing it onto his lap. He let her hand rest on his thigh as if it were the most natural place for it. The pucker returned to her brow but he didn't mention it. Bria did not seem to notice.

"I told one of them—Aunt Nancy, I think—that you ride like a Valkyrie. Aunt Lys will know that you are not overly cautious of convention and that you can hike your skirts up and tear across a field when you have cause.''

"Oh, you didn't—''

"I did.'' He was not apologetic. "I wrote about your rare smile and regal bearing. Aunt Madelyn would recognize that in herself. I told them all how you proposed to me.'' He grinned at her horrified look. "Although I admit I took so many liberties with the truth that you wouldn't recognize the event. I made it seem like a wildly romantic gesture on your part. It will endear you to all of them, but especially my mother and Aunt Laura.''

Bria tugged on her captured hand. Her palm slid over his thigh. She wished she had left her gloves on. The warmth of Luke's leg through his trousers seemed to sear her skin. "Why would you want them to like me? Why should it matter if—''

"Because I like you,'' he said simply. "And if I gave them any cause to worry they wouldn't hesitate to descend on Concord.''

"Would that be bad?''

"It would be like the second coming of William Tecumseh Sherman.''

Bria was not certain she had ever laughed at any reference to the war before. She wondered that she could now. It seemed vaguely disrespectful, as though she were dishonoring the memory of her brothers and father. Then Luke's wryly tender and faintly horrified tone echoed in her head and she felt laughter surface again. Was this healing? she wondered.

The carriage bounced hard in a rut and when Bria landed she was inches closer to Luke. She looked at him suspiciously.

"Tad?" Luke called to the driver. "Have a care. My wife thinks you and I have conspired to put her in my lap."

"Yes, sir."

The carriage lanterns bathed Bria's face in a warm golden glow. Her eyes were luminous. She did not turn away as Luke's eyes moved over her face. When his gaze settled on her mouth she wet her lips. The gesture was artless and unconscious and all the more beckoning because of it.

Luke cupped the side of her face. His thumb lightly rubbed her cheek. It was as warm and soft as a petal turned into the sun. "I do like you," he said quietly.

"I think you really do." Her voice betrayed some sense of her surprise. "I like you, too." And then she realized she meant it. She smiled. "I do."

He laughed. "We can be friends, Bree. There's nothing in our contract that forbids it."

She did not really want to think about the contract. They had drawn it up together more than a week ago. It set out Bria's expectations very clearly and it did not preclude their right to be friends. She nodded in agreement. Luke was close enough that his laughter had tickled her lips. "I'd like that. It would be a strain to pretend that it was so if it was not."

"I was thinking the same thing. Shall we seal our pact?"

Bria thought of how her brothers had sealed pacts with one another and their friends. "Do you mean to draw blood?"

"I thought kissing would suffice. But if you prefer—"

"No," she said quickly. "Kissing is acceptable." She stole a look at Tad on his perch. "As we practiced."

He let her come to him. Bria's hands went to his shoulders. They moved together slowly until her fingers brushed strands of his coffee-colored hair. She raised her face and closed the short distance between their mouths. She pressed her lips to his.

Luke's own hands balled into tight fists. To have done otherwise would have meant taking her into his arms. That could wait. For now it was enough to have her mouth moving over his, to feel the tip of her pink tongue lapping at his lips like a kitten greedy for cream. He opened his mouth and drew her tongue inside. Her fingers tightened at the back of his neck and the sound that might well have been a gasp was swallowed by him.

The first time he touched her was to set her from him. Luke took a shallow breath and let it out slowly. He searched Bria's softened features. "I hope this means you're inclined to let me share *your* bed."

Chapter Nine

She blinked. *I hope this means you're inclined to let me share your bed.* Bria was slow in assimilating Luke's words and their meaning. "I thought that was entirely understood," she said, drawing back. "I told you—"

"You told me you weren't inclined to share *my* bed. You must see the necessity of me sharing yours."

"Actually, no. I don't see it at all."

Luke glanced toward Tad. Their driver did not seem to be engaged in eavesdropping, but Luke lowered his voice to avoid that opportunity anyway. "It can't be helped, Bree. Do you think the servants won't talk if we begin our marriage in separate bedchambers?"

Bria's whisper was harsh. "We don't have a marriage."

"I am not in need of a reminder, but perhaps you have forgotten that you desired the pretense of one."

"Mother and Orrin do not share a bedroom. No one doubts they're married."

This information was not enough to move Luke from his course. "They shared one in the beginning, didn't they?"

Bria didn't answer immediately. It occurred to her that she could lie easily enough—and be found out later. "Yes," she said finally, with little grace. "But there is no rule that we must follow suit."

Luke laughed softly. "Simply because they're not written down doesn't mean there aren't any rules. You may not recognize them until you break them, but they're there. Do you really want to risk that someone—Addie or Martha, perhaps—will say something to your mother or Orrin about our living arrangements?"

It was not the living arrangements that concerned Bria, but the sleeping ones. "You've known this from the beginning," she accused.

"Well, yes."

His simple admission did not endear him to her. "I have no liking for being cornered."

"No one does," said Luke. He started to reach for her hands and thought better of it. What he would have intended as reassurance might have been interpreted as aggression. Luke pressed his palms along the length of his thighs instead. "If the prospect of sharing a bed is too alarming, I will stay in my own room and endeavor to make it seem as if I'm a regular visitor to yours. I suppose the thing can be managed that way."

Bria immediately found she could breathe more easily and think more clearly. It was as if Luke had stopped hovering in her corner. "There is the adjoining bedroom," she said after a moment. "The one Orrin showed you the first night you came to Concord."

"Mammy Komati's old room."

"Yes. We could open the connecting door so it would appear that you use it."

Luke pretended to consider this. "I suppose we could say that your snoring disturbs my slumber."

Bria's eyes widened. "I do not snore."

"How would you know?"

The logic of that confounded her. "Oh, very well. But no one will inquire why we're sleeping in separate bedrooms, not if they're adjoining."

"The servants may only speculate, but your mother will want to know. And if she doesn't, Orrin will demand an explanation from one or both of us."

Bria sat back in the carriage seat. She had her first glimpse of Concord's lighted windows in the distance. On the perimeter of the road cottonwoods were lined up like sentinels. Lamplight from the house winked and flickered as the carriage slowly passed the attending trees.

Bria sighed. "Do you mean to be the kind of husband who is annoyingly right all the time?"

"Oh God, I hope not."

He said it so fervently, Bria was forced to laugh. "Good. I don't think I should like you at all under those circumstances." She gave him a sideways glance. "And don't interpret that to mean I like you now. I'm not at all sure I do, or ever have done."

Luke's smile was wry. "I would not presume so much."

Bria snorted softly. She gave her attention to the approaching house and pretended she wasn't at all unsettled by her surrender in the very first skirmish of their marriage.

Addie opened the door for them as soon as they reached the front portico. Jeb stood behind her in the hallway, his smile only marginally more cautious in its welcome than Addie's.

Addie clapped her hands and giggled like a young girl as Luke scooped Bria into his arms and stepped across the open doorway with her. When he would have put her down, Bria clung to his neck and cast her eyes toward the long staircase. "You started this, sir. I shall have to insist you finish it."

Jeb pulled Addie out of Luke's way. "Don' it beat all?" Jeb said. "Miss Bree's really jumped the broom."

Addie pressed one corner of her apron to her eyes as she watched Luke carry Bria up the stairs. She sniffed loudly and returned Bria's tiny finger wave. When the couple turned the corner, Addie said to Jeb, "We may as well enjoy the hot tea and cakes Elsie prepared."

"Fine idea," Jeb said. "Seems a shame to waste them."

Bria released Luke's neck as soon as they were out of sight. "Oh, put me down," she said briskly.

Luke dropped her with alacrity. "You might have said that twenty steps earlier."

"I might have," she agreed. Bria smoothed the material of her gown over her midriff. For reasons she did not entirely understand, she was the one slightly out of breath. "But you didn't deserve that consideration after hauling me across the threshold."

Luke grinned. "I haul lumber," he said. "I carried you." To prove his point he lifted Bria effortlessly, put her over his shoulder, and hauled her the rest of the way down the hall and into her bedroom. There were strangled noises coming from Bria's throat but Luke ignored them. He kicked the door closed behind him and crossed the floor to her bed. He dumped her on the mattress and stayed his ground, almost daring her to hurl something at him.

What struck him was her laughter. She was bright-eyed with it. Her beautiful features were flushed and her smile was wide and open. She flung her head back and freely gave herself up to it. He realized that the strangled sounds he'd heard weren't inarticulate protests at all. She'd been trying to restrain her laughter from the beginning.

The fact that this response completely confounded him showed on Luke's face. Bria laughed harder.

Luke sat down on the bed beside her and waited for her to quiet. There was an odd little hiccuping sound that finally signaled the denouement. Bria lay back on the bed, her legs hanging limply over the edge. One of her hands rested on her abdomen in anticipation of easing the next jerkily drawn breath.

Luke leaned over her and used his forefinger to wipe tears from the corners of her eyes. "You're as bad as Addie," he said softly. "And I thought she would flood the foyer."

Bria sobered a little. She brushed aside his hand and took up her own cause. From somewhere under her sleeve she produced a linen handkerchief and pressed it to her eyes. The evidence of her smile had not entirely faded when she finished. "You act in the most surprising ways, Mr. Kincaid."

Both of Luke's dark brows arched. He stared at Bria's brilliant eyes. "*I* do?"

"You know you do. Putting me over your shoulder was not the usual thing at all. You didn't do it to make me mad, did you? Please say that you didn't mean for me to be angry about it."

"The truth is, Mrs. Kincaid, I didn't give your reaction much thought at all. You were being a bit huffy for my tastes and I sought some redress. I didn't set out to make you mad but it would have been less surprising if you had been."

Bria considered this. "I should disagree with you," she said at last. "But I can't. It's really quite troubling. I don't think I like being so amenable."

"I doubt it represents any lasting change in your character. You'll recover momentarily."

"Do you think so?"

He nodded. "I'm sure of it." Luke lay back on the bed beside her. He brought his hands together over his chest and clasped his fingers.

Bria turned her head toward him. "What do you think you're doing?" she asked.

"I'm provoking your recovery."

"You're provoking *me*." She raised one hand and pointed to the door behind her. "Your bed is in that room."

Luke sat up but not before he dropped a light kiss on her parted lips. "You're cured."

Bria found she could not manage to give him a sour look and laugh at the same time. She settled for continuing to point to the connecting door.

Luke rose from the bed. He picked up the lamp on Bria's night table and carried it with him. The key was in the lock. He turned it and rattled the knob. He glanced over his shoulder. Bria had turned onto her stomach and was watching him closely.

"There is no point in pretending it won't open," she said. "I can always check it for myself."

Luke turned over one hand in a gesture of invitation. "By all means."

Bria had not expected him to call her on it. She was certain he was bluffing. "Luke, don't tease. Open the door."

He turned the skeleton key again, twisted the knob, then pulled. The door shook under the strength of his grip, but it didn't budge.

Bria scrambled off the bed. "This is not amusing."

Luke said nothing. He stepped aside but held the lamp up so she could clearly see what she was doing. He watched her go through the same ritual as he had with similar results.

Frustrated, Bria gave the door a little kick. It had no effect on the door but it set the nerves in her foot humming. "Damn," she swore softly. "Damn. Damn. Damn."

"Stand back," Luke said. "I have bigger feet and know more curse words."

Bria looked down at Luke's boots then up at him. His lips were twitching. "The former is certainly true," she said with some asperity. "But don't be so certain about the latter."

Luke believed her. "What do you want to do?"

"You'll have to enter the room from the hall. Let me light another lamp before you take that one away." Bria accomplished this quickly, then she sent Luke out. She was sitting in the armchair removing her shoes and stockings when he returned less than a minute later. She pushed her gown over her knees and stood. "You are not going to tell me there is some problem with the outer door."

"Not if you don't want me to."

"This is not to be believed." A tendril of hair fell over Bria's forehead and across one eye. She blew it away impatiently and stalked off after Luke when he retreated into the hallway. She pushed and pulled at the door and proved to Luke that she knew something more about cursing than he did.

"Quietly," he cautioned her. "Addie and Jeb are still up. They'll hear you."

Bria sagged against the door. She closed her eyes and pressed one hand to her temple. "Can you fix this in the morning?" she asked wearily.

"Of course. I can fix it now if you'd like."

"I'd like," she said. "But that's bound to raise questions I don't want to answer tonight." She stopped massaging her temple and raised her eyes to his. "You can have the floor in my room."

"I prefer my own bed to that, thank you."

Bria realized they could not have this argument in the hallway. She pushed away from the door and, taking Luke by the sleeve of his jacket, led him back to her bedchamber. When they were behind closed doors again, she rounded on him. "You gave me all the reasons earlier why you shouldn't sleep in your own bed."

"That was when the alternative was sharing yours," he said. "Not sleeping on the floor. Taking the adjoining bedroom was a compromise that at least made sense. This does not."

"Then *I'll* sleep on the floor."

"All right."

Bria's jaw sagged a little at the swiftness with which he accepted these terms. "Are you quite serious?" she asked. "You mean to let me sleep on the floor?"

"I mean to let you share that bed with me if you have a mind to," Luke said. "Whatever else you do is your choice." He walked over to the bed and set the lamp on the table. "In the event you decide to join me, which is your usual side?"

"I have no usual side. I'm a restless sleeper. I sprawl."

Luke saw that she hoped to put him off with this news. In fact, the vision of Bria's arms and legs tangling with his was not at all unwelcome. "I'll make every effort to accommodate you."

"That will not be necessary." She went to the cedar chest at the foot of the bed and began removing blankets and linens.

Bria made a place for herself on the rug in front of the fireplace. She smoothed the blankets and tested the softness with the palm of her hand. It was nothing more than adequate.

Behind her she heard Luke's boots thump to the floor one at a time. She sat back and looked over her shoulder. He was shrugging out of his jacket. "You don't intend to change here, do you?"

"I don't intend to change at all. What I intend to do is strip to my drawers and crawl into bed."

Bria turned her head quickly and closed her eyes as if it would provide additional protection. "Don't you have a nightshirt?"

"In my own room."

"I'll get it for you."

"That's ridiculous. We're not sleeping together. Stay just as you are and I'll be under the covers in a minute."

It took somewhat longer than that. Bria ticked off the seconds in her own mind, gritting her teeth when she heard him washing at her nightstand and taking more care with his own clothes than she believed was strictly necessary. It wasn't until she heard the creak of the mattress that she finally turned on him. She had a glimpse of Luke's sun-kissed shoulders and chest as he was bringing the sheet around to cover himself. Bria spoke just to prove that her mouth hadn't gone dry.

"Now how am I supposed to change?"

"What?" Luke propped himself on one elbow. The sheet slid easily over his shoulder and halfway down his ribcage. "You sound like you have marbles in your mouth. You're not practicing oration, are you?"

"I'm practicing patience," she said clearly. "Turn your back."

"Do you want me to blow out these lamps?"

"No!" Bria held out her hand to emphasize her wishes. In Luke's haste to be accommodating, his sheet was slipping even lower. "I'll extinguish one and turn back the other."

Luke nodded. He wished he hadn't forgotten that Bria did not sleep in the dark. He made no comment as she approached the bedside table. Her clear skin absorbed the glow of the lamplight. She bent closer to the twin flames and lifted one of the glass globes. Her pink mouth puckered as if to receive a kiss. She blew gently. The light flickered and then was gone. She turned back the wick on the second lamp.

"You haven't turned away," Bria said, annoyed. She took one of the pillows from the bed and tossed it on her blankets. "You can't have both of them. Now, roll over."

Feeling rather more like Bria's pet spaniel than her husband, Luke obeyed. At least she hadn't demanded that he sit up and beg. He would have done that with a speed that would have alarmed her and embarrassed himself. The sound that erupted from his throat was somewhere between a growl and a laugh.

"What was that?" Bria asked. She was fairly dancing in place as she struggled with the tiny pearl buttons at the back of her gown.

"Nothing."

"It wasn't a snore, was it? You're not already snoring?"

"I don't snore," he said. "And I *would* know."

Bria stopped trying to work the buttons. After he'd told her there was no wife, fiancée, or sweetheart, she hadn't given any thought to his experience with other women. She let her hands fall to her sides. "Have you known a great many women?" she asked.

"How can you doubt it? Nana Dearborn. My mother. Aunt Nancy. Aunt—"

"I wasn't referring to them. I meant other women."

"Then I suppose I'd have to know what you mean by a great many and if by knowing them you mean in the biblical sense."

"More than two," Bria said. "And yes, in the biblical sense." She saw him start to turn over. "No, stay where you are. I'm not finished. I can't get all these buttons."

Luke sighed. "You should let me assist you. I have some practice with that. I've been helping women in and out of their dresses since I was in short pants."

Bria laughed softly. "You're talking about the aunts again."

"I should be wounded that you guessed that so quickly." Without looking in her direction, Luke raised a hand and crooked his finger. "I promise I'll keep my eyes closed."

Bria was not certain she believed him but she skirted the bed and cedar chest and came to stand on the side closest to him. She sat down on the very edge and heard him change position to move nearer. "Just a few more buttons," she said. "Then I can wriggle out myself."

"As you wish. I'm peeking just once to get started." He found the first button and promptly closed his eyes. "Do you really want to know about the other women?" he asked.

"No," Bria admitted. The touch of his fingers was as light as butterflies dancing on a petal. "It was the wrong question anyway. I think what I wanted to know is if you've ever been in love."

"Aaah," he said. "A very different question." Luke found another button and slipped it through the opening. He could feel the warmth of her skin through the silk and no difference in the texture. "Miss Abigail Chesterfield. I was very much in love with her."

Bria tried to turn. She wanted to see his face.

"My eyes are still closed," he said.

But that hadn't been why she wanted to look. She almost told him that. She held back the words instead and wondered why she had been moved to offer any words of regret in the first place. If she wasn't careful Luke might come to believe *she* was a romantic. "Tell me about Miss Chesterfield."

Luke laughed. "She'd have blackened both your eyes if you'd called her that. Abby was the only name she answered to and she was the best pool player on Water Street. Every boy in Five Points was in love with her."

One of Bria's brows kicked up. "How old were you?"

"Six."

"And how old was she?"

"Thirteen, I think. I thought a lot about her during the time I lived with Nana Dearborn. That's how I knew I was in love.

I thought about her more than Jack Greer and Jack was my best friend.''

"I suppose that's as good a measure of true love as any I could name. Did you ever see her again?''

Luke finished undoing Bria's buttons. He felt her rise from the bed. When he opened his eyes she was standing in front of him trying to keep the neckline of her gown in place. She could manage one shoulder or the other, but not both at the same time. He was almost thankful when she moved quickly out of the line of his vision and returned to her nest in front of the fireplace. He kept his back to her and shifted under the sheets. What he was finding was that there was no comfortable position for the heaviness in his groin—at least not one that didn't involve being deep inside Bria.

"Did you see her again?'' Bria repeated. She shimmied out of her gown and tossed it on a chair. She plucked her nightgown from a peg inside the armoire, then dove under the covers.

Luke's voice was a tad hoarse when he finally answered. He knew himself to be a voyeur even if it was only in his mind's eye. Every rustle of silk and batiste tortured him. "I saw her,'' Luke said. "I went looking for Abby as soon as I'd finished unpacking. She had one child in one arm and another hanging on her skirts. She was waiting her turn with the cue in Campbell Allen's saloon.'' He sighed. "Abby still looked wickedly lovely. I lost two dollars to her that afternoon.''

The rustling stopped abruptly. Bria's head came out from under the covers and she stared at Luke's back, frowning. "Precisely how did you lose that money?''

He chuckled. "Playing pool.'' Luke turned on his other side and faced Bria. He watched her drag the covers over her head. "What? Did you think I paid for my pleasure?''

She snorted. "There's no pleasure in it.''

Luke waited until she was finished rooting under the blankets. When her head emerged so did a handful of undergarments. She pushed them out and straightened her shift, then she folded her pillow and slid one arm beneath it. She laid her cheek against the pillow and closed her eyes. "Bree?"

"Hmmm?"

Luke's voice was gentle. "There's pleasure in it."

Bria's fingers curled into a loose fist. She made no reply. She heard the sound of his evenly drawn breaths long before she slept herself.

Addie knocked on the door to Bria's bedchamber. When there was no answer she pressed her ear to the wood. It was quiet. She frowned and looked at Martha. The tray in Martha's hands bobbled a bit as they weighed their options.

"Hard to know what to do," Addie said. "Miss Bree won't like sleeping the day away."

"Like as not she's tuckered."

Addie tried to ignore Martha's wink and grin but it was impossible to temper her own smile. "That's a fact. Maybe we should wait."

Both women started as the door was drawn open. Luke's head poked around the corner, but past his disheveled head Addie and Martha could see Bria sleeping soundly in the center of the big bed. A mound of blankets lay on the floor beside her where she had kicked them off. One foot dangled over the edge of the bed; one arm was flung across the space Luke had vacated. Her hair spilled over the cases of both pillows and her head was turned so they could see a sweetly satisfied smile on her parted lips.

"Oh my, Mr. Luke," Addie whispered. She stared wide-eyed at Bria. "Oh me, oh my."

"I'll take that as a compliment," Luke told her. He glanced down at the tray Martha was gripping. "And I'll take this as breakfast. Good morning, ladies." He had to give a small tug to get Martha to relinquish the tray. When he had it firmly in hand he nudged the door closed, but not before he caught Martha's whispered aside.

"She's tuckered, all right. I'm thinkin' my man should make me that tuckered."

"Hush, Martha." But Addie was smiling as she said it.

Luke was grinning himself as he turned away. He set the tray on the bed then eased himself onto the mattress. "You can open your eyes now, Bree. You convinced them all is as it should be. I almost believe it myself." He had the persistent ache in his groin to keep him a skeptic. Luke pushed the arm Bria had flung across the bed away from him and closer to her. "Up," he commanded. He drew his legs up tailor fashion and leaned over the tray. Lifting the lids on each of the dishes, Luke savored the aromas and announced the presence of a feast.

Bleary-eyed, Bria pushed herself upright. Her nose wrinkled charmingly as Luke investigated breakfast and the odors wafted in her direction. She ran one hand through her tangled hair and pushed it back over her shoulder. She blinked at Luke as he waved a slice of bacon under her nose. Her eyes crossed. She managed to get it anyway.

"Don't you have a shirt?" she asked. He took up a great deal of the bed sitting there like that, and everything above his waist was naked.

"Good morning, Mrs. Kincaid." He was smiling as he pointed to the chair where Bria had thrown her gown. "It's under there."

Bria turned to look where he pointed. When she came around again it was to find his face very close to hers.

"I said, good morning, Mrs. Kincaid." Luke kissed her lightly on the mouth, counting on her being too startled to strike him.

"I thought stolen moments were supposed to happen when someone was nearby."

Luke drew back. "Consider it a rehearsal. It will be a long day of performing, although you started it out well enough. I didn't expect you could move so quickly from the floor to the bed." She had brought him out of a dead sleep by diving headlong into bed beside him. "Did you hear them coming or did Addie's knock wake you?"

"I heard them on the stairs." Bria reached for a plate and served herself some eggs and another slice of bacon. "I'm a light sleeper," she lied, tucking into her eggs. The truth was she had simply slept fitfully all night and into the morning. Her shoulders and back ached. There was a knot at the base of her neck that she was afraid to massage for fear of giving her discomfort away.

"Then you weren't troubled by sleeping on the floor?"

"No." Bria reached for a warm biscuit and took a bite. It removed some of the unpleasant taste of lying from her mouth. "Not at all." There were a lot of biscuits. She could probably lie for hours if she rationed herself. "Still, you need to do something about the doors to Mammy's room."

"As soon as we've passed a proper amount of time here. Addie and Martha will expect that we won't want to leave soon." Luke held up his hands, palms out, when Bria's mouth flattened and her eyes narrowed on his innocent expression. "It was that beatific smile you gave them that did it," he said. "If you wanted to leave this room before noon you shouldn't have overplayed your hand. Tell me, what were you really thinking?"

Bria shook her head. "I don't have to show you my cards." Then she bent her head and applied herself to her meal.

"I been thinking, Mr. Luke," said Addie.

Luke looked up from his work. He was on his hands and knees on the third-floor landing, scraping paint from the wainscoting. There were flakes of white paint in his hair and on his clothes. He straightened, stretched, and brushed his trousers. "What about, Addie?"

"Mammy Komati's room."

"And?" After Bria had gone riding this morning, Luke retrieved the keys that really fit both doors and opened them just as he'd promised. Addie couldn't be referring to that. "You'll have to elaborate."

Addie pressed her hands flat against her apron. "Well, it's just that you and Miss Bree will be needing some extra space. With Mr. Orrin in the master suite and Miss Elizabeth in a large room of her own, it seems that you and Miss Bree could be a bit cramped."

Luke moved to the steps and sat down there. He tapped the paint scraper against one knee as he considered what Addie was trying to propose. "Go on."

"It's just that Miss Bree's room used to be the nursery. It's not very big. But then you have Mammy's vacant room right there beside it. Wouldn't it make a good dressing room? We could remove Mammy's bed and bring in the armoire from your room. Martha is going to move your belongings anyway. It stands to reason we should move what they're stored in."

"Stands to reason," Luke said slowly. His grin surfaced as he considered Bria's reaction to this plan. Until an opportunity for change presented itself, he had been resigned to sleeping on Mammy's narrow bed. "Have you mentioned this to Bria?"

"No, sir. She's still gone from the house and I'd like to have this settled before dinner."

"Very well, Addie. Go ahead, but don't you and Martha take it upon yourselves to move that armoire and Mammy's old bed. Some of the men working for me will help you. As for telling Miss Bree, why don't you mention it at dinner this evening? Say, when you're serving dessert?" There was no reason the entire meal should be spoiled.

Luke managed to keep Bria from going to their room before dinner to freshen up. When Addie finally announced all she had been about that afternoon, Bria simply sat back in her chair in stunned silence. Across the table from her Luke shrugged helplessly. The smile that touched his grey eyes was both innocent and mischievous.

"You might have talked her out of it," Bria said after Addie was gone from the dining room. "Did you even try?"

"No objection occurred to me. What could I say? No, Addie, don't change anything because my wife expects me to sleep in her Mammy's bed?"

"A simple 'no' would have been sufficient. You wouldn't have had to explain yourself."

"Perhaps you wouldn't have, but I think Addie would have wanted something from me."

Bria pushed away her uneaten apple dumpling. "Well, what are we to do? Have you at least considered that? I can't very well ask her to return everything back the way it was."

"No, I suppose you can't." Luke eyed her dessert. "Are you going to eat that?"

Bria shook her head. She watched him reach across the table and pull it toward him. "How can you be unaffected by this?"

"I'm affected," he said. "It's only my appetite that's unchanged." Luke did not miss Bria's heavy, resigned sigh. He took a quick bite of the dumpling to occupy his mouth with something other than a triumphant smile.

"I don't imagine that you would be willing to give up the bed."

"I don't imagine I would." He gave her a considering look. "I'm still willing to share."

Bria declined the offer that evening and for every evening that followed. At their one-week anniversary she had pale violet shadows under her eyes and enough aches to come to Addie's attention.

When Addie came across Bria catnapping in the drawing room, she realized she could no longer keep her thoughts to herself. Bria stirred as Addie placed a blanket over her shoulders.

"What time is it?" she asked sleepily.

Addie clucked her tongue gently. "Poor dear. The hall clock just struck half past eight. Would you like some help to your room? Have an early night?"

"No," Bria said quickly. The divan was comfortable. "I'm quite fine here."

Addie's dark eyes were knowing. "I should say you are. I hope I can speak my mind, but Mr. Luke hasn't let you sleep nearly enough. If Miss Elizabeth were here she'd tell you that you don't have to lie under him every night."

Embarrassed, Bria squeezed her eyes closed and moaned softly. She couldn't think of anything to say to allay Addie's concerns or make her stop talking.

"I thought Mr. Luke would have some sense about it, but the man ain't thinkin' right when he's around you. It's plain to all of us that he'd keep you in bed all day if he could." Addie patted Bria's shoulder. "You rest here a bit longer. I'll have young Jenny draw you a bath and put salts in it to ease your soreness. Mr. Luke's gone to see John. If you like I'll have a talk with him when he returns."

Bria hardly knew what to do with all the emotion welling up inside her. She was at once touched and embarrassed by Addie's worry and interest. She wanted to laugh that so much was misunderstood and cry with frustration because she could not explain it.

Bria opened her eyes and found Addie's hand. She squeezed it to reassure Addie and emphasize her own words. "Don't say anything to Mr. Luke. I'm a married woman now, Addie. I'll manage my husband in my own way."

"Mr. Luke isn't Concord," Addie said. "And he's not Orrin Foster. The day ever comes when you think you're managing Mr. Luke, you tell Addie. That's the day I'll know for sure that he's plum managed you."

Bria was not certain she liked the sound of that. Her brow puckered as she considered what Addie meant.

Addie removed her hand from Bria's and stood. "Don't strain yourself thinkin' on it," she said. "I'll just go see about that bath now."

It was late when Luke entered the bedroom he shared with Bria. He expected, as he often had, to find her asleep on the floor. Only once had she attempted to secure the bed. As soon as he slipped in beside her she woke and, realizing that he could not be moved, wearily removed herself. Tonight that was not the case. He found her in the dressing room up to her pretty shoulders in water.

Luke stopped on the threshold and waited for her to acknowledge his presence. Her eyes opened slowly. They were soft, vaguely unfocused. The lids were heavy. Her thick lashes added depth to the violet shadows. "I didn't mean to wake you," Luke said. He cleared his throat to cover the husky timbre in his voice. "I didn't expect to find you here."

"Is it so late already?" Bria was aware of his habit of coming late to their room. She was rarely asleep when he entered though she often pretended to be. "I should be getting out."

Luke picked up Bria's towel and handed it to her. He pretended not to notice that she sunk a little more deeply into the tub. Her shoulders sparkled with diamond droplets of water. "Do you require assistance?"

"No." She carefully patted her face dry and belatedly added, "Thank you."

It was the answer Luke had expected but it still had the power to disappoint him. In the presence of others Bria never seemed to make a misstep. When they were alone, however, she was often uncertain and wary. Luke started to excuse himself from the room when she stopped him.

"I've been thinking," she said quietly, "that if you'd like to . . . that is, if you want . . . well, I've been thinking that I could bear it."

For a moment he said nothing. "Bear it?" he asked finally. "Is that what you think I want from you? That you should simply have to bear it?" Luke walked out and shut the door behind him.

He was in bed by the time Bria came into the room. Only a single oil lamp remained burning, its wick turned back just the way she would have left it herself. It touched her that he had done this small thing. He never once complained about letting the flame burn itself out each night.

Bria tightened the belt of her robe as she approached the

bed. Luke was turned on his side away from her. "Are you angry?" she asked. When he didn't answer, she asked, "Are you sleeping?"

Luke rolled onto his back. He laid his forearm across his brow and stared up at Bria. "No and no."

"Oh."

He lifted the hand that lay outside the covers at his side and extended it to Bria. "Come here."

For once she didn't hesitate. Bria placed her hand in his and let herself be pulled easily onto the bed. She sat cross-legged at the level of his waist. Her robe parted and the lawn fabric of her nightgown was stretched taut across her knees. The coil of her damp hair had loosened. She could feel the uncomfortable weight of it at her nape.

"Here," Luke said when Bria started to fiddle with her hair. "Let me." He sat up and repositioned himself behind her. His fingers plucked at the anchoring pins. He set them on the bed, then unwrapped the heavy coil of dark-honey hair. "Do you trust me, Bria?"

"You know I do." Her head tipped back slightly and her eyes closed. His fingers felt very good threading through her hair. "I told you I did the evening of our first meeting."

"You were referring to my ability to restore this house," he reminded her. "I was wondering if you'd come to trust me in other ways."

"I asked you to marry me."

"You're trusting me to get Concord back for you."

"Then I don't know what you're asking. How do you want me to trust you?"

"As a man."

"I don't understand."

His fingers stilled. Luke leaned forward until his mouth was close to Bria's ear. "Yes, you do."

Bria's fingers closed into fists. Tears pressed against the back of her lids. "I'm afraid," she said on a thread of sound. "All the time I'm afraid."

He nodded. His fingers left her hair as his arms came around her. He pulled her back against his chest and nudged her head with his chin. "I don't want you to be afraid of me. Ever. I won't hurt you, Bree. Sleep with me tonight. Share the bed. There was never any reason for you to spend a single night on the floor. I won't touch you; not when you think it is something that must be borne, not enjoyed."

Luke tipped his head to one side and lightly kissed her temple. Her skin was warm and soft under his lips. His mouth trailed to the curve of her ear. He felt her shiver. The circle of his embrace tightened. "It *is* something that can be enjoyed, though," he whispered. "When you're ready, I'll prove it to you."

"What if I'm never ready?" Bria absorbed the vibration of Luke's deep and husky laughter. She shivered again.

"You will be." He leaned back and began to comb out her hair. In a few minutes she was almost boneless. Luke helped her shrug out of her robe and laid her back on the bed. She burrowed deeply into the covers he pulled over her. She didn't stir once, not when he reached across her to extinguish the lamp and not when he stretched out beside her. It was the first time since their wedding that Bria fell asleep before her husband.

It was just as breakfast was being served that Jeb announced Orrin and Elizabeth had returned. Bria's head shot up and she stared at Luke. "They're early," she said.

Luke nodded. "Three weeks."

"They must have learned about the wedding."

Luke had reached the same conclusion. He stood and came around the table for Bria. He held her chair as she rose. "It will be all right," he whispered.

"You can't know that."

"I'm only repeating what you told me when you fashioned this scheme."

She had the grace to look a shade guilty. "I think I may

have lied." Bria sighed. "You'd better take my arm. My legs are not as steady as they should be."

Luke escorted Bria outside to the portico. Jeb rushed ahead to greet the carriage as soon as it stopped and help unload the trunks.

Bria stood at the lip of the uppermost step and raised herself on tiptoe. She followed the progress of the carriage as it turned from the road into the drive. It was moving at a good clip and even at a distance Bria could see that it was not weighed down by all that her mother had packed. "Mother must be in a hurry to see us," she told Luke. "She's returning with less than half of what she took with her."

Luke refrained from reminding Bria that it might have been Orrin's anxiousness that had provoked the early return, not Elizabeth's. He waited beside her on the step until the carriage came to a halt in front of the house. Then there was no holding Bria back. She loosed herself from his arm and ran to meet her mother.

Orrin was first out of the carriage. His face was darkly flushed and anger fairly vibrated from him. None of that changed when he saw Bria. He turned to help Elizabeth but spoke to his stepdaughter. "I hope you can do something with her," he said roughly. "She hasn't stopped weeping since we heard the news. God, but I'm weary of a woman's tears. I need a drink."

Elizabeth Hamilton Foster alighted from the carriage. Her face was drawn and pale. Except for the violet bruising around her eyes, the complexion she guarded carefully with parasols and shade trees was colorless. She was a petite woman with refined features. She had delicate hands, narrow shoulders, and a tiny waist. Her fragility was magnified by the careful way she stepped down from the carriage and the quickness with which she accepted Bria's help. For all of that, Elizabeth's chestnut-colored eyes held no recognition when she turned to her daughter. She never once raised her handkerchief to stem the flow of tears.

"Mother?" Bria's heart moved to her throat. She looked to Orrin for an explanation. Her mother's current state was out of all proportion to the news of Bria's wedding. "What has happened to her, Orrin?'' But Orrin was already moving up the steps. ''What have you done to her?'' she called after him.

''Not a damn thing,'' Orrin muttered. He brushed past Luke on his way into the house.

Luke hurried down the stairs. Jeb was already supporting Elizabeth on her other side.

''I got her, Miss Bree,'' Jeb said. ''You can let go. I'll take her straightaway to her room. Do you want me to send Tad for Dr. Edwards?''

Bree stepped back. ''I don't know. Mother? Do you require a doctor? Are you hurt? Did Orrin hurt you?''

Elizabeth shook her head. The effort caused her knees to buckle. Jeb held her upright but it was Luke who lifted her. ''It's all right, Jeb. I'll carry her. Help the driver with her trunks and send Tad for the doctor. Bree, come with me.''

She didn't question that he should take charge. Bria ran ahead, opening doors for him and turning down her mother's bed. She hovered there until Luke drew her into the hallway when Addie arrived.

''There's nothing you can do for her just now,'' Luke told her. ''She's not entirely coherent. I'm not certain she knows who you are.''

Bria nodded. Her hands were cold, her heart colder. She crossed her arms in front of her chest to ward off the chill. ''What's wrong with her? I've only ever seen—'' She broke off as a horrible realization dawned. ''Oh my God, no. No!'' Bria spun on her heel and threw off Luke's effort to catch her. She ran down the hallway, descended the stairs two at a time, and threw open the doors to Orrin's study. He was slumped in the large wing chair when she charged into the room.

Bria knocked the tumbler from Orrin's hand. Bourbon spilled into his lap and the glass clattered heavily to the floor. ''Look at me, damn you!'' Bria cried. ''Is it Rand? Is that what you don't want to tell me? Is it Rand?''

Orrin looked up at her. His lips twisted derisively and his rheumy eyes were still clear enough to challenge her. ''And good riddance, I say. To Rand, to that black bastard who sails with him, and to every other soul on board. They're all gone. *Cerberus* is gone. Your goddamn Hamilton riddle is gone."

"No!" Bria was shaking. "You're making this up to hurt Mother! You're lying now to hurt us both!"

Luke had heard enough. He silently crossed the room and put his arms around Bria. She struggled at first then simply sagged against him, pressing her face in the curve of his neck. Over the top of her head, Luke kept his eyes on Orrin's. "Is it true?" he asked.

Orrin nodded. He was no longer smiling, but watching Bria's response to Lucas Kincaid closely. "The news came into Charleston last night. I expect it will be in today's paper. We didn't wait to read about it. I confirmed it with the authorities myself. Seems the ship went down in a gale off the South American coast. Only thing known for certain is that every body washed ashore was a dead one and the ship was *Cerberus*. As best anyone can tell, it was on its return voyage."

Luke laid one hand on Bria's back and rubbed it gently. Her trembling remained unabated. "Come," he whispered. "I'll take you upstairs."

Bria slept the remainder of the morning and a good part of the afternoon. She gave herself over to Luke's care absent of any protest. She heard him conferring with Dr. Edwards but had no interest in the conversation. She ate when he arrived with food and drank when he placed a glass to her lips. He spoke to her in quiet, serious tones about her mother's condition and while Bria listened intently it seemed Luke's voice simply flowed over her like a gently rolling wave. In the end she had nothing to hold onto.

Luke shared dinner with her in their room. Bria calmly accepted the news that he had informed Orrin of their marriage. She did not ask about Orrin's reaction and Luke didn't tell her about the pistol Orrin waved at him.

It was not desolation that kept Bria silent and still. The depth of that emotion would have been *something*. What she had now was nothing. She could not feel or hear the beat of her own heart. When her nails scored the delicate skin of her wrist there was no pain. Thoughts came to her slowly or not at all. There was more clarity when she observed herself taking some action than there was in the action itself.

Luke lay in bed watching her. Bria sat curled on the window seat, her knees drawn up, the side of her head resting against the pane. She was turned toward him but appeared unaware of his study. Moonlight limned her features. Her skin had the lustrous, translucent quality of the pearly underside of an oyster shell. In spite of the cool evening and the breeze that made the curtains flutter, she wore no robe, only her shift. Her fingers moved absently along the blue ribbon that gathered the neckline.

Luke pushed himself up on one elbow. His movement didn't draw her attention. "Are you going to spend the night there?" he asked quietly.

Bria shook her head. Her unbound hair fell over her shoulder. "I was waiting for you to fall asleep. I think it will be a restless night for me. I didn't want to disturb you."

"You're disturbing me now. Come here."

For the first time that day Bria hesitated in taking Luke's direction. She met his eyes and saw that they were very dark at the centers, very intent. Something outside herself pushed Bria to her feet. She padded soundlessly to the bed and when Luke lifted the covers she slipped in beside him.

Luke stayed propped on an elbow, his face close to hers. "I'm so sorry, Bria."

She nodded. Her mouth was dry. Under the sheet her hand searched for his. Her fingers closed around it. He did not resist as she lifted it and brought it to her breast. She watched him, afraid he would not understand, and she had no words to explain it.

Luke's voice was infinitely gentle. "Are you certain, Bree? It's not meant to be punishment."

She nodded. "I want to feel again," she whispered. "Even if I think I can't bear it, I want to feel again."

Chapter Ten

The curve of Luke's palm was filled by her breast. Beneath the sheer lawn fabric of Bria's shift her skin was cool. Her nipple puckered under his hand. He removed it carefully from under hers, sliding it out so that his fingers ran over her like five separate rivulets of water. They came together again below her breast, over her ribs. Her skin retracted as she drew in a shallow breath.

Luke lifted his hand and pushed back the blankets to the level of her waist. Moonlight and pale grey shadows defined the line of her throat and narrow shoulders. Her shift was like a gossamer web across her skin; her mouth a dark wound. She stared at him with eyes that were very nearly black.

He cupped her face and held it as he might have held spun glass. His fingers touched the arc of her ear and his thumb rested on the corner of her mouth. Luke bent his head and laid his lips over the small shadowed crease between her brows. He kissed her silky hairline next, then her temple. His mouth touched her cool cheek.

Luke raised his head and searched Bria's still features. He let his fingertips lightly brush her cheek; he tucked a silky strand of hair behind her ear. Luke's eyes fell on the faint pulse beating in her throat.

"Are you breathing?" he whispered.

Bria's nod was almost imperceptible, more a matter of lowering and raising her eyes.

It made Luke smile. He moved closer, changing his position so that beneath the blankets his body lay along the length of hers. His penis was heavy and rigid, engorged with blood and pressing against his silkaline drawers. There was no mistaking it for anything but what it was. Luke couldn't miss Bria's widening eyes.

"That's for much later," he told her. "I may not use it at all."

Her eyes were still wary but there was a slender smile hovering about her lips. Her glance moved away from him slowly, shyly. "I never know what you'll say."

"I surprise myself sometimes." He lowered his mouth to her shoulder and hid his smile there. He traced the line of her collarbone. At her throat he sipped her skin and left a faint mark where he worried it with his teeth. When she arched her neck he kissed the underside of her chin.

"Just as we rehearsed," he said. Then he pressed his lips to hers.

Her mouth was damp where she had touched her tongue to it. Luke nudged her lips apart. He tasted her. Running his tongue along the underside of her lips was like dipping into honey. She was sweet and warm. He pushed past the ridge of her teeth, teasing on his first foray, retreating to kiss the corner of her mouth, her jaw, the hollow just below her ear, then returning suddenly to her mouth and being more insistent this time, suckling her lips and deepening the kiss.

Bria's fingers sought purchase in the sheets, clutching the material until it was gathered in her fists. Luke's weight seemed to push the air from her lungs and his mouth stole the remainder of her breath. He was not even fully on top of her. He lay on one side of her, not between her thighs. He hadn't tried to shove her gown to her waist or trap her with his arms and legs. He really only held her in place with the pressure of his mouth and kisses that were not so different from others they had shared.

Luke lifted his head. He turned more fully on his side again and rested on one elbow so he could study her face. Bria's eyes were tightly shut. He laid a hand on her shoulder and ran it over the rigid length of her arm until he came to her clenched fist. "Bree," he said softly. "Look at me."

She opened her eyes. Luke. His dark hair was tousled and showed the tracks of his fingers through the thick of it. His sweetly crooked smile had taken a wry twist as he searched her face. Moonlight gave his grey eyes a silvery cast. His expression was faintly mocking but Bria never sensed that he was mocking anyone but himself.

Bria unfolded the fingers of one hand and raised them to Luke's mouth. She touched his lips just as he would have spoken. "I don't want you to stop," she whispered.

Luke held her hand and pressed a kiss to her fingertips before he drew it away. "You don't understand. If I think I'm forcing you, there's no pleasure in it."

"But—"

"I'm not one of them."

Bria did not have to ask who he meant. Ohio. Daniel. George. "Perhaps I should keep my eyes open this time."

Luke sat up. Without touching Bria, he levered himself over her and got out of the bed on the other side. He held out his hand to her. "If you're so determined . . ."

Bria placed her hand in his and allowed herself to be pulled up. As she scooted off the mattress her shift was rucked up to the tops of her thighs. She saw Luke's eyes drop to her bare legs. In a moment that was oddly self-aware, Bria realized she was coming to her feet with deliberate slowness, and that Luke's gaze on her legs was not entirely unwelcome. The shift fluttered to her ankles.

She followed Luke to the window seat. He sat down first,

taking the place in the corner where she had been only a short time ago. He drew one leg up while the other stretched at an angle toward the floor. He tugged her wrist and pulled her onto the seat between his thighs. His body supported her like a favorite and familiar wing chair. His shoulders and arms protected her. Her back rested against his chest.

Bria's head tilted slightly to one side. When she was still she could feel his breath shifting strands of her hair.

They sat like that for a long time. One of his hands rested on her hip, the other held her elbow. His chin sometimes rubbed the back of her head. His breathing was steady and light and as the minutes passed she felt the cadence of her own breathing match the gentle rise and fall of his chest.

"I was watching you earlier," he said quietly. "While you were sitting here. Did you know that?" Luke felt the small, negative shake of her head against his chin. "I wanted to join you, but I also wanted to look at you. You're so very lovely, Bree."

"Don't—"

"You *are* lovely."

"Is it so important?"

"I don't know. It just *is*. I wasn't flattering you."

She twisted her head a little and caught his eye. "I don't mind being flattered," she whispered.

"Liar." His fingers threaded in her hair. "You hate it." He tugged and brought her head back. Her mouth was lifted to his. He kissed her hard, without warning. When the moment of surprise had passed she was kissing him back. His other hand lay lightly against her throat. He felt the thrumming of her pulse at his fingertips. She arched a few degrees and started to twist in his hold. He broke the kiss and looked down at her. Her eyes were darkening at the centers.

It was a beginning.

Bria finished drawing the breath Luke had cut off. She sagged a little against him and felt his fingers begin sifting through her hair. The movement was as gentling as his breath at her ear. He whispered her name. The sound of it traveled under her skin all the way to her womb.

He lifted the heavy fall of her hair and moved it to one side. His mouth touched the side of her neck, then her nape. He kissed her shoulder, once where the nightgown covered it, once where it didn't. His forefinger slipped under the fine lawn fabric and ran slowly back and forth along the edge. On some passes his knuckle brushed her skin.

The strap fell. The moon's pale light was reflected on her shoulder. He kissed her there again.

Bria's skin warmed with each pass of Luke's hand across her shoulder and arm. When his kiss tripped a shiver that ran the length of her spine, it was not because she was cold or revolted by his touch. Excitement and apprehension sparked that reaction but she never thought once about leaving the embrace of Luke's body.

The other strap fell. Luke eased the material past her elbow. The neckline of her gown slipped lower until it hovered at the curve of her breasts. Her hand lifted, hesitated, then fingered the ribbon edging. She leaned forward just a fraction. The fabric fell lower across her back.

Bria swiveled her head so she could see Luke. "Breathe," she said softly. Then she let the ribbons go.

Her breasts were pale in the moonlight, the nipples dark rose. From Luke's vantage each breast was as exquisitely formed as the apple used to tempt Adam. He found that Bria's direction was needed. His breath hissed as he sucked in air between his teeth.

Luke slipped an arm around Bria just below her breasts. She fell back into the protective curve of his body, a little stiffly at first, then with more familiarity as she became used to the weight of his arm across her ribs. Her head rested against his shoulder.

"Put my hand on your breast."

Bria closed her eyes briefly. His breath had been warm against her ear. The sensitive skin at the base of her neck prickled with awareness. The undersides of her breasts lay lightly on his forearm. If she moved, breathed, there was the delicate shift in surface tension between their bodies. His skin to her skin, touching but not joined.

Her hand found his. She shaped his fingers into a shallow cradle and lifted it to within a hairsbreadth of her skin. Her chest rose and fell; her erect nipple grazed his palm. She pressed his hand against her breast and held it there.

"Look at it, Bria. Look at us."

Bria bent her head and looked down at herself. Beneath her hand, Luke's fingers were long and slender and darker than her own. Her skin looked almost colorless next to his.

"It's my hand," he whispered. "Mine."

She nodded. Bria could not mistake it for anyone else's. She had seen this capable hand gripping a hammer, taking up Apollo's reins, manipulating a deck of cards. She had watched this hand rake his hair. Bria was familiar with the tiny crescent scar on the back of his fourth knuckle. She knew there was a writer's callous on his middle finger. It was a beautiful hand. Gentle. Deft. Strong. It turned with a commanding presence when he wanted to emphasize a point. It pressed against his temple when he was thinking hard.

Now it held her breast with such infinite tenderness that Bria felt an ache in her throat.

Her voice was husky. "I know your hand."

"And this one?"

Bria watched him raise the other one and place it on her thigh. His fingers gathered the fabric of her nightgown, pulling up the the hem until it was lifted above her knee. She smiled faintly. "I know this hand, too."

Luke nodded. His fingers went still. "Good." He slipped his hand under her shift and touched the skin at the back of her knee. He felt her raise it slightly. His fingers slid along her thigh, first along the underside, then along the curve, and finally across the top from knee to hip. There was no rhythm to the caress. It was light, then firm. Long, then short. It paused on her knee and again at her hip. It moved in a straight line; it arced in a long spiral.

What was never in doubt was that the exploration had a destination and that it lay between her thighs.

Watching his hand, Bria shifted restlessly. A small sound that could have been protest or encouragement was trapped at the back of her throat. Just above her knee, Luke's fingers stilled a second time.

His mouth moved against Bria's hair. "What do you want?"

At first she could only mouth the word. She turned her head and said it again, this time with her lips close to his. "More."

Bria lifted her face. The distance between their mouths disappeared. She kissed him. Nudged his lips apart with her own. There was pressure and passion in the movement. Her tongue flicked his mouth and took his next breath as her own.

Bria released Luke's hand at her breast. She felt his palm contract around her, squeezing lightly, kneading, learning the shape and texture of her flesh. His fingertips grazed her skin. He rolled the hardened tip of her nipple between his thumb and forefinger and tugged gently. Bria's heels dug into the padded window seat and she surged backward.

Through her thin shift Bria could feel the turgid length of his penis. It pressed against his drawers and the cleft of her bottom. She started to pull away but Luke's arm slipped around her waist and stopped her.

"Here," he whispered hoarsely. "Just stay . . . a moment longer." But his hold on her relaxed almost immediately and he let her know that she was free to move out of his reach if she wanted.

What she did, whether by accident or intention, was settle her bottom more firmly against him. Caught between a laugh and a groan, Luke buried his face in Bria's fragrant hair.

The rumble in Luke's chest vibrated at Bria's back. The corners of her mouth turned up the merest fraction. Her lips parted and then she sucked in her breath when Luke turned his attention to her other breast. It swelled faintly under his touch and heat began to radiate outward from her nipple. The flush spread under her skin, up her chest and throat, and finally to her face. Her cheeks grew deliciously warm and her eyelids grew heavy. Her lashes lowered, then finally closed over her eyes.

Luke fondled her breasts, touching her on the sensitive undersides, caressing the slope toward her shoulder. He raised her arms as she leaned back and let them fall around his neck. His fingertips brushed the inside of her arms from elbow to shoulder. He followed the curve of her body to her waist. His mouth moved against her hair. He nibbled on her ear. His tongue traced the outer shell.

Bria had a vision of herself as the offering on the altar of Luke's body. The most disturbing thing about the image was that she was not shamed by it. She felt nothing but a *frisson* of pleasure that she was desired by this man. She felt nothing but a curious excitement that she might desire him.

Luke pressed the flat of Bria's abdomen. He caressed her from hip to breast, sometimes with his palm, sometimes with just the tips of his fingers. Her hands clasped together behind Luke's neck. The movement lifted her breasts. He stroked them and her bottom rubbed against his groin. There was a catch in his breath, then hers. For a moment there was no other sound in the room.

"Lift your knees," Luke said. His voice was husky. He continued to stroke her belly. "That's it. A little more."

Bria settled more firmly in the cradle of his thighs and her fingers tightened at his neck. She felt Luke's hand slip under her shift at the level of her waist. She held her breath, waiting.

His voice ruffled her hair. "Open for me."

Bria could not have imagined earlier that she would do this thing for him. Just now she could not imagine doing anything else. Her thighs parted to make room for him.

Luke kissed the side of her neck, sipping her skin in the same moment he pressed his hand against her mons. He felt her entire body go rigid and her breathing change so that it was rapid and shallow. Luke simply held her until the tension in her arms and legs exhausted her. The contractions melted away. He felt her neck and shoulders give against his chest, then her back. She was heavier in his embrace than she had been a short time earlier.

His fingers dipped into the copse of fine hair between her thighs, and lower still so that he could caress her most intimately. The soft inner folds of her skin were damp and warm and moving between them was like stirring a honey pot. Luke resisted the urge to bring his fingers to his lips. He pressed his smile against the crown of Bria's head instead.

His fingers grazed the hooded nub of flesh between her thighs. A tremor passed from Bria into him. He quieted her in his arms, his voice low and soft at her ear while he continued stroking.

Pleasure was not what Bria registered first. Other sensations, other memories, had to be peeled away. There were fleeting visions of another hand probing between her legs, fingers pushing inside her. In the beginning there was pain in that recollection that was very real to her. Heat and humiliation rose to the surface. She cringed as much as trembled from it. There was fear that made her mouth go dry and prevented her from speaking, even when what she wanted to tell Luke was only that he shouldn't stop, that she knew it was him and that he wouldn't hurt her. There was a certain amount of embarrassment that her body was wet and slick where he touched her, and that she seemed to swell and grow heavy under his hand.

Then she felt it: a tiny spark of something hot and brilliant that cartwheeled through her womb. Bria moaned softly at the back of her throat. Her eyes closed. She tipped her pelvis a fraction, pushing her mons against Luke's hand. His fingers dipped lower, even more intimately. He rubbed her clitoris and the heat and pressure built inside her.

He told her she was beautiful. This time she didn't deny that it might be true.

The sparks became too numerous to count. They never

blended; each one had a singular intensity. When Bria realized that what she was feeling was pleasure in its most elemental form, she actually cried out with the sheer joy of it. Tears came to her eyes and laughter hovered at the back of her throat. She wanted to twist around and throw herself at Luke, kiss his eyes, his cheeks, his mouth. Instead she held onto him as she was, finding purchase against his solid frame.

Her body rocked when Luke slipped two fingers inside her. She rose and fell in a natural, welcoming rhythm. His touch triggered another wave of heat and half a dozen smaller ripples. The back of her head rubbed his neck and shoulder. Her throat arched. She wet her lips with the tip of her tongue, then sucked in the lower one and caught it between her teeth. She thought she heard Luke's low, rumbling laughter at her ear, and felt the vibration of it in his chest, but she was also aware of the small cries that were coming from her own throat and the tremors that slipped under her own skin.

It might have been Luke that she sensed, but it was also happening to her. Until this moment Bria hadn't understood how the pleasure might be shared.

Behind her closed lids there were sparks of light. Between her thighs there was heat. It all came together, firing off in a series of hot bursts like a beautifully orchestrated cannonade. Her body trembled, violently at first, then more gently in the wake of rolling aftershocks. She cried out, saying "Luke!" saying it as if there were no more important thing she could have said. She gave this consuming pleasure a name and called it by his.

Luke held Bria from the moment her body seized on the verge of orgasm, shuddered in release, and was finally still. Her hands unlocked behind his neck and fell heavily to her sides. He shifted slightly in the corner of the window seat and turned Bria in his arms. Her drawn-up knees fell to one side as she curled against him. Her breathing was softly ragged. He nudged her hair with his chin and cheek and stroked her back.

He felt the cadence of her indrawn breaths change until they were even and steady.

He rested his head against the window, closed his eyes, and tried not to wish for something he couldn't have. *Take what this moment offers*. He thought about what she had already given him: the fragrance of her hair, the gentle curve of her shoulder, her softly parted mouth, the whisper of her shift against his skin. Her trust.

Luke lightly rubbed her arm and let it be.

"Luke?"

Until she spoke he thought she was asleep. "Hmmm?"

"What about you?"

He didn't open his eyes. "Me?"

She could still feel him against her hip, hard and hot and straining at the confines of his drawers. Bria laid one hand on his thigh halfway between his knee and his groin. Even through the material, she could feel the heat of his flesh and the tension in his muscled thigh.

Luke put his hand over hers. "Don't."

Bria did not remove her hand from under his, but she did straighten, separating herself from his chest and shoulder. She studied his features. Moonlight lent them a faintly grey cast and darkened his brows and the lock of hair that had fallen across his forehead. His eyes were closed but his face was not marked by serenity. Bria had seen him sleeping. She knew what his face looked like unmarked by tension or trouble. This was not that face. He was holding himself away from her, no longer able to share in the joy he had given her.

She had trusted him, but it seemed he could no longer trust himself.

"I know what's supposed to happen," she told him softly. "This other . . . This other thing you did to me was unexpected, but I know there's more. I'm not afraid, Luke. Not any longer. I'm not afraid to take you inside me."

He opened his eyes. He stared at her earnest expression, the way she leaned toward him, the small, almost defiant lift of her chin. She was watching him intently, her dark eyes grave. "Aren't you afraid it will begin to be a little like a marriage?" he asked quietly.

The shape of her mouth changed. There was a faint hint of sadness quickly masked. "No," she said, shaking her head almost imperceptibly. "No chance of that. I don't think you mean to stay so long."

Luke's heavy-lidded eyes narrowed a fraction. He didn't insult her by denying it. "How did you know?"

Bria shrugged. "I've never not known. Your being here has always seemed impermanent to me. A bit of a mystery, a bit of an intrigue. A quest, you once said. In the beginning I thought it was the treasure, but that's not it, is it?"

"No," he said gently. "That's not it."

Bria nodded. "It's just as well, I should think. For your sake." There was a hard, aching lump in her throat that choked off her words for a moment. She swallowed it back. "There's no hope of finding it now. The riddle's gone."

Luke drew Bria back into his arms and laid her head against his shoulder. He helped her raise her shift so that it covered her breasts. "Can you mourn Rand now?" he asked. "Do you feel enough to mourn him properly?"

Bria's tears were the real measure of the gift Luke had given her. His words opened the floodgate of emotion. Where she had only been driven back into numbness by the death of her brother, now she felt his loss as a terrible ache in her own chest. Every heartbeat seemed to spread the sorrow through her body. She felt it in her fingertips where she had last grasped Rand's sleeve to bid him Godspeed. She felt it against her cheek where he had kissed her. It was there at her brow, the awareness of Rand's thumb pushing back a lock of her hair. Memories were triggered by every sensation. She saw herself as a child, loping after him across the garden to the river, calling his name so that he would slow his steps. It was Rand who taught her to swim. Rand who invented Captured Indian Princess, who came to her in the middle of the night and calmed her haunted dreams, who built her greenhouse and gave her the benefit of what he had learned. She could feel the texture of his chestnut-colored hair, see the teasing gleam in his eyes of the same color. She knew the shape and length of the thin scar that a Yankee saber had cut across his cheek. In the hollow of her embrace she had a sense of Rand's shoulders filling them as they leaned on each other for support and strength.

And finally she remembered how very deeply she loved her brother. The pain in her throat, behind her eyes, in her chest was enormous. It was sharp and stinging and heavy, like a knife being twisted in her flesh by a powerful hand. Yet she never wished it away; never once prayed for rolling waves of numbness to push her under so she could drown in them. Each ragged breath she drew between the sobs was a reminder that she was alive and that she could bear it.

She could bear it.

Luke carried Bria back to their bed and laid her down. She clung to him as he straightened. He had to ease her arms from around his neck. He pressed a handkerchief into her hands and drew the covers over her shoulders.

He was gone from the room for only a few minutes, returning with a decanter of brandy and a glass. Luke sat on the edge of the bed and poured. He gave the glass to Bria when she pushed herself into a sitting position and set the decanter aside.

"Drink," he said. He had to touch his forefinger to the bottom of the glass and give it a nudge toward her lips.

Bria took a sip, just wetting her mouth with it. She felt him nudge the glass again. This time she managed a whole swallow.

"Good." He took the glass from her and finished off the drink. "Move over. First you try to drink all the brandy, then take over the bed. We need to agree to a more equitable arrangement."

Bria's mouth lifted just a fraction at the corners. "I like the way things are now," she said sleepily. She turned into him as he slipped into bed beside her. Her eyelids were heavy and swollen from weeping and the brandy was already making her warm. She looked at Luke's profile through the fan of her dark lashes. "Thank you." His lips parted and it seemed he might make a reply. "No," she said, stopping him. "You don't have to do or say anything. Just thank you."

He did not smile in return. He simply stared at the ceiling and fought the ache behind his own eyes.

It wouldn't have happened if he had been awake. Asleep he was every bit as vulnerable as Bria. He was moving inside her before he knew how he had come to be there. The bed creaked and the mattress shifted. The headboard bumped the wall.

Luke opened bleary eyes and found himself hovering over Bria. Her face was in the shadow of his but he could see that she was staring up at him, her dark eyes enormous now. At his waist Luke could feel the blankets and riding low on his hips were his drawers.

She was so hot and tight around him that drawing a breath hurt. Involuntarily his hips plunged forward and Bria moved under him. She did not rise to meet his thrust but accepted it all the same.

Luke buried his face in the curve of her neck and held himself still. She contracted around him, first intimately, then with her arms and legs. Her heels hooked over the back of his calves. "Bria . . ." Her hair was as thick and smooth as honey. The fragrance, though, was lavender. He did not want to lift his head. "Don't, Bria. I should . . ." But she remained as she was, holding him in the cradle of her body this time. Luke levered himself up higher on his elbows and tried to twist away and withdraw.

Bria tipped her pelvis upward so that he could not leave her easily and pulled on his shoulders. Her thighs tightened around his.

Luke was not proof against these tactics. He groaned softly and tried to explain. "Bria, I can't . . ."

She brought his head down and kissed him full on the mouth.

Her tongue plunged inside his mouth and found the same carnal rhythm he had shown her first with his body.

Luke's tongue stirred against hers. She was wet and hot and sweet. There was the taste of brandy on her lips. He knew that he wanted her, that he *had* wanted her for a very long time, but the full force of the passion he felt now managed to catch him off guard. It was like steeling himself for a punch and finding it still had power to rock him back on his heels.

He drew back his head a fraction. His fingers buried into her hair and he held her so she couldn't avoid him. "Am I hurting you?"

"No." Bria watched relief touch his eyes.

"You're so very tight." The words were merely exhaled. "I was afraid . . ."

"I'm not," she said. "I told you I wasn't afraid. Neither should you be."

Her stubborn little smile made his heart trip over itself. With a small expulsion of air that was very much like a groan, Luke kissed her.

Bria was rocked back with the force of his thrusting hips. She did more than lie passively under him this time. Her body responded to the movement of his, arching upward to meet him. She strained to hold onto him, and while her grip on his shoulders and legs loosened, she still contracted around him when he would begin to withdraw.

Heat spiraled through her belly as Luke moved over and in her. It was not the same intensity as before. This was warm, almost comfortable. His weight blanketed her but didn't smother. Surrounded by him now, she felt safe, not on the verge of losing control. This was good, too, she thought, vaguely reassuring, satisfying.

She watched Luke. His beautiful features were set hard. A muscle worked in his jaw. She kissed his shoulder, teased his heated skin with the ridge of her teeth. He growled deeply against her ear. Beneath Bria's fingers she could feel the taut muscles of his back shift. Against her inner thighs his flanks were firm and as finely carved. She ran one hand down his spine and then over the curve of his buttock. He reared up, closing his eyes, then plunged into her deeply.

All of Bria's senses stirred. The gentling warmth that had lulled her into complacency fled. There was a shift in the very spectrum as tiny bursts of light and heat fanned out across her skin. Her eyes widened and she grasped Luke's shoulders. His hips ground against hers and she pushed into him, not satisfied now to have only security and comfort. Her body twisted with his. Bria's heels dug into the mattress. Her back arched. Her breasts swelled under his chest. The effect on her nipples, already twin points of fire, was almost unbearable.

Luke strained against Bria a final time, arching just once before a hoarse shout and shudder signaled his release. Pleasure coursed through his lean frame as muscles contracted, then remained still. He moved again, slowly this time, and reached between their joined bodies. Luke watched Bria's face as his fingers explored her velvet folds with infinite gentleness. It required only a single stroke to give her the same pleasure she had given him.

Bria's cry was muffled by Luke's mouth. Her body trembled against his. He absorbed her shudder and it became part of his own lingering pleasure.

"Bree," he said softly. "Sweet, sweet Bree."

She did not let him leave immediately. There was still his closeness to be savored. He was really a very dear man. It was on the tip of her tongue to tell him so when he pressed a finger to her lips.

"In the morning," he said, "you will have doubts. Remember this: there is no shame unless you choose to accept it. Do you understand?"

Bria nodded slowly. "I'll remember."

He kissed her parted mouth. His lips remained a moment, then he raised his head. Luke withdrew from her. Under the covers he pulled at his drawers while Bria righted her nightshift. She lay on her back until he stretched out beside her. Her body curved into his and when his arm slipped around her waist she took it and held it there.

"I don't want morning to come," Bria whispered.

"I know." He knew because he shared the same thought.

Morning did come, of course. When Bria woke the pale mauve and grey of the dawn had not yet been burned from the sky. A thin fog pressed against the windowpanes. She closed her eyes and lay still a moment longer, not wanting to admit knowledge of the light that slipped over the sill and slanted along the window bench to the floor, or accept that Luke was absent from their bed. She stretched because she could not help herself, and found in the movement further evidence that he was gone.

Bria rose reluctantly and went to the dressing room. Luke's towel and washcloth were still damp, proof that he had left only a short time ago. She wondered if he had watched her sleep and if it had been difficult to leave without waking her. Had he struggled at all with the decision?

Bria studied her reflection in the glass above the commode. She was altogether remarkably unchanged, she thought, if one found an alternate explanation for the flush in her cheeks, the peculiar brightness in her eyes, and the heavy, faintly swollen lids. There was one, she knew. Her brother was dead and she had spent the night coming to life to mourn the passing of his.

Bria bent her head and began to wash.

Elizabeth Hamilton Foster was sitting up in bed when Bria entered her room. Lace-trimmed shams covered the pillows that supported the small of her back. The thick down comforter was folded over once across her lap. She was wearing a plain white nightgown but her satin robe was a dark, rich purple with Chinese characters along the deep cuffs and yellow piping on the lapels and collar.

Her hair was still thick, chestnut-colored like her middle son's had been. There were strands of silver woven through her hair at the temples, more strands this morning than there had been a few weeks ago, more grey now than silver.

Elizabeth was holding a cup and saucer when Bria walked in. She paused, looking at her daughter over the rim of her cup. Her hands were almost as white and fragile as the bone china. Her fingers trembled slightly as she set the cup in the saucer and placed them both on the table beside her bed. She held out her hands to Bria. Though her smile welcomed it did not transform her face.

"Bria," she said softly. "Come. Come, sit here." Elizabeth patted the space beside her, then extended her arm again.

Bria sat down carefully, afraid the smallest movement would jar her mother and break her delicate frame. Elizabeth, for all that she clung to an air of refinement as if it were the only air she could breathe, was in fact strong and resilient and sturdy of spirit. Or she had been. What had been fragile, now looked frail.

"Mother," Bria said, taking both of Elizabeth's hands. She squeezed gently and felt the corresponding squeezing of her own heart. *This is the death that has broken her,* Bria thought. *It would have broken me. If not for Luke, it would have broken me.*

Elizabeth's eyes filled with tears. She made an effort to blink them back but they dampened her dark lashes and fell over her cheeks anyway. "Hand me that handkerchief," she said, pointing to one on the table.

Bria gave it to her. Elizabeth pressed it to both eyes and dabbed at her cheeks. "Would you like your tea?" asked Bria.

Elizabeth shook her head. "Not just yet, thank you." She gave Bria a watery smile as she carefully refolded the handkerchief. "Have you had breakfast?"

"No. I wanted to see you first. Yesterday . . ."

"Yesterday I had no way of knowing that I could bear this grief. But here I am on the morning after, still alive, and another son lost to me." Her eyes remained peculiarly dry this time but her knuckles were almost as white as the handkerchief she clutched. "I'm sorry I could offer no comfort to you, Bria. I regret equally that I could accept none." Elizabeth searched her daughter's face. "And you, darling? How are you faring?"

The stinging ache returned to the back of Bria's eyes and throat. She blinked and swallowed hard. "I'm sad, Mother. So terribly sad."

Elizabeth nodded and patted the thick comforter that lay across her legs. Bria did not hesitate. Curling at her mother's side, she laid her head on Elizabeth's lap. Elizabeth's fingers lightly stroked Bria's forehead and played with the tendrils that could not be bound in the coil of hair at her nape. She rubbed Bria's shoulder and back, taking comfort from the action as much as giving it. "Rand was doing what he wanted to do, Bria. Don't forget that. I find some solace in it."

Knowing it was true made it no easier to accept. "I suppose if Rand hadn't been treasure hunting he could have been persuaded to leave Concord for his research."

Elizabeth smiled faintly. "I think you would have convinced him. The two of you could not have managed the plantation together, not like Austin and Emily Tipping. Neither of you is so biddable." She sighed. "Your temperaments are too alike and I fear one of you would have lambasted the other."

Bria had almost done that to her brother the last time he was home. He had made the usual noises about her marrying and leaving Concord. He would take over, of course—and hate every moment of it. There was also the matter of Orrin. Rand could never have learned to live with Orrin Foster under his feet. "Do you ever think the Hamilton-Waterstone treasure is cursed?" Bria asked softly. "There haven't been any Waterstones for a generation. Rand is . . . was . . . the last Hamilton male to bear the name and the direct line."

"Cursed?" Elizabeth leaned her head back against the intricately scrolled walnut headboard and closed her eyes. "I've always thought so. Your father used to tease me about it. It never changed my mind, though. I could not decide if it was the treasure that carried the curse or the riddles. Perhaps it was both. I know I liked hearing about them when I was growing up. Then it was only a legend to me. Once I entered this family it became all too real.''

"It's finished now, isn't it? As Orrin said, 'There's no more goddamn riddle.' ''

"Bria.'' Elizabeth admonished her, tapping her lightly on the shoulder. "Your language.''

"But it's true, isn't it? We're done with the riddle and the treasure. It's all lost to us and the Waterstones. Let someone else find the thing, I say, and let us be done with it.''

"Why does it worry you so much?'' Elizabeth asked. "Is that why *he's* here? Did he convince you it was for some other reason than the Hamilton Riddle? Is that why you married him?''

Bria pushed herself upright and stared at her mother. Her mouth was dry.

Elizabeth reached toward Bria and smoothed the folds of her gown across her knee. In deference to mourning, Bria had chosen a dark plum day dress from her wardrobe. "This will have to be altered,'' Elizabeth said. "It looks a little tight across the shoulders. I daresay it's because you worked too hard again during this last harvest. You have the shoulders of a farmer's daughter, Bria. I shall ask Addie to see to this. She knows who the best seamstress will be. I suppose you will need other clothes as well. Our mourning things are sadly out of fashion.''

"Mother,'' Bria said flatly. "I do not want to talk about mourning fashions or the harvest or my shoulders. I *am* a farmer's daughter. Father would be proud of that.''

Elizabeth's hand fell away from Bria's knee. She twisted her handkerchief, her expression wounded. "I'm proud of you, Bria.''

Bria sighed. "I did not mean to suggest that you weren't. I'm sorry if that's what you thought, but I won't let you steer me off course, either. His name is Lucas Kincaid, Mother. Was it Orrin who told you about my marriage?''

"Yes. Last night. Immediately after your Mr. Kincaid informed him, I suspect." She touched the handkerchief to her eyes in spite of the fact that there were no tears. "How could you?" she asked plaintively. "With no word to us? Nothing. Charleston isn't at the other side of the world, Bria. You could have sent someone. I would have wanted to be here with you." Her eyes dropped to Bria's abdomen. "Are you pregnant?"

Bria's head snapped up. "No!"

"You cannot blame me for wondering. Others will, too. The haste and secrecy of your marriage will provoke that sort of speculation. I wish you had come to me, darling. We could have discussed things of that nature."

"You've wanted me to marry, Mother. I thought it would please you."

"What do you know about this man?" Elizabeth could not bring herself to refer to him as Bria's husband. "Orrin could only tell me that Mr. Kincaid is the same man he hired to make repairs to Concord. Can that be correct, Bria? You've married a laborer?"

"Luke is a laborer the same way Michelangelo was a stone cutter." Bria rose from the bed and walked to the window. She drew back the drapes and affixed them with the royal blue rope tassels. Elizabeth's room overlooked the gardens. In her mind's eye Bria overlaid them with the beautiful landscaping plans Luke had drawn. She did not think she had exaggerated his talent to her mother. "But it wouldn't matter if he were only a handyman," she said, turning from the window. "I'm still the farmer's daughter."

"By your own choice," Elizabeth said, agitated. "By your *own* choice. You could have left Concord years ago. Austin has asked for your hand every year since the war ended. You could have been a proper lady at High Point. His sister would have stepped aside for you. Would it have been so terrible to have accepted something other than Concord?"

"Accept something else?" Bria whispered. "How can you say that after the sacrifice you made to keep Henley? Yes, Henley. We may be helpless to stop Orrin from changing the name but it doesn't mean it isn't still Henley in our hearts. Why would I want to leave, Mother, after you saved it for us?"

Elizabeth let the handkerchief remain in her lap and buried her face in her hands. Her shoulders shook with earnest sobs. What she said was unintelligible.

Bria rushed to her mother's side. She crawled into the bed and knelt beside Elizabeth, taking her in her arms. She rocked her gently, stroked her hair, and whispered words both loving and encouraging. When she thought Elizabeth could hear her clearly, she said, "Luke is a good man, Mother. I think you will come to know that. I don't know why he married me. Perhaps because of the riddle and the treasure, though he's always denied it. It doesn't matter. It never did. I would have married him regardless."

Elizabeth pushed herself gently out of Bria's embrace. She searched her daughter's face. "You love him so much?"

Bria had thought she would dread this question. Now she realized it was not the case at all. "Yes," she said quietly. "I love him so much." She pushed the linen handkerchief into her mother's hand again. "There. Dry your eyes. Do you think you will leave your room today?"

Elizabeth shook her head.

"Very well, then I shall have my own breakfast brought here."

"Don't you want to eat with your husband?"

"Luke has already eaten and is about his work. When you're feeling better I hope you will look at what he's accomplished. Orrin made a good decision to hire Luke and it was over my objections. Did he tell you that?"

"He told me." Her eyes narrowed on Bria's face but she could see nothing to advance her suspicions. "I wanted to come back immediately upon hearing that Mr. Kincaid was going to be sharing this house with you. I told Orrin it wasn't at all proper. I had to hope you would see the necessity of accommodating Mr. Kincaid in the guest house. I understand from Addie it was not that way.''

"No, it wasn't. But it was still very proper. Did Addie think to tell you that?''

Elizabeth managed to keep further criticism to herself. She pointed to the door. "Go see about breakfast. I told Addie earlier that I wanted nothing but my tea. I find I now have an improved appetite. Choose something light for me. You know what I like.''

Bria arrived back in Elizabeth's bedchamber thirty minutes later. Her mother was sitting at the round table next to the fireplace. One of the servants had come by and laid a small fire for her. It was enough to remove the chill from the room and lend some heat and color to Elizabeth's sunken cheeks.

Bria laid out the food and served her mother and herself. There were hotcakes and grits and tiny link sausages. The aroma of hot coffee permeated the air.

Elizabeth stared at her plate. "This is not a light meal, Bria. What were you thinking?''

"I was thinking this is what you like, Mother. Eat as much or as little as you want. That's entirely your choice.'' Bria cut a triangle from her hotcakes and speared it with her fork. A dollop of syrup fell back onto her plate before she got it to her mouth. "Rand loved Elsie's hotcakes,'' she said. "He could never find a cook for *Cerberus* half as good as Elsie.''

That raised a small smile from Elizabeth. "He would have taken her from under our noses if Jeb had been willing to go as well. Thank God he had sense enough to stay here.''

"I believe it was seasickness that kept him here, Mother,'' Bria said dryly. She sobered a little. "What news was there of Cutch?''

Elizabeth's fork wavered a bit. It took her a moment to find her voice. "The reports were not detailed. At least I didn't find them so, though I admit I could hardly hear what was being said to me. I understood little after I learned that *Cerberus* was lost. It would be better, I think, if you asked Orrin. He made all the inquiries. I'm afraid I couldn't.''

"Can I trust him?" Bria asked flatly.

"Bria. I know you have no liking for him, but he is your stepfather. I wish you would show him more respect."

It was an old argument, one that Bria did not wish to revisit now. "Very well. I'll ask him, but tell me first what you know. Was it at Cape Horn?"

Elizabeth nodded. "That's my recollection. Rand used to describe the treacherous waters there. The hard, high seas. The gales. The ship foundered and broke apart."

"The bodies? Were any identified?"

"I don't know. The ship's figurehead . . . the three-headed dog . . ."

"It's all right, Mother. I understand. There could be no mistaking that piece as belonging to some other ship. What of Claire? Surely a woman among the dead of that crew would have been noted."

"I heard nothing of her. But, Bria, don't forget that Claire might have remained behind in Solonesia. Rand could have been returning without her."

Bria had thought of that. "We should send word to her godfather in London. He should hear this from us."

"Yes, you're right. I will also speak to Orrin again and decide what is appropriate to write. There will be an account in the paper. Perhaps you would send one of the grooms to Charleston to collect some copies. What is the name of Claire's godfather?"

"Evan Markham. Duke of . . ." Bria frowned. "Something-or-other. I suppose it will come to me." She added a pat of butter to her grits. "It's only a few weeks until the other planters return from Charleston. Would you like to have a service for Rand here? I thought Luke and I would officially announce our marriage in November but that doesn't need to happen now. People can learn of it as they will."

Elizabeth was forced to agree. Planning any kind of reception for Bria would be awkward now. Still, she had her daughter's reputation to consider. "I'm certain we can manage something," she said. "I will think on it."

Bria would have tried to dissuade her mother but she recognized the need for Elizabeth to apply herself to the problem. "It would please me if you did," Bria said. She consoled herself that it was at worst only a half-lie.

Elizabeth and Bria both had their attention drawn to the door by a swift, staccato rapping.

"Come in," Elizabeth called.

Bria stood as Luke stepped into the room. "Luke!" She hurried to his side and came up on tiptoe. Although his arm slipped easily around her waist, his lips were cool when she kissed him. She drew back and saw that his smile, for all its endearing crookedness, did not quite touch his eyes. Bria glanced over her shoulder. "This is my husband, Mother. Lucas Kincaid. Luke, my mother."

He bowed his head slightly but made no move to approach her. "I'm very glad you meet you," he said politely. His attention swiveled back to Bria. "I need to see you now."

"But—"

"Now."

"Very well. Excuse us, Mother." Bria let Luke lead her into the hallway and shut the door. "What in the world can you be think—"

He held up his hand, cutting her off. "Your stepfather decided to tour the plantation this morning. He stumbled upon some of the repairs made to the tenant farms, Bree. He knows what's been done in his absence."

Chapter Eleven

Bria stared at Luke. "Orrin was visiting the tenant farms? This morning?" It made no more sense to her upon repeating. "How can that be? He has never gone to the farms, even when I encouraged him. And he does not usually rise before ten."

"I don't believe he's been to bed."

Bria pressed one hand to her temple and massaged it as she considered this. "Is he drunk?"

"He's been drinking steadily since his arrival. You would know better than I if he's drunk."

"How do you know that he's been out to the farms?"

"I saw him returning. He asked to see me in the study, then confronted me about the repairs. I told him I was responsible."

"Luke!" Bria's hand dropped to her side and curled into a loose fist. "You shouldn't have. Orrin's fight is with me."

"It doesn't have to be. I'm telling you this so you won't say more than you need to when he puts the same questions to you. Tell him the truth."

"The truth."

Luke nodded. He drew Bria further down the hall to be away from her mother's door and backed her against the wainscoting. He leaned toward her, bracing both hands flat on the wall on either side of her shoulders. His head dropped a fraction and his voice was soft and husky. "Do you know where I want to be at this very moment?"

Bria swallowed and shook her head. The centers of his smoky grey eyes were darkening and widening. If she let herself, she would simply fall into them. "Luke, this is not—"

He stopped her weak protest by placing a finger to her lips. "Perhaps a hint is in order."

"A hint?"

Luke replaced his finger with his mouth. His lips tugged on hers, teased. He changed the position of his head and on the next advance, deepened the kiss.

Bria's hands slipped between them. Her fingers curled on either side of his open jacket and held on, adding just enough weight to keep Luke exactly where he was.

"Is it your intention to poke her right here?"

Bria stiffened at the sound of her stepfather's voice. She turned her head away from Luke and pushed at his chest.

Luke straightened slowly, but not before he placed another light kiss on her averted cheek. "Follow my lead," he whispered in her ear. He took a small step backward, shielding Bria just long enough for her to gain some measure of composure.

Orrin made a noise at the back of his throat that was somewhere between disgust and annoyance. "Have you no shame, daughter? Your brother's death has only just been discovered. Some period of mourning is in order. If you've made Kincaid so randy that he must be serviced now, then have the decency to insist on the privacy of your bedchamber."

For a moment, Bria simply couldn't breathe. Heat flushed her cheeks.

"That's quite enough, Orrin," Luke said.

Orrin scowled. "I wasn't speaking to you. This doesn't concern you."

"You were speaking to my wife. She certainly concerns me."

"She doesn't need your protection," Orrin said. "She knows how to speak and do for herself. Tell him, Bree."

Bria looked over Orrin's ruddy features and rumpled clothes. He was standing with one shoulder braced against the wall. She suspected he would have wobbled in place otherwise. "You're drunk, Orrin," she said. None of the contempt or revulsion she felt could be heard in her voice. Bria presented a simple statement of fact. "I can think of no reason I should talk to you now." Out of the corner of her eye she saw Luke's jaw raise a fraction. She remembered that he'd asked her to follow his lead. "And I appreciate my husband's concern on my behalf. His protection is not unwelcome."

It was a measure of how much Orrin had drunk in the past twenty-four hours that he merely shrugged this off. He jerked his chin in Luke's direction but kept his eyes on Bria. "Did he tell you that I've been out to the farms?"

"Yes."

"What do you have to say about it?"

It was Luke who answered. "Bria's said this conversation can wait until you're sober, Orrin."

Orrin's laugh held no humor and his attention settled sharply on Luke. "Do you think that a few glasses of bourbon has taken my senses? It brings clarity, Kincaid. Clarity. I know it's her fine hand in this business."

Luke immediately challenged Orrin's idea of clarity and Bria's involvement. "You obviously weren't listening to what I told you downstairs. I proposed selling the used materials from this house to the sharecroppers. Some of them paid cash. Others are laboring on this house to work off their debt. Every transaction is accounted for. Every plank. Every nail. Every brick. I can show you where you turned a profit on materials that would have been thrown away. As for some of the newer materials . . . little of it was resold to your tenants, but again, there was a profit to you. I have an account ledger that I encourage you to examine."

"You're damn right I'll examine it," Orrin snapped. "I'm

not an easy mark, Kincaid, if that's your game here. You'd better be telling the truth or be very, very good. I can sniff out a hole on a page full of ciphers. I know something about keeping books and accounting.''

If Bria had not been standing so close to Luke she doubted she would have known he stiffened at Orrin's last words. She turned a little and slipped an arm through Luke's, diverting Orrin's attention to her.

"Did you approve this?" Orrin asked flatly.

"Reluctantly."

Orrin arched one brow. "You know how I feel about doing too much for the nigras."

"It wasn't charity," Bria said. "I think even kind-spirited people would agree you were hardly generous." She sighed impatiently. "Have you quite finished with us?"

Orrin looked from Bria to Luke. "I hope you made her spread her thighs wide before you agreed to accept blame for this."

Bria did not flinch at Orrin's crudity but Luke took a step forward. She hung onto his arm. "No," she whispered. "Don't."

Smiling a trifle smugly, Orrin pushed away from the wall. He staggered a bit but found his balance easily enough. "Put that ledger on my desk," he said, walking toward them. At the last moment he veered to the left and brushed past Luke. "My advice to you is to take her in hand. She'll make you her whipped dog if you don't put a leash on her first."

Bria held Luke's arm until she heard Orrin enter his own bedchamber. When she heard the door click in place, she whispered, "Luke? Are you all right?"

He did not respond immediately, and when he did it was only to nod.

Bria turned so she could better gauge his features and not merely his profile. In all the time she had known him, Bria did not think she had ever seen his expression etched with such gravity. She anticipated frustration, even anger, but what she saw was not accounted for by those emotions. Luke was grim.

Bria touched his sleeve and tugged lightly. "Luke?"

His glance finally focused on her upturned face. He raised one hand and touched her cheek. "We can't talk here. Meet me at the gazebo."

She nodded. "When?"

"An hour?"

"All right." Bria didn't move and neither did he. Luke's hand was warm on her cheek and his thumb brushed the corner of her mouth. She leaned a little into his palm.

Luke bent his head and touched her lips with his. "One hour," he whispered against her mouth. He pulled back, released her, and started to go. Just before he turned the corner to start down the stairs, he stopped and looked back. Bria was still standing in the middle of the hall, staring after him. "You don't have to be afraid, Bree." He watched the small crease between her brows vanish and her effort raised his own slight smile. "Will you make apologies to your mother for me?"

It was enough to break the thread of tension that kept Luke poised on the edge of the stairs. He disappeared without waiting for Bria's reply.

There was a light drizzle an hour later. Bria lifted her hem to keep it from sweeping the damp path to the gazebo. She kept her head low, watching her step, and was unaware of Luke's presence until he swept her into his arms and carried her the last twenty feet.

He set her down in the middle of the gazebo but kept his hands on her waist. "Speechless?" he asked when she simply gaped at him.

"Hardly. I was wondering if you think that marriage has rendered me unable to walk?"

"It was raining," he said simply. "And you were in my way."

His unexpected reply made Bria blink. "Then I suppose I should be grateful I wasn't trampled."

He grinned and touched his forehead to hers. "You most definitely should." Luke kissed the tip of her nose before he straightened. The tempo of the rain changed and the gazebo's roof began to leak. A fat droplet of rain fell in his hair, another on his shoulder. One caught Bria on the tip of her nose. "Charming," he said as she wrinkled it. He brushed it away. "Here, let's find a spot drier than this one."

Bria allowed herself to be escorted to one of the benches. She was on the point of sitting down when she looked back at the house and saw a movement at one of the windows. Someone closing it against the rain? Perhaps. She sat slowly, turning a fraction toward Luke. When Bria looked at him again it was to find he was watching her carefully. With sudden insight she understood the nature of his glance.

"It was a stolen moment, wasn't it?" she asked. Bria forced a certain lightness into her voice that was at odds with her stiffly held posture. "You knew someone was watching us from the house when you picked me up and carried me here."

"I thoroughly enjoyed sweeping you off your feet."

"Don't patronize me, Luke. That's not an answer to my question."

"No, but it's the truth." He sighed. "I knew someone was there. In fact, I'm fairly certain it was Orrin."

"It was my mother's room."

"I still think it was Orrin."

Bria didn't dispute it. "What about earlier?" she asked. "When we were in the hall and you kissed me? Orrin came upon us. I thought it was an accident but I'm thinking now that you heard him on the stairs. Was that it? Another stolen moment?"

"Yes, but it also remains true that I thoroughly enjoyed kissing you."

Bria stared at her lap. Her hands were folded lightly. The thumbnails snapped softly as she flicked the tips back and forth, one across the other.

"Bria?"

She shook her head, not certain that she trusted herself to speak. What could she tell him? "It's not what I expected," she said finally. "When we rehearsed . . . it seemed as if . . . but now I don't think I can . . ." Her voice trailed off and she shrugged helplessly.

"Last night changed things for you," said Luke, offering his perception as fact.

"No!" Bria stole a glance in his direction. "No," she said again, more softly this time, repairing the crack in her composure. "I mean, what would be changed?" Before Luke could answer, Bria forged ahead. "Did it change things for you?"

"No." He said it with such simple sincerity that there was no mistaking it for anything less than the truth. "Nothing's changed for me, Bria." Luke watched her nod, her expression a little hurt, a little bewildered. He almost told her then, knowing she had only accepted his words at face value, that their deeper meaning eluded her, but the explanation that would have cleared her features came to the tip of his tongue and remained there. A moment later he swallowed it, along with the unfamiliar ache in his throat.

Bria brought her chin up a notch. Her sapphire eyes became focused and clear, but the remoteness had returned. "Is it true what you told Orrin earlier? You can account for all the materials and show proof of a profit?"

"Yes."

"How is that possible?"

"I began creating a ledger of expenditures and payments immediately after I realized what was happening to my supplies. I know you didn't want my help, Bree, but I couldn't risk not giving it. There was not enough time for me to hide all the repairs that had been done to the tenant farms. I did what I could, and at my instruction, the men working for me did the same. We couldn't conceal everything. I had hoped to have another week at least."

"My stepfather has never shown any interest in the share-croppers or their homes. Never, Luke. I didn't refuse your help

out of hand. I truly believed I didn't require it." Bria closed
her eyes briefly and rubbed the bridge of her nose with her
thumb and forefinger. A cold shiver rippled through her slender
frame. "Oh God." Her voice was quiet, forlorn. "That I could
be so prideful."

"Bree."

"No. That's what it was. I was so surprised at having been
caught out by you that I could admit to nothing. And now it's
come to this: Orrin knows."

"Orrin thinks he knows," Luke said. "The accounts will
provide another explanation."

Bria raised her eyes to Luke's. "Will they bear his scrutiny?"

"I have to hope they will. I have some experience with
bookkeeping. My mother had a . . ." He hesitated, his dark
brows knitting briefly. "A boarder who hired me to work for
him in that capacity. I did that for several summer months
until I went away to school. I don't claim to have any special
expertise. I wasn't aware that your stepfather did."

Bria nodded, recalling Luke's reaction when Orrin told him.
"You seemed oddly struck by it."

"I was surprised."

"No, it wasn't merely surprise." Her eyes narrowed slightly
on Luke's face. "It was more. As if it held some singular
importance."

"It *is* important. I've turned over a fictional account to a
man who says he can spot lies among the numbers. I had to
work very quickly to create that account, Bree, and back it up
with what little I've been able to save. What I had an urge to
do was confess to everything right then and there."

She didn't believe that for a moment. "You're lying to
me," she said quietly. There was no hurt in her tone nor any
admonishment. "No, you don't have to explain. I'm not asking
for that. I trust you have your reasons."

Luke said nothing. He could not tell her the truth and he
would not add another lie to the one he'd told her. She was

correct that Orrin Foster's talent for accounting was of special interest to him.

Bria leaned back against the rail of the gazebo. The rain's steady staccato was comforting. "I suppose there's nothing to be done but wait," she said. "If Orrin is satisfied with what you've given him, there may be fewer consequences for all of us."

"Don't you mean *no* consequences?"

"Fewer," she repeated. "There will be some manner of retribution. Orrin won't believe in my innocence or yours. He'll only believe that he's been outsmarted. He'll want his pound of flesh."

"I considered that," he said. "I'd hoped I was wrong."

"You weren't."

Luke turned on the bench so that his back was also solidly against the rail. He stretched his legs, crossing them at the ankle. Beside him, he felt Bria's shiver. "Would you like my jacket?"

"No, thank you. It wasn't that kind of shiver."

"My arm, then?"

She glanced at him. "Yes, please."

Luke placed an arm across the rail at the level of Bria's shoulders and she leaned into him. It was easily as comforting for him as it was for her. Somehow his small sigh communicated precisely that. He wasn't surprised when Bria burrowed a bit more closely against him. They sat quietly for some time, both of them loath to break the silence. When they did speak, it was in unison.

Bria smiled faintly. "Please. Go first." When Luke hesitated, she added, "I find I am reluctant to speak my own mind just yet."

"There's no pleasantness in what I have to say," he told her.

"Say it quickly then."

"Very well. I've been asking myself why your stepfather toured the plantation when it is not his habit to do so. Especially why he toured it almost immediately upon returning to Concord. If I dismiss chance, which in this case I must, then I am left with only one explanation: someone told him what transpired in his absence.''

Bria drew in her bottom lip and worried it with her teeth. She blinked to ease the sting of unshed tears. When she felt she could trust herself to speak she said, ''I intended to share the same conclusion with you.'' In spite of Luke's sheltering arm, Bria shivered again. ''I don't want to believe it.''

''I know. It is no easy thing to accept.'' Luke rubbed her arm, infusing some warmth. ''Have you allowed yourself to consider who it might be?''

''No. It is too painful to think about.''

Luke thought about the possible suspects. Jeb. Addie. Martha. Elsie. There was Tad and his fellow stablehands and the team of laborers who worked on the house. There were the sharecroppers whose homes had been repaired through Bria's largess. John Whitney. Any of them could have reported to Orrin. The most likely ones were also the most trusted. Luke understood why Bria didn't want to think about it.

Still, it had to be said. ''Jebediah?''

Bria vehemently shook her head. ''No. It would be a betrayal of his family as well. Two of his daughters had improvements made to their houses. Elsie would have remained quiet for similar reasons.''

''Martha? Perhaps she was jealous of her sisters?''

''She was happy for them.''

''Addie?''

''She despises Orrin. She would never agree to act as his eyes and ears.''

Luke named Elsie's helper in the kitchen and the girl who occasionally helped Martha with the heavier cleaning. Bria dismissed both out of hand. Similarly, she wouldn't accept that she had been betrayed by Tad or any of the men and boys who worked with the horses. She believed the laborers could all be trusted and she could not conceive that anyone who had benefited from her arrangement to repair their home would speak of it to Orrin. Least of all John.

"That leaves chance," Luke said dryly. "And I say my luck has never been that bad. Someone spoke to Orrin, Bria. No matter how much you wish it were otherwise, that's what happened."

"Why now?" she asked.

"I would venture this is not a new arrangement. You will have to judge that for yourself. Think back to other times when Orrin has been gone from Concord. What came to pass when he returned?"

Bria considered the question. "I have never attempted anything on so large a scale as these repairs, but once I hid some money from the profits and he found it."

"Immediately?"

"No. A few weeks after he was home. But that was very stupid of me, Luke. Orrin is forever trying to find the Hamilton riddle. He would not accept that it wasn't here. I should have anticipated he would come upon my hiding place."

"All right. Other things?"

"During one malarial season I organized a school for the children of the sharecroppers."

"What happened to it?"

"The Klan." Bria's tone was flat. "No one was injured, for which I thank God. About a dozen riders came at night and burned the old slave cabin where I had arranged for the children to meet. It's the only one of the cabins that's gone now. I didn't care about the cabin. It was the books and slates and maps that were really of value."

"Did you suspect Orrin alerted the Klan?"

"Yes, but I never thought that someone here might have alerted Orrin. I just supposed he found out on his own and I resolved to be more careful. I chose to be less involved in providing assistance and simply turned a blind eye to certain activities. It wasn't until your arrival and the realization that I could get building supplies that I involved myself again. You must know I chose the men helping you carefully. It was important that they were skilled enough to assist you, but they also had to acquire the materials that were needed elsewhere at Concord.'' Bria pressed one hand to her brow. ''I fear I may have endangered them, Luke. If something happens to them, I won't be able to forgive myself.''

''It is too early to speak of not forgiving yourself, Bree. We should wait to see what Orrin discovers from my accounts. It will go a long way in helping us know how to proceed.''

He spoke of ''we'' and ''us'' so easily, Bria thought. ''I didn't mean to involve you,'' she said.

''I involved myself.''

''To help me.''

''Not entirely,'' he said. ''It was not without some regard for my own interests.''

Bria did not ask what those interests were and Luke offered no explanation. By some silent, mutual agreement they sat quietly on the bench and listened to the rain rather than the tenor of their own thoughts.

After what had passed between them the previous night, Bria had supposed it would be awkward sharing a room with Luke again. She had not let herself think a great deal about sharing anything else.

When she came out of the dressing room Luke was already cozily situated in the center of the bed. No matter which side she took, he would be cleaved to it.

Watching her, Luke grinned. He patted the space on both sides of him. ''I'm prepared to move either way.''

''I don't suppose you are prepared to move to the floor.''

His grin vanished. Luke searched her face. ''Is that what you want?''

Was it? she asked herself. ''No.'' And she realized it was true. She wanted to be with him in this room and in this bed. ''I'll take the right side.''

Luke nodded and raised the covers. Bria came around the bed and slipped in. She was wearing a white cotton nightshift. Tonight the ribbon that trimmed the neckline was pale yellow. Luke only had a glimpse of it before she turned and put out the lamp, but his fingers had no trouble finding it in the dark. He pulled on one end. There was a whisper of satin as the small bow was undone.

Bria stared up at him. Luke was propped on one elbow, watching her intently. He was not touching her, yet she could feel the heat of his hand as he fingered the ribbon.

"Did you think I wouldn't want you again?" His voice was husky. "When you fell asleep in the gazebo this afternoon, I wished it had happened here."

She remembered waking up when the rain ended. Her head was lying in Luke's lap. He had placed his jacket over her and his fingers were lightly threading through her hair. The two ivory combs and pins that had anchored it were at his side. He helped her repair her hair before escorting her back to the house. He had not demanded even a single kiss as payment, but Bria thought it was because no one was watching them just then. She found herself wishing it had been different.

"You can say no, Bree." He parted the neckline of her shift and pushed the material over one shoulder. He dipped his head and kissed the soft curve. "I've been imagining what I would do if you say no." His breath was warm against her skin.

Bria merely hummed her pleasure as his lips nuzzled the side of her neck. She arched, giving him her throat. She felt his tongue dip into the hollow.

"I was going to throw myself into the river."

She smiled a little at this bit of drama. "You're a good swimmer, Luke. It's not as if you would drown."

He kissed the underside of her chin, then her jaw. His mouth moved her ear and his teeth caught the lobe and tugged. "I wouldn't want to kill myself," he whispered. "Just get your attention."

"You have my attention." Bria caught his face in her hands.

She moved her own head to bring their mouths closer. "I'm not going to say no." She kissed him.

He murmured something that was lost to both of them. Her lips moved over his. Her hands threaded together behind his neck and she held him there. She suckled gently at his mouth, drawing out the kiss so the tempo was lilting and languorous. Her tongue played with his, twisting and darting and drawing him in. No one was watching them now, she thought. This kissing was an end in itself. Pleasure for pleasure's sake. Bria had imagined kissing him like this. She had not imagined how much it would mean to her.

Her hands parted and made twin trails down Luke's leanly muscled back. Her fingertips slipped under the string waistband of his drawers. He made a little growling sound that tickled her lips. He did it again against her neck and roused a small laugh from her. She gave him a very different sound when his mouth reached her breast.

His tongue flicked her nipple through the shift. The cotton became damp and pleasantly abrasive. Bria moved restlessly under him; her fingers tunneled in his hair. When his teeth closed over her nipple and tugged, there was a corresponding pull on his head.

Luke raised his head, a distinct gleam in his eye. "I think you should let go of my hair. Before your pleasure scalps me."

Bria's fingers unwound immediately. She blushed and looked everywhere but at him.

Cupping her face in his hands, Luke brought her attention to him. He kissed her puckered brow, then her nose, and finally the corner of her mouth. "Let's get you out of this gown," he said. "For a taste of your naked breast I shouldn't mind at all if you pluck my hair one strand at a time."

Bria's mouth opened, closed, then opened again. "That's a perfectly outrageous thing to say."

He grinned, unrepentant. "Come here." Luke helped Bria to a sitting position and made short work of her shift. He tossed it over his head to the foot of the bed. When Bria's hands lifted to cover herself, he caught her wrists and stayed them. "Some day we're going to do this in the afternoon. Perhaps by the river in the shade of the cottonwood or under a canopy of pines. There will be sufficient sunlight to dapple your skin and allow me to admire every line and curve."

"You're mad."

"I'm hopeful."

Bria could only shake her head. She didn't suck in her lip in time to fully temper her smile. She let herself be borne down to the mattress again and covered by Luke's body. His mouth closed over her breast, laving the nipple until the bud was hard and erect. She whimpered when he drew on her flesh. The suction of his mouth made radiating threads of pleasure. Bria felt the stir of heat in her fingertips, in her womb, at the back of her knee, yet he held only her breast.

Under his touch her flesh swelled slightly. Her breath caught when his mouth hovered over her other breast. Bria arched and gave herself up to the damp edge of his tongue.

This time what she clutched was the sheet. Her fingers uncurled a fraction when Luke's head moved from her breasts and paused in the hollow between them, but they tightened again, even harder this time, when he began to move lower, over the slope of her ribcage and along the flat of her abdomen.

Bria took in a sharp breath. Her skin retracted as if she could escape the sensation of his mouth. Luke shifted lower still. His hands slid under her and he palmed her buttocks. He kissed her just above the triangle of dark-honey hair at her thighs. The scent of her musk was heady. His entire body reacted with an intense sharpening of desire.

"Luke?"

He was parting her thighs, caressing the soft inner skin that was as sweetly tender as a babe's. His open mouth pressed her flesh. He kissed her. Once. Again.

"Luke!" Bria's heels dug into the mattress and she pushed at his shoulders. "No! I can't. What are you—"

He drew himself up and over her, resting some of his weight

on his elbows. Luke's heavily engorged penis pressed at his drawers and against Bria. Involuntarily her hips rolled under him.

"Don't move," he whispered, his voice hoarse.

"I didn't mean to."

"I know." His breath was slightly ragged. He closed his eyes briefly and the strain of denial showed on his taut features. "I know," he repeated, less harshly this time. He lowered his head and touched Bria's forehead with his own. "I'm sorry. I didn't think about you, what you were prepared for or wanted."

"Those are two different things."

He lifted his head and stared at her. "Hmmm?"

"Being prepared for something and wanting it. Very different. I think I wanted what you were doing to me but I wasn't prepared for it. You should have told me what you intended."

Luke's eyes darkened a fraction as he considered the merits of that. He imagined whispering every detail of his intentions in her ear. "Perhaps we'll save it all for another time."

She nodded. "If you wish." Her hips shifted again and she glanced away when Luke groaned softly.

"It's all right." He dropped away from her and pulled at the string of his drawers. It knotted. Bria's low laughter did not improve his deftness.

"Let me." She pushed his hands away and worked the knot herself. Her knuckles brushed his flat belly. Her hair fell forward as she bent her head to the task, shielding her face and her small triumphant smile when she released the string. "Perhaps we should use satin ribbons to close your drawers. You do better with them."

Luke arched a brow. The decidedly wicked look had Bria backing away. He didn't let her get far. He was able to wriggle out of his drawers and still capture her before she left the bed.

It was a frenzy after that. The sheets and blankets tangled in their legs. He kicked them away; she dragged them back. He let her take him by the wrists and hold him down so that she could stretch along his length. She kissed his face, his throat. Her tongue made a damp trail along his collarbone. When they rolled again she was under him. Her legs parted and her knees were raised on either side of his flanks.

Time only slowed once. Bria watched his face as he came into her, the tightening of his jaw, the pulse that beat at his temple, the intensity of his eyes as he studied her in turn.

Bria's hands came to Luke's shoulders. He held himself still inside of her. Her body stretched, accommodated. "This isn't wrong, is it?" she asked softly. "Tell me it isn't wrong."

So Luke told her, not because she asked him to, but because it was true. No matter what happened later, he thought, he would never count these shared moments among any that he regretted.

He moved in her then, thrusting deeply, hard. Bria clutched him and accepted the swift rise and fall of his body, meeting it with her own. There was a fierceness to their joining this time. Heat. Unchecked passion. Luke's whipcord lean frame strained against hers. The smoothly taut muscles across his back shifted under her fingers. Bria's slender legs held him. The soles of her feet rubbed his calves. A thin film of perspiration made her throat damp. Her skin glowed.

Luke rose up. His hips rocked against her hard and fast and then his own skin became too tight to contain him. Release seemed to shatter him. He gave a hoarse shout and his arms tightened around Bria for a moment, then went slack. He buried his face in the curve of her shoulder.

Bria stroked the back of Luke's head. His dark hair was damp at the ends. It curled around her fingers. His closeness was comfortable and she didn't try to push him away.

"I'm crushing you," he said.

She shook her head.

"You can't even talk."

"I don't want to talk."

"Then perhaps you don't mind if I do." He turned his mouth toward her ear and made his intentions clear.

* * *

Bria stirred sleepily in Luke's arms. Her limbs felt pleasantly heavy and when she moved it was slow, as if she were moving through water. She opened her eyes. Luke was lying partially on his side. A lock of hair had fallen across his forehead. The lack of tension in his features and the wayward lock of hair made him seem younger.

When Luke's eyes opened, Bria said the first thing that came to her mind. "I don't even know how old you are."

"Thirty-one."

"Rand's age." The stab of pain came immediately afterward. She swallowed hard.

"It's all right, Bree. You can cry."

Her smile was bittersweet. "I know. But I don't want to. Not now." She searched his face. "Did I disturb you? I didn't mean to."

"No." He glanced at the clock on the mantel, squinting in the darkness to see the numerals against the white face. "We've been asleep less than an hour."

Then it was nowhere close to morning. Bria found a certain contentment in that. "Were you a soldier like Rand?"

"I don't think so. He was an officer, wasn't he?"

"Yes. Cavalry."

"Well, I certainly wasn't an officer."

"Where did you serve?"

"Wherever I was needed."

Bria frowned. "You're being purposely vague."

"Not entirely. I did serve wherever I was sent. I was an engineer, Bria. I built railroad trestles so troops and supplies could move farther, faster. If the tracks were held by the other side—*your* side—I helped blow them up."

"You volunteered for that duty?"

He nodded shortly. His tone was equally terse. "I'd rather choose than be chosen."

Bria stared at him, wondering what it was that he wasn't

saying. Beneath the blankets her hand searched out Luke's. Her forefinger moved back and forth across the ridges of his knuckles. "Rand never wanted to talk much about the war."

"Your brother volunteered to fight?"

"Yes. So did Shelby and my father. David would have gone but someone was needed here."

It was what Luke expected. "I was conscripted, Bria. I stayed in school for the first two years of the war. I was in New York in July of '63, visiting my mother and aunts. Earlier in March, Congress passed the Enrollment and Conscription Act. That summer lottery wheels were set up in different districts and the drafting board began selecting men to serve. There was a lot of disaffection among the population. For three hundred dollars a drafted man could be exempted. The money was used to secure someone in his stead. You can see how it benefited the rich and played hell with the poor."

"Which were you, Luke?"

"I was poor, but I had a benefactor. A friend of my mother's took it upon himself to make the payment."

Bria hazarded a guess. "Her boarder?"

At first Luke did not understand. His brows drew together. "Boarder?"

"Yes. The one that let you work as his accountant."

His face cleared instantly. "Yes. That's the one. He was very good to us. At least he meant to be. I know my mother begged him to intercede for me."

"You accepted what he did for you?"

"Yes." He saw Bria try to keep her expression neutral. She failed. Her feelings were too strong. "I didn't expect you would agree or approve," he said. "I hold my own liberty at a price far greater than three hundred dollars, Bree. I recognize no man's right to tell me for what cause I must risk my life."

Bria was silent, trying to understand how Luke thought about it. "My father, Shelby, even Rand . . . they were all so eager to serve . . . it's difficult for me to imagine that you weren't."

"They were convinced that what they were fighting for was

important. I wasn't." He watched Bria shake her head slowly, quite unable to take this in. "I wasn't alone, Bree, though I'm not certain others objected for the same reasons I did. There were riots in the city that July. Thousands of men took part in them. It started as a protest against the draft and ended in a bloody melee. Telegraph lines were cut to police headquarters. Train service was interrupted. Enrollment offices were burned. Homes were sacked. The rioters beat off police with iron bars, clubs, and stones. Men climbed onto roofs so they could throw brickbats down on the police. It went on for days.

"Troops were called in. The Brooklyn Naval Yard sent marines. Two armed ships were stationed in the Hudson and East Rivers to protect the financial district from looting. Barricades, like those used by revolutionaries in Paris, were set up in the streets by the rioters. The fighting went hand to hand, house to house.

"At one point during the days of rioting the crowd targeted the Negroes. The Colored Orphan Asylum was attacked and burned. Two hundred children escaped while thousands of rioters were storming the front doors, but elsewhere in the area men and women of color were hunted down, beaten, and occasionally murdered."

Luke felt Bria's shudder. "Do you want to know if I was part of it?" he asked.

"It never occurred to me that you were," she said quietly. "I was only imagining what it must have been like and I find it's too horrible to contemplate for long."

"The city was brought to its knees before the fighting was stopped. What happened there was no protest. It had ceased to be that after the first hour of the first day. It was insurrection. Revolution. Federal troops from the Army of the Potomac were diverted to New York to make the citizens heel."

Luke turned on his back and stared at the ceiling. "This all happened within weeks of the slaughter at Gettysburg. All of the dead could not yet have been buried when the rioting began." His low, dry laughter was devoid of humor. "You must be wondering how we won the war, Bree. I can only tell you my own thoughts. It was not because we had the stomach for it, but because we didn't. We wanted it to be over and there was too much inbred Yankee stubbornness to consider surrendering. We fought on to get it over with.''

Bria bunched some pillows around her head so that it was raised a few degrees. She stared at Luke's unblinking profile. "Is that why you joined?" she asked. "You just wanted to get it over with?"

"Yes. In part. Don't misunderstand, Bree. I always thought preserving the Union was important, but it wasn't until the draft riots that I decided it was worth risking my life for. Twelve hundred people were killed in the street fighting and nothing was served by it. A month later the drafts continued without a murmur of protest. A payment had already been made on my behalf so I could avoid serving and I accepted it because the rules said I could. Then I enlisted and became my own replacement.''

Luke turned his head sideways to look at her. "It must seem like a protest of no account to you, but it was important that it be *my* choice. That's what I was agreeing to fight for. Nothing less than preservation of individual liberties extended to *all* men.''

Bria was quiet, considering that. "Do you think that's what you won?"

"I don't know. I'd like to believe that it happened in some small measure.''

"Why did you join the engineer corps?"

"It's what I could do. I wasn't a marksman. I couldn't get off two shots in a minute with the army's standard-issue Springfield, but I knew how to blow up a bridge with a few sticks of dynamite.'' Luke breathed in the fragrance of Bria's hair. He wrapped one strand around his index fingers. It was spun like silk thread. "Do you think I'm a coward, Bree?"

"No!"

"But when I told you I accepted the draft payment—"

She interrupted him. "I didn't understand. I thought—"

"I was a coward," Luke finished for her. "It's all right. I've considered the question myself. Every man wonders how he'll act when faced with certain terrible choices."

"You can hold your head up, Luke. You acted on your conscience." Bria hesitated, then plunged ahead. "You didn't want to tell me, did you? Did you think I would judge you?"

"You *should* judge my actions. They speak for me."

"Then they speak well of you." She moved closer and placed one arm across his chest. "Was my good opinion so important?"

Luke didn't answer immediately. Whatever her opinion, it would not have changed his own thinking, but he could admit that he cared very much that she could accept his choices. "Yes," he said finally. "It was."

It was no simple admission that Luke made, but a confession. Bria did not think she had mistaken that and she was moved by it. She started to say something but Luke stopped her.

"Sleep on it, Bree."

She smiled a little at that. He had managed to keep her from saying something foolish. "You promised that you would try not to be so annoyingly right," she whispered.

Luke chuckled softly. He fell asleep only after the easy cadence of Bria's breathing assured him that she had, too.

Three days passed before Orrin summoned Luke and Bria to his study and announced that everything in the house restoration accounts was in order. He gave this news in the morning shortly after he rose and before he had his first drink. Orrin's tone was civil, his manner conciliatory. He congratulated Luke for the quality and quantity of work that had already been accomplished and for finding a way in which to turn a small profit on materials that were of no further use to them.

Orrin had very little to say to Bria. She was left with the impression that it was somehow important to her stepfather that she hear the praise he had for Luke, that she was in effect being punished for having none of it heaped on her.

The peculiarity of the audience with Orrin stayed with Bria. She found herself considering its implications at odd moments. "He hasn't forgotten or forgiven," she told Luke later. "You should be thinking what you can do to get back in his good graces."

"What about you?"

"I was never *in* his good graces. I can't go back."

Luke gave it some thought and invited Orrin to play cards that evening. He shamelessly allowed his father-in-law to win on that occasion and on three subsequent nights. It was only on the fifth evening that he started to get a little of his own back. By then Orrin's humor was sufficiently restored to accept some modest losses.

The beginning of November brought the gradual return of the planters and their families. They came from their summer homes in Charleston and on the offshore islands along the coast. Some of them carried virtually all their possessions in a caravan of wagons. Sometimes families stopped at Concord for rest and refreshment on their way to their own homes. Orrin complained bitterly in private that his home was becoming a way station, but he was expansive in his welcome when faced with his guests.

Because Elizabeth was often indisposed, it was left to Bria to entertain the women and children. The planters themselves usually found their way into Orrin's study and emerged hours later a little less steady on their feet. Their wives were philosophical about it. Their children giggled.

The visits were both a relief and a trial for Bria. She welcomed their beginning and their end. She looked forward to lying in Luke's arms at night and thinking on all that had passed during the day. He simply let her talk about whatever came to her mind and when she came around to her brother, as she invariably did, he listened even more closely, allowing her to mourn, allowing her to heal.

The memorial service for Rand was planned for the third Sunday in November. That morning marked the first time Elizabeth Foster left the plantation since returning from Charleston. Entering the church on her husband's arm, she appeared as brittle as old china. A fine web of wrinkles creased the corners of her mouth and eyes. Her skin was pale against her black satin gown and bonnet. In contrast, Orrin looked remarkably healthy. His countenance was sober, even if his liver was not. He had imbibed enough to get him through the rigors of the service but not so much that he was in danger of drawing comment.

Luke observed how much the service meant to Bria's mother. The church was crowded enough to force people to stand at the back. Elizabeth seemed to take solace and strength in the volume of the turnout, accepting it as a tribute to her son and as a measure of the respect she was still afforded. She remained dry-eyed throughout the service and later, through all the condolences that were given to her.

The formal announcement of Bria's marriage to Luke was made that afternoon at the reception back at Concord. Orrin and Elizabeth made it jointly and acted as if there was nothing at all unusual about informing their guests of a wedding in the middle of a wake.

"Did you see the way they all looked at my belly?" Bria asked. She was sitting at the window seat, brushing out her hair. It was after midnight and the last malingering guests had finally gone.

Luke came into view from the dressing room. A towel was riding low on his hips. He held the knot in place with one hand while he raked his damp hair with the other. Beads of water still glistened on his shoulders. "That might be where the women were looking. I observed a great many stares in the area of your breasts."

"Luke!"

"It's true. They were—" He stopped because Bria was shaking her head frantically. She had cried out his name to get his attention, not to admonish him. She was sitting up on her knees, entirely turned toward the window. She yanked the curtain back and pressed her face to the glass. When she called his name a second time he was at her side and looking off in the same direction.

He had no difficulty finding what had drawn her eye. Every flicker was perfectly outlined against the night sky.

They watched helplessly as the first fireball erupted.

Chapter Twelve

Glass shattered in the explosion. "My greenhouse!" Bria scrambled off the window seat, eluding Luke's efforts to stop her.

He followed her into the dressing room. "I'll go," he said, picking up a pair of trousers.

"I won't stop you."

Which meant, Luke supposed, that he should show her a similar courtesy. He yanked on his pants and reached for a shirt over Bria's head as she stood dressing in front of the armoire. She was quicker with her satin wrapper and slippers than he was with more suitable clothing. Luke caught up to her in the hallway where she had been slowed by her mother.

"Luke and I will handle it, Mother," Bria explained hurriedly. "Stay in your room."

Elizabeth grasped Bria's arm with surprising strength. "Don't leave me."

Luke passed Bria and took the stairs two and three at time. He sprinted down the hall and out onto the verandah. On the horizon to the west, the bright orange, crimson, and yellow flames of three separate fires lent their color and light to the black sky.

Luke started down the verandah steps but stopped when he heard shouting from inside the house. He had no problem recognizing the voices. When he backtracked he found Orrin and Bria standing toe-to-toe outside the study.

"Thank God you're here," Orrin said, watching Luke's approach over Bria's shoulder. "Maybe you can talk some sense into her. Tell her she can't have my guns. She'll get herself killed."

Luke pushed right past Orrin and took down two of the shotguns that were mounted above the mantelpiece. "They're loaded?" he called to Bria.

"Always. There are more shells in the desk."

Luke found them easily. When he returned to the door, he handed one of the rifles and some extra shells to Bria. "I assume you can use this."

"Probably better than you."

Luke glanced at Orrin. "What do you know about the fires?"

"Not a goddamn thing." Orrin's florid features were set belligerently.

"He won't tell you, Luke. It's the Klan." Bria spun on her heel and hurried down the hall.

Luke swore softly under his breath. "Is she right?"

Orrin's shoulders were squared off as though he anticipated being pinned back against the wall. "How the hell would I know?" His eyes darted past Luke and toward the stairs. "Go back to your room, Elizabeth. This doesn't concern you."

"Bria's gone, Orrin," she said softly. The lamp that she carried lighted her face and threw her shadow along the wall. The shadow was hardly more substantial than she was. "I should go after her."

Orrin's eyes narrowed on Luke. "Do you see?" he demanded. "Bria's place is here, with her mother. Now, step aside so I can go to my wife. You, Kincaid, need to go after your own."

Luke caught up to Bria again in the stables. Apollo was being saddled for her while she paced the area outside his stall.

Luke leaned his shotgun against the wall and began to saddle a horse for himself. In a few minutes they were mounted and heading out of the stableyard.

"Forget the greenhouse," Bria called to him. "We need to get to the outlying farms."

They rode hard in the direction of the glow among the treetops. Bria's shift was hiked up to her knees. The tail of her dressing gown snapped in the wind as Apollo charged down the road. Her hair fanned out behind her, waving and whipping like a flag. In profile her features were stark, grim.

"John!" Bria called the name out as soon as she realized the origin of one of the fires. "It's John Whitney's place!"

Luke nodded. He leaned forward and urged his mount not to lose any more ground to Apollo.

They had to slow once they reached the woods that separated John's homestead from the edge of the cultivated fields. Through the trees they could see the house was fully engulfed in flames. When they reached the clearing they crossed the open ground quickly, pulling their mounts back only when they felt the heat of the fire on their own faces.

Bria dismounted immediately and unsheathed her shotgun. "John!" She turned a full three hundred and sixty degrees, her eyes narrowing as she surveyed the uneven ground visible in the circle of light. "John! Where are you? John!"

Luke called after her when she started to move closer to the house. He saw her hesitate and thought she meant to listen to him, but as she went forward again he realized it was only the blistering heat that gave her pause. He kicked at his mare's flanks and urged her forward, then turned her quickly to block Bria's path. "Get back, Bree." It was a voice he had never used with her before and it guaranteed he meant to give her no quarter. "Get back or I swear I'll take you to the house over this saddle."

Bria stared up at him, her expression anguished. "John," she said hollowly. "We have to find John."

Luke scanned the area. The ground around them had been

trampled by horses' hooves. Clods of earth lay scattered among the holes. There was some evidence of footprints on the soft soil but most of the work had been done from horseback.

Behind them a portion of the roof collapsed. Sparks showered the sky and scattered light farther across the field. It was then Luke saw the odd feathering of grass that led into the woods northwest of the house. The grass lay oddly brushed to one side in some places, swirled and broken in others. It formed a flattened trail, like a carpet runner rolled out for royalty. Luke's eyes narrowed as he tried to make sense of what he was seeing.

"Mount up, Bree."

"What about John?"

"They took John with them."

She backed away out of Luke's shadow and tried to see what had brought him to that conclusion. At her height Bria did not have the same perspective as Luke. "What if you're wrong?"

"If I'm wrong and he's in that house, then he's dead and there's nothing we can do."

Bria flinched at Luke's tone but not at his logic. She thrust her shotgun back in the scabbard and pulled herself into Apollo's saddle. Her eyes followed Luke's outstretched arm and finally saw the trail and understood what it meant. John had not just been taken away. He had been dragged.

Far in the distance, so that it was only a faint glow over the treetops, another fire erupted. "The church is that way, Luke! *Their* church."

Luke pressed his heels hard into the mare and she shot forward. Bria followed closely. Apollo would have overtaken the mare but Bria would not give him his head. The terrain was uneven and presented a danger to both animals. When they reached the woods they had to pick their way through the trees. Bria could not imagine how the night riders had pulled John among the brambles and tree trunks.

Halfway into the woods they splashed through a swiftly running stream. It was too dark to follow the trail any longer so they kept heading in the direction of the fire. Their pace increased again as the wood became less dense. By the time they entered the clearing the horses were ready to cover the ground at a full gallop.

Luke counted five men on horseback. Every one of them was hooded and robed in white, lending them a ghost-like appearance in the firelight. Luke only wished that was what they were. All of them were armed but their guns and rifles were not drawn. It was unnecessary. They had gathered their mounts into a loose circle to surround their quarry. The threat of more violence, of death, was there without going for their weapons. Men, women, and a few children were huddled in the middle of the circle, facing outward, watching their tormentors with wary, fearful, and, in some cases, hostile expressions.

The riders did not see Luke and Bria approach until they were a third of the way across the clearing. By that time both of them had their shotguns out. The fire crackled loud enough to muffle the pounding of the horses' hooves. Slender, jagged flames crawled up the side of the small church and fanned across the roof. The light and shadows thrown across the gathering were both eerie and menacing.

Luke and Bria slowed their mounts to a walk but continued forward at a steady pace. Luke could see now that there were more children than he had first thought. Their parents had them protected in the very center of the group. He also saw that one of their number was already down, lying on the ground being tended to by a woman. It required another surge of flames for Luke to recognize the woman as Addie and the man as John Whitney.

Ten yards from the circle of riders, Bria reined in Apollo. She lowered her shotgun and took dead aim at one of the hooded men. "Get off my land now," she said. "And I won't shoot one of you just because I can."

A few of the horses shuffled in place but none of the riders left the group. The hooded figure Bria aimed at raised his right hand slowly, palm out. The loose-fitting robe lifted, too. It fluttered a bit in the breeze like a flag of surrender. "This has nothing to do with you, Bria. Go on your way."

"That was my greenhouse you torched. This is my land. That building belongs to me."

"I beg to differ," he drawled. "This is Foster's land. I can't believe you've forgotten that. Our complaint is with him and these nigras. You shouldn't concern yourself or your husband there. Go on back and get yourself decent. Unless you planned to join us. You're nearly dressed for it."

Bria ignored the chuckles this last comment brought. She readjusted her aim. "You can be satisfied with what you've accomplished tonight. You've terrorized these people enough. Now go."

Luke heard the unspoken threat in Bria's tone. He kept his shotgun leveled on another member of the group. The mare stayed steady under him and his aim did not waver. He made certain the riders could see the repeat action on his rifle. He could get off three shots before any of them drew and his concentration on their group communicated his intent to do it. He was prepared to kill, not injure.

Luke knew the moment the riders were going to back down. four of them took their eyes off their leader and began to look to each other for direction. With this small dissension in the ranks the will of the group was broken. Uncertainty was transmitted to the animals and the horses began to shuffle nervously; one of them actually began to back out of the circle.

The leader was quickly aware of the uncertainty that surrounded him now. He reacted decisively to halt it. The hand he had lifted toward Bria was raised higher. He twisted it once in a gesture that essentially dismissed the troop.

The signal pulled them together again. Almost as one they turned their mounts and fled toward the river.

Bria and Luke did not lower their weapons, even when the riders disappeared.

"Addie?" Luke called, urging his horse forward. "How's John?"

"He's alive, Mister Luke, but just. Wrists burned raw from the rope they used. He's got a dislocated shoulder. Belly and feet are all tore up." Her breath caught on a sob. In the firelight the tears on her dark face glowed like embers. "They drug him. *Drug* him. He pulled himself up on his feet and *ran* behind the horses. He wants to live, Mister Luke. My John wants to *live.*"

Luke stopped her. "We have to hurry, Addie. Can you ride with him, keep him up in the saddle?"

Addie had no idea but she was game. She nodded her head vehemently. "I can, Mister Luke. I can do that."

It was accomplished with more efficiency than Luke could have hoped for. Bria took charge of the children and families and moved them to a point of safety away from the burning church and in the opposite direction the riders had gone. She stayed huddled with them until Luke had Addie and John mounted on his mare. John faded in and out of consciousness and leaned heavily against Addie for support, but he was able to stay upright. Her small frame shouldered his weight as if no effort was required.

Bria provided their escort back to the main house while Luke remained to assist the others. Three families had been targeted by the Klan. All of them had had repairs completed to their homes, but only one family had been burned out. They stayed at the church to make certain the fire didn't spread. The women wept softly while they comforted their children. The men remained silent, stoic yet somehow resigned.

Luke memorized their guarded, tormented expressions, and thought about the faces he hadn't been able to see, the ones that remained hidden under the hoods. His grip on the rifle became bloodless.

"I could have killed them," he told Bria a few hours later. He was sitting in the kitchen with her, drinking a cup of coffee. He had her chair turned slightly sideways so his feet could rest on the rungs under her seat. "There was a moment, while I sat with the others watching their church burn, that I regretted I hadn't fired a single shot.''

Bria's heels were hooked on the edge of her seat. She hugged her knees to her chest, her nightgown pulled taut over them. Her coffee cup remained untried on the table top. ''I thought you said you weren't a marksman.'' Belatedly she realized how inane the comment was. ''I'm sorry, I'm not thinking clearly.''

''You're tired.''

''No, I'm not. I'm so wide awake I'm not certain I'll ever sleep again, or want to.'' With her eyes open or closed, Bria could clearly see John's bruised and battered body, the dark skin shredded across his belly and arms so that bloody layers of tissue were laid open. She and Addie had made him as comfortable as possible in the overseer's cabin. Jeb and Elsie lent their assistance, bringing fresh water and sheets, shredding bandages, and scrubbing the wounds clean.

In some ways John's silence was harder to bear than his injuries. The pain Bria saw in his eyes seemed unrelated to his raw wounds. The tears that made his dark eyes glisten appeared when he watched Addie kneel beside his bed, not when Jeb cleaned dirt and bits of twisted hemp from his savaged wrists.

''I didn't realize how much John Whitney loves her,'' Bria said. ''Addie, I mean. It was so very clear tonight. His eyes followed her everywhere.''

''She staying with him?''

''Yes. I left her my rifle.''

One of Luke's brows kicked up. ''Is that a good idea?''

''I don't know. I was afraid to leave her without protection.''

''Bree, you know what will happen to her if she points a gun at a white man. What if I stay with John tonight?''

''You'd do that?''

''Of course. I like John. Addie, too. I don't really think there will be another raid this evening—the Klan accomplished what it set out to do—but I don't mind taking up a post in the cabin.'' He saw Bria gnaw absently on her bottom lip. She picked up her coffee cup and held it between her palms while she considered his offer. Luke was fairly certain he knew the bent of her thoughts. "In the event you're still wondering what sort of marksman I am, I can tell you I improved."

"A lot?"

"Enough." One corner of his mouth lifted. "Would I be correct in assuming you have some small concern for my safety?"

"You may assume anything you like."

The creases at the corners of his mouth deepened. Luke's eyes regarded her warmly.

Bria was not proof against the double assault of that crooked grin and smoky grey glance. "Oh, very well. I don't want you dead."

Luke found that he still had it in him to laugh. "A singularly compassionate declaration."

"After all, you haven't won Concord yet."

"Yes, there's the wager to consider."

His wry tone raised Bria's own small smile. She sipped her coffee. "Would you mind if I sat with you?"

Luke didn't answer immediately. His expression gradually sobered as he considered her request. "I didn't want you out there with me tonight," he said finally.

"I know, but it wasn't your place to say whether or not I went. It was mine. They could have killed you without me there. You must be aware of that."

"Orrin was sending us a message. I don't think it was his intention to have either one of us killed."

"Perhaps not. But then he doesn't have control once he sets them loose. You saw what they did to John. I doubt very much my stepfather specifically ordered that. It's more likely that he said something vaguely threatening, like 'teach them a lesson.'" Bria put her coffee down, most of it untouched, and hugged her knees to her chest. "You recognized some of them, didn't you?"

"A few. I met all of them earlier, I think. Probably shook

hands with most of them. They were guests here at Concord. I believe you had your gun leveled on Austin Tipping.''

Bria nodded. ''What gave him away?''

''His shoes. I noticed them when he cornered you this evening shortly after the announcement of our marriage.''

''You noticed his shoes,'' she said with quiet incredulity.

Luke shrugged. He could have told her that he had to look at something besides the way Tipping was openly admiring her. ''How did you recognize him?''

''His horse. That's the way I knew them all. Sam Daniels. William Adkins. Franklin Archer. Jim Poling. You *did* shake hands will them tonight. My mother and I accepted their most heartfelt condolences about Rand.'' She sighed. ''Do you know they meant their regrets, Luke? Even that bastard Austin. They would be deeply hurt if they thought I didn't realize that. What they did tonight to John and the others, to their church and homes, wasn't supposed to make me think less of them. They see their actions as actually protecting something Rand and the rest of my family fought for.''

Bria impatiently swiped at the tears that gathered at the corners of her eyes. Her next breath shuddered through her. ''That isn't why Shelby and Rand and my father went to war, Luke. It isn't why David died at home trying to take care of us. They were fighting because they didn't want to be dictated to. They were fighting for independence.''

''I know,'' he said quietly. He set his coffee cup beside hers. ''Come here.''

Bria raised her head a fraction and stared at him through eyes still luminous with tears. ''Where?''

Luke patted his thigh. ''Here.''

She surprised herself by not hesitating. There was not the slightest qualm about accepting the invitation. Bria very much wanted to have Luke's arms around her. She moved from her chair to his lap so quickly and easily it seemed her feet never touched the cool kitchen floor. She placed her arms around his neck to anchor her to his side. Belatedly it occurred to her that perhaps he'd heard someone coming. Her glance turned toward the door.

Reading her thoughts, Luke smiled. "There's no one there, Bree. Not that I'm aware of. Orrin was passed out in the study when I went there to return my rifle. I don't think he'll rouse himself until late morning. When I checked on your mother she had fallen asleep in a chair in her room. I think she meant to wait for you."

"I should go to her." She made no move to do so, however. Luke's loose embrace was too comforting to leave it just yet. "In a little while," she added.

Luke nodded. He could smell the faint scent of wood smoke in Bria's hair as she laid her head in the crook of his neck and shoulder. It reminded him there were still things left unsaid. "What about your greenhouse, Bree? You said that what the Klan did tonight wasn't meant to be a personal affront. How do you account for the greenhouse?"

She was silent for some time, thinking it through. "I'm not certain Austin and the others are to blame for the greenhouse," she said finally. "It's occurred to me that that may have been entirely Orrin's doing. I'll know better in the morning when I can look around the area. There would have to be some evidence of the group if they set the fire. I'm not sure we'll find that. Orrin might have acted alone."

"He would do that?"

"If he didn't think the others would go along. Orrin had time and opportunity to set the fire. That's all he needed. Perhaps you didn't notice, but there were a number of occasions when he was absent from my mother's side this evening."

Luke had noticed. "I saw him retire to his study during many of those times." He'd thought it was because Orrin needed to fortify himself with drink. Looking back, he realized that Orrin hadn't always gone alone. He had invariably been closeted with one or more of the men who had attacked John. Orrin had used the occasion of Rand's wake to make arrangements with the

Klan. "You've been expecting something like this, haven't you?"

"Yes. Of course. I told you my stepfather would want his pound of flesh." She thought of all she had seen tonight, especially John's tortured body, and couldn't repress another shudder. "I hadn't anticipated he would demand it in quite so literal a manner."

"Is this the end of it?" asked Luke.

"For now. Until Orrin gets it in his head that I've undermined his authority again."

"This wasn't precisely in Orrin's head, you know. You *did* undermine his authority."

"I know." It was hardly more than a whisper. "I know I'm to blame for what's happened."

Luke lifted Bria's chin. "That isn't what I meant. You're not responsible for Orrin."

"You said it yourself, Luke. I knew the risks. I knew what he was capable of."

"So did everyone else."

"Not the children," she said stubbornly.

"Their parents were willing to take the risk *because* of their children. I took them back to their homes tonight, Bree. I know none of them holds you responsible. They're wondering the same thing I am: who betrayed them?" Luke felt her stiffen in his embrace. "You have to open your mind to it, Bree. Someone told Orrin what was going on. That's the only reason he discovered what you were doing."

"It doesn't seem possible."

Luke did not repeat it was the *only* possibility. If Orrin was indeed finished exacting his revenge, then Bria would have time to consider what had brought them to this pass. "I'm going to go over to the cabin now. Why don't you go to bed?"

She sat up and let her arms fall away from his neck. "I still want to go with you." Bria searched his face. "You can't tell me that it's too dangerous. You already expended some energy earlier convincing me it wasn't. You can't have it both ways, you know.''

"Both ways? I'd settle for *my* way."

He looked so endearingly grumpy about it, that it raised Bria's smile. She slid off his lap. "I'm going to check on Mother and change out of these smoky clothes. I won't be long. Don't shoot me when I come to the cabin." She started to go. Luke's hand snaked out and attached itself to her wrist. Before Bria could divine what he had planned, she was back on his lap with his mouth covering hers.

Sometimes, she thought, Luke's way *was* better.

Orrin listened to Bria's report of the damage the following afternoon. Instead of taking her meal in her bedchamber, Elizabeth had joined them in the dining room. Luke was late to the table but no one had started eating. The tension between Bria and her stepfather was thicker than the creamed chicken over their biscuits.

"So what you're telling me," Orrin said heavily, "is that the Klan came on my land, burned out two homes and a building the nigras were using as a church, and almost killed John Whitney."

"John may still die," Bria said. "He was not doing well this morning."

Orrin slapped the table with the flat of his hand. Bria and Luke didn't flinch, but out of the corner of his eye he saw Elizabeth's head snap up. Well done, he thought. He deserved to have her attention in this matter. "How do you know if he is well or not? Have you been to see him?"

"Addie is nursing him in the overseer's cabin."

"You took it upon yourself to put him there?" he asked sharply.

"I told her she could," Elizabeth said with quiet dignity. She felt three pairs of eyes turn in her direction. Orrin looked surprised. Bria, pained. Only Luke's expression hinted at admiration. "I wanted to consult you, Orrin, but you were asleep in the study and I know how you don't like to be awakened. I thought you would want John well cared for. He is, after all, one the better workers here at Concord, and a lot of the others respect him."

Orrin broke in. "That's enough, Elizabeth."

She barely paused. "They stay because he does. If John dies, I think you can expect that a lot of them will leave. You know yourself that there are barely enough hands now to cope with the rice production."

"Are you quite finished?" Orrin asked flatly.

Elizabeth responded by simply averting her eyes back to her plate. In her lap, her hands trembled. She jammed her fingers together to still them.

"Good." Orrin picked up his fork. He ignored the chicken and biscuits in front of him and waggled the fork at Bria instead, using it to punctuate his point. "As soon as he's on his feet, he's leaving there. This brush with the Klan should have taught you all something, Bria. They won't stand for coddling the nigras. I don't want them down on our heads again, making trouble here at Concord. It may go worse for us the next time."

"It hardly seems to have affected you," Bria said. Under the table she felt Luke nudge her foot. She kicked him back. "You were not stirred to action last night. Luke and I could have used your assistance dealing with the riders."

"My assistance?" Orrin did not feign his astonishment. "What would you have had me do?"

"Precisely what we did. Run them off." She ground her heel on the toe of Luke's boot when he nudged her again. "Mother is not wrong about the need to keep workers here at Concord. You should be considering your duty to protect them, not—"

One of Orrin's thick brows rose in a perfect arch. "Not what?" he asked.

Luke had managed to free his foot from Bria's heel. He risked nudging her again, this time more firmly.

Not ordering the Klan to terrorize them was what Bria wanted to say but she finally heeded Luke's cautionary tap. "Not ignoring them," she finished lamely.

Orrin said nothing, but it was clear he was suspicious of her reply. He turned to Luke. "What do you say, Kincaid? Did you have need of me last night?"

"It would have placed you in harm's way, sir. The truth is, I did not particularly want Bria's assistance."

Watching Bria scowl at her husband, Orrin smiled broadly. "Well said. Finding her difficult to handle, are you?" He lightly tapped the tines of his fork against the tabletop. "You should have sent her upstairs with her mother. Kept her out of harm's way." He tucked into his meal with more enjoyment than one usually reserved for creamed chicken and biscuits. "So what do you think of the way they do things here in the South? Renegade Klansmen taking the law into their own hands. Not what you're used to in New York, is it?"

"I wasn't aware any laws had been broken," Luke said. He picked up his fork and began eating. A moment later he saw Elizabeth and Bria do the same.

"It's their damnable code," Orrin said. "It's not what's written down. It's what's *not* written down. It took me some time to learn, but what I've gathered is this: doing anything for the nigras beyond what the law requires will bring the Klan down on you and them. There's no keeping it secret, either. They always find out. Isn't that right, Bria? Didn't the Klan find out about your school?"

For a moment the reply stuck in her throat. She knew very well how the Klan had discovered its existence. "Yes," she said. "They did."

Orrin turned his attention back to Luke. "Most of the planters south of these parts are still reeling from reconstruction laws that gave the freemen forty acres and a mule if they were of a mind to farm for themselves. No one wants that here." He washed down another bite of biscuit with a large swallow from his wine glass. "It doesn't matter what I think about it. There are many people who don't agree with the Klan's methods but find their existence necessary. I don't try to push my opinion on them. Being a Yankee, they don't care to listen anyway."

Luke realized there was more fact than fiction in what Orrin was telling him. What Orrin failed to relate was his culpability in last night's raid on Concord. Luke was not prepared to challenge him now, not without evidence to support his accusation. Bria and he had investigated the greenhouse. It wasn't the work of the riders on horseback. No more than two men had set the fire. Because there was so little in the greenhouse to burn they carried in lumber and rags soaked in lamp oil and set a bonfire inside. When it got hot enough, the windows exploded. Luke knew he would not easily forget the look in Bria's eyes as she wandered around the wreckage of her experiments. There was nothing that could be saved from her years of work.

Luke took a deep breath and let it out slowly. "I didn't realize when I sold the building materials that it would have such consequences. Perhaps someone should let them know you made a handsome profit. They targeted tenants who'd made repairs to their homes. They might have assumed you sanctioned it, even that you gave the bricks and lumber away."

Orrin considered that, then he waved his hand dismissively. "I'm sure you're right, but changing the Klan's view presumes one of us would know how to reach one or more of them."

"I'll speak to Austin myself," Elizabeth said. She did not look up from her plate but felt everyone's attention on her in spite of that. "I've known for years that Austin Tipping was in the Klan. I believe he helped organize it in this community."

"Mother!" Bria's fork simply fell out of her nerveless fingers. "You've never said a word. How could you possibly know that?"

Bright patches of color appeared in Elizabeth's otherwise pale face. She looked up and regarded her daughter steadily. "Rand told me. Austin approached him about joining years ago."

"Rand? But he—"

"I didn't say your brother joined, only that he was approached. We didn't discuss it at length. Rand had no interest in Austin's proposal. Austin seemed to accept it. In any event he knew Rand was never here long enough to be of any real help."

"Austin Tipping," Orrin said softly, shaking his head. "I'll be damned. He was right here, in my home, spreading his regrets as easy as a bull spreads his chips."

Bria stared at her stepfather, marveling at his ability to act as if this was all news to him. She opened her mouth. Closed it. Her lips parted again and she felt Luke's gentle tap on her foot. "Excuse me," she said. "I'm going to check on John."

"I'll do it," Elizabeth offered. "I know you were up most of the night. You couldn't have slept more than a few hours. Why don't you go to your room for a little rest? I'll come for you if I need you."

Bria agreed, not because she felt particularly tired, but because she felt it was important to accept her mother's overture. Elizabeth was still too often confined to her room, listless and melancholic. Her full mourning attire sapped her complexion of what little color it possessed. With her skin pulled taut of the bones of her face, her small features remained pronounced. "Thank you, Mother," she said, forcing a smile. "I'd like that."

Luke stood and helped Elizabeth out of her chair, then Bria. When both women were gone he returned to his chair and his meal. "Care to play a few hands of poker?"

Pleased, Orrin raised his wine glass. "You read my mind."

Bria brushed at her cheek. A moment later the same tickling sensation tripped lightly across her skin. Eyes still closed, she brushed her cheek again.

Smiling, Luke let his index finger trail between her brows and down her nose. She wrinkled it and batted at his hand. The bed creaked as he sat down. He bent and kissed her silky temple.

"You're not going to let me sleep any longer," she whispered.

"No."

She stirred, stretching her fingers and toes with feline grace. "Does Mother need me?"

"No." There was an infinitesimal pause. "I do."

Bria's eyes opened wide. Although she was fully alert now, her voice was still husky with sleep. "You do?"

"Hmmm." He watched a faint flush color her complexion from the neck up. During the past few weeks he had become familiar enough with her body to know that this rosy color began flowering in the valley between her breasts. Bria was all buttoned up in a gown as dark as the finest burgundy. The bodice fit her like a cuirass. With honeyed hair framing her face, she managed to look tempting and inviolable at the same time. "I need your advice," Luke said.

"My advice?" Bria blinked at him. "I thought you wanted . . . that is, I thought . . ."

Luke glanced to the window, then back at Bria. Outside the room, night was chasing day but twilight would hold steady for another hour. The idea of sharing this bed with Bria, her body uncovered by everything but twilight, certainly had appeal for Luke. "I like what you're thinking, Mrs. Kincaid. And in the middle of the afternoon."

Bria's mouth flattened. She pushed at his chest with both hands and struggled up to a sitting position. "You don't know what I was thinking," she said tartly, shooting a look toward the mantel clock. "And it's hardly the middle of the afternoon. In fact, I don't know how I slept so long. The day is all but gone." She ran her fingers over her hair where it had been softened by sleep and attempted to restore a measure of order.

Luke failed to keep his crooked grin in check or the amusement out of his smoky-grey glance. While her hands were occupied he was able to steal a kiss. Her mouth was warm and sweet and he was allowed to linger longer than he'd imagined.

Bria slipped her fingers between their lips and gently pushed him away. "You mentioned something about advice," she said coolly. It was her turn to smile when she saw him blink. "Your kisses are very nice, but they don't addle my brain."

"I'll accept that as a challenge."

She leaned back against the headboard and arched a brow. "The advice?"

"Orrin has invited me to play cards with him and some friends Saturday night."

"Where?"

"Here, I suppose."

Bria shook her head. "They don't always play here. Sometimes the games are at Austin's. Sometimes Sam's. They don't take turns or rotate the games among all the players. The location is usually happenstance."

"Does it matter where it is?"

"It could, especially if they're setting some sort of trap for you. I think you're safer here at Concord than on the road to or from the other plantations. Who are the other players? Did Orrin mention any names?"

"Your friend Austin, of course."

She frowned a little at Luke's modifier. He had said similar things in the past and she had never taken issue with him. Bria decided she did not want it to continue. "He's not my friend, Luke. He was *never* my friend. David was going to marry his sister Emily. Austin's never seriously courted me. He knows I was raped. For years he thought I would be grateful to be his mistress. Marriage was an offer only very recently." Bria saw the tips of Luke's ears redden. That he had the grace to look abashed touched her. Her voice softened. "Was Orrin filling your head with Austin's virtues?"

"Actually, it was your mother. I just came from visiting John. Your mother was still there. She talked a great deal about Austin. In spite of what was done to John, I think she regards

Austin's participation in the Klan as youthful high spirits. She certainly believes he is a better match for you than I am.''

"My mother is not herself, Luke. It's the only thing I can say in her defense. She isn't thinking clearly. I don't know if she's even capable of it any longer. Even Orrin is making allowances for her. Before the announcement of Rand's death, he would not have tolerated any part of her behavior at the table this afternoon. He most definitely would have forbid her caring for John.''

Luke considered this. It had not occurred to him before that Elizabeth was perhaps thinking more clearly—and cleverly—than her daughter or husband could credit. He said nothing to Bria. His suspicions were half-formed at best. "I have not spent nearly enough time with her," Luke said. "I'd like to know her better.''

Bria did not try to hide her pleasure. She reached for Luke's hand and squeezed it. "Thank you. You're very kind." Her fingers unclenched slowly; she retracted her hand. "Now tell me the others who are invited to the card game.''

"I believe we met them all last night," said Luke. "Sam Daniels. William Adkins. Franklin Archer. Jim Poling.''

"Dear God.''

"What do you think? Do they mean to take my money or my life?''

Bria simply stared at him; the last vestige of her smile disappeared. "For someone contemplating either of those possibilities, you sound too cheerful.''

He shrugged. "Tell me what you think they're planning.''

"How can I know that?" she asked plaintively. "Is that why you've come here? You expect me to advise you as to their intentions?" Bria shook her head. "No. I'm not going to do that. My advice is that you refuse to join them, whether the game is here or elsewhere.''

"That doesn't make sense, Bree.''

"Of course it does," she said stubbornly. "If they mean to kill you, it does.''

"But what if their intention is simply to take my money? I think they're the kind of men who would consider that a good lesson. And it provides the opportunity for me to take Concord with a wager. If Orrin believed he held the upper hand, he could be goaded into making such a rash bet. This is what you've been hoping for, isn't it?"

It had been. "Not precisely," she said slowly, hedging a bit. "I expected to orchestrate the game. I would have been particular about the guests, and the game certainly would have taken place here."

"You could do that?"

"Of course. I have in the past. Not often, and always at my stepfather's request, but I *have* made the arrangements for him."

"Then you want me to let this pass."

"Yes."

"And if I say I want to do it anyway?"

Bria shut her eyes briefly. Unbidden, the shattered remains of her greenhouse came to her mind. "I don't know," she whispered. There was an ache in her throat. "Do you?"

Luke cupped the side of Bria's face. His thumb swept lightly across her cheek. "Yes," he said. "I want to do it."

She held his hand to her face, then turned just enough so that her lips lay against the heel of his palm.

"Bree?" Luke pulled her into his arms and held her. She was shaking. "It will be all right," he said against her ear. "You'll see. Everything will be all right."

Bria did not know how that was possible, but she let herself be lulled into believing it. He made it easy for her with his gentling voice and secure embrace. For good measure, he would addle her brain with kisses later. She was not so much resigned as looking forward to it.

* * *

"Have you seen Luke?" Bria asked Martha as they passed on the back stairs leading from the kitchen. "He was with Orrin after dinner and now he's disappeared."

Martha shook her head. She had an armful of linens in front of her. Her chin rested on the top of the pile. "Maybe he's gone to see John," she said.

"I just came from there. My mother's not there, either."

"If they're together, then they could be strollin' the gardens."

It was rather late for that, but Bria suspected Martha was right. She had not noticed anyone walking the garden paths when she returned from John's, but then she hadn't really been looking at that point. "Thank you, Martha." Bria stepped lightly down the stairs and made her way out to the verandah.

A sliver of moon helped her find two figures walking slowly along the fine gravel path at the garden's center. She waved to them but there was no response. Rather than join them, Bria chose to sit on one of the wicker chairs. She turned it so she had a full panoramic view. Even at night there was a certain beauty in the garden's dark symmetry. The carefully manicured hedgerows were a deep grey-green. The last of the blossoming roses looked almost black. The hardy petals of late-autumn flowers were gilded at the edges by moonlight.

Bria drew her legs onto the chair and spread her skirt around her. She hugged herself, tucking her hands under her arms. It was a moderately cool evening and she had come outside without a shawl, but she had no intention of returning for one. The slight chill was not entirely unpleasant. She breathed deeply and found her mind was clearer and her spirit refreshed.

Above the steady sound of the river rushing by on its way to the sea, Bria heard another, less familiar sound. It was easily identifiable, for all that she hadn't heard it in such a very long time. The light, tinkling sound was her mother's laughter.

Elizabeth Hamilton Foster was laughing.

Bria found that with her next breath the air was even sweeter.

She rested her head against the back of the chair and closed her eyes. Several minutes later, Bria heard the crunch of gravel as her mother and Luke approached the verandah. She sensed them pausing on the uppermost step when they saw her.

"I'm not sleeping," she told them. "I've had enough of that for one day."

"I thought you'd gone back to your room after dinner," Elizabeth said. "I wasn't certain you were feeling at all well."

"I did and I wasn't." Bria opened her eyes. She couldn't know it, but even in the shadowed verandah they sparkled. "I find I'm completely rested and recovered. Martha said I might find you both out here. It's been a long time since you walked in the gardens, Mother."

Elizabeth nodded. She unwound her arm from Luke's. "Your husband suggested it and was kind enough to offer his escort. Do you know he has plans to enlarge the garden?"

"Does he?" Bria resolutely squashed the pang of regret that surfaced. She remembered very well the detailed drawings she had found in his room. He had never shared them with her and she had never come across them again. "What sort of plans?"

"A reflecting pool. Wildflowers. Mazes. Exotic fish in the pond. It's marvelously well thought out, Bria. I shouldn't wonder that when it's completed I'll be less than enthusiastic about spending summers in Charleston. It will be a pleasure to stay here and observe every day in full bloom."

Her mother's enthusiasm was not feigned and Bria's own smile was sincerely felt. She avoided looking at Luke. "It sounds splendid."

"Oh, it is." Elizabeth went to Bria's side. She placed one hand on the back of the chair and bent to kiss her daughter's cheek. "Good night, dearest." She straightened and headed for the door. When she brushed past Luke she paused long enough to squeeze his arm lightly.

Bria watched her mother disappear into the house. While she was looking away, Luke came to stand in front of her. He bent so that his arms were braced on either side of her. She only had to lift her head a few degrees to be nose to nose with him. His eyes were distinctly warm as they darted over her face.

"Would you like to see my drawings for the gardens?" he asked.

Her voice was soft, throaty. "I would."

Luke nodded. "This way." He took her hand and led her to the music room. He lifted the polished lid of the grand piano and retrieved his rolled up drawings from the case. "Elizabeth hasn't seen these. I made sketches for her as we were walking this evening." To prove his point he showed her the crumpled bits of paper in his jacket pockets. "Come on." He closed the lid and took her hand again. They were halfway up the stairs when he stopped and thrust the rolls into her hands. "Take these." Once her arms were full he backed her against the wall and kissed her until the only breath she could draw was his.

Surprise and pleasure made Bria unsteady on the steps. Luke grasped her elbows and held her in place, never taking his mouth from hers except to ask her not to crush his drawings. She murmured something incoherent against his lips. He felt the vibration all the way to his toes. Before he completely lost his own bearings and took her right where they stood, Luke pulled Bria the rest of the way up the stairs and down the hall to their bedchamber.

There was no lamp lighted in their room and Bria hadn't asked anyone to lay a fire. The draperies were closed at the window. Darkness did not impede them in any way. As soon as the door clicked into place behind them the drawings slipped free of Bria's nerveless fingers. Luke kicked them out of the way and pressed her against the door. She came up on tiptoe as his mouth fell on the sensitive hollow just below her ear. Bria clutched at his jacket for support.

It was not the depth of the hunger that shocked her. It was the depth of all the emotions that accompanied it. Her heart tripped over itself and hammered hard enough that she thought he would have to feel it. The roar in her ears was the rushing of her own blood.

Luke's fingers tugged at the tiny buttons at Bria's throat. He loosened enough of them to push the neckline over her shoulders. The wide cambric straps of her chemise fell next. He buried his face in the curve of her neck, drawing in her fragrance as he sipped her skin.

Bria's breath caught. Her eyes closed.

''I love you.''

Chapter Thirteen

Luke's head lifted. His eyes narrowed as he tried to search her face in the dark. From what he could see she was as stunned as he was. "Bree? Do you mean it?"

She nodded slowly. She hadn't intended to say the words aloud, but she wouldn't call them back, either. "I told my mother weeks ago."

His brows came up. He cupped her face in his hands. "You told your mother? Weeks ago?"

"Mmm. Yes. Yes, I did." Bria could not pull her eyes away from his. The wide, dark centers of his eyes were ringed with silver. She thought his vision must be sharper than hers, that his gaze was faintly predatory. A shiver ran through her. Bria had a glimpse of Luke's white teeth as he smiled. It appeared he understood the nature of her shiver. She inhaled sharply and then his mouth was on hers.

Damp. Warm. His tongue flicked her lips. She opened for him. His knee nudged her legs apart. She was damp there, too. And more than warm. Hot. If he knelt at her feet and raised her skirts and put his mouth there . . .

The image was so erotic that Bria felt herself slip a little against the door. Luke caught her. He held her loosely by the wrists and raised them first to the level of her shoulders, then a few inches higher. He touched his forehead to hers. His breathing was ragged. "Is it all right, Bree?"

She nodded. It was different, this way he kept her to him. He held her up, not down. Bria tilted her head under him, opening her mouth and taking his hungrily. She heard him moan softly, then his body was thrust fully against hers, pressing her back so that she could feel the rigid length of him through their clothes. His hips ground against hers. She pushed back. Her breasts swelled above her corset. She ached for him to touch her there.

Luke drew back and sucked in a breath. He released her wrists but her hands didn't fall. He opened four more buttons at the front of her gown, then lowered her arms himself, pushing down the sleeves of her gown until the bodice settled around her waist.

"Don't move." Luke kissed her for good measure, then he went to the bedside table and lighted a lamp. His hands actually shook as he carefully replaced the hurricane glass. His face was bathed in the warm glow of the lamplight until he stepped in front of it and became a silhouette.

Bria stood exactly as Luke had left her. She could not look anywhere else as he approached again. His face was in deep shadow, yet she felt his eyes touching her everywhere. It was as if he had never stopped kissing her mouth or her throat or the curve of her shoulder. She bit her lower lip to stifle a whimper.

Luke's glance dropped away from Bria's face to her grey silk corset. "My God," he said softly. "You're wearing armor."

It was not so much his comment as his frustration that raised Bria's small smile. "You have no idea how true that is." She looked down at herself. The stiff whalebone stays and rein-forced stitching at the front kept her spine rigid and diaphragm flat. Drawing a breath was never particularly easy. Now, with Luke hovering over her it was doubly hard. She whispered, "I should like to be out of it, please."

That fit with Luke's plans. "Turn around."

Bria faced the door. She placed her palms flat against the inlaid panels and rested the top of her forehead between them. She felt the heat of Luke's hands a moment before his fingers touched her skin above the corset. There was just the hint of pressure as his thumbs ran down the line of lacings. He pushed her gown lower over her hips so that it fell to her feet.

Luke pulled on the ends of her laces. He thought he heard her actually sigh as he loosened them. He leaned forward and kissed her bare shoulder. When his hands were finally able to slip under the corset, he spread his fingers and forced the laces farther apart. Luke made short work of it after that, flinging it away from them when he was done.

Bria hummed her pleasure as Luke lifted her chemise and massaged her skin where the whalebone stays had marked it. He rubbed her back with the heels of his hands, then her sides from under her arm to her waist. Every stroke brought him closer to her midriff and the sensitive undersides of her breasts.

She pushed away from the door and leaned back against Luke's chest when he finally cupped her breasts. Bria felt her immediate response: the tender swelling of her nipples, the firming of her flesh. He caressed her. Stroked. His mouth was in her hair, at her ear. He kissed her temple, the downy skin of her cheek. His thumb and forefinger closed over one of her nipples and rolled it with just enough pressure to wrest a cry from her.

Luke paused. He breathed her name and held her in a close embrace. After a moment he helped her step out of the puddle that was her satin gown and led her to the bed. He knelt at her feet and removed her shoes and stockings. Bria leaned back on her elbows, watching his hands as they slipped under the lace-trimmed hem of her chemise where it rose above her knees. His hands slid over her thighs. He found the side button closure on her drawers and undid it. She lifted her hips to assist him. His fingers brushed the back of Bria's knees, tickling her as he pulled the undergarment off.

Bria was left wearing only the soft cambric chemise. Her shoulders were bare. The straps lay loosely over her upper arms. The fine linen fabric was virtually transparent. Luke's gaze slid over the beautifully full curves of her breasts. Her aureoles were a darker, dusty rose and Bria's arousal was perfectly defined by the pearly nipples.

His hands rested on her knees. He raised his head and looked at Bria. Her eyes were heavy-lidded, lowered to half-mast. Her mouth was lush and sulky and damp. His glance dropped briefly to the shadow between her parted thighs and when it lifted again he communicated his question with nothing more than the tiniest arch of one dark brow.

Bria's lips parted. A wave of heat washed over her. Then her head dropped the smallest fraction and she gave herself up to Luke's hands and mouth.

Luke raised Bria's knees and supported them on his shoulders. He palmed her bottom and brought her closer to the edge of the bed. Her chemise rolled under her and over her thighs until the hem was at her hips.

The first touch of his mouth made Bria's fingers curl in the comforter. Her elbows collapsed under her and she stretched, arching, flexing her fingers, and spread her arms wide across the bed. It was exquisite, this intimate caress of his lips and teeth and tongue. Flames darted where he touched her: tiny, licking, jagged flames that turned her blood to heated quicksilver.

Uncertain of what she wanted, Bria reached for Luke. His tongue flicked in her again, deeper this time and she forgot what she wanted from him. Her hand stopped in midair and fell on her abdomen instead. Her fingers twisted in the chemise, raising it higher over her flat belly. The thin fabric was like a whisper of air against her skin, warm and insubstantial. She laid her palm across her diaphragm and felt it contract as she drew in a sharp breath. Her thumb found the slope below her ribs and passed back and forth, tracing the line.

Bria's head fell to one side. She sucked in her lower lip and caught it between her teeth. Her heels pressed hard against Luke's back and her hips lifted. He held her firmly, probing, exploring. His mouth was hot against her skin. The edge of his tongue was gently abrasive and relentlessly applied. To keep from crying out, Bria pressed her lips tightly together and breathed through her nose. The air felt thin, inadequate. There was darkness on the edge of her vision and sharp, piercing pleasure at her open thighs.

She gasped, drawing a raw, ragged breath and arched high off the bed. Bria's hand fell across her breast. She lifted it slowly, lethargically, moving her fingertips across the nipple. That absent touch created a firestorm of sensation.

Every fragile thread of pleasure was pulled taut at the same time. Bria felt her limbs contract, her neck arch. Her eyes opened wide. Her shoulders pressed hard into the mattress while her spine lifted. The orgasm rolled through her, flushing her skin, tightening the smooth muscles of her legs, extending her fingers and toes.

Luke sat back on his haunches and gently let Bria's legs fall against the bed. He laid his hands on her bare knees, his fingers spread, and raised himself up. Beneath his palms he could feel the faint tremors that vibrated under her skin.

Aftershocks.

Never looking anywhere but at Bria, Luke shrugged out of his jacket. He tossed it somewhere behind him, then removed his shirt and silkaline undershirt.

Bria pushed herself up to a sitting position and drew her legs to one side on the bed. Her chemise slipped back to her hips. She fingered the lace hem while she watched Luke undress. The carpet muffled the sound of his boots thudding to the floor. She still blinked. Twice.

Luke's thumbs slipped under the waistband of his trousers. A smile edged his mouth. "Do you want to help?"

Bria stared at him. Her fingers stilled. She realized she hadn't touched him nearly often enough and she wanted to do this now. Unaware of her slow, fluid grace, Bria came up on her knees and pulled Luke closer with just the lift of her thick lashes and the beckoning gleam in her eyes. She placed her hands between his thumbs and began to unfasten the button fly of his trousers.

Her knuckles brushed his skin. She felt him draw in a breath when her fingers grazed the rigid length of him through his drawers. Bria pushed at his trousers and Luke shucked them off. The outline of his arousal was clearly visible. There was no mistaking his body's response to her. Bria looked up at him.

Both of Luke's brows were raised and his head was tipped to one side. The look in his eyes was both expectant and questioning. *Well?,* he seemed to be saying.

Bria pulled the side tapes on his muslin drawers, loosening the waistband, then unfastened the single button at the front. There was only the briefest hesitation on her part before she pushed them quickly down over his hips.

The confrontation with Luke's full erection could have given Bria pause, except her eyes were closed. Chuckling at her temerity and her timidness, Luke rid himself of the drawers and socks. He knelt on the edge of the mattress and bore Bria down to the covers with him.

"You can open your eyes again," he whispered.

"They're open."

He looked at her more closely. The heavy fan of her lashes was lifted just a fraction above her lower lids. His deep, husky tone held mock horror. "You were peeking!"

"I was." She made the confession seriously, as if what she had stolen was more than a glance. Bria reached between their bodies and began to explore what she had helped uncover but only glimpsed. Her eyes were open wide now, but she was watching Luke, not what she was doing.

Bria lightly scored the underside of him with her fingernail. Luke shivered. When she manipulated the heavy sac at the base he stayed her hand, but not before she wrested a low growl from deep in his throat. Bria's fingers closed around him and she moved over the length of him, cautiously at first, then with more confidence when she saw his response.

"It won't break," he said. His hand went around hers and he showed her that he wasn't at all fragile. Luke groaned softly as Bria easily found the exact rhythm and pressure. "Or at least I won't mind if it does."

His own eyes closed so he missed the siren's smile in hers. Luke fell on his back and gave himself up to Bria's attentions until he knew himself to be close. He gripped her arms and stopped her, but made no attempt to move over her. "I want to come inside you. Here. Like this." Luke helped her straddle him. He cupped her bottom and urged her upward. "Go on. Put me inside you."

Bria released her breath in short, quiet bursts as she guided him into her. She felt herself stretch to accommodate him. She leaned forward and pushed back with her pelvis, taking him completely inside her, her palms on his shoulders. Luke's hands moved from her hips, over her rounded buttocks, and then up the gentle, inward curve of her spine all the way to her shoulders.

Bria's head dipped lower. She stretched over Luke, offering her breasts to his hands and his mouth. His tongue flicked her nipple. He caught the bud between his teeth and tugged; he suckled her while her hips slowly undulated and her breathing became charged with excitement.

Bria raised her torso. She looked down at herself, at the damp nipple that seemed iridescent in the lamplight, and lower, to where their bodies joined. It stunned her, this vision of herself with this man. That she could be with him, unashamed and unafraid, was beyond her comprehension even while she celebrated it as fact.

Her sapphire eyes shifted to Luke's face. He was absorbed in the pleasure of watching her: the lift of her breasts, the roll of her shoulders, the tilt of hips. Bria unfastened her hair and shook it out, running her fingers through it in a manner she'd learned from Luke. When she leaned forward this time, her honey-colored hair spilled around her and shielded her face from the lamplight.

She kissed him on the mouth. Slowly. Deeply. Her tongue swirled around his, probing and retreating. She licked his lips and caught the lower one between her teeth. Bria worried it as gently as she did her own. She placed her mouth close to his ear and whispered her intentions: "I will always love you."

Her body rocked, rising and falling, taking Luke deeply inside her with each thrust. She contracted around him, deliberately at first, then without conscious thought. Her body's memory of pleasure took over and she acted on what it wanted, almost without a will of her own.

Luke felt a need to shed his skin. It was too small for him now, every part of it stretched taut across his lean frame. The muscles in his arms and legs tightened. There was tension across the plane of his chest and abdomen and he drew in a breath, held it, then drew another without releasing the first. His fingertips pressed whitely against Bria's bottom. His head was thrown back so the cords of his neck stood out in sharp relief. Blood thundered in his ears.

Luke twisted, toppling Bria so that she was under him. He came buried deep inside her, driving hard between her open thighs. Bria's slender body trembled beneath his but he hardly felt it against the rush of contractions that seized him.

He was not particularly eloquent. There was no rash declaration of love. Luke's words were half-formed and mostly unintelligible, but his skin fit again, and he was grateful for that.

Bria lay back, bereft of strength and the motivation to acquire any. Closing her eyes, she didn't protest as Luke eased off her and collapsed on his back at her side. She was aware of her uneven breathing, then his, then how their breathing slowly melded and became one, as if they were drawing on the very same air.

Bria made a small sound, something between a sigh and a hum.

Luke turned his head slowly to look at her. "Did you say something?"

She made the sound again. "I don't think so."

It was simply too much effort to smile so Luke just contented himself looking at her. In profile her exquisite features were serene. Her complexion glowed. Her mouth was slightly parted, still dewy and swollen from his kisses. At the base of her neck, where her hair fell back, he could see the faint bruise he had raised on her skin. Blood stirred in his groin. Not enough to make him erect, but enough to confirm his body would entertain the notion.

Luke turned on his side. He lifted his head and managed to support it by propping it on his elbow.

Bria felt him move. She opened the eye closest to him and cast him a wary glance. There was a little bit of alarm in that breathy, humming sound now. She slithered out of bed before he could trap her with an arm around her waist. Luke had a vaguely predatory aura about him, like a big cat who was perfectly sated but was keeping close watch on his meal in the event he found room for more. Bria grabbed her rumpled chemise at the foot of the bed and held it up in front of her breasts and belly.

Luke arched one brow and let his wicked glance slide to where her covering fell short. From his angle he still had a nice view of silky flanks and a glimpse of smoothly rounded bottom.

Bria put out one arm, trading modesty for safety in the event he suddenly pounced. She skirted the bed and padded quickly to the dressing room, aware of Luke's head swiveling to watch her progress. *It would serve him right if he got a crick in his neck,* she thought as she bent over the washbasin and sluiced her flushed cheeks with cool water. But when she was face-to-face with her own reflection, she had to admit that she was flattered . . . and satisfied . . . and well, yes, happy.

Luke roused himself to turn back the comforter and slide in under the quilt and sheet. He cradled his head in his hands and listened to the sounds of water splashing in the adjoining room. Bria seemed to be taking a long time going about the business of her sponge bath and it finally occurred to him that offering to help her was the surest way of getting her back to their bed quickly. He was opening his mouth to make that offer when she appeared on the threshold wearing a fresh lawn chemise that was only fingertip length.

"You're gaping," she said.

He didn't tell her he had been prepared to render his services as her handmaiden. The truth was that once she was framed in the doorway like a Renaissance painting, warmly radiant in the full spectrum of golden light, his jaw *had* dropped another fraction. Her observation was accurate. He was gaping.

Bria watched Luke close his mouth and swallow hard. It was the bobbing Adam's apple that she found so endearing. When he lifted the covers, Bria closed the distance to his side with a few light steps and an eager scramble onto the bed. She settled in, stretching herself along the length of his body, a little disappointed to find he was wearing his drawers again.

"Armor," he said dryly. "Because you're certainly not wearing any."

She pressed her smile against his chest. Her bare legs rubbed his. "Will you turn back the lamp?"

He reached behind him and extinguished the wick. It provided them with another opportunity to adjust their positions and find the perfect fit of curves to angles. Darkness just made it more interesting.

Bria's head rested in the crook of Luke's shoulder. She laid her arm across his bare chest. "Do you remember the afternoon we spent in the gazebo? It was raining and we sat on the bench waiting for it to stop."

He remembered everything about that afternoon. "Hmmm."

"It was the day after . . . that is, the afternoon following the first time we . . ."

"Shared this bed?"

"Yes, that's right." Content with this euphemism, Bria

plunged on determinedly. "Well, you should know that I lied to you. You suggested that things had changed for me because of the way we spent the previous night. And I said that they hadn't."

"That was the lie?"

"Yes. You were a little smug about your observation, I suppose. That's what prompted my lie, at least in part. I didn't want to admit that it chafed that you showed me special attention because Orrin was approaching or watching. Those stolen moments hurt a little. Just a few hours earlier I had admitted to my mother that I was in love with you. I didn't offer that to appease her, but because it was true. I simply couldn't tell you, not when I didn't know how you felt."

"And what's changed?"

"I have," she said quietly. "*I* have. I told Rand once that I could only playact at emotion. I could capture the nuances perfectly—the expression, the tone, the exact gesture—but it all came from what I observed in others, not from what I felt. I didn't have to experience an emotion. I only had to know what it looked like." Bria tucked a heavy lock of hair behind her ear and made an imperceptible swipe at the tears at the corner of one eye. "I had no center for pain, Luke, but I also had none for pleasure. It was as if my life was happening to someone else, as if I were watching from the balcony and never once appeared on stage."

Bria shifted so that she had a better look at Luke's shadowed profile. "Until you," she said. "You pushed me front and center. It's not about sharing this bed with you . . . at least not entirely about that. It's splendid, what you do to me here, but it's an expression of loving you, not the reason why I do. That would have something to do with the way you leaped from the wall to save Apollo the first day I met you. And the way you covered me at the river after I fell in. You listened to me chatter on about my experiments in the greenhouse." Her voice dropped to a mere whisper. "You listened to me about . . . about the rape . . . and you accepted it and made it possible for me to accept it. You're clever and talented and generous and patient. And then, well, there's your crooked smile.''

Luke cocked his head and looked down on the crown of Bria's head. ''It's crooked?''

''Mmmm. Perfectly so.''

''Imagine that.''

''I do. Often.'' She sighed. ''I don't want you to think that I expect you to return a declaration of love. That same afternoon I lied to you, you also said nothing had changed for you. I don't think you were lying.'' She hesitated. ''Were you?''

''No, Bree, I wasn't lying.''

Bria said nothing for a moment. The breath she took in was shaky but she spoke in a carefully modulated tone. ''I can admit I'm disappointed, but I'm not going to shatter. I was the one who set the terms of our marriage, the one who didn't want it to be real. I can hardly demand that you alter your feelings in the service of mine.''

Annoying tears gathered in her eyes and Bria blinked them back. ''We've talked before about it being your intention to leave Concord and I want you to know that I won't try to keep you.'' Her smile was a trifle wobbly and she was glad he couldn't see it. ''At least not with restraints. I'm not above trying to change your mind about loving me.''

''You can't do that,'' he said quietly.

Bria had no response. She hadn't anticipated he would be so discouraging.

Luke slipped his arm out from under her head. He turned on his side and slid a few inches lower so they could be face-to-face. ''Look here.'' When she was slow to respond, Luke took her chin in his hand and nudged it in his direction. ''Look at me.''

Bria turned her head. Darkness shrouded his features but Bria had no difficulty imagining them, particularly the smoky grey eyes.

''Listen to me carefully, Bree. I want to be certain you understand what I'm saying.''

The note of gravity in his voice made Bria's stomach clench and her head feel thick. She had to concentrate very hard to hear him above her own inner turmoil.

"You can't change my mind because I already love you. I didn't lie when you put the question to me at the gazebo. Making love to you —and that's the proper term, Bree— changed nothing for me." He let her chin go. His fingers trailed lightly over her slender neck. "Nothing you said could have persuaded me to marry you if I hadn't loved you. I didn't know what we would make of this marriage when you were so determined not to want one, but I was willing to risk it."

Bria simply could not move sound past the lump in her throat.

"Bree? Were you listening?"

She nodded.

"Are you crying?"

She shook her head.

"Breathe," he told her gently. He touched her lashes with the pad of his thumb. They were damp. "Just breathe."

Bria sucked in a shaky breath, then a second one. She sat up just enough to level her body over Luke's. "I *do* love you," she whispered. Then she began kissing him. His brow. His temple. The corner of his mouth. His jaw and the underside of his chin. She lingered at his lips again, probing with her tongue ever so gently.

She held his face in her hands and raised her head. "Why didn't you tell me before now?"

Luke understood immediately that she had a plan for torturing him. His manhood was rising with comfortable pressure against the cradle of Bria's thighs. "You wouldn't have believed me," he said. "At the very least you would have been suspicious. You know it's true, Bria. You would have thought I was trying to trick you into something."

"That's not—"

"You didn't understand about love then. You said it yourself, you playacted at emotion and that's never been part of what I wanted from you. I was willing to be patient until your head and your heart sorted it out."

Bria simply stared at Luke, falling in love with him all over again.

They made love slowly this time, with none of the frenzy of their earlier encounter. They nurtured their desire. Touching was enjoyed in its own right, not as a means to an end. Textures. Fragrances. Tastes. All of their senses were engaged.

They slept sharing the same pillow, their foreheads almost touching. For a while, beneath the blankets, their fingertips were interlaced.

Luke was shaving at the basin when Bria walked in the dressing room. He watched her out of the corner of his eye. She yawned so widely that her eyes became mere slits, then she stood on tiptoe and stretched, arms reaching toward the ceiling. Her short chemise rose with her efforts and he had a glimpse of a triangle of dark honey hair.

He jerked as the razor cut him. A thin line of blood appeared at the curve of his jaw and ear. Pain came a moment later.

Bria was immediately all concern. "Oh, you've cut yourself." She hurried over to his side, found the alum powder while he blotted the wound, then applied it.

The look Luke gave her in the mirror was frankly ironic. "As if you didn't have anything to do with this battle scar."

"Hmmm." She smiled and stood on tiptoe again, this time to kiss him just below the scratch. "In the future, Mr. Kincaid, surrender your weapon when I walk into a room. Otherwise you may cut off your nose to spite your face." Bria laughed and danced away as he growled low and made a grab for her. "Finish your work there. I'd like to have something smooth to rub my cheek against."

They had breakfast with Elizabeth in her room. It would still be hours before Orrin woke and the three of them were not above enjoying the respite from his unpredictable moods.

"Tell me, Bria," Elizabeth said. "What did you think of Luke's gardens?"

Over her plate, Bria's hand stopped in midair. Her fork dangled from nerveless fingertips. "I didn't actually see Luke's plans," she said. Although she tried for a careless tone, she sounded more apologetic and faintly embarrassed. The swift color in her cheeks didn't help her any. "I was rather . . . umm, tired, when we . . ." Her voice simply trailed off when she glimpsed both her mother and Luke simply smiling at her. Elizabeth looked quite pleased for her. Luke, on the other hand, looked quite pleased with himself. She kicked him under the table.

He raised both brows at her but stuffed half a muffin in his mouth to keep from laughing.

Bria changed the subject. "Mother, Orrin's invited Luke to play cards Saturday night. What do you make of that?"

Elizabeth put down her fork, sat back in her chair, and dabbed her mouth carefully with her napkin. It was not an exposition of good manners, but calculated to give her time. "It could be that your stepfather is trying to make amends. He does feel terrible that he accused Luke of stealing from him."

"He said that to you?" asked Bria.

"Not those exact words."

"What were his *exact* words?"

"I'm sure I can't remember them precisely." She saw Bria was perfectly willing to wait her out and she caved. "If you must know, he blames you. If Luke was involved at all, Orrin thinks he is simply too much in your thrall to be held accountable."

Luke was glad he had finished his biscuit and hadn't yet started his coffee. He would have choked or spewed.

Bria reached across the table and patted the back of Luke's hand. "I know you're as surprised by Orrin's perceptiveness as I am."

Luke scowled at her.

Chuckling, Bria took back her hand quickly and looked at

her mother. "Then you don't think Orrin means any harm to Luke?"

"Harm? No, I don't think that. It's much more likely he intends to empty his pockets." She glanced at Luke. "*Do* you have money?"

"A little. Perhaps I can't afford to play."

"I'll stake you."

Bria and Luke both stared at Elizabeth, twin expressions of surprise on their faces.

"I have some money saved. Orrin gives me an allowance." She added less defensively, "I don't mind spending it on a worthy cause."

"And the worthy cause?" Luke asked.

Elizabeth's soft smile was a shade wistful. "My gardens. If you could win at the table using my money, how could Orrin object to expanding the gardens at my expense? It would be a lovely tribute to Rand, don't you think, Bria?"

"Oh, Mother," Bria said, almost sighing the words. "Yes, it would be lovely." She glanced at Luke and saw that he wasn't going to object. "But it might also be dangerous. Luke isn't certain that the game will be here. I don't like the idea of him going to play at Austin's or Will's. Not after what happened here with the Klan."

"One has nothing to do with the other. Not all of Orrin's friends are members of the Klan. And don't you think they've had their fill for a while? They've settled their score with you for the time being."

Bria's appetite fled. "With me? There was never any score to settle with me. Orrin thinks he has reason to be angry and he engaged the Klan to make his point. He has no proof that I've wronged him in any way. He's plainly mean-spirited, Mother. He attacked me by attacking the coloreds." Bria's voice dropped to a whisper. "He could just as easily have hurt you as John Whitney. Before Rand's death, he would have." Bria saw her mother's eyes fill with tears. She wondered which words she should call back, then realized it was none of them.

She couldn't ease her mother's pain by pretending any part of what she'd said was a lie. Instead, Bria asked, "*Has* he hurt you, Mother?"

Elizabeth dabbed at her eyes and shook her head. "No, not the way you mean. And even so, it wouldn't be your place to do anything about it. That remains my responsibility." She drew in a shaky breath. "If I'm to have any dignity, it must be my responsibility."

Luke nodded, drawing Elizabeth's attention toward him and cutting Bria off. His narrowed, grey eyes searched her features and when he spoke there was less question in his voice than conviction. "Orrin's angry with Bria because she married me. It has almost nothing to do with selling the building materials to the sharecroppers or the improvements they made. All of that simply provided a convenient target for his anger and a method for concealing the roots of it from Bria and me."

Luke watched Elizabeth's chin come up slightly. Her chestnut eyes were still shining darkly with tears but their expression was no longer tragic. "But you knew, didn't you?" he asked.

Elizabeth made the faintest gesture of assent with her eyes.

"Mother," Bria said softly.

Luke lifted his hand a fraction, halting Bria before she said more. His gaze never left her mother. "Have you always known, Elizabeth, about Orrin's feelings for your daughter?"

Bria started to come out of her chair. "I don't want to talk about this. Luke, please, you're distressing her."

"I'm distressing you," he said calmly. "Your mother's been living with this knowledge for a long time, maybe since the beginning of her marriage to Orrin."

"Not from the very beginning," Elizabeth said quietly. Out of the corner of her eye she saw Bria slowly sink back into her chair. "But soon after. It just became harder for him to conceal it. I saw the way he looked at her, the way his eyes followed her entrance and exit from a room. It riled him that she hated him so much, but I think it was a relief as well. It helped him keep his distance. He fought his desire, you know."

Beside her, Bria ducked her head and moaned softly.

Elizabeth went on. "He took to calling her vile names. He drank more. Woke late. Showed less interest in Concord. He gambled with his friends. Bria doesn't remember a time when he wasn't coarse or surly, but a time like that existed, at least briefly. I suppose it was in his nature to turn out the way he did. Perhaps the gallant, considerate side he first showed me was the sham, but I didn't mistake that it was there.

"When I met Orrin Foster I was grieving for my husband, my sons, my home, and"—she glanced sideways at Bria, her dark eyes both infinitely tender and sad—"and my daughter. He showed me great kindness during our short courtship. I was not so grief-stricken that I couldn't see that, but I may not have been able to see past it."

Luke nodded. "You wanted to save your home."

"And my life," she said, though the admission cost her. "It was a frightening time. The freemen were rioting, looting plantation homes. A few whites were killed. People were scared while I was plainly terrified. There were taxes that I couldn't pay, workers I could offer nothing to. The fields had been lying fallow and couldn't immediately produce. My only surviving son had some idea in his head that restoring our fortune lay in finding a treasure, and my daughter had become someone I no longer recognized.

"When Orrin entered my life I saw a way to save us all, but Rand resented me for marrying again, and Bria was tormented by it. I don't know what I could have done differently. This plantation was my children's heritage. My motives weren't entirely selfish."

Bria did come out of her seat then. She knelt beside her mother's chair and slipped her arms around Elizabeth's tiny waist. Her head lay against her mother's breast. "Oh, Mother, we never thought ill of you. Rand understands what you did for us. Claire made him see that. I *know* she did. He came to recognize what kept us here."

Elizabeth stroked her daughter's head. Her fingers lingered

over the downy hair at Bria's nape, just below the intricately wound coil. It was almost as soft as a baby's. Her baby. Tears gathered in Elizabeth's eyes, making them beautifully gentle and luminous.

Bria lifted her face and looked up at her mother. "It's my fault that Orrin hit you, isn't it? You said he drank and gambled and a host of other things, but you never mentioned once how he hurt you. And you accepted it because you were protecting me. The two of you fought about me, perhaps not directly, but I was there, at the root of it, just as Luke said."

As she considered her words, Elizabeth drew in her bottom lip and worried it in exactly the same fashion Bria often did. "There is no part that is your fault. No blame that should be attached to your shoulders. You did not entice him. To Orrin's credit I think he was unsettled by his attraction to you." She saw Bria's skepticism. "I know it's difficult for you to believe Orrin has any moral code, but you must see now he does. Coveting his wife's daughter caused deep shame in him. He doesn't want to desire you, Bria, but he can't seem to help himself. He has never acted on his feelings, has he?"

"No," Bria said quickly.

Luke raised one brow at both women. "Before one or both of you suggest the man for sainthood, allow me to suggest that Orrin has *always* acted on his feelings for Bria, but acted in opposition to them. The consequences of that have had no less impact than if he had slept with her. They have only been different." He ignored their single gasp and went on. "Orrin has heaped abuse on both of you for years and you accepted it because in your own way each of you was protecting the other. I'd say there was considerable damage in that."

Bria drew back from her mother. She stood slowly, the crease between her brows appearing as she continued to stare at Luke. "It's Orrin," she said quietly, faintly accusing. "That's why you're here. You always said it was never about the treasure. It's Orrin Foster that's brought you to Concord." Her voice grew steadily more confident. "You know him, don't you?

From somewhere before. Or you know something about him. That's why you asked about family photographs and why you've asked questions about him from time to time. I'm right, am I not? This is why you're going to leave me. When you've settled with Orrin, that's when you're going to leave.''

Bria sat down suddenly. The silk and satin fabric of her deep emerald gown rustled. Breath rushed out of her.

''Are you quite finished?'' Luke asked calmly.

Bria nodded shortly.

Elizabeth's chestnut-colored eyes darted from one to the other. ''I think there is much more here than I understand.''

''Most definitely.'' He turned his smile on Elizabeth. ''Will you excuse us?'' He picked up another muffin, gave it a little toss as he stood, caught it again, and looked dead on at Bria. ''I think we should finish this in private. Would you like to walk or retire to another room?''

Bria glanced at her mother, seeking advice.

''Accept the invitation to walk, dear. I find there is something about walking that clears one's mind.'' And, in the event that Bria misunderstood, Elizabeth added, ''It's *your* mind I'm thinking of.''

Luke finished his muffin before they left the house. He brushed off his hands when they reached the verandah, then started down the steps. Bria followed at a slower pace until she saw his destination was the stable.

''We're riding?'' she said. ''Why didn't you say so? I would have changed.''

''I didn't say so because you would have changed. You can ride sidesaddle.''

''I don't like—''

He shrugged ''Then ride astride.''

''You wouldn't mind? What if we met someone?''

That stopped Luke in his tracks. ''Are you the same woman who rode hell-bent for leather across these fields in her night-gown and robe only a few nights ago?''

There wasn't a defense she could mount in the face of that so she remained silent.

Once they were far afield Luke finally slowed his mare to an amble. Apollo chafed a bit at the restriction but Bria brought him around. She looked back at the house. All that was visible through the trees and outbuildings was the roof. It fairly gleamed in the morning sunshine. The air was clear, the sky a field of blue. None of it brightened her mood. She felt as if a single dark cloud was suspended over her head. Any moment it would pelt her with rain or hail or—

"What in the name of heaven is going through your mind right now?" Luke asked.

It was odd that he should mention heaven, she thought rather gloomily, when she was reckoning with a lightning bolt about to pierce her heart. "Did you bring me this far from the house so no one could hear me scream? I told you I wouldn't try to keep you from leaving. I meant it, Luke. If loving me isn't enough reason for you to stay, then I can't imagine what is."

Luke supposed he had invited that outburst. In the future he would tread more carefully. "I didn't bring you out here to listen to you scream or to keep it from anyone else. I insisted we leave your mother's room because I wanted privacy. There are certain things I'm going to tell you that must remain with you. They're not meant for anyone else's ears."

"My mother—"

"Anyone else's ears," Luke repeated with a certain intensity. "Do you understand?"

Bria nodded slowly.

"Is there some question in your mind that I love you?"

"No."

"Good. Has it occurred to you that if I have to leave for any length of time that I would return?"

It had never occurred to her. Not once. She had always envisioned him going and never seeing him again. She stared at him, suddenly stricken by the obvious.

Luke put it into words. "I'm not your father, Shelby, or Rand. If I go, I'm coming back. I promise you that, Bree."

"They said the same thing," she said on a thin thread of sound. "Exactly the same thing."

There was a tightening in Luke's chest and a corresponding pressure against his heart. "I'm sorry. I know they meant it because I mean it, too. But they offered it as comfort when they couldn't have known how it would turn out. I'm not going to war or out to sea. At the very most I'll have to go back to New York County with your stepfather."

"Then I was right that your being here at all has something to do with Orrin."

"Yes."

"Can you tell me what it is?"

"What do you want to know?"

She thought about that. There was part of her that wasn't certain she wanted to know anything at all. Her agitation was sufficient to make Apollo stir. Bria absently patted him on the neck. "I suppose I want to know why you have to go back to New York with Orrin."

"A promise I made."

"To whom?" As soon as she asked the question, she knew the answer. "Your mother and aunts."

"Yes. That's right."

"Then all this time you've known Orrin."

"No. That's what's made this so damnably difficult. I can't be certain even now that Orrin is the one I want."

Bria tried to make sense of that. Luke was being forthcoming in only the most enigmatic manner. "No photographs," she said softly. "Is that why you wanted a picture of him? So you could have sent it back?"

"Yes. I've made sketches but it's been eleven years since my mother and aunts last saw him. There have been a lot of changes during that time. He's heavier in the jowls. Broader across the middle. His hair is thinner and greying. Aunt Lys and

Aunt Nancy think it could be him. Everyone else is reserving judgment until they confront him.''

"But surely Orrin Foster is not so terribly common a name."

"I don't suppose it is."

Bria's mouth flattened in frustration. "Could you be any more abstruse?"

Luke sighed. He kicked his mare and headed her toward the riverbank. Apollo and Bria were immediately beside them. "Are you certain you want to know?"

"No. I'm not. But that doesn't mean I shouldn't know. Didn't you bring me out here for exactly that purpose? I wish you wouldn't try to protect me. Not about what's important to you."

Several minutes passed before Luke answered. Until he spoke the only sounds were the steady plodding of the horses, the distant run of water, and the voices carried by their own inner thoughts. "Very well," he said finally. "But there are other things you must know first."

With sudden perception, Bria realized that Luke was talking about himself. Having to reveal something more about himself was at the root of his real reluctance to talk.

"I've mentioned my mother's boarder before."

Bria nodded. "The one who hired you to help with his accounts."

"Yes, well, that was his way of putting some money in my pockets. The work was genuine enough but he didn't require my services. He had a score of employees working for him in the same capacity. It was simply an apprenticeship for me . . . and it kept me off the streets and away from the gangs. My mother was set on me going to college. I was not so enthusiastic about the prospect. Life with my mother and my aunts was rather unusual. They're all rather . . . mmm, free-spirited. I couldn't imagine how I would fit in at any university, even with Nana Dearborn's strict upbringing behind me. I couldn't tell my mother or any of the others. It would have hurt them to know I was blaming them for putting this opportunity in front of me and keeping me from it at the same time."

Luke risked a glance at Bria. Her head was bent forward at a slight angle. He could see that her brow was puckered. She was concentrating on his every word. "I wasn't being fair, of course, but I didn't know that then," he said. "I saw that I had other opportunities in the neighborhood. I knew I could make a good living and have some influence. It would have been graft and gambling mostly. The word was out that I was showing promise."

Bria's head snapped up. She didn't turn to look at Luke, but the crease between her brows deepened.

"My mother knew what I couldn't bring myself to say. It was no secret from my aunts, either. They got together and agreed it was time to call in a favor from Mr. Morrison."

"The boarder," said Bria. When Luke didn't confirm her statement immediately, Bria thought he hadn't heard. Her head swiveled in his direction and posed it more as a question this time. "You're speaking of your mother's boarder, aren't you?"

"Yes," he said, not looking at her. "The one I told you was our boarder." Luke inhaled deeply and let it out slowly. "Bria, Mr. Conrad Morrison was more of an occasional boarder."

"Occasional? You mean seasonal. He stayed in summer and went—" She stopped because Luke was shaking his head.

"I mean he came and went as he pleased and took a room when the mood was on him."

Exasperated, Bria threw up both hands. "I have no idea what you're trying to tell me. Can you not say what you mean plainly?"

"Conrad Morrison did not rent rooms from my mother. He rented women. My mother is a madam, Bree. Back then my aunts were all prostitutes." Luke paused a beat. "Have I said it plainly enough?"

Chapter Fourteen

Bria blinked and brought Apollo up short. She had asked for plain speaking and received exactly that. Keeping her eyes focused steadily on the ground in front of her, Bria picked up Apollo's reins again and brought him abreast of Luke and the mare. "I'm not terribly adept at masking my surprise," she said.

"You used to be better."

"That was when I rarely felt anything at all. It's much more difficult now."

Luke nodded. They were only fifty yards from the riverbank. He pointed to a location downstream where an outcropping of flat rocks were dipped in sunshine. They rode another three-quarters of the way before they dismounted and tethered the horses. Bria took off her shoes and socks and sat down on the portion of the rock closest to the water. Luke found a natural cradle in the stone carved out by wind and water and sat there.

"I know you have a hundred questions," he said.

Bria raised her skirts up to her knees and dipped her toes in the water. She kicked at the surface lazily. A tiny rainbow spray of droplets formed in the air. "More than a hundred. But I'm waiting for you to tell me what you want me to know."

She glanced over her shoulder at him. He was leaning back on his elbows, his long legs stretched out in front and crossed casually at the ankles. He had opened his jacket and loosened his shirt at the neck. "Although you could start by telling me who Nana Dearborn really was."

"Exactly what I said. She was my grandmother. My mother was her only child. I'm not a bastard, Bree. My mother ran away from home at sixteen to marry Patrick Kincaid. She had me at an appropriately decent interval and Patrick stayed around a few months after that. One day he went to work and never came back. That's how my mother remembers it. No warning. No news. She waited as long as she dared for him to return. There were rumors that he had sailed on a packet for China and my mother was inclined to believe them.

"She swallowed her pride and went back to her own mother. Nana offered to take me but wouldn't let her step foot in the house. My mother refused. We went back to the city, to Five Points where she could afford the rent, and she supported us with jobs cleaning homes in the better parts of town. That lasted until she was raped by one of her employers." Luke saw Bria's shoulders stiffen and her dangling legs pause in their lazy circling, but she continued to stare straight ahead. "She was dismissed when she tried to bring it to the attention of the authorities. Her unwillingness to go quietly meant no one would hire her. She worked for awhile in the saloons and gaming hells in the Five Points but it was dangerous and not very lucrative. After a time, my mother discovered she was pregnant."

Bria lifted her legs out of the water and drew her knees to her chest. She wrapped her arms around them and settled her chin on their caps. *Pregnant.* She remembered how very much she had dreaded that possibility after the rape.

"Are you all right, Bree?"

She nodded. "Go on."

"My mother visited an abortionist. Madame Restell. I understand she was notorious for her Infallible French Pills. I don't remember any of this, Bria. Some things Mother told me. Some I overheard. Aunt Madelyn gave me a few home truths from time to time when she thought I needed to hear them." Luke leaned his head back and basked in the autumn sunshine. Behind him he could hear leaves rustling as a squirrel scurried through the thicket looking for fallen nuts and berries. "It was Madame Restell who suggested that my mother see Flora on Greene Street. Flora managed a successful brothel. She was particular about the girls she hired and the clientele she catered to. She also had a daughter enrolled in a prestigious boarding school who was unaware of any aspect of her mother's profession. I don't know if my presence on my mother's lap had anything to do with her being hired, but Flora took her in and allowed me to live there."

"You grew up in a brothel," Bria said. She had to say it aloud because she couldn't quite believe it.

"At Flora's, yes. Until Nana Dearborn convinced my mother that I should be with her. Nancy, Lyssa, Maggie, Laura, Livia, and Madclyn—my mother's closest friends at Flora's, the ones I knew as my aunts—finally began to believe that Nana was right." Luke's shoulders rolled in a careless shrug, but his chest was tight. "So she sent me away. I've told you all that before. By the time I returned to my mother's, she had her own place. The Ruby Star. Everyone who worked for her had the name of a precious gem. My aunts were now Beryl, Topaz, Emerald, Garnet, Pearl, and Opal."

Bria glanced back at him, one brow arched in disbelief. "Can you possibly be telling me the truth?"

Luke crossed his heart and countered, "I could not make this up."

She supposed that was true. She turned around and supported herself on one arm, letting her legs fall to the side. Bria pleated her skirt with her free hand and kept her attention on Luke. "Did you know the Hamilton riddle was about seven gems? Not exactly the same ones your aunts used . . . umm, profession-ally. The Hamilton stones were called the seven sisters."

He shook his head, a faint smile lifting the corners of his mouth. "There's a highly exclusive brothel in New York named The Seven Sisters. Mother wanted to use the name but she couldn't buy it from the owner."

Bria's mouth twitched. "The Ruby Star has a certain elegance."

Luke rolled his eyes. "Bree, she chose it only because calling it The Red Light was too obvious a stab at Nana Dearborn, even for my mother."

"Oh."

"Indeed," Luke said dryly. "However, patrons tended to agree with you. The Ruby Star has become extraordinarily successful. My mother has important business contacts because she is discreet. She made money because she learned to listen to them. Bankers are happy to take her earnings and invest them. She has holdings in half a dozen profitable companies like Northeast Rail and she owns hundreds of acres north of Central Park that, with a combination of good fortune and shrewdness, will probably make her a millionaire before the decade is out.

"My mother finally matched Flora's success. In the last five years she's surpassed it many times over. It's not something that's widely known and that is at my mother's wish. She's called herself Ruby Dearborn for so long that most people don't know that she ever had another name. It's Mary Kincaid who quietly holds the land and the stocks and the certificates."

"Then you're wealthy."

"You sound disappointed."

"I suppose I could get used to it."

"Don't become accustomed to it too quickly," he said. "My mother is wealthy. I'm not. And while she may settle a portion of her fortune on me someday, in her last letter she threatened to disinherit me altogether if I didn't finally settle the business that brought me here."

Bria fell silent, considering all that he'd told her. "How does what you've said connect to my stepfather? I can't work that out.''

"I take it the name Conrad Morrison doesn't mean anything to you."

She shook her head. "The only time I've heard it is today, when you—'' She stopped as something niggled at her brain. "There was a Morrison from New York who . . ." Her voice trailed off and the crease between her brows relaxed. "I'm sorry. I can't remember.''

"It's not surprising. You would only have been fourteen or fifteen when he committed suicide. That's what most people remember about him if they recall the name at all. His steel mills and iron foundries were sold off piecemeal to pay creditors and no longer bear his name. He was always a favorite of my mother's. It was at his encouragement that she set up her own establishment. When she left Flora's he patronized her new place and helped build her clientele by telling the right people about it. He used his business acumen to help her make investments. Even so, in the beginning it was difficult and she had to put a lot of money into the business itself. Liquor. Bribes to the proper officials. Doctors. Furnishings. Protection money.''

Bria nodded slowly as something he once told her came back. "That's why she couldn't pay for your draft substitute during the war.''

"Not exactly. It was about that time that some of her investments were losing money. She was also paying more out in bribes than ever before. But mostly she went to Mr. Morrison for help because I asked her not to purchase my draft ticket. She went to him as a way of getting around her promise. He had already helped her get me away from the Five Points gangs and into his alma mater. He was more than happy to keep me out of the war.''

"He must have cared very much about you.''

"I think he did,'' Luke said quietly. "I'm certain he loved my mother. I got the courage once to tell him he should marry her. I stood my ground, prepared for him to backhand me, and instead he just agreed with me. Something about the way he said it convinced me that he'd already asked her. My mother turned *him* down.'' He released a deep breath slowly. ''I never asked her about it, but I did ask my aunts. It was their general opinion that she said no because she loved him too much.''

Bria felt tears unexpectedly well on the rim her lashes. One tracked down her cheek when she tried to blink them back. ''That isn't why he killed himself, is it?''

Watching her, Luke's smile was soft. ''Why, Bree, you *are* a romantic. No, I'm certain that had nothing to do with it. Mr. Morrison's suicide happened while I was away fighting. It was very close to the end of the war and I was in Tennessee at the time. I didn't learn of it until all the letters reached me months later in Virginia. Armed with the entreaties from my mother and my aunts, I was able to muster out and return home.''

Bria impatiently brushed the tears from her eyes. ''I'm very sorry about your Mr. Morrison, Luke, but I still don't understand how Orrin is involved. All of you are from New York. Orrin came here from Philadelphia.''

''I told you Mr. Morrison had clerks doing the accounting for his many businesses. All of them were overseen by one man. That man embezzled a fortune and was clever enough to make it appear that Morrison had raided his own companies. The steel and iron produced at his factories was needed for the rails. Orders couldn't be filled. Investors pulled out. Creditors thought Morrison was hiding the fortune he made in the first years of the war. When he couldn't produce it, they turned on him. He was more devastated by the loss of his good name than the loss of his fortune.''

''So he killed himself.''

''That's what his murderer wanted everyone to believe.''

Bria's luminous eyes widened. ''His murderer? But—''

''Morrison supposedly used a Remington to kill himself. A single shot through his temple.''

''And?''

''And Morrison owned only Colts. He had a contract with

Colt to supply the raw materials they needed. He wouldn't have used a Remington.''

"Luke, he was in mourning for his good name and his company. He took his own life. He wasn't thinking clearly.''

"He didn't own a Remington revolver, Bree, and Mr. Morrison was left-handed. The shot was through his right temple.''

"You might have said that first. If it was murder, then why was it reported as a suicide?''

"The police thought it would assist them in catching the murderer if he thought he'd gotten away with it. They considered it less likely that he would flee. Even after it was clear that they wouldn't find him in New York, they didn't come forward with the truth.''

"If Mr. Morrison's death has always been named a suicide, how do you know differently?''

"It was my mother who found him,'' Luke said. "The body was still warm when she came upon it. My aunts were all waiting for her in a carriage around the corner from Morrison's brownstone. They saw someone leaving by the alleyway. Later, when they gave their description to the police, it was a good match for Morrison's senior accountant. It took the police some time to sort through the evidence and accept what my mother had been saying all along. By the time they acknowledged they had a murder, not a suicide, it was already too late.''

Bria remained pensive. "Is it Orrin?'' she asked finally.

"A man named Walter Wingate was Morrison's accountant. The embezzlement scheme can certainly be attributed to him, but there were two others involved. Both men are dead now, probably by Wingate's hand, though proving it would be impossible without Wingate's own confession. I followed the trail of one to Pittsburgh. The other to Atlanta. That was in the early months of the search. Two years ago I thought I'd found Wingate himself in Savannah. I spent months there with nothing to show for it. In the end I had to retrace my own steps and consider what information I had gleaned in a new light. All of that eventually led me to Charleston and Charleston led me here.''

"So Orrin Foster is Walter Wingate.''

Luke nodded. "I think so. I need to take him back to New York to prove it. My aunts can place him at Morrison's brownstone for the murder and the police still have a case for the embezzlement."

"The embezzlement." Bria did not so much say the words as breathe them. "If my stepfather *is* Wingate, then Concord . . .'' She couldn't finish. The consequences of what Orrin may have done were too sweeping to contemplate.

"The back taxes on Henley were paid for with money stolen from Morrison. It represents only a fraction of what was taken. Orrin's bank accounts and investments will reveal the whole of what was embezzled. I know money went toward improvements at Concord, and Orrin chafed at every dollar spent, but it was still a very small amount of what he has available."

"Do you have evidence?" she asked. "Have you seen his accounts?"

"I've looked through the house for them, searched the rooms . . . his study. I've never been able to locate them. There's no safe. No secret drawers in the desk."

"He would have had them with him while he was in Charleston."

"I thought of that, but I had to look anyway."

"I think he might actually move his account books around," Bria said. "I used to believe he occasionally tore up his study or some other room in the house because he was searching for the Hamilton riddle. Now I'm thinking that it's not that way at all. It could be that Orrin forgets where he puts his papers. It would be just like him to think Mother or I would want to poke into his business." She ignored Luke's patently skeptical look. "I think he moves his personal investments and accounts around to keep us from finding them."

Luke considered that. "You could be right."

Bria felt sure she was. "Luke, what does this mean for Henley? Can Orrin even lay a proper claim to it?"

"Probably not."

Bria's expression remained unchanged although her eyes slipped away from Luke's. She nodded slowly. "I didn't think so," she whispered. "What about you, Luke? How were you involved in all of this?"

"Mary Kincaid," he said, half sighing his mother's name. "All of my aunts with the exception of Laura were quick to support her. She took a minute or so longer to make up her mind, but there was no question that she would be pulled in." Luke took a deep breath, filling his lungs with crisp autumn air as he gathered his thoughts. "By the time I arrived home Wingate was long gone and the police were still investigating in only the most haphazard manner.

"Morrison had no wife or children. His parents died years before he made his fortune and he had no brothers, no sisters. For all intents and purposes Mary Kincaid and her best friends were his family. My mother cared deeply that Morrison's name be cleared. When she realized the police weren't doing enough to make that happen she hired Pinkerton men to help. That lasted until I was enlisted. The Pinkerton detectives turned over what they had gathered and gave it to me. That was close to nine years ago. I've been plodding along ever since, picking up architectural commissions as I was able."

"Your quest," Bria said softly. "It's been your quest."

"Perhaps in the beginning."

She glanced at him, uncertain.

"Don't you know yet, Bree? You became my quest."

Bria's head tilted to one side and her eyes narrowed. She studied Luke in the manner of one trying to appreciate a novel work of art, intrigued by its originality but skeptical of its promise. "Can that be true?"

"It's true."

"But I asked *you* to marry *me*. As I recall, you tried to talk me out of it."

"All part of my plan."

"You had a plan?"

"I had ideas."

"Mmmm." Her brows lifted a fraction. "Tell me . . . on our wedding night . . . did you do something to the doors leading to Mammy's old room?"

"No. I did something to the keys."

"The keys!" His crooked grin turned her insides out. He looked enormously pleased with himself again and Bria couldn't even pretend she minded. "One of your better ideas."

"Thank you."

Bria smoothed her gown over her lap. Her expression sobered slowly. "What have you decided to do about Orrin's invitation for Saturday?"

"You know what I've decided. I haven't changed my mind. You heard Elizabeth. She's agreed to stake me."

"I don't know if she should do that. What if Orrin found out?"

"I'm not going to tell him, at least not beforehand. Are you?"

"No, of course not."

"And your mother certainly won't tell him . . ." Luke waited to see if Bria would mount another protest. When she didn't, he went on. "What about you? Are you going to add your money to the pot?"

Bria didn't want him to go at all. "I know it was what I wanted, Luke, what everything hinged on, but things are different now. Even if there was no risk, can Orrin properly wager what doesn't rightly belong to him? If he bought Henley with money he stole, then Mr. Morrison's heirs or his creditors could make a claim against it. Have you considered that?"

"Yes. Long before you did. I think we need to put the plantation back in your hands, then work out the rest. There still is the matter of proving Orrin is Wingate. That will take time, and in the absence of more compelling evidence than the testimony of Ruby and all six of her precious gems, it might never happen.''

"Don't you think people will listen to your mother or your aunts?''

"They're prostitutes, Bree,'' he said, matter-of-fact. "You were listening when I explained that part, weren't you? You didn't show much reaction to it.''

"I've never been confronted with anything quite so astonishing. I'm certain something will come to me. All the same, I don't think that what they do necessarily makes them untrustworthy. Just the opposite, I would imagine. You said yourself that discretion counts for a great deal in their . . . um, profession. A lawyer could make something of that.''

"Perhaps.'' Luke remained doubtful. "Still, it remains true that you could have Henley in your control while things are sorted out.''

Bria's mouth and chin were set stubbornly. "If your life is what is really at stake, then I'm not interested.''

"Very well.''

"Then you won't—''

Luke cut her off. "I'll use your mother's money and what savings I have. That's all I meant.''

Bria stood because she saw there was no changing his mind. "I think I'd like to ride alone for a little while.''

He came close to reaching for her as she brushed past him. Instead he stayed exactly as he was, staring out over the river but having no vision save Bria.

On Saturday evening Bria stood at the front door of the main house and watched Luke ride away on Apollo. Orrin had set off in the carriage a few minutes earlier.

"I don't see why Luke couldn't have gone in the carriage,'' Elizabeth said, stepping outside to join her daughter. "Surely it's safer for both of them if they travel together.''

"Orrin insisted,'' Bria said. "He pointed out that if one of them felt the need to leave the game early, then the other wouldn't be obligated to go along.''

Elizabeth appeared a bit surprised. "Then I suppose Orrin was being thoughtful.''

Bria turned toward her mother when she could no longer see Luke. "If Orrin was being thoughtful, then he was only considering himself. He doesn't believe Luke has enough skill or a stake large enough to keep him in the game. He wants to be certain that he can stay when Luke is run off by the others.''

"Bria," Elizabeth chided. "You don't know that.'' She saw by the stubborn line of her daughter's mouth that Bria wasn't going to change her mind. Elizabeth changed the subject. "Dare I hope that finding you out here means you and Luke made amends before he left?''

"We weren't fighting, Mother.''

"That's because you weren't speaking.''

"That's not true. We spoke.''

"Not often. And when you did, the tone was so civil and impersonal the two of you might as well have been meeting for the first time. It's been going on for days. Even Orrin remarked on it to me.''

Bria stepped back into the house and held the door for her mother. "I imagine Orrin hopes it will put Luke off his game,'' she said dryly. She saw by Elizabeth's small start that she had correctly divined Orrin's thinking again. Bria sighed. "I simply didn't want Luke to go. There is nothing more to our disagreement than that. He knows my objections and I know his reasons. I made certain he had Apollo because I wanted him to have the very best horse to carry him back safely. I don't know that there was anything more I could have done or said.''

"Did you say farewell?'' Elizabeth asked softly.

"I came outside to see him off.''

"But did you speak to him? Wish him well? Tell Luke you love him?''

Bria hadn't said a word. Only her eyes had pleaded with him to remain at Concord and only after his back was turned.

She had merely been intractable before that. Bria shook her head now, answering her mother.

"Oh, Bree. Never let him go without saying you love him."

Bria stared at her mother for a long moment. "Did you say as much to Orrin? Did you once consider withdrawing your support from Luke to keep him here?" She turned her back on Elizabeth and crossed the entrance hall to climb the stairs. On the lip of the first step she paused briefly to glance over her shoulder. "I thought once I could pit Luke against Orrin to get what I wanted. I was wrong, Mother. People can't be manipulated to act in predictable ways. There is more here at stake tonight than money for your gardens."

Bria thought she saw her mother's eyes flinch at this last remark, but the flicker of apprehension or hurt was so quickly masked that she questioned what she had seen until she reached her bedroom. There, confronted with Luke's absence again, Bria forgot all about what she had glimpsed in her mother's eyes.

Franklin Archer's home was twelve miles southwest of Concord. The plantation was a few thousand acres of farmland and pasture and boasted a large carriage house and stable that most of the planting community envied. The gracefully curved portico welcomed visitors to the house. When Orrin and Luke arrived they were shown directly into Franklin's study by the Archer family's longtime butler.

Austin Tipping stood when Orrin and Luke entered the room and greeted them both warmly. He was tall and slender, with long, tapered fingers and rather delicate hands. He held one out to Orrin, then Luke, and gave them both solid handshakes. "Help yourself at the sideboard," he said. "Frank was called upstairs to settle some family dispute. He's regretting he didn't make arrangements for his wife and daughters to go to his mother's for a few days."

"Precisely why I didn't want to host this game at Concord,"

Orrin said. "We would have to contend with Bria pressing her ear to the door all evening, or finding excuses to disturb us just to assure herself that Luke here wasn't being cheated." He clapped Luke hard on the back. "Isn't that right, Kincaid? Bria doesn't trust us not to take advantage."

"I don't know about taking advantage, sir," Luke said. "I think she's worried about you taking my life."

Austin Tipping was the first to laugh. To Luke's ears it sounded genuine. Orrin's heartier chuckle was the one that seemed forced. None of them pursued the topic. Luke prepared a drink for himself and Orrin, then took a chair at the table opposite Austin. Frank Archer joined them a few minutes later. He settled his bulk into the chair beside Luke and heaved a long-suffering sigh.

"Somebody deal the damn cards," he said. He pulled on one of his thick eyebrows so several of the coarse silver hairs stood at attention. "The only ladies I want to see for the rest of the evening are in that deck."

Austin picked up the cards in front of him and began shuffling. "What about Will? He's coming, isn't he?"

Franklin shrugged. "He'll get here when he gets here."

Orrin opened the box of chips and organized the bank, giving the players what they asked for. "What about Sam and Jim?"

"I heard Jim Poling's laid up with a sprain," Franklin said. He tapped the table impatiently with fingers the size of sausages. When Orrin passed him his chips he divided them into smaller piles and began tapping them. "I can't say about Sam. I didn't hear that he *wasn't* coming so I expect he will."

Austin dealt the cards. He eyed the pot in the middle of the table. The cherry wood was buffed to such a gloss that the chips were reflected in the finish. "Everyone in? Jacks or better to open. Nothing wild." He glanced at Luke. "I'm assuming Orrin told you this is a friendly game. There's no limit except a gentleman's own conscience. You understand?"

Luke hadn't opened his own hand yet. "I understand."

The first several hands certainly proceeded in a civil fashion.

Luke won one, but the rest were taken by Austin. Franklin grumbled good-naturedly about his damnable luck while Orrin suffered his losses in silence. They broke once when Sam arrived and again when refreshments were brought in. It was only after one of them observed that it was unlikely that Will would be joining them at so late an hour that the play began in earnest.

Luke sensed the change in the atmosphere immediately. It was not any one thing that stood out, but a subtle shift in mannerisms and posture. While Sam's wide brow remained creased, the furrow had deepened. His eyes went from watchful to vigilant. Orrin actually tempered his drinking. He lifted the glass often to his lips but took smaller sips. Luke observed him once going to the sideboard and cutting his bourbon with more water than was to his usual taste.

Franklin's staccato rhythms changed depending on the hand he was dealt. Luke was well aware that the others had long ago figured that out. They put up with their friend's nervous tapping because it gave them the clearest signal about the cards he held. If it was a good hand he drummed his fingers. If it held nothing, he beat his forefinger against the table. The only time Franklin stopped being a one-man band was when he was bluffing. At that point he could only concentrate on his demeanor.

Austin was the most skilled player, but he hadn't cut his teeth at the gaming tables in Flora's brothel. Until he was six, Luke had watched some of the finest card sharps in New York take a seat at Flora's. While his mother worked upstairs he brought drinks to the back room, lighted cigars, opened new decks. The players didn't merely suffer his presence; sometimes they paid for it. They called him Little Lucky and asked him to stand at their side. He could be roused from his bed, sometimes after midnight, to join the game in the hope his appearance would have some effect on the outcome. In turn, Luke learned from the New York masters. Once he had been seated on the lap of Gentleman George James while the man's winning streak extended to twenty-three straight hands. He saw Jesop Fitzgerald, the fire and brimstone evangelist of Lower Manhattan, play out a bluff to win a man's soul and six hundred dollars. Little Lucky was there to witness Jack Fine accuse Edmund Benning of cheating and settle it with a derringer. It was this last incident that convinced Mary Kincaid that her son would be better raised by her own mother. Nana Dearborn arrived in a carriage the following day to take him away from Greene Street.

Luke was not particularly bothered by Austin's skill at playing the game. His skill at manipulating the cards was another matter entirely. In addition to that, Austin, Sam, Franklin, and Orrin were playing against him as one. He had seen it done before. One man would take a loss while feeding winning hands to another player. Only deft dealers could manage it. Luke acknowledged that Austin Tipping was good enough to get away with it if Sam's earlier effort hadn't alerted Luke to the possibility.

Luke never called them on it. He doubted any one of them would accept being named a cheat, just as he doubted he could win any confrontation with them. The memory of Jack Fine's concealed derringer was very much on Luke's mind. He countered their cheating by folding early so that he had less to lose. It took some effort on his part not to be obvious about it. The last thing Luke wanted was to call attention to his own skill as a player.

Conversation was acceptable around the table. This was, after all, a friendly game. They discussed Grant's presidency, the last harvest, Franklin's daughter's upcoming wedding, and Captain Matthew Webb, who swam the English Channel in August. They were of similar minds on a number of topics and most especially Webb. There was sound agreement that it was, as Sam put it, "a damn fool thing to do."

Between anteing, raising the bid, folding, raising again, and calling, the subject of the Klan came up. Luke joined the conversation because it was expected. He asked questions about the organization as if he had never met any of the hooded riders.

They responded in kind, explaining why it was needed to protect the property of the whites.

"The magistrates have failed us," Sam told Luke. The others, save Orrin, agreed. "Too many coloreds took office after the '68 election. The rice crop is failing. Can't get the nigras to do a damn thing during the lay-by time."

"He means after the harvest," Orrin said. "Sam, are you in or out?"

"I'm in." Sam studied his cards. "Where are we?"

"Three dollars."

"Oh, hell." He threw in some chips. "There. Three dollars and I raise two." He folded his cards neatly in front of him and continued the thread of his thinking. "Like I was saying, you can't get them to do the ditching or mend the trunks. Pay them a decent wage and they drink it away."

Franklin saw Sam's raise. He tapped the table with his fore-finger. "When they get drunk they get ornery. They imagine slights; they talk uppity to our women. The Klan keeps order. Isn't that right, Orrin?"

Orrin lifted one brow. "If you say so. Hard for me to know when they're keeping order on *my* land. Burning *my* buildings. Torturing a man who works for *me*."

Sam chuckled. "Take the long view, Orrin. The nigras won't be stealin' from you in the future."

"Of course," Orrin said dryly. "The long view." He jerked his chin at Luke. "What do you think, Kincaid?"

"I think I'll fold." Luke threw in his cards and sidestepped the question entirely by leaving the table. He wished he could see the looks they were exchanging behind his back. They were actually trying to recruit him to the Klan. Orrin's rather terse objections were merely to demonstrate all opinions were toler-ated.

Luke's rebuff assured that the game continued with less chatter after that. The play became more intense as conversation lapsed into concentration. Shortly after midnight Sam excused himself to lie down on the chaise near the fireplace and fell asleep. The game continued with just four players.

Luke began to win more often than he lost after that. The pots grew steadily until Franklin declared they were too rich for him. The less Luke seemed to care about the outcome, the more Orrin Foster did. Occasionally Luke caught him flashing a look of disgust at Franklin and the sleeping Sam, rebuking them for deserting him. Austin stayed in until the clock in the entrance hall struck three. His narrow face was pinched as he pushed away from the table and went in search of coffee.

Luke looked down at the stacks of chips in front of him. "More than enough to restore Elizabeth's gardens," he said. "I'm prepared to go if you are."

Orrin's eyes were red along the rim but clear and focused at the centers. "What?"

"I'm prepared to leave."

Orrin shook his head. "What did you say about Elizabeth?"

"She staked my play tonight," he said casually. "She knew I couldn't possibly have enough money otherwise. She warned me that all of you are serious about your friendly game." For good measure, Luke punctuated this last statement with a crooked grin. "Elizabeth was right, of course. I would have had to excuse myself before Sam fell asleep if she hadn't helped me." He feigned earnestness when Orrin glowered at him. "I wasn't wrong to accept it, was I? She was insistent and it was in support of a worthy cause."

Orrin swore softly as Franklin laughed. "Kincaid, you're trying my patience."

"He means," Austin said, "that you're playing with his own money."

Luke's brows knit. "I don't understand."

"Elizabeth doesn't have a penny that I haven't given her," Orrin said. "Everything she has belongs to me."

Sam roused himself to a sitting position on the chaise and offered his own sleepy observation. "If you gave it to her,

Orry, doesn't that make it hers? Is there any bourbon left? I certainly feel a second wind at my back.''

Austin poured two fingers of bourbon for Sam and carried it to the chaise. ''The expression is 'three sheets to the wind,' '' he said. ''And it describes you perfectly.''

Sam was not offended. He thanked Austin for the drink and clutched it as he rose rather clumsily to his feet. ''Of course, it does seem wrong somehow. Like you were playing against your wife. Or yourself.'' He took a swallow. ''Or some non-sense like that.''

Luke gathered up the cards. ''You could always try to win it back.'' He shuffled the deck with indifferent ease. ''I'm not anxious to lose, you understand, but it seems reasonable to make the offer since you didn't know how I came by my stake. I suppose there are some that would say that what Elizabeth owns is yours, whether you gave it to her or not.''

''That's what I would say,'' Franklin offered. ''In fact I say it all the time to my Amanda, not that she pays me any mind.'' A chuckle rumbled in his barrel chest. ''No mind at all.''

Orrin Foster leaned back in his chair. His eyes were partially hooded as he watched Luke shuffle the cards. ''What sort of wager are you proposing?'' he asked. ''You must have something in mind.''

Luke paused in his shuffling long enough to indicate the stacks in front of him. ''All of it against what you have.''

''That seems unequal. You've been winning lately. I've merely held my own. You have twice as many chips.''

Luke shrugged. ''I understand your reluctance. I imagine something seems not quite right. I stand to lose so much more than you that you must be suspicious of my motives. My uncle Morrie would tell you to walk away from the table now. That's how he advised me when it came to accepting a suspect wager. Walk away.''

''Uncle Morrie's advice seems sound,'' Orrin said. ''Have you ever taken it?''

''No. I can't seem to get the hang of walking away, but I

don't judge another man poorly for doing so. Uncle Morrie would say that it makes them smarter than me.'' Luke lost his shuffling rhythm and fumbled with the deck. A few cards dropped on the table. He scooped them up and fit them back in the deck.

''You missed this one.'' Austin Tipping hunkered down beside Luke's chair and picked up a card. He started to hand it to Luke, then turned it over at the last moment. It was a four of clubs. ''I wonder if any of us would still feel kindly toward you if it had been an ace.'' He let Luke pluck it from his fingers this time and stood.

Luke resumed his idle shuffling. ''We could always agree to even stakes,'' Luke said. ''I would naturally accept your marker for what you lack in funds right now.''

''So I would face the possibility of losing even more?'' asked Orrin. ''No, I don't think your uncle Morrie would advise that.''

''Probably not. He was generally too cautious. People said that was true of him in business, but I don't think he made his fortune by being overly cautious.''

One of Franklin's thick brows lifted. He ambled back to the table and sat down. ''You have an uncle with a fortune, Kincaid? Orrin had us believing Bria Hamilton had made a poor match in every sense. Did you know about this, Orrin? The Yankee comes from money.''

''Of course he comes from money. He's extorting a fortune from me for restoring Concord.'' Orrin's smile was tight, his eyes shrewd. ''And that didn't change once he became my son-in-law. He works for me less and charges more. I believe you're exaggerating anyway, Frank. Or at least you took a meaning from my words that I never intended.'' Orrin shifted his heavy-lidded stare back to Luke and posed his question so that it was edged with sarcasm. ''So, Kincaid, are you an heir to Uncle Morrie's fortune?''

Luke's eyes settled on Orrin Foster's face. He spoke quietly. ''Uncle Morrie wasn't any relation at all. He was a family friend and he died owing people. There's no fortune to claim.

Even a cautious man like Conrad Morrison can lose all his money.''

Luke was aware that the others reacted to Morrison's name. Sam whistled softly. Austin sat down. Franklin drummed his fingers harder. But it was only Orrin's reaction that Luke cared about, and at last he was rewarded for his patience. Orrin Foster's ruddy features drained of color. Before he caught himself and slammed a shutter over his expression, there was guilty recognition for the name in his eyes.

Orrin pushed himself upright in his chair. His hand shook slightly as he reached for his tumbler of bourbon. He clutched the glass like a lifeline and raised it to his lips. He took a single, deep swallow. His voice was steady when he finally spoke. ''What do you want?''

''Concord.''

''Impossible.''

Luke shrugged.

Franklin stopped drumming his fingers. ''What the hell is he talking about, Orrin? It sounded like he wants you to wager Concord.''

Sam rose from the chaise for the second time during the evening. He was fully alert now. ''Are you serious, Kincaid? Didn't you hear what we said about this being a friendly game?''

Austin Tipping's eyes darted across the table from Orrin to Luke and back again. ''I never cared much for Henley ending up in Yankee hands, Orrin. You know that because I never made it a secret. Now, if Kincaid here was a true son of Dixie I could be persuaded to take up his cause. However, he's a Yankee, same as you, and he has the woman promised to me. Adding insult to injury is the fact he calls that industrialist swine Uncle Morrie. I say you should accept the wager, but make certain it's better than one-sided. If Kincaid wins he gets Concord. What is he proposing that you'll win, Orrin? He doesn't have enough on the table to match against the plantation. Surely your wife doesn't have funds in that amount as collateral.''

The look Orrin cast in Luke's direction was expectant. "Well? Austin's right. What are you putting on the table?"

Luke reached inside his jacket and came away with a fountain pen. "May I have a piece of paper?" Franklin got one from his desk and handed it over. Luke folded it a third of the way from the top, creased it, and tore it off. Using his hand to shield what he wrote, Luke scrawled something on the paper, then folded it in half when the ink was dry. He slid it across the table toward Orrin. "Read it, then listen to my wager."

Orrin didn't reach for the note immediately. Caution was in order. There was really only one outcome to any wager, Orrin thought. What was placed on the table didn't matter now. It was what would happen later that counted for something. Orrin knew he was making his wager with a dead man.

Drawing the note slowly toward him, Orrin picked it up and held it close to his chest. He opened it and looked down at what Luke had carefully penned. *Walter Wingate*. Orrin remained virtually expressionless as he stared at the words. No one at that table was privy to the roar in his ears and the hammering of his own heart. All they could see was the flush that rose above his shirt and loosened cravat. In a few seconds his previously pale complexion was returned to its rosy hue.

Orrin refolded the note with care and slipped it in his vest pocket. "Very well," he said to Luke. "I'm listening, though I can tell you I don't know what I'm supposed to understand by your marker. It doesn't mean anything to me."

Franklin plucked at his heavy eyebrows. "Aren't you going to tell us what it is, Orrin?"

Orrin ignored him. "Kincaid?"

Luke stopped shuffling. He placed the deck in front of him and let his hands fall back to the arms of his chair. "I'm willing to remove myself from your life," he said flatly. "If you win you keep Concord and I go back to New York. Alone. You have my marker there that I'm giving you your life back."

Sam thumped his tumbler on the table. Bourbon splashed the polished surface. "What the *hell* did Kincaid write, Orrin?"

"And if you win?" Orrin asked with dead calm.

"I get Concord and you still have my word and my marker."

Orrin's smile rose slowly and it held no warmth. "You're proposing your silence as collateral against Concord. Have I understood you correctly?"

"Yes."

Sam Daniels rapped his drink against the table again. "Silence about what, Kincaid? Orrin, I don't think you should be agreeing to this. Does it have something to do with Klan business? It does, doesn't it? You Yankees—"

"Stay out of this, Sam," Orrin snapped. "I know what I'm doing."

Austin Tipping expressed no doubt. Luke saw him catch Franklin's eye, then Sam's. They immediately settled back. Sam cleaned up the droplets of bourbon on the tabletop with a handkerchief. "I was wondering," Austin said, turning to Luke. "What you meant about going back to New York alone."

"Exactly that," said Luke.

"You would leave Bria?"

"I would divorce her."

Orrin's brows shot up. "Does she know this?"

"No."

Austin Tipping's sigh held a certain satisfaction. It brought Orrin's attention to him. "I don't see how you can't accept," he said.

"That's because you're not wagering your plantation."

"True enough." Austin's pale eyes shifted to Luke. "How many hands?"

"One."

"Who deals?"

Luke shrugged. "We'll cut for it."

Sam finished buffing the table and pushed his handkerchief deep in his trouser pocket. "One of us should deal. Keep it neutral."

"I agree," Orrin said.

It was hardly neutral, Luke thought. Especially if Tipping dealt the cards. "Who chooses the dealer?"

"You can cut for that," Austin said. He pointed to the deck in front of Luke. "May I?"

Luke pushed it toward him. "You'll find they're shuffled."

"Yes. I noticed that." Smiling politely, Austin deliberately split the deck and lifted the corner of each stack. He fanned the cards so both stacks were efficiently intermingled. He lifted the deck and tapped it lightly on all four sides to trim the edges. "Who will cut first? Orrin? Kincaid?"

Luke pointed toward Orrin. "He can go."

Austin extended the deck toward Foster and released it. "Go ahead."

Reaching for it with credible nonchalance, Orrin cut the deck a third of the way down. He looked at the bottom card first, then showed the others. "Ten of hearts." He set his small stack back down and pushed the cards to Luke. "There's room to do better."

There was more room to do worse. Luke tried not to think about that. He cut the deck more than halfway and showed the card to them before he looked at it himself. Their expressions told him all he needed to know. He examined the card out of habit. "Seven of spades. You choose the dealer, Orrin."

"Then I choose Tipping."

Luke nodded. He had expected nothing else. He gestured with his hand that Austin should go ahead. Luke pretended to distract himself with his drink but he watched Austin manipulate the bottom of the deck as he shuffled. When Austin stopped and prepared to toss out the first card, Luke pounced. He placed one hand firmly on Austin's wrist and lowered it to the table. "You don't mind if I cut, do you?"

"Now, see here," Orrin snapped. "Are you—"

"You can cut," Luke said calmly. "Austin accidentally flashed me the bottom card as he shuffled. I don't think it's fair that I know what it is and you don't."

Orrin frowned. "What is it?"

"Ten of hearts. The same card you cut earlier."

"Is that right, Austin? You flashed him that card?"

"If I did, it was as Kincaid said—an accident."

"Show it to me," Orrin said. His tone implied that Austin Tipping did not have accidents of this nature.

Luke was satisfied to watch Orrin's distrust surface. Orrin Foster would always see himself as an outsider even when he was a member of an inner circle. Sam Daniels was quick to believe Luke's wager of silence with Orrin had something to do with the Klan. Orrin had probably not missed that Franklin was similarly convinced. Orrin was now in the position of wondering where Austin Tipping stood.

Austin slowly lifted the deck and held it out so they could all see the bottom card. Ten heart-shaped pips were displayed.

Luke shrugged. "There's no need to cut the deck now," he said. "Orrin and I have the same advantage. Go ahead. Deal."

Chapter Fifteen

He had the winning hand, or what should have been the winning hand, in his jacket pocket. He had taken the cards immediately after the hand was played, before they were gathered back into the deck. He was certain no one had seen him. In light of what had been lost this night, it was a small victory. Still, he took some pride in having managed the sleight of hand without detection.

It was too dark to study them now. The crescent moon slipped behind heavy clouds for minutes at a time, making it difficult to see more than a few yards in front of him. He suspected that what he would find when he returned to Concord was that they were marked in some way. He wondered why he hadn't suspected that at the outset. The answer came to him quickly. He had seriously underestimated all of them and their notion of a *friendly* game.

Fallen leaves stirred on either side of the road as he passed. There was movement in the underbrush. Deer. Raccoons. Occasionally something would take flight overhead. Lost in his own thoughts, he barely noticed his nighttime companions. When he did, he was unconcerned.

He considered what he would do after he examined the cards

and identified their markings. How would he confront the others without challenging them? They would all call him out, one after the other, and he would have to face them across a distance of twenty paces. The image that came to him actually raised his smile. He realized he didn't know if Southern gentlemen still dueled for their honor, or if it was an antebellum custom that no longer had any place in their lives.

Too much had changed since the war. He felt for the cards in his pocket and fingered them, as if he could assure himself of their value by doing so. Three queens. Two fours. He should have won the hand. Whatever trick they had managed, it was better suited to riverboat gamblers or robber barons. It had no place in the game they played.

He was only a mile from Concord when a single shot brought him down. The pain in his chest and the report came almost simultaneously. He slumped forward and dropped the reins. His last thought was that they had no honor at all.

Luke heard the melodic strains of Haydn before he entered the house. The notes were played so quickly they seemed to chase one another out the music room window until they scattered across the lawn. By the time he reached the verandah, he was humming softly to himself.

Consulting his pocket watch under a trio of sconces in the hallway, Luke confirmed it was just shy of six o'clock. He had wondered if anyone would be waiting up for him; now he wondered who.

Pale yellow light defined the edges of the music room doors. Luke did not announce his presence by knocking. He pushed apart the doors . . . and stood there frozen.

It was Bria.

She didn't see him. Her face was a tribute to fierce concentration. It fairly glowed in the light from the candelabra. Her eyes were closed. Her full mouth was pressed into a flat line. The familiar crease between her brows was there, deeper than usual.

There was a faint wrinkle in the otherwise perfect line of her nose. Sheets of music were scattered on the floor around the bench. None of it rested on the stand. Her head bobbed ever so slightly, marking time to her internal metronome while her fingers flew across the keys. Tendons rippled across the back of her gracefully arched hands, testimony to the hard work of her accomplishment.

This was the music she had buried inside her. The melody. The joy. Passion and harmony. It hadn't been destroyed after all. Somehow she had kept it safe, even from herself.

Luke crossed the hardwood floor almost soundlessly, his steps masked by Bria's light staccato accompaniment. He stood in the curve of the grand piano and watched her and thought that at the end of everything, this was his reward.

Bria's fingers stilled over the keys without warning. Even before she opened her eyes she knew he was there. "Luke!" She pushed away from the piano, nearly tipping the bench as she came to her feet and launched herself at him. "I knew it was you! I knew it!" Wrapping her arms around his neck, Bria lifted herself on tiptoes and kissed him full on the mouth.

Luke held her close. Here it was again. The melody. The joy. The passion and harmony. The fierceness of her concentration was wonderfully familiar to him. He tasted her mouth and breathed in the fragrance of her hair. In his ears he heard the last refrain she had played.

Bria drew back slowly. Her hands unclasped at his neck so that she could cup his face. She looked up at him. His eyes were the exact color of mist. "You're crying," she whispered. "Why are you crying?"

He smiled in response, kissing the pad of her thumb when she ran it across his mouth.

She prompted him again, touching his lips with hers and saying his name so softly it was merely a sweet breath against his skin.

"The music," he said finally. "It's the music."

"Because of you." Bria stopped the sideways motion of his

head when he would have denied it. "No, you *do* have something to do with it, so let me properly say so. I hardly knew what to do with myself this evening, all the long hours of waiting for you ahead of me, and I found myself here, at the piano, and for the first time in years I felt music stir inside me unaccompanied by dread. I wasn't afraid of what I heard in my head and when I touched the keys, I realized I was no longer afraid to express it. *That's* what you've given me."

He stood there mutely, searching her face, accepting what she told him not because he believed he had given her anything, but because *she* believed it was true.

"I love you," she whispered against his mouth. "I'm so sorry I let you go without a kind word. Even Mother took me to task for it." She kissed him sweetly again, then drew back. Taking his hand, she led him over to the upholstered bench in front of the fireplace. A small fire had been laid for her comfort earlier in the evening and Bria had added wood throughout the night. "Warm yourself here," she said. "Your hands are cold. I'll get you something hot to drink."

Luke would have preferred that she simply held them but she was already on her way out of the room, bent on looking after him, and determinedly avoiding any discussion of the night's other events. He was standing in front of the fire, rubbing his hands together, when she returned with a tea service.

Bria set the tray down and poured them each a cup of tea. Luke turned his back on the fire to face Bria, but remained standing. She sat on the bench and lifted her skirts a few inches to let the warmth reach her feet.

Luke glanced down at her shoes and noticed for the first time that the soft leather was damp at the toes. There was also a wet stain ringing the hem of her dress. "Where did you go tonight?"

Vaguely surprised by the question, Bria followed his eyes to her feet. "Oh. My shoes. Well, I walked down to the river a short while ago. I was restless and my fingers were cramping from playing. A walk seemed in order."

Luke set his cup aside and hunkered down in front of Bria. He unlaced her shoes and removed her damp stockings. He rubbed her feet to warm them and chuckled when she sighed gratefully. "I suppose it was too much to expect that you would have gone to bed."

Bria simply snorted her derision. "Mother retired to her room before midnight. Addie disappeared around that time. Jeb and Elsie went to their rooms even before Mother excused herself." Her tone conveyed she believed they were all faint-hearted.

"Then they all missed your concert."

"I suppose that's true. No one came around to investigate the noise I was making."

"Certainly that was their loss." He straightened and picked up his teacup. He sipped it, watching Bria over the rim. She was putting forth considerable effort *not* to ask him any questions about the outcome of this evening's game. He let her wrestle with it.

Bria's eyes shifted casually toward the bank of windows. All the drapes were drawn back but it was still too dark outside to see anything beyond her own reflection. "You didn't mention Orrin," she said finally. "Did he return with you?"

"He was still at Franklin's when I left."

"Mmm. I imagine they had business to discuss?" The tiniest inflection at the end made it a question.

"That's possible." Luke's tone was indifferent. He finished his tea and set the cup down. "Bed."

Bria blinked. "You're not going to tell me, are you?"

"Tell you what?"

It was an effort not to grit her teeth. "Tell me the outcome of the game. You're making me break the promise I made to myself."

Luke's confusion was quite real this time. "What promise?"

"That I wouldn't ask you anything about it so I could prove to you that I didn't care. I only wanted you back safely. That's all. Truly. And now that you're back I'm being eaten up with curiosity and it isn't fair that you're tormenting me. You may as well tell me because when Orrin arrives, he will. Even if it went badly for him." She saw Luke open his mouth and she quickly held up her hand. "No, I don't want to know. I've changed my mind. It's more important that you know I don't care about the outcome."

"Why shouldn't you care about the outcome? I did."

"That's your right. You were taking all the risks. I was left behind to do all the worrying."

"Not all the worrying. I did some on my own. They tried to recruit me to join the Klan. I hadn't thought to expect that. I had no idea what the consequences of my refusal might be. As it turned out, there was only blessed silence on the subject once I turned away from the conversation."

"They wanted you to join them?" Bria had not been able to anticipate that either. She shook her head slowly. "Didn't they recall you faced them down with a shotgun a short time ago?"

"That incident certainly wasn't mentioned. I believe they think it was your influence. Nothing like that was said, but it makes sense that they would draw me away from you to get my thinking on the subject. I'm very much an outsider, so they covered that ground carefully."

"Incredible," she said softly. "It's beyond anything I—"

Luke interrupted her. "Bed."

Bria jumped to her feet. "Of course." She put her cup beside his and took his arm as if he could no longer support himself. She heard him chuckle but paid no attention.

"You're quite sure you don't want to know?" he asked. "I won't be offended."

"I don't want to know. It's not important. Nothing is, except that you're here and all of one piece." She paused beside the piano to extinguish the candelabra. Their shadows were cast on the wall by the fire in the hearth. "Unless you want to offer some sort of hint. A hint would not be out of the question. I wouldn't be breaking my promise and it would have the consequence of making me more kindly disposed to you once we reach our bedroom.''

Luke squeezed her arm and stifled a yawn as they passed through the music room doors. ''Bree, if by 'kindly disposed' you mean you will allow me to sleep, I'll tell you anything.''

''A less secure woman would be offended by that. I, however, am merely never going to forget you said it.''

''That's a relief,'' he said dryly. ''I wouldn't want to offend you. Look in my jacket pocket if you want your hint.''

Bria's arm dropped away from his. She searched Luke's impassive expression for a long moment before her hand slipped inside his jacket. She felt the stiffness of a folded piece of paper filling out the pocket. ''This is what you want me to have?''

He nodded. ''Go on. take it.''

Bria slid the paper out and carefully unfolded it. She had to go under one of the wall sconces to read it clearly but she recognized her stepfather's scrawl before she made out a single word.

Offered this day as payment for all debts to Lucas Dearborn Kincaid: The property known as Concord, formerly Henley, is forfeited this 30th day of November to Bria Hamilton Kincaid, the daughter of my wife Elizabeth Hamilton Foster. Said property shall include all holdings : livestock, crop stores, outbuildings, tenant farms, and the house proper. It shall include funds set aside for the management of the property in the amount of eight thousand dollars.

Respectfully submitted under no duress,
Orrin Foster.

In the sight of God and before these witnesses:
Austin Tipping
Samuel Daniels
Franklin Archer, Esq.

Bria saw the paper tremble in her hand before she realized she was the source of the movement. She looked over her shoulder at Luke. Her voice was no more than a whisper. "Is this true?"

"I didn't think you would be satisfied with a hint. Yes, it's true."

Bria threw herself so hard at Luke that he actually rocked back on his heels. He heard the note bearing witness to this night's events crumble in Bria's hands. He gingerly extracted it from her fist while continuing to return her kisses and replaced it in his pocket.

They might have gone on as they began—a few tentative steps up the wide staircase interspersed with unintelligible murmurs of the heart—if it had not been for sudden shouts and cries rising beyond the house. Bria and Luke broke apart. His hands settled on her shoulders when he saw the alarm in her face.

"I'll see what it is," he said quickly. "Wait—" He stopped. She would not wait. He saw that. He had made her wait all evening. This time she would be at his side. "At least let me lead this time." Without waiting for an answer, Luke turned and hurried down the stairs and hallway. He sensed Bria only a narrow step behind him.

They were met on the verandah by Tad and another stablehand just as dawn broke in the eastern sky. An orange crescent of sun colored the undersides of clouds shades of mauve and rose and pink and laid its light along a narrow band on the horizon.

Tad and Geordie stopped so suddenly on the dewy stone steps that their bodies vibrated with the effort to remain upright. Geordie was a younger version of his cousin Tad, a shade slimmer, less contained in expression and energy. His hands twitched nervously as he waited for Tad to speak up. His dark eyes darted from Luke to Bria as if he expected them to have divined the purpose of their visit before a word was said.

"It's the master," Tad said with a credible effort to sound calm.

Geordie slapped his thigh with his fist. "He dead. Sure as I'm standing here in my nightshirt and britches. He dead. Took the buggy right up to the stable door, just like he always do, but then he didn't holler for me or Tad. The mare snufflin' against the door is what roused me. Saw him first and called his name. Thought he was drunk. Pardon me, Miz Bree, but that's what I thought and I aim to say it truly now, jest so you know it wasn't any of my doin'. He dead. Tad will tell you. Tell them, Tad."

Tad glared sideways at Geordie. "Seems like you already told them." His expression became infinitely gentle when he looked back at Bria. "I'm sorry, Miss Bree. Geordie's scared and his mouth outruns his feet and his brain, but he's told you the truth. Mr. Foster's dead. Looks like a bullet in his chest."

Bria wavered on her feet. Her knees held but the edges of her vision darkened. She felt Luke's arm slip around her waist and did not pretend she didn't need the support.

"Where is he?" Luke asked. "Did you move him?"

Geordie shook his head vigorously. "Didn't touch him at all. I was scared, just like Tad says, only I ain't no more. I left him like I found him. Went straight away to Tad and then we both come here, shoutin' like, to get your attention."

They certainly had his attention, Luke thought. He tested Bria's ability to stand on her own, then eased his arm away from her. "Show me," he said tersely. He let the stablehands lead the way across the yard, realizing belatedly that Bria was still following, albeit at a slower, more cautious pace this time.

Orrin Foster's body was slumped across the buggy seat. He was no longer holding the reins but part of the leather ribbons were caught under his side. The buggy whip was lying on the floor at his feet. Even before Luke stepped up he could see the stain of dark blood on Orrin's jacket. He bent down and undid two buttons. The mortal wound was revealed in full crimson bloom.

Luke looked over his shoulder. Bria was standing back, her face pale, her features very still. He shook his head slightly and he thought he heard her soft moan. "Tad. Geordie. Unhitch the buggy and one of you stable the mare. The other can help me carry Mr. Foster inside."

"I'll help." It was Jebediah's deep, sleep-filled drawl that made the offer. "I heard the shouting. Elsie said I should see what it was. Damn, but I didn't think I was going to see this." He scratched his head, his brow deeply furrowed. "Miss Bree, you go on back up to the house. Your mama's gonna have to know. Give me and Mr. Luke here a chance to fix him up before you tell her. It ain't fittin' she should see him like this, even if he was a no account husband to her."

Bria lifted her eyes from Jeb to Luke. "I'll get Addie to help me with the linens." She turned and started back to the house, her head bent low. She could not make sense of the tears that made her vision liquid. Was she really crying for Orrin Foster? Or was it something else she did not dare name?

Luke watched Bria go and while the others were similarly distracted by her retreating figure, he reached into Orrin's inside jacket pocket and plucked out the note that bore Orrin's true name. Blood stained the paper and darkened the ink. The script was almost illegible. *Walter Wingate*. Luke thrust it in his own pocket and stepped down as Tad and Geordie began to unhitch the buggy.

"You have any ideas about this?" Luke asked Jeb.

"Plenty of ideas," Jeb said. "Not too many folks going to miss him. But do I know who might have pressured the Lord's smiting hand? I'm not thinking I do."

There was a discordant thump as the horse and buggy were separated. Luke frowned. "Carefully," he told the stablehands.

"That wasn't us," Tad said. "Something slid off the seat in the buggy." He straightened and looked over the front board . . . and whistled softly. Reaching inside, Tad lifted a silver-plated Remington off the floor at Orrin's feet. "Mr. Luke. You'll want to see this." He held up the gun.

Luke recognized it immediately. He'd seen one like it before in New York. The police had shown him the Remington that had killed Conrad Morrison. It was the twin of this one, or it appeared to be. The ivory handle bore five stars in relief, underscored with a Union banner. Remington had made only one hundred of the revolvers. They were sold in pairs, cased in a walnut box lined with black velvet. They had been distributed to Union officers who distinguished themselves at West Point. The revolvers became sought after by collectors after the war, but Morrison was not a collector of Remingtons. Luke wondered about Walter Wingate.

In his searching through the house, he had never uncovered a walnut case with a missing Remington. He also had to admit that he hadn't been looking for it. It had never once occurred to him that Orrin Foster would keep such a critical piece of evidence in his possession.

"You think he killed hisself?" Geordie asked, sidling up to Luke. "Seems strange someone would shoot him and leave the gun behind. Could be they was scared, though." He eyed the revolver closely and whistled under his breath. "That a Colt?"

"Remington," Luke said. "Right here. You can see the mark."

Geordie and Tad both peered closer, almost bumping heads. Luke separated them. "Have any of you seen this before?" He let Jeb look at it closely. "I've never known Orrin to carry a gun." He was met by three blank stares, all impossible to interpret. Luke didn't press for information. He tucked the revolver into his trousers and looked to Jeb for help. "Let's take Orrin in. Is there anything in the stable we can use as a litter?"

They made a makeshift litter with a pole, a piece of lumber of almost equal length, and a horse blanket. It held Orrin's ample weight all the way to his room. Bria was waiting for them in the hallway. She pushed open the door and let them inside. Lamps had been lighted on either side of the bed and on the mantel. The basin was filled with water and a stack of towels sat on a nearby chair. Fresh sheets had been placed across the bed in order to clean and prepare the body. They would be removed when that was accomplished.

"I can't find Addie," she said as Luke and Jeb passed with the body. "She isn't with John and she isn't in her own room. Elsie's gone to the kitchen to make breakfast. She needed to be busy, she said."

Jeb nodded. "We passed her. She's up to her elbows in flour, preparing to feed the mourners."

Bria hadn't been able to think that far ahead. She watched Luke and Jeb place Orrin on the bed. His body depressed the mattress but didn't stir. If he hadn't been so quiet she could have made herself believe he was simply drunk. "I suppose someone should send for Dr. Edwards. Perhaps the sheriff. I don't know—"

Luke interrupted her quietly. "I sent Tad off for both of them." He removed the gun from his trousers. "Have you seen this before?"

Bria's eyes widened with surprise, not recognition.

"Never. Where did you find it?"

Sensing his presence was of no help now, Jeb excused himself and went in search of Elsie.

When they were alone, Luke told Bria about finding the revolver and its possible origin. "Who would know he had it?" Luke asked.

Bria's teeth pressed against her lower lip. "Why do you think anyone would know? That Orrin knew was enough. He killed himself with it, didn't he?"

Luke could see that Bria very much wanted to believe that. His voice was gentle. "Let's wait and hear what Dr. Edwards and the sheriff have to say. I think Elizabeth needs to know now. Shall I ask Jeb to get Martha and one of her sisters to prepare the body? Then I can go with you to see your mother."

Bria nodded. "Yes. Thank you."

"I'm going to need a photograph, Bria. Of Orrin. It will help with identification. I'll make the arrangements."

"Very well." She stopped Luke just as they would have parted in the hallway. "Could it have been the Klan?" she asked.

"I don't know." He had wondered the same thing himself. "There was some talk tonight at the table, Bree. A suspicion, I think, that Orrin might have been thinking of betraying them in some fashion. You should know it was prompted by the wager. Orrin and I conducted it with a certain amount of secrecy. I didn't confront him about being Walter Wingate in front of the others." Luke reached in his pocket and withdrew the stained, folded note. He opened it across his palm and showed it to Bria. "I gave him this."

Bria's eyes narrowed as she concentrated on the script. "Walter Wingate," she said finally. She looked up at Luke. "This is how you let him know you were aware of his identity?"

He made a slight nod. "It forced him into the wager. He never denied it and didn't want the others to know." Luke put the note away again. "But perhaps it made them suspicious in other ways."

Bria took his hand and squeezed. "I don't blame you, Luke." Tears gathered along the rim of her lower lashes. "There were so many times I thought I wanted him . . ." She could not say the word now, but she could also not deny that she had thought about it. "I considered doing it myself. You know he was frightened of me. He believed I could. I pointed a pistol at him once. Held it on him in front of my mother and Rand and Claire . . . in the entrance hall." In some ways it was difficult to believe that she had done it. "It was after Orrin shot Cutch. I could have killed him. Rand stopped me, but I could have done it then, Luke."

She swiped at her eyes impatiently. "Go on. Find Jeb and ask him to send Martha to Orrin's room. I'll wait for you outside Mother's. She must be sleeping hard, not to have heard the commotion."

Luke kissed Bria's damp cheek. "I'll be a few minutes. No longer."

Bria nodded, watched him go, then went back inside Orrin's room and set out his best suit and shoes for Martha to use. She saw the Remington where Luke had left it on the nightstand. She stared at it a long time before she picked it up. Turning it over in her hand, she studied the five stars on the ivory handle. She ran her finger over them. Finally she opened the cylinder and counted the bullets. Four. Two had been discharged. If they both had been fired tonight, then it wasn't a suicide. Orrin couldn't very well have shot himself twice at such close range.

Steeling herself, Bria put the revolver down and checked Orrin's wound. There was only a single entry wound just left of the center of his chest. It would have been awkward for him to have pulled the trigger, but Bria assured herself it could have been done in such a manner. The alternative . . . she could not let her thoughts drift in that direction.

Bria fled the room just as Luke was turning into the hall from the rear stairs.

"I thought you were going to wait for me outside your mother's room," he said. Her face was pale, the sapphire eyes enormous. "Are you all right?"

"I put out clothes for Martha to use." She could see Luke was waiting for more but she offered nothing. Instead, she led the way to Elizabeth's room.

Luke tapped lightly on the door. There was no answer. He looked to Bria for direction. She knocked more loudly, then twisted the handle and walked in. Except for the small amount of natural light slipping under the closed drapes, the room was dark. Bria could make out the shape of her mother in the bed but little else. She went to the window and drew back each panel of drapery and secured it.

Luke stared at the sleeping figure in the rocker. "Addie." He did not say it with the intention of waking her, but merely to point out to Bria that the housekeeper had at last been found.

Bria turned around and saw her. She frowned. "I certainly didn't expect that she would be here. Wake her gently, Luke. She looks exhausted. I'll wake Mother."

A three-legged stool covered in delicately cross-stitched roses was sitting beside the fireplace tools. Thinking that Addie would be less alarmed if he was not looming over her, Luke pushed it within arm's length of the rocker and sat down. He touched her wrist just below the tight sleeve of her dress. "Addie? It's time to get up." She stirred, pulling her arm away and cradling it against her with her other arm.

Luke glanced at Bria. She was being similarly unsuccessful with her mother. Luke studied Addie more closely. She was drawing each breath hard so that she sounded almost as if she were snoring. There were abrupt little pauses where she seemed to stop breathing all together. On one of those pauses, Luke leaned closer. At the exhale, he smelled spirits on her breath.

His brow furrowed. Addie did not typically drink in the evening. He had spent enough time with her to feel confident of that. Even during the harvest celebration she drank very little. Luke looked more closely at the dress Addie was wearing. Though she was small herself, this gown looked uncomfortably tight. The color of it was plain enough, but the material looked rich. It was something much finer than the cotton and wool dresses in her wardrobe.

Luke gave Addie's shoulder a gentle nudge. He almost fell off the stool as she bolted upright, her dark eyes wide with fear. Before he could make her understand that she was safe, Addie had shot to her feet and thrown her arms widely to the sides. Luke had to duck to avoid being struck in the head.

"Addie!" It was Elizabeth who called to her from the bed. The voice was husky from sleep but carried absolutely authority. "It's Luke and Bria come to wake us. Now calm yourself."

Addie Thomas actually woke on her feet. She blinked once. Twice. Full alertness changed her expression from alarm to embarrassment. She sank slowly back into the the rocker. Her eyes darted once toward Elizabeth then back to her lap. She stared at her clasped hands and was uncharacteristically silent.

Luke caught Bria's puzzled glance but his own face remained expressionless. His gaze shifted to Elizabeth. She was already situating herself in bed like a queen seeking comfort from her throne. She had pushed a small pillow behind her back and neatly folded down the thick comforter across her lap. Her nightgown was embellished with satin ribbons along the neckline. Elizabeth had pressed all of them neatly in place with her fingertips. Now her hands were lightly patting down her hair, smoothing back those few strands that had been disturbed by sleep.

Bria eased herself onto the bed near her mother's side. The hem of her gown rose as she lifted her legs onto the mattress.

Elizabeth looked at her daughter's bare feet and frowned. "Where are your shoes and stockings, Bria? It's much too cold to be walking around the house with neither."

Luke did not hear Bria's reply. He was temporarily distracted by Addie shifting her position in the rocker, drawing her feet up under her gown. He glimpsed ten bare toes before they disappeared under the hem of her dress. His eyes darted, looking for the shoes and stockings that belonged on those feet.

"Why is Addie here?" Bria asked.

Elizabeth's narrow chin came up. "You can't have come here to ask that. Whatever has happened needs to be said directly."

But Bria wasn't ready to do that. She leaned closer to her mother and settled her cheek with a kiss. The scent of alcohol was unmistakable. Drawing back slowly, she gave Elizabeth a questioning glance.

Elizabeth's mouth flattened and her chestnut-colored eyes became remote. Her expression almost dared her daughter to challenge her.

Bria kept her silence. She had not come to raise these concerns with her mother. Elizabeth was correct on that count. Indeed, there had been no concerns of this nature until now. "Luke and I apologize for disturbing your sleep, Mother." Her gaze shifted briefly to Addie. "And Addie's. It can't be helped, though. We have news that could not wait any longer."

Elizabeth pushed herself even more upright. "Is it Rand?

Has there been some word? I've never given up—'' She sank back because Bria was shaking her head slowly, a pained look replacing the worried one. "Tell me. What is it?"

"It's Orrin. He's been shot."

"Shot?" Elizabeth merely mouthed the word. She started to push back the comforter but Bria stayed her hand. Although it was reedy and thin, Elizabeth found her voice. "I must go to him. Addie! Did you hear? You must help me. We'll need bandages and salves. A poultice like Mammy used to make. You know how to do that." She looked pointedly at Bria's hand covering hers and then even more intently at her daughter. "You haven't said where he's been shot. Has someone sent for Dr. Edwards?"

Bria did not remove her hand. If anything, the pressure became greater. "He's dead, Mother. A bullet struck him in the heart."

"His heart? But . . ." Her shoulders slumped and the lines of Elizabeth's face sagged with bewilderment. Her hand turned over beneath Bria's. This time Elizabeth's fingers curled around her daughter's. She squeezed, looking for strength outside of herself. "Who? Was it Austin? Was there a duel? Orrin always fancied himself avenging some slight in that manner. He thought it distinguished a gentleman of breeding. I don't think it occurred to him that it isn't done any longer. I never told him. He would have pressed for one if his honor was challenged." Tears swam in her eyes. She blinked them back as her liquid gaze turned to Luke. "Was it the card game, Luke? Were there words?"

"I don't know," Luke said. "I left before Orrin. I explained to Bria that there were certain suspicions surrounding my wager with him. The others thought the secrecy around my marker had something to do with Klan business."

It was difficult for Luke to tell what Elizabeth actually heard. She made a more concerted effort to get out of bed this time, pushing away from Bria and kicking at the comforter.

"My gardens weren't worth this price. Not this." Elizabeth's voice sank as she twisted her hands together. "I want to go to him. Is he here? Did someone have the decency to bring his body here?"

"He's here," Bria said. She did not elaborate on the manner in which Orrin had arrived. "Luke and Jeb put him in his room. Martha is preparing him."

"I should do that." Elizabeth took her dressing gown from where it lay folded across a nearby chair and slipped it on. She belted the sash firmly and stepped into her butter-yellow leather slippers. "Come, Addie. You will help me. Martha's never done this before."

Addie leaped from the rocker as if seized by an invisible rope that tethered her to her mistress. She quickly wiped her eyes with the back of her hand and followed Elizabeth to the door. On the threshold she paused and looked back at Bria. She opened her mouth to speak, her dark eyes uncertain and faintly pleading; then Elizabeth touched her elbow and urged her into the hall.

The door closed with a decisive click and then there was silence. Bria's eyes immediately sought out Luke. "I'm afraid," she said. "Luke, I think she might have . . ." Bria's soft voice simply trailed away. What she was thinking was too frightening to put into words. She looked at her husband helplessly. "What are we going to do? The sheriff . . . Dr. Edwards . . . they're on their way. If my mother speaks to them, they'll . . ." Bria lay down on the bed and hugged the pillow Elizabeth had used to support her back. Her mother's scent was there, comforting in its familiarity.

Luke rose from the stool and pushed it out of the way. He looked around the room, surveying the chest of drawers, the vanity, and the armoire. His gaze finally returned to Bria on the bed, then lowered to the dark space under the frame. He crossed the room and dropped to his knees, searching under the bed with his arm. His hand came across a small decanter first. He pulled it out and saw that a third of it remained. Removing the stopper, Luke raised it to his nose. "Scotch."

He pushed the stopper back in and laid the decanter on the bed.

Bria reached for it and pulled it close. There was a certain edge of despair in her voice. "That's what I smelled on my mother's breath."

"Addie's, too," Luke said.

Bria felt as if her heart were being squeezed. She whispered Addie's name reluctantly, as if saying it aloud would make everything she was thinking too real.

Luke continued to search under the bed, dropping forward to look when his arm couldn't reach any deeper. There was only one other object under there. Luke left it where it was. He pulled himself up and sat on the edge of the bed. His features were still with thought. A muscle worked in his cheek. "There was an instant earlier, Bree, when I thought it was you."

Her eyes snapped open and she stared at Luke's back.

He twisted slightly so he could see her face. "When Tad and Geordie told us Orrin was dead, and I saw the wound, I thought for the space of a heartbeat that it might have been done by you. Your dress was stained at the hem, remember? And your shoes and stockings were wet. You'd been out of the house not so long before I returned. It occurred to me that you might have killed Orrin and arrived back just before I did. I know what a good rider you are. You know shortcuts across this property that I don't. Tad and Geordie would have covered for you. They would do anything to protect you."

"You considered all of that in the space of a heartbeat?"

He nodded. "And dismissed it."

"Why are you telling me now?"

"Because you're entertaining a notion that has no evidence to support it. The fact that your mother and Addie shared a drink means nothing. Elizabeth may have difficulty falling asleep and asked Addie to sit with her. One of them suggested a drink to encourage sleep. It may have been as simple as that."

It was what Bria wanted to believe. The thought that the liquor had been needed to bolster her mother's courage in taking

Orrin's life was hard enough to bear. The alternative that she and Addie had toasted his murder was even worse. "It's true, what you say." Bria pushed at a lock of hair that had fallen across her cheek. "There was a moment when I thought it was you."

It would have been more surprising to Luke if she hadn't suspected him. "Go on."

"He murdered the man who thought of you as a son. That was motive enough. By your own admission, you left the card game before Orrin. I imagine Franklin and the others will support that. I've never seen that Remington before and we both know how unlikely it is that Sam or Austin or Franklin owned a similar one. It occurred to me that you might have brought it with you from New York for the sole purpose of killing Orrin. You're a good enough shot to have done it."

"So we have enough suspects to offer up to the sheriff." Luke's fingertips left furrows in his dark hair as he raked it back. "Will you let me handle it, Bree? Follow my lead and say as little as possible. It will be difficult enough to contain your mother so she doesn't show her hand. Addie will need your help not to bring attention to herself. She can't be considered a serious suspect, Bree. You know they'd hang her."

Bria nodded. "What will you do?"

He did not answer her directly. "Get your shoes and stockings from the music room and put them away, then go to your mother. If Addie is still wearing Elizabeth's dress, encourage her to change it without placing any importance on it. Can you do that?"

"Yes. But what are you—"

Luke leaned across the bed and placed his mouth over hers. He could feel the tension in the line of her lips slowly disappear. Her breathing relaxed to the point that she sighed. "Ask me later," he said as he drew back. He would have answers for her then—after the fact. Right now he had no plan. "Go on. I'll join you in a little while. I want to talk to Jeb before the sheriff arrives."

Bria released the pillow and the decanter and slid off the bed. "There are only four bullets in the revolver, Luke. I checked it when you left the room. If one of them is in Orrin, where is the other?"

Luke had no reply for that. He couldn't even tell her not to worry. "I'm glad you said something," was his only response.

Nodding shortly, Bria stopped in front of the vanity mirror and smoothed the skirt of her gown, then the bodice. Over her shoulder she saw Luke pick up the decanter and set it on her mother's nightstand. For the first time Bria realized there were no glasses anywhere. Elizabeth and Addie had drunk straight from the decanter. The vision that came to Bria's mind had a certain desperate quality. She blinked, removing it from her mind's eye, and hurried from the room.

Once Bria was gone and her footsteps had faded in the hallway, Luke searched Elizabeth's armoire. He found Addie's dress, stained by wet grass along the hem, at the knees, and still damp in places. Her shoes and stockings were similarly cold and damp. Bits of leaves and mud clung to the soles and heels. There was another gown hanging on the inside hook. He recognized it as the one Elizabeth had worn at dinner that evening. He inspected the hem. His fingers came away dewy with moisture.

Searching further in the bottom of the armoire, Luke found Elizabeth's shoes. Her stockings were stuffed inside. There would have been no suspicion if the women had handled their clothing in the usual way, but neither had been thinking clearly. Luke carried the gowns over to the window and examined them more closely in daybreak's light. Addie's had a stain on the sleeve that could have been blood. Luke raised it to his nose and confirmed it. He found a similar stain on Elizabeth's gown, just at the wrist. A petticoat was hanging beneath the gown. The bottom was frayed where the ruffles had been torn away. A bandage? he wondered. He recalled how Addie had cradled her arm. Four bullets, not five. Had she been injured?

Gathering up all the soiled clothes, undergarments, and shoes,

Luke placed them at the foot of the bed. He dropped to the floor again and this time when he reached under the frame he came out with the case he had seen earlier. It was nine inches by twelve and three inches deep. When Luke turned it in the light he could see the polished walnut finish was smudged by fingerprints. Fingerprinting was a relatively new technique, not wholly reliable, and with many detractors. Luke didn't know if the sheriff was aware of the technique of inking a fingertip to make an identification or if the method was confined to the forensic detectives in cosmopolitan cities like New York, Paris, and London. What Luke did know was that there were too many different prints on the case to support it being handled by Orrin Foster alone. Whorls. Arches. Loops. They were all represented in at least one clear print.

Luke added his own to the case as he lifted the brass latch and opened it. The black velvet bed where the pair of Five-Star Remingtons should have lain were both empty. Snapping the lid closed, Luke latched it again and tossed it onto the pile of clothes. He scooped up everything into one armload, added the decanter at the last moment, and left the room.

Outside of Orrin's bedchamber Luke used his foot to rap on the door. Bria came to answer it. When she saw the pile of clothes in his arms, she blanched.

"Careful," he whispered. Over her head he could see Elizabeth and Martha tending to Orrin's body. Neither of them spared him a glance. "Where is Addie?"

"Changing."

"Good. Can you get your mother and Martha out of here for a few minutes?"

"But—"

"Tell them anything. I need a few minutes. That's all."

"All right." Her eyes were uncertain. "I'll think of something."

Nodding briskly, Luke slipped into an adjoining room and waited. He heard voices rising. The tenor was confusion, not anger, as Bria herded her mother and Martha out of the room.

Luke dropped the bundle of clothes and the decanter. From the middle of the pile, he extracted the walnut case, and slipped it under his arm. When he could no longer hear the women, he left the room and went to Orrin's.

The body had been washed. A sheet covered Orrin to his waist. Above that his skin was pale. The bullet wound was not immediately visible in the mat of hair that covered his fleshy chest. It was small and dark and looked more like a third nipple than a mortal wound. His blood-stained clothes were on the floor. Luke stepped around them as he moved closer to the bed.

Picking up one corner of the sheet that covered Orrin, Luke wiped the walnut gun case clean of every fingerprint. Holding it with the sheet to protect it from picking up his own prints, Luke examined it by the bedside table lamp to make certain he had rubbed the finish clear. Lemon oil had been used so often to polish it a thin sheen still remained.

He sat on the bed and held the case out to Orrin as if he expected the man to rise up and take it. Carefully holding the box with the sheet, Luke took Orrin's right hand, then the left, and added ten prints to the box in a manner that one would expect to find. He smudged some around the latch and a few more on the surface, then examined it again. Satisfied with the result, if it should become important to anyone, Luke slipped the case into the drawer of Orrin's nightstand.

Almost as an afterthought he picked up the revolver. There were no clear prints on it. Just to be safe he placed it in Orrin's right hand and pressed. "I won't make the same mistake you did," he said softly. "I *know* you're right-handed."

He replaced the gun on the nightstand and came to his feet. "Did you even know who did it, you bastard?" With that, Luke left.

It was eleven o'clock when the doctor arrived. Sheriff Joseph Allen came shortly after that. Luke escorted the sheriff up to Orrin's room where Dr. Edwards, Elizabeth, and Bria were all gathered. The doctor stood as Allen entered and held out his hand. "Good to see you again, Sheriff, though the circumstances could be better." Edwards's voice dropped as he indicated the women still seated beside him. "This is more than anyone should have to bear. First Rand. Now Orrin. Of course you know about the rest of the family. Seems the men are a cursed lot." The doctor heaved a heavy sigh and scratched behind his ear. He was a large man with greying hair and deep-set eyes. His beard covered the lower half of his face and was almost completely white. His lips were barely visible below his mustache. He glanced toward the body. "Have a look for yourself."

Allen greeted Elizabeth and Bria solemnly in turn before he went to the bed. Orrin was dressed now in his best evening suit, his arms flat at his sides. Allen looked over his shoulder. "I'd appreciate it if you ladies left. There's no need for you to see me undo your handiwork."

Bria offered no protest. She took her mother's arm and escorted her outside. It was only as she closed the door that she risked a pleading, anxious look at Luke. He acted as if he hadn't seen her at all.

As soon as the women were gone, Sheriff Allen bent over the body and opened the jacket and shirt. "That boy you sent to me . . . Thad?"

"Tad," Luke said.

"Yes. Tad. He said it was a chest wound."

"That's right."

Edwards sidled over to the foot of the bed, his arms folded across his chest. He watched the sheriff search for the puckered wound. "Not much to look at, is it? Clean and neat. I left the bullet buried there. No need to remove it."

"Where did it happen?" Allen straightened and closed Orrin's shirt. He rebuttoned the jacket and made an attempt to smooth the material. He shoved his hands into the pockets of his own jacket and rocked back on his heels. In his fourth term as sheriff, Allen was familiar with almost everyone in the county. If he hadn't met someone personally, then he knew of them. His amiable nature made him accessible and non-threatening. It was easy to forget he was also a politically shrewd and cautious man. He looked to Luke for an answer to his question, his dark eyes merely questioning.

"We don't know. Somewhere between Franklin Archer's place and here."

"That's twelve miles."

Luke nodded. "Probably closer to here, though I can't find anyone who heard the shot. He was in a buggy. The mare just ambled home."

"I see. Hard to believe she would amble twelve miles."

"That's what I thought."

Allen twisted around and looked at the gun on the nightstand. "This the revolver Tad said was found in the buggy?"

"Yes."

The sheriff picked up the gun and examined it, turning it over in his hand, testing the weight and grip. He opened the cylinder, spun it, then emptied the bullets into his palm. He laid all four of them on the nightstand. Without warning, he leveled the gun at Edwards.

In spite of the fact that he knew the gun was empty, the doctor flinched. "You'll put me on that bed beside Orrin, dammit. Put that down."

Allen swiveled his aim to Luke. "How about this, Doc? The right distance? Closer? Farther away?"

"I can't say."

"You treated enough wounds during the war. You must have some idea."

"Then I'd say closer." Edwards scratched his beard under his chin. "Much closer."

Allen twisted his hand and turned the barrel of the gun on himself. "Like this?"

The doctor nodded.

Both of Allen's brows lifted, his skepticism plain. He regarded Edwards first, then Luke. "You'll have to convince me."

Chapter Sixteen

Dr. Edwards prompted Luke. "Go on. Show him." He indicated the sheriff with a wave of his hand. "Show him what you showed me."

Even with the doctor's encouragement, Luke still hesitated. Some show of reluctance was in order, he thought, before revealing family business of this nature. Eagerness would make him seem like an outsider. He had to be seen as protecting the Hamilton family because he was a member of it.

Reaching in his pocket, Luke extracted Orrin Foster's marker and held it out to the sheriff. "There was a game at Archer's this evening."

"Figured as much," Allen drawled. He took the piece of paper, unfolded it, and began to read. His expression remained unchanged until he was finished, then he cocked one eyebrow in the doctor's direction. "Are you telling me Foster would have killed himself over losing Concord?"

The doctor scratched the back of his neck with his fingertips. "I never had much dealings with Foster. Fixed a brace for him once when he almost killed himself jumping fences. Saw him for bursitis a couple of times. Dried him out on two occasions when alcohol poisoning was nearly the end of him. I can't say that I know what he would do about losing this place.'' Edwards raised his eyes and regarded the sheriff squarely. ''But losing Elizabeth? That could surely have made him take a gun to himself. Losing Concord meant losing her.''

Joe Allen considered the doctor for a long moment. ''I take it that you're still sweet on her.''

The tips of Edwards's ears reddened but he didn't flinch. ''I don't deny it. I've been happily married to my own Harriet for almost thirty-four years, but I dare you to find any man my age in Charleston County that doesn't still think fondly of Elizabeth Denton. She had her pick of beaus before she settled on Andrew Hamilton and there were a score of hearts broken the evening she pledged herself to him.''

''Broken hearts,'' Allen repeated. ''No one took a pistol to himself that night.''

''Most of us thought about it,'' Edwards said. ''We didn't have the same fool mix of courage and cowardice that Foster had.''

Sheriff Allen glanced down at the bed. Orrin's still features offered no answers. ''Seems like he would have pointed the gun at his head.''

''Maybe he did,'' the doctor offered. ''And changed his mind. Maybe the gun went off when he lowered it. Maybe it went off when he raised it. I don't think we can know exactly what happened.''

The sheriff lifted the gun and examined it again. He turned his attention back to Luke. ''Tell me about this card game,'' he said flatly.

Luke went over the evening's events carefully. His account was largely truthful and he knew it would be supported by Archer, Tipping, and Daniels. He did not mention the note he passed to Orrin with the name Walter Wingate on it, nor did he speak at length of what prompted Orrin to put Concord up in the first place. He allowed the sheriff to draw the conclusion that it was Orrin's drinking that had brought him to that.

''I've played some cards with Orrin before,'' Allen said. ''I suppose I always left the game too early. He never got drunk enough to offer his property but I've seen others do damn fool things like that. Did you goad him into it?''

Luke shook his head. ''No sir, he asked me what *I* wanted.''

''And you told him Concord.''

''I did. I didn't expect him to accept. I don't think anyone else did, either.'' Luke doubted any of the others would talk about the note he had passed to Orrin. They wouldn't be eager to discuss Klan business with the sheriff or, in the event Sheriff Allen was connected to the Klan, they would not want to admit how vulnerable they had made themselves by trying to recruit Luke. ''Look, Sheriff. Orrin wasn't entirely pleased that I married his stepdaughter. He hired me to restore his home. He gave me the opportunity because I was a Yankee and it was the only bond we had. I didn't particularly respect or like him and I saw what he was doing to Concord, to my wife, and my mother-in-law. When I had an opportunity to do something about it, I seized it.''

''You took advantage of his liquored wits.''

Luke didn't apologize for it. He merely shrugged. ''He was level-headed enough to write out this marker.'' Luke held it up before he slipped it in his jacket pocket. ''There was no coercion.''

Joe Allen raised the gun. ''No, I don't suppose you had to use this.'' He pointed to the five stars on the ivory handle. ''I've never seen one like it. Have you?''

''No,'' Luke lied easily. ''Not before tonight.''

''Then you didn't know Orrin had it with him?''

''No. We rode separately to Archer's, remember?''

''And why was that again?''

Luke repeated the same reasons he had first stated, knowing full well Allen hadn't forgotten a single detail. ''Orrin has a collection of guns in his study. You're welcome to look through those, though I understand the weapons were really Elizabeth's first husband's.''

''I'm familiar with them,'' Allen said. ''I don't recall ever seeing this among them." His eyes shifted to Edwards. "What about you? Did Orrin ever show you this?"

"No, but I've seen one before. During the war. I tended a Yankee officer who had one. I asked him about it. You have to allow that it's unusual. They came in pairs, he said, though he only carried one. Remington made them and the Union boys handed them out to outstanding officers."

Allen's lips pressed together. He looked at the weapon, then at Orrin. "Then this certainly never belonged to Andrew Hamilton or any of his boys. The Union wasn't giving them to Lee's good men." He put the Remington on the table beside the four bullets he'd emptied earlier. When he turned back to Luke and the doctor his expression was thoughtful. "Mind if I look around? I have some questions for Mrs. Foster and Miss Bria. I'll want to talk to the house nigras, of course. They always see more than they let on. Could be that one of them knows something about this gun." He rubbed the underside of his chin. "Could be one of them knows when and where it was fired before. I have to wonder about four bullets in the chamber instead of five."

Edwards held up one hand. "You can talk to the nigras, but I'm going to insist that you leave Elizabeth be. She's already told me she's never seen the gun. That should be good enough."

Allen hesitated, considering how much pressure he should apply. Luke's sentiment about Orrin Foster echoed in his own mind. *I didn't particularly respect or like him* . . . Allen felt similarly. He had no real desire to find a murderer, especially if his search led him to one of the other men at the card table. Making trouble with Archer, Tipping, or Daniels had consequences that could mean his removal from public office. Orrin Foster had not belonged and that would never change now. Nor was it terribly wise to poke in his widow's direction looking for answers. The simplest course would be to support the doctor's findings or connect Orrin's death to the other outsider: Lucas Kincaid.

The sheriff's sigh was heavy. "As near as I can tell, Kincaid, you got everything you wanted when Orrin signed his marker. Is that about right?''

"Yes, sir."

"So you have no real reason to wait for him along the road and murder him."

"No reason at all."

The sheriff nodded. "And you, Doc? You're swearing it's possible that Foster could have done this to himself?"

"There's no doubt it's possible," Edwards said, his conscience eased somewhat by the fact he could say this with absolute certainty. "No doubt at all."

Allen rocked back and forth slowly, taking this in. "I'd still like to look around," he said finally, looking at Luke. "Maybe talk to Jebediah. That's your house nigra, isn't it?"

"Ask Jebediah anything you like."

"I heard there was some Klan activity out here after the memorial service for Rand. Could be Orrin's death has something to do with that. The freemen have been known to retaliate."

"Orrin didn't have anything to do with the Klan," Luke lied. "My wife's greenhouse was destroyed and Orrin was furious about that. The sharecroppers wouldn't choose him as their target."

There was sense in what Luke said, Allen knew. And something that didn't quite ring true. He had always considered that Orrin was involved with the Klan in some way. There was no question that his card playing friends were. "Send Jeb up here," Allen said. "I'll see him alone."

Luke and the doctor waited in the study while the sheriff met with Jebediah. Edwards sat behind Orrin's massive desk and sipped tea from a delicate china cup. It rattled the saucer each time he set it down. Luke tried not to let it rattle his nerves. He leaned farther back into his chair and stretched his legs.

Edwards watched him over the rim of his cup. "I'm doing this for Elizabeth, you know."

"Doing what, sir?"

"Whatever it is that I'm doing," Edwards said obliquely. "Orrin was a thorough bastard to her. I've been summoned out here to look at sprains and dislocated collarbones more times than I can count since she married him. Bria always sent Jeb for me. I generally pretended my visit had nothing to do with Elizabeth. Made it a point to act like it was a social call. It was better for her that way; Orrin didn't seek immediate retribution. I couldn't protect her any more than that. Elizabeth's a proud woman and was deeply ashamed of what he was doing to her. She never once admitted to me that a single bruise was caused by anything other than her own clumsiness. I suppose she forgot that I knew her to be the most graceful, accomplished dancer in Charleston County. She was *never* clumsy. She didn't know how to be."

The doctor drained his cup and set it down. "She was also a crack shot." Edwards caught the flash of surprise in Luke's eyes before it was shuttered. "You didn't know that, did you? Her daddy taught her. She used to hunt with him. She had eyes as sharp as the hounds had a nose. I imagine the passage of years and the lack of practice would have some effect on her abilities."

Edwards shrugged. He continued without looking at Luke directly, as if speaking to himself. "The sheriff didn't know Elizabeth like I did. He's too young for that, but he's a good man trying to do a difficult job, and he hasn't been elected four times without figuring his way around the politics of any situation. I imagine it's all going to work out. People around here want to do their best by Elizabeth Hamilton." Now the doctor's gaze speared Luke. "I don't suppose you're any different."

Luke didn't respond immediately. He had to deny, not defend. When he found the right words, his tone was carefully neutral. "I don't understand what you mean."

Edwards's smile was a slim, knowing one. "Of course you don't. And I'm just rambling. You can forget what you heard."

Both men turned toward the study doors as they slid open. Bria stood on the threshold. "Mother's finally resting," she said. "May I join you?"

The doctor and Luke came to their feet. "Certainly, my dear," Edwards said. He gestured to her expansively, as if he were welcoming her into his own home.

Luke pointed to his chair. "Would you like some tea? I can ring for another cup."

"No, thank you." Bria searched his face. He did not seem at all upset that she had come to him. His features were relaxed, untroubled. Then Bria had a vision of herself sitting across the table from him, each of them holding five cards. He was playing poker now, she realized, with the doctor, with Sheriff Allen, and now with her. There was nothing in his face to give away his hand and nothing to tell her what had already transpired. She sat down where Luke had been. He remained standing but he leaned against the chair and placed one hand on her shoulder. Bria reached back and laid her fingers over his.

"We're waiting for the sheriff," Luke told her. "He's with Jebediah. He's trying to find out if anyone's seen the Remington before."

"Unusual gun," Edwards murmured.

Bria nodded. "Do you suppose he might have taken it from Franklin's this evening? I hope the sheriff thinks to ask about it there."

The doctor scratched the back of his neck absently. "Allen's thorough. He'll ask whatever he thinks is necessary."

They all fell silent as footsteps approached from the hallway. The sheriff entered the room carrying a walnut case across his open palms. He hesitated slightly when he saw Bria. His head bobbed once in the manner of a greeting and he said her name. "Miss Bria. I don't know if it's fitting that you're here."

"It's Mrs. Kincaid now, Sheriff, and if my husband doesn't ask me to leave then I want to stay." She glanced at Luke to see how he would respond.

Luke didn't look at Bria but his hand tightened gently on

her shoulder. "My wife can hear anything you have to say. She will hear it from me when you're gone, so she might as well hear it from you."

Allen nodded. "As you wish." He set the case on the desk carefully. When Edwards leaned forward to get a better look, the sheriff put out one hand to block him from touching it. "Jebediah convinced me he's never seen the Remington before, but he knew what might have held it. He described a box to me that he saw from time to time in different locations. He swears he never touched it because he knew it must have belonged to Orrin. The last thing he wanted was trouble with him." Allen glanced at Bria. "Have you ever seen it before?"

She shook her head. "Never," she breathed softly. The honesty of her response was clearly in her eyes. "Where did you find it?"

"Jeb took me to a few places he had seen it. The music room. One of the guest bedrooms. Orrin's wardrobe. When we didn't find it we made a more thorough search of Orrin's room. I found it in a drawer in his bedside table." The sheriff flicked the latch with his fingernail and lifted the lid. "Come closer."

The doctor half-raised himself out of his chair to peer over the lid. Bria stood and took a step toward the desk. Luke came up just behind her. All three of them stared at the bed of black velvet with its twin depressions. While they looked on, Allen pulled the Five Star Remington out of his waistband and laid it in one of the niches. It was a perfect fit.

The sheriff closed the lid over the gun and watched all three of his on-lookers draw back slightly. He spared each one of them a glance before his eyes came to rest on the box again. "I wouldn't expect that any of you would be knowledgeable about fingerprinting, but if you look carefully at the case in the right light, you can make out prints on the polished wood. As near as I can tell this case was touched by just one other person besides me. I'm satisfied that the person was your stepfather, Mrs. Kincaid. I don't know if it will come as a shock or a relief, but I'm inclined to side with Dr. Edwards here, and judge that Orrin killed himself. The doctor thinks Mr. Foster would have been despondent about losing Concord, but more heartsick about losing Elizabeth. Knowing your mother even as little as I do, I can't find fault with that reasoning. There are a lot of people in Charleston County who were sorry to see Henley fall to a carpetbagger after the war.'' He glanced at Luke. "If you'll pardon the expression, Mr. Kincaid. No offense meant.''

"None taken," said Luke. "Go on.''

The sheriff rested one hip on the edge of the desk and folded his arms casually across his chest. "Most of us were sorrier still to hear that Henley had become Concord. Conquered. It had that ring to some of us. It was your brother, Mrs. Kincaid, that put it in my mind. Rand used to call it that.''

"Rand had a peculiar and dark sense of humor," Bria said, but she was smiling at the memory. She felt Luke's arm go around her shoulders. "And no particular love for Orrin.''

"Don't I know that," Allen said. "I imagine that if Rand were here now it would have crossed my mind that he killed Orrin.''

"Don't you mean," Luke said, "it would have crossed your mind if you hadn't already concluded Orrin killed himself?''

Allen's smile was rather like a salute. "Yes. That's exactly what I meant. It's clear to me now that Orrin died by his own hand. It would take an exceptional shot or dumb luck to have caught him in the heart at night. As for the bullet missing from the cylinder, it's impossible to know when Orrin might have fired it.'' He tapped the walnut lid. "I will speak to Franklin Archer and the others, of course. I suspect they will have nothing to say which will change my mind. I'm certain they will agree that Orrin was capable of this after witnessing his loss.''

The sheriff stopped tapping on the lid and lifted it again. "There's something I need to show you. I don't know if it would ever come to light otherwise.'' He removed the revolver and laid it on the desk. "Under here.'' He ran his nail around the edge of the velvet lining until he found the opening. He gingerly inserted two fingers inside the slit. "There are some papers under the lining. I haven't looked at them so I have no idea what Orrin was hiding." He manipulated them around his fingers, curling them until he could pull them out without a tear. "I wanted you to examine them with me." He held them out to Bria. "I believe it's your right."

Bria saw that her hand was trembling as she reached for the papers.

"There are more," Allen said. "It would be easier if—"

"Here," Edwards interrupted. He held up the letter opener he found in the desk's middle drawer. "Allow me. I'm the surgeon, after all." Before anyone could stop him, he used the sharp-edged opener like a scalpel and gutted the lining. "There. And not a mark on them." He plucked a dozen or so sheets of onion skin paper from the bottom of the case. "Take these, Bria. From all the numbers I see, I'm guessing they're a record of Orrin's accounts."

It was exactly what they were. Orrin's entries were meticulously detailed and listed accounts, investments, holdings, locations, and interest. Bria could only give the papers the merest oversight before she had to sit down. She passed them to Luke who placed them on the desk so Allen and Edwards could see.

"Good Lord," Edwards said under his breath. "Look at this money. These investments. Bria, did you have any idea?"

She simply shook her head, stunned by the enormity of what the sheriff had presented her. *It all belongs to someone else.* The thought spun through her mind and turned her stomach over. The sheriff and doctor believed this incredible wealth would go to her mother. Only Luke and she knew it was all stolen from Conrad Morrison.

Edwards had seen enough. He sank back into his chair and stared vaguely up at the ceiling. "Good Lord," he whispered again.

The sheriff straightened, too. "It would seem Orrin Foster

was worth rather more than he let on. I didn't guess that he could be secretive."

"Miserly," Bria said softly. "And afraid. My stepfather thought if my mother and I knew anything about this money we would make demands on him."

"Was he right?" Allen asked.

"Probably. There was always something that needed to be done here. Orrin had a difficult time seeing this plantation as an investment that would eventually return his money." She pointed to the accounting sheets. "He expected more, I think."

The sheriff nodded. He stood, looking from Bria to Luke. "It would be interesting to know about the missing gun, but I don't think there's anything more I need to do here. I'm satisfied with my conclusions." He smiled faintly. "Or at least I can live with them. I'll show myself out. Are you coming, Doc?"

Edwards heaved himself out of his chair and picked up his leather bag from the floor. He opened it, searched the contents, and withdrew a small brown bottle. He gave it to Luke. "Laudanum. For Elizabeth if she complains of headaches or not being able to sleep. I don't expect coming into this fortune will ease her mind in the least. Give it to her sparingly."

Luke's hand closed around the bottle. "I understand."

The doctor nodded in Bria's direction. "Don't be afraid to take a little yourself. You look as if you could use the rest." Although Bria's wan smile acknowledged that she heard him, he knew she wouldn't take a single drop. Stubborn to a fault, he thought, just like her mother. "Very well," he said. "I'll be back for the services and to check on you and Elizabeth."

"Thank you, Doctor," Luke said.

Edwards extended his hand. "Thank you." There was a faint emphasis on the second word. The doctor lifted his black bag under his arm and pointed to the open doors. "After you, Sheriff."

Luke set the bottle of laudanum down after both men had gone. He opened his arms to Bria. "Come here," he said. She didn't require a second invitation. "You couldn't stay away, could you?'' His voice was soft against her hair, and infinitely tender in its admonishing. ''I thought that when you saw those accounts and investments you were going to blurt out that it all belonged to someone else.''

Bria found that she had it in her to smile. She raised her face and looked up at Luke. ''That was the exact thought I had. How did you know?''

''I know you,'' he said easily. ''You didn't expect it to be so much.''

She shook her head. ''Never. I understood that Mr. Morrison was wealthy, but this . . . I never once considered what that might mean. I'm realizing that Yankee rich is different than Dixie rich. What will we do with it, Luke? We can't keep it. It belongs to Morrison's heirs.''

''I told you, he didn't have any family. There may be some second or third cousins with an interest but they don't have a claim.''

''Creditors?''

''They were paid off by selling the mills and foundries.''

''Why didn't you tell the sheriff about Orrin being Walter Wingate?''

''Because it would have complicated things. No one here needs to know who Orrin really was. My mother and aunts will know I found him.''

''But they wanted to clear Morrison's name. You were supposed to prove there was no suicide.''

''They will have to settle for a private settling of accounts, rather than a public one,'' he said. ''I think they can accept that when they consider the alternative.''

Bria frowned. ''What alternative?''

Luke cupped Bria's elbows as if to hold her steady. He watched her face carefully. ''I didn't kill Orrin Foster.'' There was no change in her expression. ''But if I reveal that Orrin is Walter Wingate, people will always wonder if I did.'' The crease between Bria's brow deepened. Luke drew in a breath and released it slowly. "Conrad Morrison had one beneficiary in his will, Bree. I am his heir."

She sagged a little in his arms. "You?"

"You said it yourself once. He thought of me as his son."

"You."

Luke smiled faintly. "Me."

"But why didn't you tell me?"

"For several reasons, I suppose. I never really expected to find all the money. I didn't know it was in that case, Bria. I never saw the case before this evening and I've been through this house looking for something that would connect Orrin to his past. When you asked me to win Concord for you it was an opportunity to win something back for myself. I didn't want the money, only the chance to take it away from Orrin. I knew it represented only a fraction of what he had stolen but it was *something*."

Bria closed her eyes briefly, nodding her understanding.

"I might have felt differently about it if I hadn't met you," Luke went on. "You made it easy not to care about the money. Taking it back for you was infinitely more rewarding than taking it for myself."

She looked at him doubtfully.

"It's true." He paused. "And then there's the final reason I didn't tell you: I'm a better poker player than you. I didn't think you could help but give it away. You practically telegraphed your thoughts to the sheriff and Dr. Edwards tonight. If you had understood how closely I was connected to this fortune I believe I'd be on my way to the county jail. I think Sheriff Allen was willing to turn his head only so far. For your mother and you he made allowances. For me?" Luke shook his head. "It would have been much more difficult establishing my innocence."

Bria stood on tiptoe and kissed one corner of his mouth. "It might have meant pointing a finger in some other direction," she said. "That's what you meant. If you're innocent, and it's not a suicide, then someone has to be guilty. My mother. Addie. Me.''

"I wouldn't have done that. Not to any of you."

"I know." She regarded him steadily. "So who killed Orrin?"

"You heard the sheriff . . ." He stopped because Bria was shaking her head, refusing to accept that answer. "I don't know. That's the truth. I found the revolver case under your mother's bed and moved it to Orrin's bedside table where I hoped it would be found. I didn't know about the papers and I somehow doubt that your mother or Addie did. It might have been one of them that fired the gun. Maybe they both did. Perhaps it was neither. They know what happened, though, and I can't imagine that they'll ever say. Can you?"

"No. They mean it to be their secret."

"Then we'll leave it at that."

Bria nodded slowly. She leaned into Luke and pressed her forehead against his shoulder. She felt his arms close around her and she settled into the circle of his embrace. Bria might have simply fallen asleep there but Luke led her up to their room. They drew the drapes, blocking out the afternoon sun, and lay on the bed together. They slept for a time and held each other, sharing everything in a deep, abiding silence.

It was two weeks after Orrin's burial that Addie and John Whitney left Henley. John's wounds were healed enough for him to travel and he could not be persuaded to stay. Bria was not surprised when Addie joined him. She only wondered that her mother accepted Addie's leaving so well. It had seemed to Bria that Elizabeth had come to rely on Addie even more since Orrin's death. Now Bria asked herself if what she had thought was reliance was, in fact, the plotting of old friends as thick as thieves.

Bria stood in the cabin that John had vacated a few hours earlier and surveyed what had to be done. She would ask Martha to sweep it clean and strip the bed. There was the faint scent of liniments and medicinal herbs in the air. It was not unpleasant except as a reminder of all that John had suffered at Orrin's urging.

"It would make a good schoolhouse," Luke said, coming up behind her. "Your mother said I could find you here."

"Hmmm. I suppose that's better than burning it to the ground."

"I think so," he said dryly. "We can tear out that wall dividing the rooms and have one large one. I can find some men to help me make tables and benches for the children. You'll be happy with it."

Bria knew he was right about that. She liked the idea of having children close to Henley again. "I think Mother can be persuaded to teach them from time to time. Jebediah will take a turn at it, too." She wandered into the bedroom and looked around. Something colorful on the nightstand caught her eye and she approached it. At a distance she thought it was a miniature portrait, then she realized she was looking at a face card. Bria glanced over her shoulder at Luke. He was standing in the doorway, his hands braced on either side of the frame. "Look at these. John must have forgot them." She held up the small stack of cards and fanned them open.

Three queens and two fours. A full house with one neat hole blown through the center of all five.

"Whatever do you think this is?" Bria asked.

Luke's recognition was immediate, his reply quietly intense. "Put it down, Bree. It's a dead man's hand."

Elizabeth rested her head against the back of the wing chair and closed her eyes. Music transported her. It was easy to imagine that Bria was not alone at the piano. She could see Andrew standing nearby, ready to turn the pages for his daughter. His smile was encouraging as he watched Bria's fingers fly over a difficult passage. Elizabeth wished she could see him in something other than the uniform she had made for him, but no other vision would come to her mind. He had been so proud to wear the uniform, in no small measure because her hands had fashioned it. His broad shoulders filled out the double-breasted frock coat and the blue-grey wool was almost the same color as his eyes. The gold braid on the sleeves distinguished him as an officer.

It flashed briefly in the candlelight as he reached for the sheet music.

"Mother?" Bria's hands dropped away from the keys. The last echoes of music were silenced when she took her foot off the sustaining pedal. She swiveled on the bench to see her mother more clearly. "Is something wrong?"

Luke leaned forward in his own chair and turned his head in Elizabeth's direction. Her features were still, peaceful. There was color in her cheeks that was not easily explained by her proximity to the fire. A faint smile, enigmatic, bittersweet, had changed the shape of her mouth. Diamond-like in their clarity, tears studded the dark curve of her lashes.

Elizabeth opened her eyes to find her daughter and son-in-law staring at her intently. "I'm not dead."

Luke grinned, but Bria was not amused. "That's a horrible thing to say, Mother."

"Do you mean you wish I *were* dead?" Out of the corner of her eye she saw Luke's grin become even wider. He, at least, did not treat her like one of Bria's fragile rice seedlings.

"Mother!"

The tears on Elizabeth's lashes fell because her eyes crinkled with laughter. She removed an Irish linen handkerchief tucked under her sleeve and dabbed her eyes and cheeks. "You are far too easy to tease, Bria. It is no wonder Luke and I take such delight in it."

Luke groaned and slumped in his chair. "You're cruel, Elizabeth, to include me. Bria will always forgive you. She is not so easily persuaded when it comes to me."

Elizabeth shrugged. "So you will have to beg. I'm certain you both will enjoy it."

Bria's eyes widened and her cheeks flushed with color. "Mother!"

"Is that the extent of all you can say this evening?" Elizabeth was smiling widely now, thoroughly enjoying herself as Bria rose so beautifully to the bait. She came to her feet and eliminated the distance separating her from her daughter. Bending, she kissed Bria's warm cheek. "I'll turn the pages for you," she said. "Just as your father did."

Bria nodded, too moved to speak. She made room for her mother on the bench. Their skirts overlapped so that dark emerald velvet and satin sapphire were like a wave of blue-green water rising up from the floor.

Luke left his chair and joined them as Bria began to play. Her fingers moved nimbly over the difficult and exhilarating measures of *Ode to Joy*. He rested one hand on Elizabeth's back and felt the slight rise and fall of her shoulders as the music did the same. Candlelight spilled over Bria's dark-honey hair so that it shimmered with liquid strands of gold and copper.

The room was comfortably warm. The fire in the hearth crackled at odd moments, lending its own peculiar accompaniment to the swell of music. Outside, a cold and steady drizzle etched the window panes. Night made the glass a dark mirror and reflected the images of Luke, Bria, and Elizabeth standing in a circle of candlelight.

Christmas still lingered in the air. Jeb had removed the tree four days ago but bayberry candles and pine boughs on the mantel kept the fragrance of the holiday close at hand. They had celebrated Christmas quietly. It was not so much in observation of Orrin's recent passing that they chose to pass the day in this manner, but because they had had so little time alone in the weeks following his death.

When word of Orrin's suicide reached the neighboring plantations and Charleston itself, Concord became host to a constant stream of visitors. They came with condolences and a surfeit of curiosity. Austin Tipping and his sister were among the first to arrive. Sam Daniels and Franklin Archer came shortly afterward. Dr. Edwards and his wife stood near Elizabeth while she accepted the expressed regrets of the mourners. Days after the burial service friends still came to sit with Elizabeth and offer what measure of comfort they could. For the most part they restrained themselves from asking pointed questions about the nature of Orrin's death or the fortune it was rumored he had amassed and hidden from everyone.

There was widespread interest in the card game that preceded Orrin's suicide. Luke did not deny or confirm any of the things he heard whispered about. He also noticed that the others who were there that night had little to say, but privately they each asked him if he had known the extent of Orrin's wealth. Tipping, in particular, looked ill as he posed the question, and Luke suspected he was wondering how he had failed so thoroughly to win Bria's hand or even a moderate degree of her regard.

Shaking his head slowly as he returned to the present, Luke watched Bria's hands move swiftly over the keys. There was beauty and grace and strength in the power of her expression. He tilted his head so he could see Elizabeth's profile more clearly. She was watching her daughter with rapt admiration, the diamond droplets of tears back in her eyes, the smile on her face perfectly serene.

When Bria raised her hands and the last strings ceased vibrating, Elizabeth cried out softly, "*Brava*, darling. *Brava*." She raised her face to look at Luke. "Thank you."

His eyes were questioning. "Elizabeth, I didn't even help turn the pages."

"You helped my daughter find her music. I know you didn't intend it as such, but it's a gift to me as well. Bria couldn't be sharing it now if it weren't for you."

Embarrassed, Luke ran his fingers through his hair. "I don't think—"

Holding up one hand, Elizabeth stopped him. "It doesn't matter what you think," she said tartly. "It matters what *I* think. God blessed us the day you came to Henley. I don't pretend to understand the whys and wherefores of it, but I know you found Bria, not the other way around. You might have arrived here under the pretense of restoring this house, but you've done much more than that. You've restored a woman's soul. Now stop shifting back and forth as if you're going to expire from accepting one grateful mother's mere compliment. That's better. I do appreciate how you listen. It must be the influence of your beloved Nana Dearborn. Bria's told me how highly you regarded her."

Luke almost choked, but he managed a cough instead. He didn't dare glance in Bria's direction. Her expression of innocence would have made him want to laugh outright. When Luke could trust himself to speak, he said, "Yes, ma'am. Nana Dearborn was a powerful influence in my life."

Elizabeth nodded, satisfied with that answer. She slid off the bench and went to the tea service. "I have something I want to tell you both," she said, pouring herself a cup of tea. She offered the same to Bria and Luke but they shook their heads in unison. "I would have liked to have said something earlier but promises and caution forbade me. Today I received a post from Addie and now I can tell you the whole of it."

Bria gathered her skirt to one side as Luke lowered himself slowly on the bench beside her. If she hadn't already been sitting, she would have felt the need to do the same. "You know where Addie is, Mother?"

"No." Elizabeth returned to her wing chair. "Nor John. And if I knew, I would not say. They didn't ask me to keep silent—it's a promise I made to myself that certain things should end with me." She paused and sipped her tea. Her expression was thoughtful. "Other things, I believe, should be shared."

"You don't have to explain anything," Bria said.

"I know I don't. I want to." She replaced her cup in her saucer and set both on the table at her side. "I don't know how you managed to make Sheriff Allen believe Orrin's death was a suicide, but I suspect you did it because you thought I murdered him.''

Bria started to deny it but Luke took her hand and squeezed it. He said, ''It's true, Elizabeth. Dr. Edwards was helpful as well.''

A pale wash of color touched Elizabeth's cheeks. ''He's still sweet on me.'' Her chin came up a notch. ''But he wouldn't have been so accommodating if he'd suspected Addie. He's with the Klan.''

Bria's brows lifted. ''The Klan? But how do you—''

''Orrin told me. He knew a great many things about our friends and neighbors and he found some odd pleasure in telling me what he knew. I suppose he thought it would make me think differently toward them, hold them in less regard perhaps. In truth I didn't judge them at all. I would not give Orrin the advantage of knowing my opinion. He wanted so much to be accepted he would use anything he learned from me to make a place for himself. I was able to keep my silence on many things—no matter what pressure Orrin brought to bear.'' Elizabeth held Bria's gaze a moment. ''Addie was not so fortunate.''

''Addie.'' Bria breathed the name softly. ''He was questioning Addie?''

''Always. At the end of every season, when Orrin and I returned from Charleston, she was the first person he went to. You mustn't blame her, Bria. She had no choice. Not after what Orrin did to her husband. He threatened the same to her. The Klan. A lynching. Orrin felt betrayed when Durrel left. He arranged his murder and has been torturing Addie with that knowledge in one way or another for years.''

''You *know* all this?'' Bria felt her chest tightening. It was difficult to draw a single breath. ''But you've never said—''

''To what end? She stayed because of me, because of what she thought Orrin would do to me if she left. I know you, Bria. You could not have remained silent. You would have tried to do something because you believed there was something that *could* be done. You are not so different from Rand. You both tilt at windmills.''

"I would have stopped him," Bria said quietly.

"He *was* stopped." Elizabeth's velvet gown whispered against the brocade upholstery as she stood again. She went to the fireplace and stirred the logs with a poker. For a few moments the snap of the flames was the only sound in the room. "Orrin got his information about what you were doing for the sharecroppers from Addie. She couldn't have known how badly it would turn out. When Orrin deliberately selected John to be beaten and dragged ... when he told Austin and Sam and the others to burn the church ... when he ...'' Elizabeth stopped. Her hand tightened around the poker until her knuckles were bloodless. "It was too much," she said at last. "Too much to be borne.''

Bria started to go to her mother but Luke stopped her. "Let her finish," he said. "She wants to say this."

Elizabeth put down the poker and turned her back on the fire. "I knew that Orrin had a revolver he kept hidden. Jeb informed me the first time he came across the case. There was always only one gun in it. That was years ago, shortly after I married Orrin. I never gave it much thought. It was simply one of Orrin's eccentricities, I decided.''

She took a deep breath and expelled it slowly. "After what happened to John Whitney ...'' Her voice trailed off. Several moments passed before she continued. "It required a thorough search to find the case, over a period of days, but it turned up among Orrin's favorite wines. The opportunity to use it presented itself soon after that. Knowing Orrin would be returning from Franklin's, most likely without escort from Luke, seemed to offer the best chance. It was not a particularly thoughtful plan, merely my only plan. The day before the card game I went down to the river and fired the revolver, just to make certain I could. I didn't know Addie followed me. She was frightened, afraid I meant to use the gun on myself. I had to tell her the truth to keep her from going to one or both of you."

Bria frowned. "But weren't you concerned that she would go to Orrin?"

"No," Elizabeth said simply. "It never once entered my mind."

Luke nodded, understanding that Addie would not have betrayed Elizabeth in this manner. "She involved John, didn't she?"

In an absent, vaguely nervous gesture, Elizabeth smoothed the rich velvet fabric of her skirt. "Yes. I didn't anticipate that. They tried to talk me out of it, of course, and I allowed them to believe they were successful. I even gave John the walnut case for safekeeping."

"But not the gun," Luke said.

"I'm not certain I like being so predictable," she said. "You're correct. I didn't give him the gun. When John realized it, I was already on my way to meet Orrin. I knew I would have to wait for him. Hours, probably. It was easy for John to find me. Addie came with him."

"How could I not know this?" Bria asked.

"You had no reason to think I was anywhere but in my room."

Bria remembered that well enough. "I didn't think John was well enough to walk."

"He wasn't. He came anyway."

Luke rubbed the bridge of his nose. "Bria and I have known for some time that John was there that night. He left some playing cards in his cabin that belonged to Orrin."

Elizabeth nodded. "Yes. Three queens. Two fours. Orrin was carrying them in his jacket. You must have had a considerably good hand that night, Luke, to have beaten a full house."

"Four of a kind. It wasn't supposed to happen that way. Tipping intended to deal Orrin an even better hand from the bottom of the deck. I stopped him and arrived at a better outcome for myself. Orrin didn't seem to know the cards were marked. I think he believed he had the winning hand. His friends had been playing him for a long time with their friendly game.''

"No doubt. Austin Tipping has not done well by his father. Robert was a kind and honorable man. One has only to scratch the surface to discover Austin is neither. I have always liked his sister but I can't be entirely sorry that our fortunes have not been tied to theirs.''

Bria did not want to hear about the Tippings. "Mother. What about Orrin? What happened?''

Elizabeth looked at her daughter, puzzled. "But you know what happened. He was shot.'' She saw immediately this did not satisfy Bria. "I have no intention of telling you by whom. I promised Addie I would let you know that in the end I did not act alone. She and John must have suspected I would break that promise. I imagine that's why John left the cards where you could find them. He wanted to be certain you knew he was also on the road to Franklin's that night.''

"But you had the revolver,'' Bria said.

"I did in the beginning . . . and perhaps again, when it counted most, but I dropped it when John tried to wrest it from me. It lay there on the ground between the three of us and we all wanted it.'' Elizabeth's eyes held her daughter's. "You must ask yourself if you would be better for knowing the truth. How can it matter if I pulled the trigger? I had the intent. I carried the gun. Addie and John where there to protect me. Anything they may have done would have been in the nature of an accident. I was the one who had a plan.''

No one said anything for a long time. Elizabeth returned to the wing chair and resumed drinking her tea. Bria studied her hands in her lap and wondered what else she could have done to save her mother from this pass. Luke's gaze shifted from Elizabeth to Bria and back again and he learned then what Orrin Foster had never understood: Orrin had feared the wrong woman.

Bria lifted her head and looked at her mother. "John. Addie. Where are they going?''

"Far away from here," Elizabeth said. "Some safe place."

Bria did not press for more information. "You gave them money?"

"Yes. It was the very least I could do. Addie intends to write again when she and John are settled. I believe she means the next letter to come to you."

"I miss her."

"As I do."

Bria stood and went to her mother. She sat on the floor at Elizabeth's feet and laid her head against her mother's knees. The velvet was soft against her cheek. Elizabeth's hand came to rest lightly on the crown of Bria's head. She stroked her hair and hummed the first bars of a lullaby she remembered from her own childhood.

Luke left the room quietly. He did not think he would be missed.

Bria stirred sleepily. She stretched her toes and fingers first, then her arms and calves. Her back arched, her neck. Her shoulders rolled. When her body was fully engaged she turned and bumped into Luke's broad chest.

She lifted one eyelid and peered at him. He was watching her with both eyes open. The centers of them were wide and very dark. It was not the look of sleepy sensuality. There was an intensity, a directness, that came with full knowledge of his own desire. This look was for her alone.

Bria's feline stretch became an abrupt little shiver.

Luke's laughter was low and a little wicked. "I know you're awake."

"I don't want to be." She buried her face in a pillow. "You have a very loud stare."

Luke wasn't certain he heard her correctly but he knew better than to ask her to repeat herself. He laid his hand at the small of her back instead and began to massage. He had no difficulty interpreting her soft, satisfied moan.

It was not long before Bria raised her head and began pressing kisses along the length of his collarbone. The damp edge of her tongue flicked at his throat. He raised the hem of her nightshift and cupped her bottom. She rubbed against his erection.

Luke's urgency was tempered by Bria's exploration. "Are you in a hurry, Yankee?" she drawled.

"I've been awake longer than you."

"I'm not certain I'm awake even now. You'd better kiss me."

The kiss was deep and slow and thorough. There was nothing Yankee about it. His tongue glided over hers like sweet, thick molasses and it seemed to go on forever.

When he came into her it was the same way. He filled her, held her, and moved in her as if all urgency had fled and time would only be marked in the passage of hours.

He kissed her breasts. Adored them. He sucked the rosy nipples into his mouth and laved them with his tongue. He kissed her flushed cheeks, the underside of her jaw. He buried his face in the curve of her neck and breathed deeply of her fragrant hair. Her skin was musky and warm. Her hair smelled as always of lavender.

She raked back his sleep-tousled hair with her fingers. Her eyes searched his face and found it at once familiar and curiously strange. His mouth was set narrowly, the dear, crooked grin absent. The cool grey color of his eyes was nearly eclipsed by the dark pupils. His skin was pulled taut; a cord in his neck stood out. He was holding himself still and the effort cost him. His features were cut from pleasure and denial because he knew both in that moment.

Bria's heart swelled. "I keep falling in love with you."

His head lowered and his mouth rested near her ear. He wanted to hear that all the days of his life. He told her so.

They made love once and again. The house stirred around them but they didn't leave the warm comfort of their bed. They heard Martha chattering to one of her sisters in the hallway.

The covered contents of a breakfast tray clattered on the way to Elizabeth's room. Outside, Tad and Geordie were exercising the horses and from the kitchen the delicious smell of Elsie's peach cobbler wafted in the air.

"I do not think I want to move today," Bria said. "At least no more than I already have."

Luke was raised on one elbow. Now he lifted an eyebrow at her. "Saucy remarks, Mrs. Kincaid? And no blush to soften it."

"I haven't the inclination to blush. I am most thoroughly compromised." She raised her hands above her head and stretched again. The sheet slid deliciously over her tender breasts and she smiled with sybaritic pleasure. Bria laughed when she saw where Luke's interest had strayed. She pushed at his chest and sat up herself. "Show me your gardens," she demanded. "It will be spring in mere months and I've never properly seen them."

"Not properly, perhaps. But I know you've seen them."

At first Bria did not know what to say. "You do?" she said finally.

"Mmm. I do. They were under my bed before I moved in here. You didn't roll the paper as tightly as I do."

"What makes you think it was me? Addie might have—"

"Addie might have found them, but she wouldn't have looked. Martha or Jeb, either. What did you hope to find?"

"Exactly what I did. It was just after you showed me your plans for the house. I wondered if you had others and went to your room to look for them."

"You could have asked."

"No, I couldn't have. I didn't want you to know I was interested."

"In the plans or in me?"

Bria bent forward and kissed him on the mouth. "Don't you know yet? One is not so different from the other." Her words had the effect of raising his crooked grin. It was both sheepish and mischievous and Bria had to scramble quickly to elude Luke's playful grab.

Luke watched her drop to her knees over the side of the bed and search for the plans beneath it. "I thought you didn't want to move at all." He pretended to understand her muffled reply. "If you say so."

Bria wriggled out from under the bed and held up the plans. She dropped them beside Luke, then found her dressing gown and slipped into it. She handed him his and ignored his disappointed look. "Bring them here to the window," she said. "You can show me how it will look from our room."

They sat on the bench, the landscaping plan between them as Luke described his vision of pools and mazes and an artist's palette of colors blooming all year long.

Bria pressed her nose to the windowpane and looked as far as she could to the east and west. Her breath misted the glass. "We'll put exotic fish in the pools."

"If you like."

"And Mother will have a party in the spring with paper lanterns winding all the way to the river."

"Not this spring," Luke said. "In a few years, when the gardens are more mature."

"She'll start planning it now." Bria pointed to where the wild geraniums and coneflowers would have their home. "You'll make love to me here."

"And here." He showed her where the rhododendron would bloom in the wood. "And here."

"In the pond?"

Luke looked to where his finger had strayed. "Here." He moved it to center of the maze.

"That's better."

Laughing, Luke rolled the plans, secured them, and dropped them to the floor. He sat back and drew Bria between his splayed legs. She came without hesitation and leaned comfortably against his chest. "You stayed with your mother for a long time last night," he said.

She nodded. "We talked about so many things. It was good for both of us. I did not realize it was possible to love her so much and understand her so little." Bria turned her head to get a better look at Luke. His eyes were thoughtful. "What about your mother, Luke? When am I going to meet her?"

"Do you want to?"

She was a little hurt that he would ask. "Of course I do. Why wouldn't I?"

"I told you what she is, Bree."

"You told me what she *does*. I want to meet your mother. Mary Kincaid. You're not ashamed of her, are you?"

"No!" More quietly he said, "No, but I would understand if you had reservations."

"I do. But they all have to do with whether or not she thinks I'm good enough for you. What if she thinks you could have done better? She might think I married you for your money."

"I was hardly a wealthy man when you married me."

"But you are now. Or you could be if you would tell my mother that what she inherited is rightfully yours."

"I'm not worried that she'll squander it, Bree."

"She could marry again."

"Then we'll explain it if that time comes. For now, it doesn't matter. My mother is satisfied that Orrin was Walter Wingate. She's accepted that she cannot entirely clear Conrad's name. That also will come in time. Right now she is anxious to meet you."

"She is?"

"That's what she wrote. A visit can't be very far in the future."

"You mean we're going to New York?"

"That would be the surest way to miss her. I believe she intends to come here."

"Luke!" She moved away, turned, and poked him in the chest with her forefinger. "How long have you known this?"

"Since yesterday. Her letter came in the same post as Addie's."

"And you're only telling me now?"

"Your mother had revelations of her own last evening. Mine could wait."

"But this morning—"

He gave her an arch look. "This morning I wasn't thinking of my mother." Luke pulled Bria back in his arms when she had the grace to blush. "Not so saucy now, are you?" He wrapped his arms around her and tugged on her earlobe with his teeth. "Do you think—"

Bria nodded before he could finish. "All the time," she said. "It's indecent how often I—"

He cut her off with a kiss. "Then do the decent thing," he said against her mouth. "Show me."

Epilogue

The carriage bounced along comfortably, stirring up a smal dust cloud in its wake. The road from Charleston to Henle had not been particularly improved and occasionally a rut woul lift the passengers off their bottoms. None of them rose ver far, squeezed as they were into their seats.

"It was very kind of you to share your carriage with us,' Mary Kincaid said. "We really are so anxious to reach m son. We might have been left at the side of the road for hour longer if you hadn't offered your assistance." Her soft gre eyes were clearly grateful as she held out her hand to the ma seated across from her. "I am Mary Kincaid. And these ar my sisters." She smiled. "In spirit, at least."

Six women turned glowing smiles every bit the equal o Mary's in the direction of their Good Samaritan.

All the attention was a bit overwhelming. Two redheads, blonde, three brunettes, and Mary Kincaid herself with hair a dark as bittersweet chocolate. The smiles were open, friendly and on some faces, just a bit flirtatious, in spite of the fact tha he was traveling with his wife.

Mary withdrew her hand. "You must be wishing that you had been able to repair our carriage. We have completely taken over." She gestured to their gowns that spilled out from under their cloaks. The carriage was filled with the rustling of satin and silk and colors as bright as gemstones.

"Neither my wife nor I had any inclination to leave you at the roadside. Your presence was an omen of good things to come."

"Us, do you mean?" Lys asked, removing her jaunty hat because the ostrich plume kept dipping and tickling her cheek.

"An omen?" Livia rearranged her skirt at the next bounce so Maggie was not sitting on it.

"A *good* one?" Madelyn asked, her dark brown eyes suspicious.

"How could that be?" Laura and Nancy chimed in as one.

Mary Kincaid's handsome features were apologetic, though a faintly crooked smile played around the edges of her mouth. "Please forgive us. We have much more curiosity than good manners properly dictate. Your remark is a rather startling one, you have to allow."

There was not much room for the man to stretch, but he maneuvered a little space for himself by lifting his wife onto his lap. There was a round of gentle laughter and an exchange of knowing smiles, and, most notably, not a single protest from the woman in his arms.

"Have you ever heard of the Hamilton and Waterstone riddles?" he asked.

"I believe I have. Something to do with a treasure, I think. My son wrote to me about it."

"Really? Then you know about the seven sisters?" He watched Mary and the other women look at one another in an odd, secretive fashion, but he could not divine what passed between them.

"Perhaps you should explain," Mary Kincaid said cautiously. "It doesn't seem likely that we would be familiar with the same seven sisters as you." She couldn't imagine he was speaking of the infamous New York brothel of the same name.

He began to recite. "Seven sisters, cursed every one. Seven

sisters, all alone. One more lovely than the other. Each, at heart, as cold as stone.''

There was silence.

At last, Lys spoke. ''Not very complimentary, is it?''

Maggie nodded and felt compelled to point out, ''There was the part about one being more lovely than the other.''

''He's not talking about my heart,'' Nancy said. ''I challenge any of you to find a warmer one than mine.''

He felt all eyes on him, including his wife's. ''Perhaps you should explain,'' he said to her.

''I think so.'' She slipped one arm around his neck and faced the others. Her lovely features were animated with good humor. Her dark eyes held their attention. ''The seven sisters are seven precious gems. That was all that was meant by their hearts being as cold as stone. It's a riddle, after all, and meant to mislead and intrigue at the same time. My husband should have gone on to finish the Hamilton riddle. The last lines make it clear that when the sisters are reunited they will be placed upon their throne.''

Madelyn poked Maggie with her elbow. ''On our throne. Did you hear that?''

Maggie rolled her eyes. ''I was right here, the same as you.''

''When my husband and I saw all seven of you, your gowns as perfectly splendid as a rainbow of precious stones, it wasn't possible to pass you by. We're treasure hunters, after all. At least we were. We've closed that chapter of our lives.'' She looked at her husband for assurance.

He nodded. ''We have.''

''Then you found your treasure?'' Mary asked.

His smile was enigmatic and he did not answer the question directly. ''If we had known it was possible to find gems like yourself along the road to Henley, we might not have left at all.''

''He called us gems,'' Livia said, pleased with this pronouncement. ''Just as if I were Opal.'' Which she was, in her

New York boudoir. She giggled at her small foray into humor and then fell silent when Laura gave her a quelling look.

Mary Kincaid cleared her throat delicately. "You say you're going to Henley? But that is our destination also. I understand that until most recently it was called Concord."

"I've known it as Henley," he said curtly.

Mary noticed his wife frowned disapprovingly. She ventured, "Then it's just as well they're using that name again."

Taking his cue from his wife, his tone improved. "What takes you there? You mentioned a son?"

"Yes. Lucas. He has recently married. I am going to meet my new daughter-in-law. By his every account she is a most lovely and accomplished young woman."

"Hah," Nancy interjected. "As if our Luke would tie himself to anyone who was not."

Lys nodded. "Yes, but I wonder how she responds to surprises."

"I'm certain she will be gracious," Mary said. "It's bred in the bone here. The same will be true of her dear mother. Luke is the one who will be looking for cover. He'll think it's a siege."

"Then your visit is unexpected?"

"Yes. And yours?"

"Most unexpected." There was a glimmer of a smile at the corners of his mouth. "Apparently everyone thinks we're dead."

Mary Kincaid blinked. "Dead?"

He nodded. "Our ship foundered off the coast of Argentina and was lost at sea."

Three voices came together as one. "But how did you survive?"

"By having the good fortune not to be on *Cerberus* when she went down. I sold her in Papeete before we left the South Seas. After months in tropical waters, she wasn't yare enough to finish the voyage home, and we—my wife, myself, and the crew—were all anxious to get here. None of us wanted to wait while the hull was repaired. We left *Cerberus* in Tahiti and made our passage on a whaler.''

His wife picked up the story. Her clipped English accents were nothing like his honeyed drawl. ''The captain promised a straightforward voyage home for the price we agreed upon, but he was not at all honorable. Had he strayed from course one more time I believe there would have been a mutiny.'' She sighed and absently tucked a strand of dark brown hair behind her ear. ''I know, because I would have led it. Still, it seems churlish to be ungrateful. We missed the storm that left *Cerberus* wrecked. We heard about it only after we arrived here. People were so perfectly astonished to see us. The stories tumbled out one after the other. We left Charleston as soon as we could arrange it. There seems to be no end to the things that have happened since we've been away.''

Rand Hamilton smiled warmly at Mary Kincaid. ''Including, it appears, the marriage of my sister Bria to your son. At least that is one of the things that was told to us.''

Mary's lips parted slightly. She pressed one gloved hand to her mouth to suppress something between a hiccough and a gasp. ''Oh my,'' she said at last. Out of the corner of her eye she saw every one of her dear friends determinedly contain their curiosity behind vapid, polite smiles. ''Rand Hamilton.''

''The very same,'' he said. ''And this is my wife Claire.''

''Oh my,'' Mary said again. ''Luke has written of you, of course. Of both of you. He said how very sad Bree was at your passing. He feared she would . . .'' Mary shook her head and her expression brightened slowly as she looked from Rand to Claire. ''It no longer matters, does it? You're both here now. It will be a most exceptional homecoming and what a privilege for us to witness it. That is, if you have no objection. You might want to reconsider your hospitality.''

''Abandon you on the road?'' Claire asked. ''I think not.''

''My son might thank you.''

"I most sincerely doubt that."

Mary smiled. "No, you're right. He wouldn't thank you. He dearly loves us all, but you can see for yourself that as a group we're . . . well, we are a bit crushing."

Rand felt the full force of six more happy, rather hopeful smiles turn on him and began to form some small understanding of what his new brother-in-law faced. "There is room enough for all of you at Henley." He would take Luke fishing, he thought. Often. "You will find it very comfortable."

"Luke has written the very same to us," Mary said. "Although I do not think he meant it to be construed as an invitation." She bit her lip and looked anxiously ahead to where the road widened, trying to get a glimpse of Henley as Luke described it.

"It's miles yet," Rand said.

Mary Kincaid visibly relaxed. Her smile became a trifle self-mocking. "A mother worries about her son. But then, you must be all too familiar with that."

He was. "My mother will be grateful for your presence. And Bree. I imagine she will find all of you a treasure."

Livia giggled. "It's a fact that we're a treasure." She fell silent abruptly when Nancy kicked her under cover of a cascade of petticoats.

"About the treasure," Madelyn said smoothly.

"Yes," Laura chimed in. "The treasure. Did you—"

"Find it?" Maggie and Lyssa finished together.

Claire's laughter drew Rand's adoring eyes toward her. "More than you know," he said softly. He glanced briefly at the seven sisters, a slight smile edging one corner of his mouth. "But that's altogether another story."

Bria sat cross-legged at the foot of her bed and ran a brush lazily through her hair. The ends curled slightly around her hand as she pulled the brush through. She made a half-hearted attempt to straighten the neckline of her shift when it fell past her bare shoulder. The small negative shake of Luke's head stopped her. It was there, in his eyes, the undeniable fact that he liked looking at her. She opened her mouth to admonish him, then closed it. His boyish grin, so endearingly crooked, simply undid her.

Bria merely shook her head and tapped his outstretched foot with the tip of her brush. "I hope we have girls."

That announcement, more than the toe tap, drew Luke's attention away from Bria's shoulder. "Is there a particular reason?"

"If our sons have your smile you cannot expect me to discipline them. They will be young ruffians as children and rogues as young men. Someone will have to take them in hand, Luke. I don't think I'm up to it."

"So you would punish me with beautiful little girls that I'll spoil as toddlers and have to lock away as young women." He considered that a moment. "Yes, that seems perfectly fair."

Bria tossed the brush aside and threw herself forward on the bed. She propped her chin on the back of her hands and stared at Luke. "Would you mind if our babies were girls?"

"I like girls." He reached out and touched a heavy lock of hair that had fallen over her shoulder. His fingers sifted the soft strands. "Are we going to have babies?"

"I hope so." The corners of her mouth lifted a bit dreamily. "I wouldn't really mind boys, you know."

Luke chuckled. "Perhaps we could start with one of each."

"Twins? I don't think that's the sort of thing either of us can make happen by wishing it."

Wrapping one hand around her wrist, Luke pulled Bria closer. "Hmm." He bent his head and touched his mouth to hers. "I was willing to do rather more than you wished."

"Really?" Smiling, Bria slipped her arms around Luke's neck and stretched along the length of him. "Then you've seriously underestimated me."

It was not a mistake that Luke particularly minded making. There, in the sweet oasis of their bed, supremely unaware of a certain carriage wending its way toward Henley, Luke and Bria made love.

Teasing. Playful. Laughter was their treasure.

ABOUT THE AUTHOR

Jo Goodman lives with her family in Colliers, West Virginia. She is the author of twenty historical romances (all published by Zebra Books) including her beloved Dennehy sisters series: WILD SWEET ECSTASY (Mary Michael's story), ROGUE' MISTRESS (Rennie's story), FOREVER IN MY HEAR' (Maggie's story), ALWAYS IN MY DREAMS (Skye's story and ONLY IN MY ARMS (Mary's story), as well as her Thorn Brothers trilogy: MY STEADFAST HEART (Colin's story MY RECKLESS HEART (Decker's story), and WITH AL MY HEART (Grey's story). She is currently working on he newest Zebra historical romance, the first of a new four-boo series set during the Regency period (to be published in Jun 2002). In the meantime, TEMPTING TORMENT, the conclud ing chapter in the McClellan trilogy (after CRYSTAL PAS SION and SEASWEPT ABANDON) will be republished i the fall of 2001. Jo loves hearing from readers, and you ma write to her c/o Zebra Books. Please include a self-addresse stamped envelope if you would like a response. You can als e-mail her at jdobrzan@weir.net and visit her website www.romancejournal.com/Goodman